ILLUSIONARY

BY ZORAIDA CÓRDOVA

HOLLOW CROWN
Incendiary

Illusionary

BROOKLYN BRUJAS
Labyrinth Lost

Bruja Born

Wayward Witch

THE VICIOUS DEEP
The Vicious Deep

The Savage Blue

The Vast and Brutal Sea

Star Wars: Galaxy's Edge: A Crash of Fate

The Way to Rio Luna

ILLUSIONARY

ZORAIDA CÓRDOVA

LITTLE, BROWN AND COMPANY

New York Boston

Copyright © 2021 by Glasstown Entertainment
Map illustration by Karl Vesterberg

Cover art copyright © 2021 by Billelis. Cover design by Marci Senders and Karina Granda. Cover copyright © 2021 by Hachette Book Group, Inc.

Little, Brown and Company
Hachette Book Group
1290 Avenue of the Americas, New York, NY 10104
Visit us at LBYR.com

First Edition: May 2021

Little, Brown and Company is a division of Hachette Book Group, Inc. The Little, Brown name and logo are trademarks of Hachette Book Group, Inc.

Library of Congress Cataloging-in-Publication Data
Names: Córdova, Zoraida, author.
Title: Illusionary / Zoraida Córdova.
Description: First edition. | New York ; Boston : Little, Brown and Company, 2021. | Series: Hollow crown ; [2] | Audience: Ages 14 & up. | Summary: "Renata and her enemy Prince Castian must team up to find the fabled Knife of Memory and bring peace to the kingdom of Puerto Leones." —Provided by publisher.
Identifiers: LCCN 2020036603 | ISBN 9780759556034 (hardcover) | ISBN 9780759557871 (ebook)
Subjects: CYAC: Fantasy. | Princes—Fiction. | Memory—Fiction.
Classification: LCC PZ7.C8153573 Ill 2021 | DDC [Fic]—dc23
LC record available at https://lccn.loc.gov/2020036603

ISBNs: 978-0-7595-5603-4 (hardcover), 978-0-7595-5787-1 (ebook)

Printed in the United States of America

LSC-C

Printing 1, 2021

FOR MYSELF

ILLUSIONARY

WANTED

RENATA CONVIDA

FOR CRIMES AGAINST THE PEOPLE OF PUERTO LEONES, MURDER, COLLUSION, AND THE ILLEGAL USE OF ROBÁRI MAGICS. LAST SEEN ON THE CAMINO MAYOR LEAVING ANDALUCÍA WITH THE DISSIDENT REBEL WHISPERS. CONSIDERED ARMED AND LETHAL. GOOD CITIZENS OF THE KINGDOM HARBORING RENATA CONVIDA OR ANY MORIA MUST REPORT TO THE SECOND SWEEP IN EXCHANGE FOR A 10,000-PESO REWARD.

APPROVED BY JUSTICE ALESSANDRO

KINGDOM OF PUERTO LEONES
YEAR 40 OF HIS MAJESTY KING FERNANDO'S REIGN
317 A.C. OF THE THIRD AGE OF ANDALUCÍA

Song of the Moria Queen

I'll sing you the song
of the Moria Queen.

Lost to the oceans
and lost twice to me,
but I remember her
in my dreams.

I'll sing you the song
of the Moria Queen.

Her heart was aglow
with a thousand stars.
Her smile had me bend
at the knee.

I'll sing you the song
of the Moria Queen.

I'll find her once more
in the hollow of night,
in the after, the gone,
in the salt of the brine.

I'll sing you the song
of the Moria Queen.

I'll sing you the song.

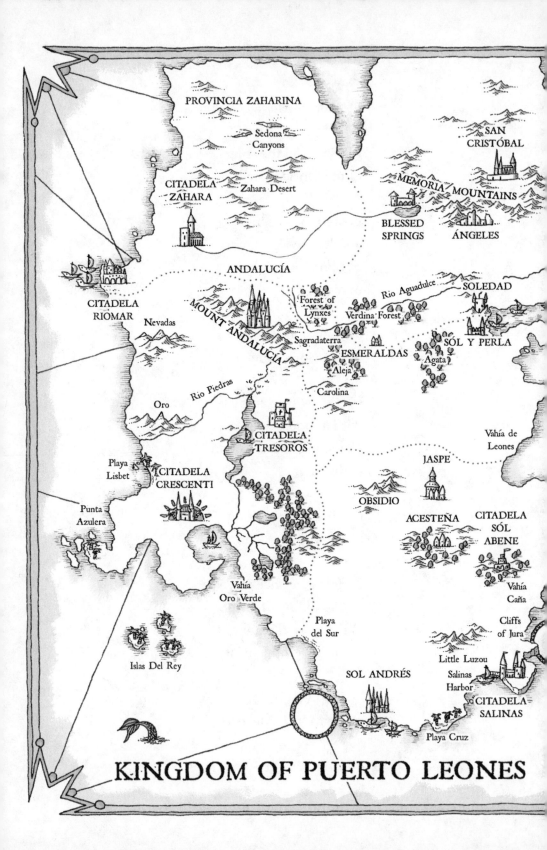

KINGDOM OF PUERTO LEONES

PROVINCIA ZAHARINA

Sedona Canyons

SAN CRISTÓBAL

CITADELA ZAHARA

Zahara Desert

MEMORIA MOUNTAINS

BLESSED SPRINGS

ÁNGELES

ANDALUCÍA

CITADELA RIOMAR

Nevadas

MOUNT ANDALUCÍA

Forest of Lynxes

Rio Aguadulce

SOLEDAD

Verdina Forest

Sagradaterra

ESMERALDAS

SOL Y PERLA

Aleja

Agata

Oro

Rio Piedras

Carolina

CITADELA TRESOROS

Vahía de Leones

Playa Lisbet

CITADELA CRESCENTI

JASPE

Punta Azulera

OBSIDIO

ACESTEÑA

CITADELA SÓL ABENE

Vahía Caña

Vahía Oro Verde

Cliffs of Jura

Playa del Sur

Islas Del Rey

Little Luzou

Salinas Harbor

SOL ANDRÉS

CITADELA SALINAS

Playa Cruz

N

S

Cliffs of
Memoria

KINGDOM of
DAUPHINIQUE

CASTINIAN SEA

LITTLE
DAUPHINE

EMPIRIO
LUZOU

ARBOLO
GULF

Porto
Cebou

ISLA SOMBRAS

PROLOGUE
317 A.C.

As Fernando, king of Puerto Leones, Keeper of the Peace, and true heir of the Fajardo dynasty, watched the young soldier drown, he realized that there was something very wrong in his kingdom. Not only had he been forced to repeat his questions, but when faced with His Majesty's wrath, the boy would not give satisfactory answers.

While most people thought Fernando cruel for the sake of cruelty, he always learned the name of those he executed. At the time of death, he would speak the name of the deceased so that they would have no reason to utter his once they ventured into the afterlife.

The drowning boy's name was Delios Urbano. Seventeen and a recent military draft, with no family left to bear his shame. His crimes were simple. His negligence had aided the Moria insurgents who disrupted the Sun Festival with an attempt on the king's life.

Between gasps for air, Delios begged for forgiveness but still could not explain why he had abandoned his post.

The morning after the Sun Festival, after Justice Méndez had been attacked, after the rebels had escaped, and after the dungeon had been emptied of prisoners, Delios Urbano had been found in one of the palace courtyards, reeking of his own filth and stale liquor. He would have remained in the dungeons, but after nearly a fortnight of dead ends and failure to crush the rebels, King Fernando had had enough. If he couldn't have answers, he'd settle for blood.

"Please," the boy sputtered.

King Fernando brushed a cold droplet of water from his cheek. He ushered the guard aside and plunged Delios's head back into the barrel. The boy's scream turned into a gurgle. And then, with a final tremble, he was still. He had failed his kingdom for the last time.

"Delios Urbano, may the Father of Worlds forgive your crimes," Fernando said.

Then two of his youngest but most loyal personal guards unceremoniously dragged the body out of the room, where it was deposited on a cart with the others, ready to be delivered to the apothecura's study for research.

"It is done, Your Majesty," Analiya assured, then offered him a handkerchief.

Fernando dried his hands, his eyes drawn to the blood staining the stone floor and walls. This was the place where Justice Méndez had been found, alive, but barely. King Fernando understood the message quite well. In a single night, his enemies had nearly destroyed everything he had labored to build. In the days that followed, he'd refilled the dungeons, interviewed every single subject in the palace. It hadn't changed a thing. His weapon was in the wind. Méndez was far gone. The prince *taken*. And no one could explain to the king *how* it had all happened. He was surrounded by traitors and fools. Fury burned through his veins, igniting the hate that always simmered in his heart. When he turned around, he nearly stumbled on a set of iron manacles.

Analiya picked them up and presented them to the king. The metal was warped, as if it had been melted while being worn.

"What could do such a thing?" Nazar asked, then reached for the string of wooden prayer beads tucked under his black uniform.

Not what. *Who?* Renata Convida. The Robári who had saved his life, and then revealed the viper that she was.

Fernando threw the manacles against the wall. Cracked a chair in half. Kicked the barrel onto its side. The water that held the last breath of half a dozen men washed away the blood of others. He panted hard and fast, blinking until his sight was clear. "Seal this room. I want to see him."

Analiya led the way out of the putrid mazelike tunnels. Unlike Nazar, she did not flinch at the human waste that was caked to the muddy dungeon steps. A pity he'd never had a daughter like her.

They reached the end of a corridor that emptied onto the courtyards between the palace and the cathedral. King Fernando inhaled deeply in the flickering torchlight. Incense and stale aguadulce clung to the air even as they made for Justice Méndez's bedchamber.

"Your Excellency." Analiya spoke firmly. "You should not have to see this."

"Oh," Fernando said, "but I do."

Justice Méndez was as close to a friend as he had ever had. They were going to reshape the known world. Harness the unnatural magics of their enemies so that Puerto Leones could roar into a new age. He'd sacrificed everything for it. But the Father of Worlds demanded more and more. Now it was up to Fernando to finish what he'd started nearly four decades ago.

He entered the dimly lit chamber. Justice Méndez sat on the edge of his bed. His gray eyes gaped at nothing. His skin had the texture of crumpled parchment. He'd been bathed and brought to his rooms for comfort. The apothecuras had tried everything, despite knowing that there was no cure for this ailment. Someone had placed the Bible of Worlds in his hands, in fleeting hope that it would jog the devout man out of his sickness. But Méndez was experiencing far worse than a sickness. He was a Hollow, empty of memory and mind. Alive in body alone.

King Fernando had seen the work of Robári before. This particular strain of the Moria disease drained memories. Someone had tried to explain it once, how their cursed Lady of Shadows had given these Moria the ability to steal memories by imbuing the Robári with her own lifeblood. Both king and justice had believed they could look beyond subduing the monstrous magics and instead wield them for the good of the land. They had been so close.

"Is there nothing that can be done?" Analiya asked.

"The body in this state will not eat or sleep or speak," he said. "It will simply fade. A fate worse than death, they call the Hollows. I've already let him suffer too long. I must give him mercy."

King Fernando unsheathed a dagger hidden inside the breast of his black doublet. The hilt was encrusted with sapphires. An engagement gift from the first woman he'd made the mistake of loving. He did not know why he carried it so close when he had wanted nothing more than to forget her. Heavens knew he'd tried. The rest of the world already had. Perhaps it was the chaos of the day, but he thought of her, the queen that never was.

As quickly as it had arrived, he swallowed the sentiment away. Fernando pulled Méndez to his feet and into an embrace. The frail body was cold even through his tunic.

"I will avenge you, old friend. I swear it."

Then the king of Puerto Leones stepped back and drove the blade across Justice Méndez's tender throat. Arterial blood sprayed his face, his clothes, the linens. Méndez released a long, gargled breath. King Fernando did not clean his blade before sheathing it, and he did not wait for his guards before leaving the room.

"Make the arrangements for the funeral. Spread the word to every citadela, every village, every forsaken hamlet and hovel on the pilgrimage roads, that Justice Méndez has been murdered by the rebel Whispers." He handed Nazar a slip of parchment with a list of names. "Assemble these people in my chambers."

"Your chambers?" Nazar asked, confused. Then, as if realizing his mistake in questioning the king, he stammered, "Right away, Your Majesty."

King Fernando stopped on the exposed walkway that bridged two of the palace towers. The blue mosaic pillars glinted in the moonlight. "I have a special request for you, Analiya."

"I am your servant, my king."

He handed her an envelope stamped with his seal. "Be sure this invitation is delivered. I want you to escort her back yourself."

Analiya bowed, snapped her boots together. "Yes, my king."

Fernando returned to his wing. He had to prepare for his guests and a mystery he'd been unraveling since the night of the attack. He'd been betrayed yet again. And this time, everyone would see what happened to traitors.

The fireplace roared. Ten crystal goblets brimmed with wine, but no one drank. The bottle chilled in a silver bin, and condensation rolled down the glass almost as quickly as the sweat that poured from each person assembled around King Fernando's parlor. It was rumored he never had guests in his apartments, not unless it was a concubine or his wife. In attendance was everyone he'd summoned. All except one.

There was the justice, Alessandro. Perhaps it was because Méndez's blood was still dried on his skin like a dusting of freckles, but the sight of Alessandro made the king's upper lip sneer. The justice's new robes were cut too wide at his weak shoulders. To his left was his wife, Lady Nuria, Duquesa of Tresoros. She was, perhaps, the only person in the room not sweating, though her dark eyes roamed the tapestries and the elite members sharing the table, then Nazar and General Hector guarding the door.

King Fernando had uttered only "Please remain seated" before taking his place at the head of the table. He wanted them to sweat. Wanted their own anxieties to crack them apart wondering why they had been called here, of all places, during a time of unrest.

The young Duque Arias cleared his throat and tugged his cravat loose. Lady Roca fanned herself. The royal priest's ninety-year-old eyelids fluttered closed. Duque Sól Abene tugged at his black beard. Fernando's beautiful queen picked at the lace of her bodice, pouting full lips. These affairs were not for her, but she needed to see. He needed her to tell every one of her maidens, her confidants, her secret keepers, both in Puerto Leones and in her home country of Dauphinique across the sea, about this meeting. He wanted everyone to know what happened in this room.

"Are we waiting for someone, Your Majesty?" Alessandro motioned to the empty seat. When the king said nothing, the justice pressed. "And why is Leonardo here? He is but a servant."

Nuria rested her delicate hand on her chest. The sienna-brown skin there was unblemished. King Fernando noticed the way her eye twitched at the sound of her husband's voice. The attendant in question, Leonardo, gave his mistress a shake of his head.

The heavy tread of boots echoed in the halls, and everyone turned to the door.

Analiya entered, bowing to her king before making way for a young woman. The foreigner swept into the room with her head held high. She was dressed in fine green silk trousers embroidered in shimmering beads and threads. Her doublet had a high collar and tails, with tapered sleeves. Thin gold bands decorated her fingers and slender neck. She had the bronze skin, high cheekbones, and thick black hair common to the people in Empirio Luzou. Although the green of her eyes was more akin to the eastern regions of Puerto Leones. Like her father.

"Lady Las Rosas," King Fernando said, half-amused. "Thank you for answering my invitation."

She gripped her hands at her back, like someone who would never stop being a soldier. But though she stood there, she did not bow. The king watched the way the elite families of Puerto Leones reacted to her title. The distraction was exactly what he'd hoped for.

"You are too kind, Your Majesty," the girl said, her full mouth tugging into a false smile. "But I am no lady, as I cannot inherit my father's title."

Fernando ignored the girl's barb and gestured to the empty seat to his left. "Sit."

Lady Las Rosas did as she was told.

"Have you been enjoying your return to your father's nation, Lady Las Rosas?"

A muscle tensed at her square jaw. "At the court of Empirio Luzou we allow for less formality. It's Leyre. Your Highness."

"But we aren't in Luzou, are we? And because of the circumstance, you are by every right half-Leonesse. Before his recent trial for treason, your father amended his will, naming you the sole heir to his lands and trading company."

The lords and ladies in attendance perked up at this news. Duque Arias eyed the girl's pretty mouth, her eyes made sultry by dark green powder dusted on her lids.

Leyre Las Rosas must have had excellent training because her shock, if she'd felt any, didn't register on her face. She picked up her goblet but, realizing no one else was drinking, set it back down.

"This was news to me, as my father has been in your dungeons for weeks," she said.

Fernando ignored the resentment in her words. When she first arrived at the palace, the memory thief was to turn the traitor Las Rosas into a Hollow in front of the entire court. But Renata's power failed. Another likely deception, no doubt. The king gripped the arm of his chair and let the memory pass.

"How very fortunate for your father that his executioner escaped this very palace the night of the Sun Festival," he said. "I have transferred Lord Las Rosas to Soledad prison. In the meantime you will take up his seat in this gathering. Now, I need every person here to help me solve a mystery."

The room was quiet enough to hear a fly buzz before landing on the lip of Alessandro's wine.

"How did the great palace of Andalucía, the jeweled capital of this kingdom, allow itself to be attacked by a handful of half-starved rebels?"

There was a collective held breath, followed by the faint plop of the fly falling to the wooden surface, dead.

"No one?" King Fernando tented his fingers. The lion's head of his family ring was the only adornment he allowed himself during the somber occasion. He glanced around the room. "You were all there. One of you *must* have witnessed something out of the ordinary. Something to help me piece together how I have been betrayed."

King Fernando traced his finger along his alabaster cheekbone, rubbing away the dried blood. He wanted them to see him this way. He wanted to make them feel as if their blood would fill his tub and he would bathe in it.

"I have told you everything—" Alessandro began.

"And you will tell me *again*," Fernando shouted. "Spare no details. Mistakes were made by all, even by my most trusted friend, Justice Méndez. May he rest in peace."

"May he rest in peace," they echoed.

One by one they recounted the Sun Festival. Even his wife, the young queen, wasn't excused from this inquiry. She accounted for every moment it took her to get dressed, and the tour of the grounds she gave her parents, the king and queen of Dauphinique.

"And where did you disappear to during the dance?" her husband asked.

Queen Josephine's mouth was a perfect circle of surprise. Her lovely black skin caught the gleam of the fireplace, and a part of him loved to see her squirm. "One of the courtiers from Dauphinique. I showed him the statues you built for me in the garden."

King Fernando glanced at Analiya, who corroborated the queen's evening with a single nod.

Then came Alessandro, who spoke the longest, reminding them all how he had never trusted Renata Convida, the Robári who had made a Hollow of Justice Méndez.

Lady Roca confessed to a marital indiscretion but claimed she'd rather die than aid the rebels. She vouched for all her ladies, who had spent most of their night watching Prince Castian dance with the memory thief.

"How he held her—" Lady Roca said dramatically.

"Like he'd claimed her," Duque Arias chimed in. He finished unknotting his cravat and shoved it into his pocket. "I saw them. If

Méndez hadn't interrupted them, I was sure Castian meant to—" The duque looked at Lady Nuria, who kept her face impassive. "I thought he meant to bed her."

"Instead she tried to kill him," Leonardo said softly.

"*You* were in the library when the prince was attacked!" Alessandro pointed a finger at the attendant. "How do we know you weren't aiding her?"

Leonardo cleared his throat and sat forward in his chair. "I was, uh, engaged with a paramour of mine. That room has always been empty."

Lady Nuria reached out and squeezed the boy's shoulder, ignoring the round of titters from the others. "I'd hate to think what would have happened if you hadn't been up there to save the prince from certain death."

Lady Roca clucked her tongue. "I could have *sworn* I saw Prince Castian in the ballroom at the same time we heard the screams of his attack."

"Perhaps the other Moria created a distraction," Alessandro offered. "While the wretch Renata attempted to murder him."

"What about you, Lady Nuria?" King Fernando asked. "You spent quite a bit of time with her, if I recall."

Nuria stiffened. Her onyx eyes locked with the king's. There was shame there. "I beg your forgiveness, Your Majesty. I had been attempting to convince the girl to remove one of my memories."

"What memory would that be?"

Her chest rose and fell quickly. She touched her temples and squinted as if trying to see into a far distance. "I no longer have it. But I know it was between myself and ...Castian."

Alessandro did his best not to grimace at the prince's name. Even if Nuria no longer possessed the specifics, they could all guess at the intimacy of the memory. As the table began to descend into chatter and unkind whispers, General Hector stepped forward from his post near the door.

"Pardon me, Your Majesty, but we should be asking how a band of rebels was able to get into the palace in the first place. The Robári never left her room. I saw to it."

"Perhaps she snuck away when the drink made you pass out," Alessandro accused.

Stunned silent, General Hector retreated, nursing his wooden hand against his chest.

King Fernando's chair grated against the floor. He sauntered to the fireplace, letting the flames kiss his fingertips. The pieces of that night were coming together, but there were still things he could not explain.

"Why save my life and then try to kill my son?" he asked.

"To destroy the king's last heir, of course," said Duque Sól Abene.

At the implication of his dead son, King Fernando felt something ancient and withered within him stir. After Castian drowned his baby brother, the king had feared Penelope's madness had weakened his last heir. But Fernando had set the boy right. Castian proved strong. Ruthless. Clever in a way that troubled even Fernando. There was a duplicity to his son that the king could not figure out. But soon, he'd have the answers he needed.

"This is what I know," the king said, returning to his seat. "We were attacked in our own home by our enemies. Our justice was murdered. Hundreds of prisoners were freed. A small infantry was slaughtered. They were able to attack Soledad prison and take years' worth of progress and kidnapped my son."

"There were dozens of them," Alessandro intoned quickly. "We were outnumbered. I swear, on my life, we will get them back."

King Fernando cut his black eyes to Alessandro. "My new justice, you don't have the marrow to do half the things Méndez did.

Do you know what I see in this room? Lies. Excuses. They have my son. What do we have? I am left with no choice but to . . ."

Alessandro dabbed a cloth at his face. Lady Roca was positively green. The priest roused from his sleep to mutter a prayer for their souls.

". . . raise a toast," King Fernando said.

Despite their confusion, every person picked up their crystal goblet.

"One of these glasses contains alacrán venom. There is a liar among you. If you have been true and faithful, drink."

Eyes darted from one person to the other. The queen drank first, followed by Lady Nuria and Leonardo. Then Alessandro. Lady Las Rosas and Duque Sól Abene. Lady Roca. The priest.

"Your Majesty," Duque Arias said, looking up at King Fernando. He was the only one who hadn't tipped back his drink. He reached for the inside of his doublet. Analiya and Nazar were on the lordling, drawing their swords. "Please, I beg you, let me explain!"

Duque Arias was a scoundrel and a poor loser. He'd lost several of his family's lands repaying gambling debts. Fernando had once sailed with his late grandfather, the decorated admiral Joaquín Arias, and he'd been forgiving of the young duque's behavior, as his father was killed in the Battle of Riomar. This louse of a boy was not the voice he'd expected to step forward. King Fernando arched a brow but nodded once. "Go on."

"Castian was at my estate a few months back for a night of revelry. I lost a wager. He bet me any item in my manor. I believed he'd go for my father's hundred-year-old cask of aguadulce, but instead he took something else."

"What did he claim?"

The duque's voice rasped. "My grandfather's chest from his

admiral days. It isn't worth anything. Seashells and compasses and an old senile sailor's logbooks full of gibberish. Maps to places that don't exist. I offered him gold, land, anything, but nothing would do. Castian wanted it. My mother's furious with me, more so after losing that ship to pirates. I thought—you see—the night of the Sun Festival, while the prince was preoccupied, I went to his room to take it back."

"You *stole* from the prince?" Alessandro asked incredulously.

"I didn't! I never found it. I've been racked with guilt since the news that Castian was taken." Arias shook so hard that wine sloshed from his cup, but he did not lower it. "I should have come forward. I don't know what use Castian would have had for my dead grandfather's ramblings. I swear—"

King Fernando gazed upon the lordling and smiled. Clever boy, his son. All these years and Fernando had never considered...

"You are forgiven, Lord Arias. I am a benevolent king. Remember that, when you leave this room. As for the rest of you, return to your provincias. Increase patrols along the major routes. Freeze outgoing ships in the ports. Gather those of fighting age and send them to the training yards. Speak to your people. Tell them that now, more than ever, we must be vigilant against the threat of the Moria. War will not be easy, but it will all be over when my son is returned, and our enemies have surrendered. Now go."

One by one, they left the room.

"Not you, Lady Las Rosas." King Fernando beckoned.

"You honor me with so much attention, Your Majesty," she said, lowering her eyes.

"*Honor* is perhaps not the word you wish to use, but it is good to know the Luzouan court hasn't robbed you of your manners."

The girl frowned and clenched her fists but remained silent. She glanced at the door, the windows, but they were the only ones in the room.

"I'm not going to hurt you," he assured her.

"Then what do you require of me, Your Majesty?"

"You left a promising naval career to help your mother run a small trading empire. You find rare and beautiful objects for her to sell from all the corners of the known world. Recently you haven't been able to do that due to her illness. Combined with your father's imprisonment, you must be adrift."

"I have managed."

"It has been a trying time and so I will be direct, Leyre Las Rosas." He spoke her name softly. *Lay-reh.* "Your father's life is in my hands. And I need your skill as a tracker of rare things."

"You presume I care about what happens to my father," she said, her alto voice hard.

"When we arrested your father, I visited his house. I like to see for myself the homes of those who betray me, and do you know what I found?"

She shook her head.

"A man who loves wine. A man who loves his daughter. A man who loves this kingdom. I know your father was framed. But by whom? I can only guess the Whispers, though that would be difficult to prove in a trial. I could be persuaded to pardon him, to show my benevolence. You see, I have read every letter you've ever written to your father. He's kept every parchment you've scrawled on since you could write. Despite being the bastard product of an affair, you are his, and he loves you. I give you his fate, Leyre. All you have to do is find the object I desire. Two, but they come in a set."

He picked up Duque Arias's wineglass and drank. "This was a very good year. The bottle is a tempranillo from your family's region, I believe."

Realization dawned in Leyre's jade-green eyes. "Were any of the glasses poisoned?"

"No."

"How do you know someone wouldn't rather drink the poison than face your wrath?"

Fernando cocked an eyebrow. "At the very least that would show conviction. I'm more interested in ferreting out the cowards who don't want to die. The Fajardos have always taken chances. Do we have a deal?"

"What will happen to me if I fail?" she asked.

"Your father would remain in Soledad prison. You would return to Luzou, and the Las Rosas estates would be remanded to the crown." He flashed a smile at the way she simmered with rage. That was the key.

She offered her hand, and when they shook, she did not let go first. "What is the object I am to track?"

King Fernando got up to pull open a hidden compartment on the fireplace mantel. He retrieved a wooden box and laid it in front of her. "Inside is everything you need to find that which was taken from me."

Leyre reached into the box and pulled out a golden sextant, small enough to fit around her fist. Diamond constellations were etched in the gold.

"It's beautiful," she said.

"There's more."

She kept digging and pulled out a slip of parchment with an illustration of a magnificent weapon. She scoffed. "You want me to find you a knife?"

"It's not just any knife," he said with a fervor he didn't mean to display. "It was taken from me long ago. I thought it lost to time and space. But I've discovered a plot that threatens everything I have ever worked toward. Now I *know* someone else is searching for it. He will lead you to the location, but what he doesn't know is that you need this sextant to get there."

"And after I have the weapon?"

"Kill him."

She frowned. "Whose life am I taking?"

His own blood and bane. "My son, of course. Prince Castian."

1

I REMEMBER STANDING IN THIS MARKET SQUARE NOT LONG AGO, AND I DON'T know what has changed more: the village or myself. The old dirt road is now paved with worn cobblestones. New wooden stalls form crooked rows offering dates and imported nuts by the barrel. A vendor, whose teeth have as many holes as the hard cheese he's peddling, offers me a sample that I decline. Faces I know so well are etched with wrinkles and gray. When did the inn at the top of the hill add two more stories?

In the back of my mind, a girl whispers her name to me over and over again. *I am Renata Convida,* she says, and she repeats it until I feel myself slowly fade away.

I remember standing in this market square, but this memory is not mine.

I am Renata Convida, and I am trapped inside my own mind.

My body, numb and still, is planted in front of a market stall. I'm aware of the baker asking a question, but the sounds of the stolen memory imprison me. The corners of my vision blur with color, like looking at the bend of light through a prism—laughter and music warped behind glass. Then all of it, the village green, the baker, everything, is leached of color. I am slipping into a void that swallows my memories whole, where there is nothing but a terrifying quiet.

But somewhere, a sound hooks my belly and tugs me back to reality.

"I *said*, are ye going to stand there," the haggard baker shouts, "or are ye going to buy something?"

Perhaps it is the shrill pitch of her voice that frees me from the occurrence, but I'm so grateful that I gladly return her grimace with a smile. These moments have come and gone over the last two weeks. They start with an uneasy sensation in my gut and end with me trapped inside a memory that's so vivid it feels as if someone is possessing my body and mind. This one lasted the longest.

All my life, my power has been as much a mystery to me as it was to the elders of my people. I can steal memories from the living, and they become mine forever. I have taken so many memories that I have a vault in my mind, the Gray, to store them. Sometimes memories slip out like frail ghosts. But this, whatever it is, feels different. I walk down a road, and without warning, I am overcome with the sensation that I am not myself. I see a familiar face, and it takes every ounce of strength not to call out a name. I stand in this market, and I see the way it used to be.

I've discerned that I can snap out of a memory occurrence when I go through my mental list of reminders: *I am Renata Convida. I am a Robári. I am of the Moria people.* Once I was a rebel, one of the Whispers. Now I am just a traitor. It has been thirteen—no, fourteen—days since I betrayed my people and chose to follow my enemy, Prince Castian. Though, to be fair, they betrayed me first.

The smells of candied walnuts, ale, and bread remind me of where I am: the quaint village of Acesteña, in the Sól Abene region of the kingdom of Puerto Leones.

Bread.

That's what I left the inn to get.

The baker scrutinizes me. Like most people from the Sól Abene provincia, she has a fair complexion, obsidian eyes, and thick black brows. Her hair, white as milk but still full, must have once been black, too. Her simple brown tunic is dusted with flour. Her shrewd stare lingers on my clothes—cream blouse with long sleeves and a modest high collar, deep blue linen skirt with a dusty hem. My hair, dark as crow feathers, is braided in a crown, and wisps unravel at my temples because I have never been good at this sort of thing. My scarred hands—which would give me away as a Robári— are gloved in delicate white lace. But here, in Sól Abene, married women keep their hair tied back and their hands, legs, and necks covered, so I do not stand out. At least I hope not.

"Two loaves, one hazelnut tart, and an olive oil cake, please." I dig into my pocket for my coin purse.

The baker's wrinkled scowl turns into a pleased nod. "Here for Carnaval, are ye?"

I nod. We are not here for Carnaval de Santa Cariña, but the festivities are the perfect cover. While the village is full of revelers from all over the provincias, Castian and I will appear to be two tourists enjoying the culinary offerings and dulcet sounds of bag- pipes when we meet with Castian's informant.

"And honeymoon," I say sweetly. I *hope* it's sweet. Whenever

I try to sound like Sayida from my old unit, I end up shouting in people's faces and smiling as though I am deranged. Sayida would probably get free braided sugar bread.

The baker turns away from me. Yes, definitely deranged over sweet. She wraps the olive oil cake in brown butcher paper and ties it up with pretty gold thread. "Don't look very happy about it, do ye?"

I blanch. I should be used to the brusque nature of the Sól Abene provincia by now.

"Don't worry, dearie. Yer still a bit young for it, ain't ye? Why, my first marriage was for love. Love can survive anything, except the plague, of course. My second marriage was for the bakery. If the first one doesn't work, make sure ye outlive the second so ye will always have a trade."

Still speechless, I dig deeper into my coin purse, wishing it was large enough to hide within. "Uhhh—thank you. That is very wise."

"Wisdom is free. The bread and cakes will be twenty pesos."

"Twenty?" Neighboring vendors crane their necks. I lean closer and lower my voice. "A week ago, my—husband—bought this and paid ten."

The baker purses her thin lips. "Aye, but a week ago, the king hadn't doubled the tax on wheat. Not to mention the fees for the olive oil coming down from Provincia Zaharina. Barely breaking even now, aren't I? I'm giving ye the loaves on the house on account of yer honeymoon. Fifteen for the cake. Five for the tart."

Doubled the tax on wheat. Again. Last time this happened, the king and justice were funding their war efforts. I should count myself lucky. When I traveled with my rebel unit, we stole, scavenged, and hunted for food during missions. Now I have a purse full of coins. Of course, it is still stolen because I took them from Castian this morning after he'd left for the day with nothing but a note that read *I will return for supper.* ~~Your~~ *Your husband.* I balled it up and threw it into the dying embers of the fireplace. Then I dug into the hidden pocket in his pack that he thinks I don't know about and stole a few coins.

But twenty pesos for some sweets is an indulgence we don't deserve. After a fortnight of searching for Dez and the Knife of Memory, our trail has gone cold. Dez, once my unit leader, was the one who taught me how to hide my tracks. I thought I knew him well enough to find him. It was what Castian counted on. But perhaps Dez didn't teach me all his tricks. Perhaps he doesn't want to be found—not even by me.

The longer we go without a trace of Dez, the more the prince and I fight. I convince myself that the battles have earned me these cakes, and so I count out the large pesos and place them on the baker's outstretched hand. She pockets them inside her apron, hands over the baked goods, and moves on to other customers.

On my way through the market, I'm hit with a wave of nausea. That's usually how the occurrences start, followed by the sensation of someone taking a hatchet to my skull. I hurry down the road toward the inn, holding my basket against my chest. I try to focus on the hillcrest ahead, focus on the present and not the stolen memories trying to overtake me. Each labored breath gets me a few paces closer. I slip through the foot traffic and try to name the smells—roasted meat, vinegar, salted fish imported from several coasts. I try to recite my list of grounding truths, when I realize someone is watching me.

A bead of sweat stings my eyes, but I still see him. A bearded young man with strange blue eyes and a speckle of blood on his cheek. He weaves through sheep herded by a girl in a pale green dress. How long has he been following me?

I stop to smile at an elderly couple. He stops, too, and when the couple moves away, he keeps coming toward me. I pick up my pace. My heart leaps to my throat. Does he recognize me from the wanted leaflets? Most of them are poorly rendered and could be any girl in Puerto Leones with brown eyes and black hair. Besides, the Second Sweep would be looking for a filthy rebel, not a recent bride on holiday.

When I glance over my shoulder, the young bearded man shouts, but I can't hear him over the music and ruckus of the market. I notice the knives at his hip and the crude sack over his shoulder leaking blood. I remember the stories the Whispers would tell in the dark of rogue hunters who work for the king. They're not military or honorable. They simply hunt Moria, like me, cutting our body parts to sell as trophies.

I run.

My thighs burn from the quick uphill climb. I drop a loaf from my basket, but I keep going. I hate the fear that licks its way between my ribs. This is not how I'm supposed to get caught. Anger needles at me because I know I should have stayed in our room. I shouldn't have left without Castian.

I reach the top of the hill, and the man yells for me again. This time he says my name. Not the name written in the leaflets. *Wanted: Renata Convida. Robári. Murderer.* Instead he calls me by a name only my father ever did.

For a moment, the inn vanishes. The marketplace is gone. There is only a void of black ahead and behind me. I squeeze my eyes shut. This can't happen again. Not now.

"Nati!" His deep voice is right against my ear. "What's gotten into you?"

The present returns in a cold rush. I drop my basket and succumb to the pressure at my temples. All at once I realize that I'm in Castian's arms. I cling to the worn cotton of his tunic and feel his racing heartbeat under my palm as he holds me upright. *Castian* is the strange bearded man. I had completely forgotten about his illusion, the face he was wearing.

I can't afford to forget.

"I—I didn't realize it was you," I say, and push off him. Gather my bread. The olive oil cake is a little smooshed, but even covered in dirt I'd eat it. "You scared me."

I leave him at the top of the hill and resume my retreat to the inn. His long legs allow him to catch up to me in a few paces.

His hair is a muddy brown, matted at his temples. He tugs on his short brown beard. "I *scared* you?"

"Maybe you should have chosen a more memorable face!"

"Maybe you should just tell me the truth."

"What are you talking about?" I wince at the headache that started building in the market.

A grumble starts at the back of his throat. "Something is wrong, and it would be advantageous to the remainder of our mission if you wouldn't shut me out the way you've done since you *chose* to follow me out that window."

We reach the Sagrada Inn. One of the servant girls who moon after Castian watches us yell at each other as she arranges a flower arch over the door. I whirl to face him. There's dirt on his forehead. I want to brush it away, but I clench my fist around my wicker basket.

He sighs, defeated, and says, "We should go upstairs."

"No, go ahead. You're the expert on honesty. What exactly do you think I'm keeping from you?"

I know he won't say it. Not when we might be overheard. It isn't fair of me to dare him.

"Ahem," comes a high-pitched cough from a source I've come to know too well. The innkeeper and owner, Doña Sagrada. Her graying hair is neatly twisted in a bun, and a festive red rose is pinned behind her ear. She smooths the front of her apron and beams wide brown eyes at Castian. "I thought I heard my favorite lovebirds. You certainly fight and make up like a married couple, Señor Otsoa, but please keep it down. We've had some complaints from the adjoining rooms. I've told them that you're here for Carnaval on your honeymoon. Which reminds me, your deposit won't cover any damage to the bed."

I think of how yesterday, I may or may not have thrown Castian's boots at him when we were discussing his brother. How once again we lost his trail. How once again I failed.

"I assure you—" I begin to deny any sort of marital bliss, but Castian interjects with a dizzying smile.

"That we will show more restraint."

"It's no bother at all. Now, did you bring it?" Doña Sagrada asks Castian, clapping her plump little hands together.

Castian avoids glancing at me, but even his Illusionári magics can't hide the red creeping up the open front of his tunic, to the tops of his cheeks. He hands over the bloody sack. "Yes. I had luck and caught two of them. One is for you."

"Oh, Señor Otsoa!" The matron beams, resting her hand on his muscular forearm. "Bless you!"

"Please, I told you. Call me Will."

"What is it?" I ask.

The innkeeper clucks at me. "Ruin the surprise, Marcela, why don't you! But when Will said you'd been craving the rabbit fricassee that we ran out of, I said the butcher only had beef and pork for Carnaval, but if he caught me a rabbit, I'd whip it up for you."

Yesterday, after we hurled cruel words at each other, I was tired and hungry. We ate fried pork and salted potatoes, and I said offhandedly that I missed the rabbit fricassee. Then I crawled into my pillows and covers on the floor and went to sleep in front of the fire.

Castian won't meet my eyes, but he is an expert at charade in a way that I am not. He gently takes my basket. I didn't realize he had picked up the loaf I dropped in my haste.

Doña Sagrada nods. "It's my great-grandmother's recipe. She was a cook in the old palace for the Sól Abene royals back in those days. The Duque Sól Abene himself still comes to eat here when he isn't in the capital. He always comes home for Carnaval, but I don't expect him during these troubled times."

I smile painfully. "Yes, you've mentioned that." Once or fifteen times.

Castian quickly takes the innkeeper's hand and kisses it. She blushes and gives me a look, as if she thinks I'm the luckiest new bride in the whole kingdom. "We thank you, Doña Sagrada. Truly."

We. Me and Castian. A bolt of pain drives between my eyes, and I can't tell whether it's my broken mind or just the hatred for him I haven't been able to shake.

As we follow the matron inside the tavern, I catch sight of a red uniform. Two young soldiers belonging to the Second Sweep are sitting at a table drinking from glass pints. They're laughing, and before one of them can look up at me, I whirl around and cling to Castian like I can't get enough of this man, my husband. He doesn't bat an eye, but I feel him tense.

"We will be in our room, Doña Sagrada," he says, and the roughness in his voice tells me I'm not alone in fearing the closeness of the king's presence.

The innkeeper places the back of her hand on my forehead. Her knuckles calloused but warm. For a flash, I remember something I had locked away for so long: my own mother checking my temperature. I only see her face for a moment, but it's enough to make me wobble. Castian tightens his grip around my waist, and I don't fight him. For now, I'm grateful that I'm not alone, even if I have to be with him.

"Oh dear. You're flushed, Señora Otsoa. I'll send up fresh water and a manzanilla tea. It worked wonders for me in the first few months I was with child."

Castian is so startled that I can see his illusion flicker ever so slightly in the gold that shimmers in a lock of his hair.

"That would be lovely!" I say, saccharine and shrill. "Let's go, *darling.*"

I yank Castian by his hand up the stairs, leaving the kind and clueless innkeeper clutching a bloody bag full of game. I spare one glance at the soldiers, getting up without paying, as they return to their patrol.

Castian fumbles with the skeleton key and unlocks our door. When he slams it shut, his illusion falls away, revealing the true blue-green of his eyes, his long golden hair curling against broad shoulders. A rough ridge breaks the straight line of his nose, and the thick brown beard returns to burnished gold scruff.

"We need to talk," he says, then looks down at his feet.

I set the basket of baked goods on the table. "Let's."

But we only stand there, neither saying a word. I might prefer the fights to moments like this.

There are so many things we should discuss. I'd start with the fact that we've been here a week and this is the first time guards in royal red have arrived. I still have the thick scar on my neck from my last tangle with the Second Sweep, soldiers Castian once trained himself and are now commanded by the king and justice. Then there's Dez, Castian's brother and my former—everything. How I didn't deny Doña Sagrada's herbal tea because I fear the possibility that she may be right. There's the not knowing whether our quest will make any difference or maybe push the kingdom closer to destruction. And then there is our very tangled past. How Castian, years before he was this monstrous prince, was my very best friend. My only friend.

Castian and I agreed to work together, but how can we, when we don't trust each other? He's right, I have been keeping something secret. But when I look at him, truly look at him, I know something else is wrong.

"What is it?" I ask.

He withdraws a balled-up piece of parchment from his pocket. Even as I stand right in front of him, he doesn't meet my eyes. I take the parchment but watch his features. Anger in the furrow between his brows. Hurt in the single tremble of his bottom lip. Denial in the way he inhales deeply, crosses his arms over his chest, and sighs.

I uncrumple the parchment, prepared to see a new sketch of my face with a new reward. Instead, there is a single sentence scrawled across the center.

Stop following me. I'm already gone.

It's Dez.

2

NO MATTER HOW MANY TIMES I READ THE WORDS, THEY DON'T FEEL REAL. I TUG off my gloves and run my fingertips along the familiar handwriting. What did I imagine? That the ink would be raised, like the rivers of scars that run across my hands? That I'd be able to lift some sort of memory from this?

Stop following me. I'm already gone.

I spent weeks believing that Dez had been killed. His execution in Andalucía might have been an illusion created by Castian, but the desperation and the grief I endured was real.

"Dez knows we're tracking him," I say.

Castian puts as much distance between us as possible. The honeymoon suite is the biggest room in the inn. There's a private bathing tub, a fireplace, a bed large enough to fit a small Leonesse family, a dining table for two, and plush rugs and throw blankets, which over the last few days, I've hoarded for myself. And yet this space has never felt so suffocating.

I rub the emerald wedding ring I've worn since we left together. "Dez knows that *I* know he's alive."

Castian is aware of this, but I have to say the words because otherwise I'll convince myself that this is a cruel trick.

"He must have been following me," he says, pushing open the curtains. Afternoon rays glint off the silver hand mirror and brush on the table. He rolls up his sleeves, pours water from the pitcher into a porcelain basin, and scrubs his hands with a bar of soap. "He pinned it to the tree where I'd set my trap."

"He couldn't have gone far," I say. "The village has one main road. He'll want to avoid the patrols there. He'll take the woods."

"You said Andrés was the best hunter among the Whispers. He could be anywhere by now."

I crush the parchment in my fists. "What do you want me to do? Nothing?"

Castian leans on the vanity and cranes his head back, like he's searching for strength from the Six Heavens. "It is clear my brother does not want to be found."

I angrily close the distance between us, but my delicate slippers don't give me the stomping effect I would prefer. He turns to face me, drying his hands on a towel as I slap the crumpled parchment against his chest.

"You're the one who convinced me to come with you. You're the one who wanted to find him."

Castian simply lets the message fall to our feet. I want him to be furious. I want him to want to *do* something.

"That hasn't changed." Exasperation steels his words. "But my informant is arriving tomorrow with the forged documents we need. The Second Sweep is downstairs. Even if I cloak us with an illusion for as long as my strength will hold, do you have any idea where Andrés would go from here?"

Hearing Castian speak Dez's birth name is still so strange. Dez himself didn't reveal it to me until the night we slept together. The night before he was captured. No, the night before he *let* himself be captured. When did Dez notice us? Has he been watching Castian and me pretend to be married all this time? Dez was the best hunter and tracker in the Whispers. But what's left of the rebels fled to safety across the sea.

Stop following me. I'm already gone.

There's a tightness around my chest, and I have to remind myself to breathe.

"No," I admit. "I don't know where Dez would go from here."

Castian opens the doors leading onto a narrow balcony. The cool breeze carries the scent of the Acesteña forest and the roasting meats from down below. Villagers mill about preparing for tomorrow's festivities. Everything outside this room continues, and I have never felt at such a distance from the world. I grip the rail and inhale deeply, but my heart still races, my mind fires too quickly.

I think of my old rebel unit. Are they safe? And why should I care, after they left me to rot? I think of the king's weapon, somewhere out there, and the chaos we left behind in the capital. The growing patrols in even the smallest hamlet. I worry that the damage I have done to my mind may be irreparable. Worst of all is that there is a small part of me, like the first drop of water signaling a storm, that is glad I'm not alone. Even if I am with the prince of Puerto Leones.

"What happened to you earlier?" Castian asks tentatively.

I know that he means the occurrences, but I don't want to talk to him about it. Not after reading Dez's note.

I realize I'm hungry and leave him on the balcony. After a

moment of hesitation he follows. I break off a piece of the fresh bread from my basket and offer it to him.

"I'm sorry I took your pesos without asking. You can't blame me. I'm a thief."

Castian plops the bread in his mouth and shuts his eyes. I wonder if it's the first thing he's eaten today.

"You could have asked me for the coin," he says.

"Well, what if you'd left for good? What if this morning you'd decided that you changed your mind and returned to your father?"

Castian gestures in the direction of the forest. "I left to hunt."

"I didn't ask you to."

"I know you didn't ask me to. I just—I wish you'd have waited for me. We promised that we wouldn't venture into the village alone. And I wouldn't leave you without a word," he adds harshly, strangling the air with his fists. His knuckles are scarred, and I remember the spiked gauntlets he liked to wear. How slick with blood they were after he was finished. "You should know that by now."

"All I know of you, of the man that you are, is what I've seen for myself. The destruction you left behind. You might have hidden your Moria powers from the king and Puerto Leones, but that doesn't make you the same as those who have suffered and died under your family's reign for decades."

I see the hurt that flashes across his face. As still as he is, Castian resembles a gilded statue. Despite my frustration, my breath catches at the sight of him because he is so impossibly, infuriatingly beautiful. I thought that long ago, once. How can someone so hateful look the way he does? But Prince Castian is made of shadows and lies. He orchestrated his reputation for years. And to what end? The kingdom is no closer to being fixed by his actions, and now we are here, bound by a single purpose: the hunt for his brother and the legendary Knife of Memory. It seems we are no longer in search of one of those things.

He turns and kneels in front of the fireplace. He does that when he's upset. Gets eerily calm, then busies his hands with something to do. This time he's moving my makeshift bed on the floor and sweeping away the soot.

"We won't be able to move forward if all we do is lash out at each other," he says. "We can't keep secrets or lies. Not if there is to be trust between us."

Part of me doesn't want to move forward. Part of me wants to stop this quest, find a quiet corner of the world, and live out the rest of my days. Isn't it enough that I have to live with the memories locked inside my head, the ones that have been coming undone bit by bit every day? I was once a weapon that led to the death of thousands of Moria and Leonesse alike. Now I'm left with tattered thoughts and little understanding of who I'm supposed to be. And there it is, isn't it? The answer to my own traitorous weakness. I may not want to move forward, but I owe it to the memory of my parents to try. To mend a kingdom Castian and I both helped break.

"Fine," I say.

"No more lies."

"I have nothing to hide, Castian."

He goes to retrieve new logs from the corner, but it's empty. He grunts. Scratches the side of his neck. Twists the marriage band around his finger. It's made of oak carved with runes of unity.

"Is what the innkeeper said true? Are you—"

It takes me a breath to realize what he means. I grab a wilting flower from the vase in front of me and throw it at him. He catches it and swiftly ushers it into the dead fireplace.

"It's a highly unlikely suspicion," I snap. It's true that my monthly bleeding is late. Late enough that I've been worried since we've arrived in Acesteña. "Moria apothecuras taught us that these things are affected by stress on the body and heart. I'd say the last weeks have been full of that. Though I have considered that my nausea might be the side effects of your Illusionári magics. Every time you hold me while you're glamoured, I want to throw up."

His lips twitch, as if he's trying to suppress a laugh. "It's good to know I provoke such a strong reaction from you. Did you feel this way the night of the festival?"

That was the night everything went wrong. The Sun Festival. I remember us dancing across the ballroom and then beating each other bloody. I remember wondering why Castian knew my childhood name, the one only my father had called me. I pressed my fingers to his bare skin with every intention of ripping every memory from his head, but it didn't work. I wonder if it was because part of me, deep down, recognized him from when we were children and truly didn't want to hurt him.

"No," I say. "Your magics didn't affect me that night."

"You can rule me out. I've learned to control my magics to minimize the side effect, Nati," he says earnestly. "I wish you'd told me."

"When I knew for certain, I would have."

"Are you sure of that?"

"What happened between Dez and me is not your business. The Whispers all drink irvena tea, which would make a pregnancy highly unlikely."

"But not impossible."

I rub my hands across my face. I wish Sayida were the one asking me these questions. "No. Not impossible."

"Then perhaps we should find my brother to reunite you with your *dear heart*. Even though he knows exactly where to find you and left again."

"I *hate* you." The words froth at my lips like venom.

The cruel, violent prince I know is back. His blue-green eyes dark and cold, his lip a snarl. "I hate you more."

Castian's glamour slides back into place. Stomping past me, he slams the door.

I yank the ring from my finger and throw it into the pile of cinders. I sit on the floor until I stop trembling. My anger melts into the kind of heartache I first felt on the day I believed Dez was dead. Why am I still grieving for someone who is very much alive? *Because he was once everything to you*, I answer.

I wish I could take everything I said to Castian back. There's something about him that makes me so angry. Working with him seemed bearable if I could see Dez again and convince him to join us in our search for the mythical weapon. But spending every day and night pretending to be Castian's wife is harder than I thought it'd be.

Letting go of a long, tired breath, I dig through the cinders to find the wedding ring. When Castian lent it to me for our disguise, I didn't ask why he'd had it at the ready. In my tired state it seemed that princes carried their riches with them. But there, in that seaside cave, he'd been so prepared, like he'd spent his whole life ready to one day run away. I wonder if it was once worn by his former fiancée. Why would it matter?

I clean the gold band and emerald, then slip it back on my finger. What would my old unit say now? *Renata Convida, the wife of our enemy.* But Castian isn't my enemy. He's the only person who chose me.

For this to work, for us to destroy his father and right the wrongs of the past, I have to find a way to quell my anger.

Tugging on my gloves, I go in search of him.

I cut through the lunch crowd filling the tavern. He isn't among the gathering on the green. Women make flower crowns and lace masks. An old man plays the bagpipes, and several inn guests lounge on blankets under the sun. He wouldn't go back to the market at the busiest time of day. He'd want to sulk and perhaps add to his scarred knuckles by hitting something. Then it occurs to me: the woods.

When I pass the inn's courtyard, a rhythmic thwacking sound catches my attention. Before he left, Castian was going to make a new fire, but we were out of logs. Of course, he's cutting wood.

I catch a glimpse of him through the lines of laundered sheets blowing in the breeze. I think of the lavanderas I met when I was in the palace, and suddenly, I miss the afternoons we spent washing linens. Those girls took me in. And I used them to steal memories of the prince.

Castian is right. I haven't been completely honest with him. I start to step forward, but then I hear voices. A trio of servant girls from the inn huddles behind stacks of crates watching the shirtless man. I want to laugh until I hear what they say.

"That Wilmer Otsoa could split me in half, and I'd die happily," one declares, exaggerating her husky voice for effect. "How does a musician wind up with all those muscles and scars?"

"Maybe ye should offer, Silvia," another girl suggests. "Look at the way he's chopping those logs. That's a man who hasn't found pleasure in a very, *very* long time."

"Silvia will not offer *anything*. He's just married. That's a sin!" the youngest pipes up.

"Marriage don't make ye an expert in matters of the *flesh*." The girl emphasizes the last word.

They fall into hysterics. I yank the sheet that blocks me from their view.

"No," I say, smiling at their yelping, reddening faces, "but practice does."

I hate you.

I hate you more.

Those were our exact words mere moments ago. But being

laughed at by these girls who are barely older than I am reminds me of the years I spent under similar scorn. I tell myself that they rankle me because they are taking a liberty with a man who is supposed to be my husband. That is a disrespect a young wife wouldn't tolerate. I tell myself that we have to keep up our charade. If the people around us don't believe that Castian and I are married and in love, then we would open ourselves to scrutiny. I tell myself that we can't afford to lose our cover.

And that is why I march across the grass to where he is chopping logs. He hasn't glamoured away the scars on his bare chest and across his shoulders. He's being careless because of our fight.

Castian stops midswing, and his eyes track me, as prey might track its hunter. I cup one hand on the back of his neck, threading my fingers through his hair, and yank him against me.

"What are you—?"

"They're suspicious," I whisper quickly. "We have to—"

He makes a fist against my lower back, and I feel his entire body tense with revulsion. He presses me tight against his chest, glistening with sweat. My arm is trapped between us, right over his heart. I can feel his pulse, as frantic as my own.

Then he meets me halfway. Our teeth collide, but his rough kiss softens. His tongue chases away the sting of his bite, and I feel an ache deep in my belly when he makes a gruff sound at the back of his throat. He must hate this. I hate this. Don't I? Why can't I stop myself from raking my nails along his scars?

My breath hitches when he squeezes me harder, lifting me in the air. When he pulls away, his calloused thumb traces the side of my cheek, down to my neck where he unpins my braid. He winds it around his fist and tugs ever so slightly.

"Don't use me like this, Nati," he whispers, then presses a final kiss on my exposed neck, right over a thick white scar.

Speechless, I return to the inn, keenly aware of the girls watching me with a combination of awe and jealousy as they finish their chores.

When I get back upstairs, I run to the privy to relieve myself.

"Thank the Mother of All," I say. I have never been so relieved to find that I am bleeding.

I go back downstairs and pay Doña Sagrada for a hot bath and new undergarments. There is no being demure around a woman her age, though I assure her I was never with child to begin with. She takes my coin and leaves me a fresh towel and a couple of sea sponges.

She pats my cheek and says, "Don't worry, soon you'll have a litter."

In my bath, I scrub myself clean. I lick the inside of my lip where Castian's teeth cut me from the force of our kiss. I remind myself that it was a necessity. Why do people love newlyweds so much? I can't fathom. In the last town we were in, we held hands in public and shared a chaste closed-mouth peck to sell our charade. Then when we reached our room we shot to our separate corners. But today was different.

I replay the shock in his eyes, the tension with which he held me, like he was fighting to not shove me away. The way his voice was almost pleading. *Don't use me like this, Nati.*

I finish washing my hair, insert the sea sponge for my bleeding, and rinse with the cold water that's left. When I step into our room, I barely recognize the suite. My makeshift bed on the floor has been folded away. The fireplace is lit and crackling. Supper has been set under a porcelain serving dome, three fat candles drip around a fresh bouquet of wildflowers.

And there, at the foot of the bed, is Castian, doing the best he can to brush hundreds of petals off the blanket.

What a perfect start to the romantic dinner with my fake husband.

3

"I DIDN'T DO THIS," CASTIAN ASSURES ME. PANIC FLOODS HIS FEATURES.

My hair is still damp and loose over my shoulders, and when I step closer, I notice his is, too. He smells like soap and woodsmoke.

"I didn't imagine so." I chuckle and shove my dirty clothes in my pack.

"Doña Sagrada truly outdid herself." He throws rose petals into the roaring fire, then rubs his palms together.

"I'm ready to talk." I take a seat at the table and lift the serving dome. The savory steam from the rabbit fricassee makes my mouth water. "Honestly."

Castian sits in front of me, dressed in a loose black tunic open at the chest. The candlelight makes shadows dance along his forearms as he ladles our meal onto large plates. Here is the prince of Puerto Leones serving me dinner, making sure my plate is full first. I pour wine into the crystal goblets. Then we stare at each other, and I'm not sure who should begin.

"Ren—"

"Let me speak," I say softly. "It's taken me hours to work up the nerve. I *have* been keeping something from you." He sits back, and I'm uncertain about the way his stare makes me feel, but I know I have to try for the good of our mission. "There is something wrong with my memories."

He leans forward on his elbows. "What do you mean?"

I bite my lower lip. I've never really spoken to anyone about my magics except for Dez and my old mentor, Illan.

"There is a part of my mind where all the memories I've locked up live. Every Hollow I've created is in there, but so are most memories from my own life. I call it the Gray. I've never known another Robári well, so I don't know how to control it or whether I can ever be rid of it. But once a memory is taken, I can't give it back."

I take a sip from my glass. He keeps watching, waiting.

"I feel like I'm losing control of the Gray," I confess. "Méndez was the first Hollow I've made in years."

"You've been reliving his memories," Castian whispers.

"Yes, but something worse has been happening to me. If I'm in a place, a memory will slip out that belongs to that location, and I cease to exist. When I was in the market earlier, I forgot why I had gone in the first place. Then I forgot your glamour, and I thought you were going to attack me."

He rakes his fingers through his golden hair. "I apologize for frightening you."

"You couldn't have known. This is new to me, too." I drink from my wine goblet. "The night the Whispers kidnapped you, I was trapped with the Ripper. I let him—I let Cebrián take my magics."

Castian says nothing, but nods in understanding. I don't know what to do with that feeling.

"I wanted it to be over," I continue. "My unit had used me as bait. The Whispers wanted me dead. I wanted to end. But when Cebrián used his power on me, it felt like it bounced back. I don't know what happened, but I could see his last memory—he was watching you play with dice. Then my memories of the escape from the palace all returned. I realized it was *you* who helped me escape, not Dez. And since then, the Gray has been spilling out, releasing bits of my own memories along with the others. I'm afraid they're taking me over. What if—what if the next time a memory is sparked, I'm lost in that moment forever?"

He holds his fork in a vise grip, prongs up, and if we were other kinds of people, if we were friends, I'd joke about how he looks like an ancient sea god. But we aren't, we are just Castian and Renata.

"I will find a way to help you."

"It's not that simple. How many Robári have you ever known?"

"Only you." A smile tugs at his lips when he drinks.

"Exactly. There's no helping this, Castian. At least you have a grip on your magics. You're not ripping at the seams like I am."

"Yes, I am, Nati." He holds my stare. "I want to tell you that everything is going to be all right and that we're going to find the Knife of Memory, but the truth is, I am more terrified of what will happen once we do. How do I even start to heal this kingdom when I can barely get you to look at me without murder in your eyes? How am I supposed to lead Puerto Leones if I can't survive you?"

The fire crackles. Someone outside is singing in preparation for tomorrow's Carnaval.

"I won't matter when this is over," I tell him. "I'm going to set things right. And then I'm never going to step foot in Puerto Leones again."

He refills our wine and drinks deeply. "Perhaps you shouldn't use your magics until we find out more. It's not worth hurting yourself."

My entire life, my magics were all anyone wanted from me. The king and justice used me to rip images from the minds of their enemies. The Whispers, my own people, did the same. But Castian is the first person in my recent memory to propose something else. I don't trust myself to speak so I nod.

"That's settled." He looks down at his food and pushes the peas and perfectly cubed potatoes across his plate.

"You used to do that when we were little," I say, and take a bite of my rabbit. Doña Sagrada's family recipe is exquisite. The meat is tender and melts on my tongue, though the fricassee is still hot, and I burn the tip of my tongue eating too quickly.

Castian's laugh is deep, his smile wide. "Of all the things that you suddenly decide to remember about me, it's my aversion to peas?"

"In the process of being honest with each other, I have to confess I have more memories of you. Recent ones."

I tell him how I gathered memories from people in the palace—his chambermaid, a demoted general, and Lady Nuria, his former fiancée.

"Nuria deserved better than what I could give her. I thought breaking our arranged marriage would free her. I was wrong. My father had other plans." He shifts uncomfortably in his seat while eating around the peas. After a while he says, "You have the memory of Nuria and me—"

"Two actually," I say quickly, using the rest of the bread to sop up the gravy.

He winces, embarrassed. "No wonder you hate me."

"When she offered up her memories, I thought it was so that she could move on from you. But I wonder if she wanted me to understand you beyond the stories of the Bloodied Prince."

"And do you?"

I chew longer than I need to because I don't know how to answer this. "It was difficult to piece you together. Imagine my shock these past days realizing you've always been hiding under your magics."

"I don't want to lie to my kingdom," he says, voice low with lament. "I don't want to kill. I don't want my family's legacy to be ruin. But this is the only way I could help my country."

"No, it wasn't." My heart beats quickly, and I can't tell whether it's because I'm angry or because I remember that Castian got up before sunrise to catch this rabbit for me. "You could have joined the Whispers. You could have killed your father long ago. Instead, you chose to play games. To create illusions over the citizens of this kingdom. I remember the Battle of Riomar, and those deaths *weren't* an illusion."

"You think murdering my father is so simple?" His laugh is dark, his eyes glossy with tears and regret. "You have no idea what my father is capable of. It's so easy for you to think that, isn't it, Nati? Your world is either the Whispers or the justice. I am either a murderer or a rake ruining the women in my life. But what you fail to realize while you're casting judgment upon me is that the Whispers conspired with my own mother to let me believe I killed my baby brother. I lived with that truth as a boy and as a man." He shoves his plate away, fork clattering on the porcelain. "Do you remember me as a child? My mother locked away with her ladies, always in a stupor. Parents kept their children away from court. When we met, you thought I was a servant boy because I was always filthy."

I pick up my goblet and sit back. "Am I supposed to feel sorry for you? You were my only friend while I was a prisoner in your father's castle. *Your* castle."

"I'm not comparing our tragedies. It doesn't matter who suffered the most because we're here now. I'm doing the best I can now. Is it enough?"

"It has to be."

The sun is long set, and the candles are half burned down into puddles of wax. We keep sipping our wine in silence, testing the waters between us. An unfamiliar sensation spreads across my shoulders, my chest. Is this what it feels like to share a burden?

"You have to ask yourself if you truly want to continue this journey with me. I need your help. That hasn't changed."

"I'm not going anywhere," I say. "What about your informant? Can we trust them?"

"With my life. The search for my brother led us here, but we can't go much farther without documents. And as I am currently being held captive by the Whispers, I can't use my usual resources to procure us passage out of the kingdom."

I raise my glass. "Here's to the runaway prince of Puerto Leones."

He tries to suppress a grin but clinks his glass against mine. "I normally wouldn't celebrate before we're aboard the ship, but I know the hardest challenge is yet to come."

"Do you mean the part where we use a decades-old captain's log to chart our route to a mystical Moria island that *supposedly* holds this knife?"

Castian leans back languidly, ever the confident prince. "Precisely."

"You never told me how you discovered that logbook."

He offers a genuine smile, narrow eyes and all teeth. "It's a long story for when I've consumed less wine. But I won it off Duque Arias."

"The *gambling* runaway prince of Puerto Leones," I amend. "We have a map to Isla Sombras, a secret ally, and threadbare hope."

"I'm sorry about today," he says quickly, as if he's been holding it back. "I don't hate you."

I wish that I could say the same thing, but something's wedged inside my heart. Like a splinter buried so deep the skin just grows around it. "I'm sorry I kissed you like that."

"I'm not." Cas's gaze flickers from my lips to his plate of peas. "What I mean is we have to keep up this ruse for a period of time, but you don't have to do anything you revile. We can set rules. Boundaries."

I see the moment again—the laughing girls, the flutter of his eyes. I clear my throat. "For the sake of peace, I will admit that kissing you isn't the worst thing I've done on a mission."

"High praise."

"Perhaps we limit our shouting to the safety of our room, the way married people fight?"

"I don't know. I can't recall my parents willingly talking or being in the same room together." His smile falters, but only for a moment. When he looks at me, his sadness is gone, carefully veiled by bright turquoise eyes and that smile. "Did Doña Sagrada leave us dessert?"

"No, but I did." I fetch the cake wrapped in butcher paper. We clear the dirty dishes onto a tray, and I undo the gold string.

"Is that...?" He doesn't even finish his sentence before breaking off a piece and biting down.

Frosting from the olive oil cake is smeared across the wrapping where it fell. Castian wipes it and licks his fingertips. Just like that, a memory unfolds like a letter tucked safely in a drawer. I smooth out the creases and watch it:

Castian and I sneak down to the kitchens. He's barefoot,
and I've borrowed a pair of his trousers to run better in

case we're caught. We cut two giant slices of olive oil cake
and devour them, licking icing off our sticky little hands.

I think about what life would have been like if I'd never been taken from my family and if he'd never grown up trying to craft the reputation of a murderous royal. Perhaps we never stood a chance to be anything other than what we became, and we were always going to be a little bit broken. The memory slips back into my mind, but it isn't painful like the others.

I watch Castian eat half the cake before I indignantly claim my share. When we've eaten every morsel and drunk all the wine, we linger in a comfortable kind of quiet we haven't been able to find since we began our journey together.

"I'll leave the tray outside," he says.

In the bathing room, I change into my sleeping chemise and underbreeches. I brush my teeth and unsnag the tangles in my hair.

When I step back into the room, Castian is carrying two pillows off the bed.

"What do you think you're doing?" I ask.

He looks up, a deer frozen in the woods. He's taken off his shirt as he does when he sleeps. His underbreeches hang low on his hips. "I was going to sleep on the floor tonight."

"Your princely hide will bruise if you sleep anywhere but a feathered mattress."

"I've served in the military since I was eleven, Nati. Believe me, I can take it."

"Doña Sagrada took every blanket except for this one, and you'll freeze to death in the middle of the night." I pull back one side of the bedspread. "Simply stay on your side."

Tentatively, I crawl under the covers. There's something in the way—a strange pillow full of beans. It's warm to the touch. "Why would Doña Sagrada leave us this?"

"It's a heating pad," Castian says, scratching the back of his head. "For your—woman—lady—affairs."

I find myself enjoying his inability to form words. "What do you know of it?"

"Nuria had one," he says, by way of explanation. Then he climbs into bed with me. We lay on opposite sides, staring at the ceiling.

"I don't sleep," he tells me.

"Then what do you do?"

"Listen to you snore or mutter, mostly."

I reach out to punch him, but the bed is fit for a king, and I only hit mattress. "I do not."

His eyes flutter. "Tell me about my brother."

I turn away from him and hug the heating pad to my lower belly. The tight pain there eases, and my eyes flutter. "What do you want to know?"

"Anything. Everything."

But I can't get the words out, not without breaking apart. So I close my eyes and fall into the pit of the Gray.

When I wake, the sun is rising, and the room is an oven. I realize the warmth is emanating from Castian. I'm in the crook of his arms, my palm splayed over his heart, his hand on my thigh.

His eyes are shut, and as I slip from his embrace, he remains completely asleep. I would laugh if he didn't look so vulnerable. A sleeping prince out of a fairy tale.

I push away the realization that we wound up holding each other in the middle of the night. I've had to huddle with other people in my unit before, even Margo and Esteban, who hate me. But this is *Castian*. It can't happen again. It won't. I take a step back, and the floorboard groans loudly.

Castian jolts awake, drawing the knife he keeps on the bedside table and breathing hard and fast.

I hold my hands up in defense. "It's me."

Is this why he does not sleep? I know that feeling, the one that tells you the nightmares will find you, no matter what. Or in my case, the memories.

Except last night I dreamed of nothing. I saw only black.

"Sorry to wake you, princeling," I say. "But we have to get ready to meet your informant."

Outside, music booms, voices shout. The Carnaval de Santa Cariña has begun.

4

AFTER A QUICK BREAKFAST OF FRIED EGGS, SPICY SAUSAGES, AND BREAD, CAS-
tian and I step out of the inn and into the fray. All of Acesteña and
people from all over the kingdom flood the market square. There's
a parade of children in matching costumes, bagpipers, and women
twirling in bright skirts. A horse-drawn carriage decked in flowers
carries a young couple dressed in silver and green. Vendors ring
bells to signal their stalls are open for business, offering wine and
food and trinkets.

"How are we going to find your informant in all of this?" I ask
Castian.

He runs a hand along the short tuft of his beard. His eyes scan
the crowd. "High noon at the seafood stall."

"That's hours from now."

Castian reaches for my hair and removes a bit of dandelion fluff stuck in my braid crown. "We blend in. Walk around the stalls. Watch the parade. If you're still hungry—"

"You'll rue the day you threaten me with food."

Castian smirks and offers me his arm. We're dressed in the best clothes we have. His cream linen tunic has a high collar and intricate blue embroidery that matches the long bell sleeves of my dress. They're in the regional style, and the first items he bought when we arrived. I thought it an unnecessary expense, but now the newlyweds we are supposed to be—Wilmer and Marcela Otsoa—don't stand out.

We buy two slices of olive oil cake from the baker, pinxos of cubed pork and beef, sausages, a sample of cheeses, and two pear ciders. Castian picks a relatively quiet spot near the gazebo where we can spread our blanket and eat with an advantageous view of the crowd.

"I've never been to a festival like this," I say.

"The Carnaval de Santa Cariña is singular to this region. Despite how small the village is, people journey from all over to watch the pageantry. I'd say it's when the vendors make most of their business for the year."

"Understandably." I pick up the wooden pinxo and bite off one of the lamb cubes. "I could eat a dozen of these."

Castian begins to stand. "I can go get more."

I grab the hem of his sleeve and laugh. "I wasn't serious."

He frowns and points at the remnants of our feast. "The way you've eaten more than half of your share is very serious, *wife*."

My eye twitches when he calls me that. But then I realize, it is the first morning that I haven't had an occurrence. My mind is as clear as the blue sky above. I offer Castian the last sliver of cheese I was about to eat, and he devours it right out of my fingers.

"Don't you two look lovely!" Doña Sagrada says, beaming as

she walks up to us. She's in her festival best—a green dress that matches the emerald gems dangling from her earlobes.

"Join us, Doña," Castian says.

The innkeeper takes a seat on our blanket and immediately inquires about my health and the food last night. It's almost refreshing having her take my mind off the impending meeting. Castian's kept the identity of his informant a secret. As a former Whisper, I understand that too well. I lived and died by the grace of our hidden allies. But after our conversation last night, I wish I had waited before sending out my own letter beseeching a friend for help.

"Will you return to the capital after your honeymoon?" Doña Sagrada asks us.

We look at each other. We never decided on our story after leaving Acesteña, and a mild panic brings a stutter to my lips.

"Perhaps," Castian says with a dreamy stare. He's better than I am at coming up with lies, and people like the innkeeper hang on his every word. "There are still places in this great kingdom we long to see. Citadela Crescenti on the southern coast. The Zahara canyons in the north. We have all the time in the world."

I suppose it does no harm to create such a fantasy. To imagine that we truly *do* have all the time in the world.

"If you ever find yourselves back in Acesteña, please come back to the inn. There's so much you haven't seen. The Sól Abene estates are marvelous. Did you know that Queen Penelope was from here? Bless her soul. Shame what happened to her family's castle after she died so suddenly."

I glance at Castian. The anguish in his features overwhelms me because I know what it is like to miss your mother so much it renders you helpless.

"Poor King Fernando," Doña Sagrada continues. "So much tragedy. I do hope this new marriage to Queen Josephine is fruitful."

"What's the story behind this saint?" I ask brightly, switching the subject. "I don't believe I know anything about her."

"Well, Santa Cariña was said to have lived near here in Galicia valley. This was centuries ago, when the kingdom of Sól Abene had its dominion, of course. There was a terrible drought. Santa Cariña was an ordinary person then. She and her husband could not stand watching the people suffer, and so they made a bargain with the old gods. They gave her rain, but at a great price."

"Saints require sacrifices, don't they?" I ask.

Doña Sagrada nods sternly. "Santa Cariña and her beloved sacrificed themselves into the lake. The old gods were so grateful, their tears became rain. This is the day we celebrate life. Every year, there's a reenactment in front of the cathedral. Don't miss it!"

Doña Sagrada stands and quickly joins the revelers in scarves and lace masks. There are bagpipes and flutes, guitars, and tambourines. Children run across the lawn. Tiny crystals in the shape of raindrops line hems and cuffs.

I want to ask Castian whether he's all right, but his deep frown answers that. We drink our pear ciders and sit side by side until it's time to meet his informant.

At noon, we buy two briny oysters as big as Castian's hands from the seafood stand. We wait for a moment, stealthily watching for some signal. An old man compliments my dress, but then takes the hand of his husband and keeps walking. Strangers offer us friendly cheers or tell us we're blocking the path. High noon comes and goes. We retrace the perimeter of the market square again and again. We buy so many more oysters that all I can taste is salt.

"What if they had trouble at the tolls?" I whisper. "What if they were caught? Perhaps they were expecting to see you alone?"

Castian is tense as the lanterns strung from stall to stall are lit and the reenactment begins. Crowds amass by the flower arch in front of the cathedral. The couple who were in the parade now stand with the priest. Her dress is covered in raindrop crystals, and she wears a golden headpiece that looks like an aura. The young man is dressed in green, a silver scarf around his hips.

The old priest walks as slow as the seasons change, but his voice thunders. He recites the story of Santa Cariña while the lovers representing the saint and her husband dance to his words.

"Hear me, my great sky! Take my heart and soul but spare the people of Sól Abene," Santa Cariña says.

"Spare us all," the crowd murmurs. "Blessed be the Father of Worlds."

The priest leads the revelers in a prayer.

"Excuse me, miss," a familiar voice says just before I feel a hard shove on my shoulder.

Castian moves quickly between us, reaching for the knife in his boot, when I recognize my friend.

It takes all of me not to scream Leonardo's name and embrace him. His bright green eyes crinkle at the corners as he smiles. His flop of black curls is dusted in beige powder, and his somber servant garb is dirty, but it's him. I know it is.

"No problem at all, traveler," I say, squeezing Castian's hand in mine. "What are you doing here?"

As the priest's prayer comes to an end, the music resumes, and the three of us move our little cluster just outside the buoyant crowd in the market. Leo eyes Castian from head to toe, but all he sees is a stranger. I try to convey that the stranger is trustworthy. We have much to speak about.

"We must hurry," Leo says, glancing back at the main road that snakes from the valley into the village green. He opens his simple black vest and reveals a pendant. Three mountain peaks with a sun at the center. The personal crest of Lady Nuria, Duquesa of Tresoros. "A sweep is coming."

The energy in the air shifts—the Carnaval revelers know something is wrong, too. There's the thundering sound of horses. Soldiers wearing the scarlet garb of the Second Sweep crest a hill on the main road and encircle the square. Confusion and fear mingle in gasps and whispers.

"Keep going," I say, but the rearing form of a horse blocks my path. Castian pulls me against his body, and I barely avoid having my skull cracked by hooves.

"Back in the square!" the soldier demands.

Castian's fingers dig into my shoulders, leading me back into the fray.

"What do we do?" I hiss. "And do not say we need to remain calm."

I remember the town of Puerto Dorado. Anyone harboring Moria families and deniers of the Father of Worlds was ordered to be turned over. Every house was searched, and every store cellar was emptied, but all they did was arrest the town drunk and a man who had ancient reliquaries of the old gods. They watched as the justice set fire to the heretic's house. Following these usual manipulative strategies, the Second Sweep returned two days later to help the citizens and remind them that they would have been peaceful had it not been for the Moria and other dissidents.

Among them was Prince Castian.

I hated him then, and that feeling resurfaces as we watch soldiers corral the villagers in one area. Those on foot drag vendors out of their stalls, mowing over bread rolls and bins of pistachios. The bakery's pastries and cakes are crushed in the dirt. One of the men takes a bottle of wine from the vintner and yanks the cork free with his teeth. He spits it on the ground and takes a swig.

A moment later, a scream comes from somewhere across the crowd. The soldiers have grabbed the young couple dressed as Santa Cariña and her husband, ripping off their crowns and sashes, their flowers and scarves. A woman beside me sobs, and I feel myself sink into that pitch-black void where my memories live.

The last of the Second Sweep procession gives way to two closed carriages displaying the Sól Abene family seal. A man climbs out of one carriage, flanked by two personal guards. Duque Sól Abene is a severe, bearded man with sharp cheekbones and furry dark eyebrows that frame tourmaline-black eyes. His creamy white skin is flushed. I remember seeing him briefly at the palace, and though he looks the same, the bruised shadows under his eyes are recent.

"Duque!" the people shout. "What is the meaning of this? It is a sacred day, Duque Sól Abene."

A red-clad soldier steps forward and addresses the masses. He's in his midtwenties with a brutal scar running diagonally across his face.

"Pascal," Castian whispers under his breath. Of course he knows the soldier. These are his men.

"Everyone will be allowed to return to their homes after the Second Sweep has finished their inspection."

Doña Sagrada steps through the throng. Despite her small stature, she clasps her hands together and pleads to the soldier. "Why are you doing this?"

Pascal barely acknowledges her. "This is an unholy festival. It is against the laws of the Father of Worlds to celebrate heretic saints and false gods."

Castian jerks forward, but the priest beats him to it. The sagging skin of his face jostles as he tries to speak. "We have celebrated the Carnaval de Santa Cariña for centuries. We tithe to the Father of

Worlds and the crown, for we are good and loyal citizens. Queen Penelope even graced this market with her exalted presence. The Duque of Sól Abene and his family have never missed Carnaval."

"That's right!" someone shouts. Red soldiers move in the direction of the voice.

"It ends today," Pascal pronounces. "The justice has decreed all coin made on this heretical feast be tithed to the war effort. Every person old enough to carry a sword will come with me."

War. The word sparks through the crowd like fire down a candlewick.

"Please," Doña Sagrada begs. Tears race down her round cheeks. "We have sent all our soldiers. Even our youngest children. Have mercy—"

I am already moving, running to block the soldier as he raises his fist to strike Doña Sagrada into silence. I grab his fist in midair. Shock widens his eyes into black moons, and I know I have made a huge mistake. I can push him further—raise my knee to strike his gut, slam my open fist against his ear to make him lose his balance, hike up my skirt and grab the dagger at my thigh.

But I don't.

I let him shove me to the ground.

Castian is there at once. "Stand down!"

Castian's voice must sound all too familiar because the young soldier hesitates like a reflex. But the prince still looks like Wilmer Otsoa, a musician from a small village, with no power.

"Who do you think you are?" Pascal spits on Castian's face. "I'll have you gutted for treason and obstruction."

"Peace," the priest urges. "He was only protecting his wife."

Pascal scrutinizes me. Recognition strikes him all at once. "Remove your gloves. Now. Do it."

I clutch my hands against my chest as the crowd gathers around.

"Do it," Castian urges so softly that it takes me a second to understand.

I yank off my white lace gloves. Castian's familiar magics brush against my skin, cloaking the scars with his illusion.

Pascal inspects my palms and fingers, turning them back and forth. The skin there is smooth. He squeezes my wrists, and it takes all my strength not to fight back.

"Arrest them for obstruction of the Second Sweep."

There is unrest as the crowd shouts obscenities.

"Show us the order from the king!" someone clamors.

"We've done nothing wrong!"

For the first time, the Second Sweep realizes it's not terrorizing helpless farmers. The people of Acesteña *will* put up a fight.

Duque Sól Abene surveys the shifting masses. I see a man torn between doing what the people of his provincia want and what the king has ordered. Then his gaze falls on me. Am I imagining the flicker of recognition? I remind myself that we never spoke in the palace, and he's only seen me from a distance.

"This mere girl obstructed you?" Duque Sól Abene asks, arching a brow. "Was she that strong?"

There's a round of titters as people spit at the ground and recite long curses. Pascal releases me with a shove. Castian glares at the soldier, but I pull him to me, forcing him to look into my eyes. All I see is remorse. Helplessness.

Duque Sól Abene puffs out his chest and waves a dismissive hand to Pascal. Then he takes the matron's hands in his. "My dear Doña Sagrada, I apologize for this disruption. I come with news from Andalucía." He turns to the crowd. "Hear my words and repeat them to every neighbor and friend. Forgive this uncouth soldier. He does not know the ways of our provincia. But what I have raced here to say to you cannot wait. Not even for Carnaval."

The crowd settles, hanging on the edge of his silence.

"We are fighting rebel insurgents all over Puerto Leones," the duque continues. "The Moria Whispers still hold our prince hostage! His Majesty has asked me to seek help from my provincia. Many of you have known my family for generations. Believe me, I would not lead you astray.

"Take this final day to celebrate. Kiss your loved ones, because soon we will be under attack. I require every person who did not get selected for the draft to volunteer. King Fernando has allowed youths starting at thirteen to enlist. It is an honor to serve your kingdom, which needs you, now more than ever. Now return to Carnaval!"

"My lord—" Pascal starts, but his voice is drowned by the roar of the crowd.

"Doña Sagrada," he says, "my company is weary and I require your best table."

I lock eyes with the innkeeper. She nods to me and Castian as we retreat into the crowd. There is no time for good-byes. We have to leave Acesteña tonight.

5

LEO FOLLOWS US BACK TO THE INN. THE TAVERN IS EMPTY, BUT DOÑA SAGRADA IS only a few paces behind with the lord and his court. Servants hurry to assemble tables and pay us no mind as we race up the stairs. None of us talk until we're inside with the door locked and the curtains drawn. Castian—Will Otsoa to Leo—busies himself lighting a fire.

Leo begins to bow, but I pull him into an embrace. He laughs and squeezes me back. I thought I'd never see him again. He smells like a mixture of sweat and the citrus oils he massages through his dark curls.

"I've missed you, too," Leo says. He cups my cheek and brushes away my tears. "I must say I'm rather confused. Don't tell Prince Castian, but—"

I clear my throat and wave my hands to stop whatever he's going to say.

The fire in the hearth catches, and Castian stands, his eyes bore into mine. "Do you trust him?"

"With my life."

Confusion registers on Leo's face before morphing into shock as Castian's illusion falls away and reveals the kidnapped prince of Puerto Leones.

"Don't tell Prince Castian what?"

"Oh. *Oh.*" Leo staggers back a step. He looks from me to Castian. "I had wondered where—never mind. A hundred thousand apologies, my prince. Now I understand why Lady Nuria told me to find Renata and that she'd lead me to you. I'd seen you both but did not approach at first because you were so—uhh—well disguised. This is unbelievable. This is utterly—"

"Leo," I say.

"This is normal," he corrects, his voice breaking.

"You were supposed to be there at noon," Castian says, starting to pack. "What happened?"

"The only way for me to leave the palace safely was with Duque Sól Abene's company. When we were near, I tried to run ahead and warn you, but I was too late." Leo sits at the dining table, pours himself a glass of ale, and takes in the room. The fire, the fresh flowers in the vase, a few petals still on the floor. The underclothes I didn't bother to put away this morning.

"Wait. *Nuria* is your informant?" I ask Castian, who keeps packing.

I don't know why I sound surprised. The Duquesa of Tresoros has aided the Whispers for years. She sent Leo to help me escape the palace. A few days into our journey, when I was uncertain of Castian's plan, I sent her my own letter asking for help.

"My gracious lady sends her regrets and wishes she could do more, but her every move is under surveillance."

"And yours isn't?" Castian changes out of his festival garb.

"I've been Lady Nuria's spy for the better part of a year, my prince. Did you ever suspect me?"

"Truly?" Castian says, letting out a frustrated sigh as he pulls on a black tunic and trousers. "No. You're very good at playing the flirt and the baud. While we're at it, there is no Prince Castian here. I am Will Otsoa, and this is Marcela Otsoa."

"Will and Marcela." Leo licks his teeth and watches us with unfettered delight. I feel my entire body flush hot. "Your...sister?"

"His wife," I mumble, holding up my ring.

"How *delightful*," Leo says, enjoying himself far too much under the circumstances. "After Nuria received both of your requests, and the unpleasant conclave in the king's chambers, we agreed it was worth the risk to send me here." He fishes two letters from his vest.

"What do you mean, 'both' of our requests?" Castian asks.

My friend's full lips turn into a round exclamation. His green eyes bounce between Castian and me. "Didn't you each write to Lady Nuria beseeching her help?"

Castian and I reach for the letters at the same time. Leo swiftly rises and holds them above his head. "I think it safest that these disappear."

"Leo—" I shout as the letters go into the flames. He dusts his fingers, smooths out his plain tunic as if he were wearing his usual embroidered doublet, and returns to his seat.

But Castian won't let it drop. He reaches into the flames and grabs my letter. The broken wax seal is melted on the parchment and red cinders slowly burn their way up. His face is impossible to read. I can't be certain what part he's able to see as the letter turns to ash in his hands, but I remember the words I wrote in a fury after the first time we'd lost Dez's trail.

I'm traveling with my most ardent enemy, though I know it is for the good of my people. The lion cub is stubborn, graceless, and I don't trust him. You've done so much for me already, but I need your help to end this quest and be rid of him.

Castian throws the remnants in the fire. "That's that."

"Castian," I begin, but he cuts me off with a question for Leo.

"What did Nuria say?"

"She couldn't acquire what you've requested. All her ships have been seized for emergency vessels, so she doesn't have a spare to give to you. The king's behavior has been erratic. That's not the worst of it."

Castian curses and hits the wall. "Pray tell, what is the worst of it?"

"Ah, the conclave I mentioned. King Fernando summoned the elite families to his private rooms." Leo describes the evening surrounded by the elite family representatives of Puerto Leones, drinking wine he believed to be poisoned. I sit beside him and squeeze his hand.

Castian fastens his belt hard, like he wishes it might be around the king's throat. "My father loves his games. Tell me, Leonardo. Did you notice anything strange that night?"

"Other than the blood still drying on your father's face? Let me think," Leo says. "Honestly, that whole night feels like a fever dream. Lady Las Rosas was there. Though she didn't leave with the rest of us. Lady Nuria and I plotted my path to you two, but the only way to hide was in plain sight in Duque Sól Abene's caravan."

"Las Rosas?" I ask, knowing I've heard the name before.

It takes a moment for the memory to dredge up, but then it slams into me. Lord Las Rosas was the man I was supposed to turn into a Hollow for the entertainment of King Fernando's guests, to show that he had brought the Moria under his command. I pretended my magics were affected by my self-inflicted wounds and bought myself time to investigate the palace and gain Justice Méndez's trust.

Castian's hawk stare falls on Leo. "I didn't realize Lord Las Rosas's daughter had returned."

"Oh, yes. The king gave her a seat at the table and her family title along with their lands."

I take in the confused shock on Castian's face. "Why is that surprising?"

"Leyre Las Rosas is the lord's illegitimate daughter with a Luzouan woman," Leo explains, never quite losing his dramatic inflection for court gossip. "Most in attendance didn't know she even existed until that very moment."

"Everything my father does has a motive," Cas interjects. "But even I admit that giving away the Las Rosas estate was a foolish thing to do if he's building an army. Especially since he needs soldiers."

"That's just it—the reason Lady Nuria sent me." Leo's easy humor fades when he looks at me. "The king has urged the elite back to their estates and provincias to spread the word of the prince's kidnapping and Justice Méndez's death. Justice Alessandro is marching toward Citadela Crescenti with Lady Nuria."

"It's her provincia," Cas admits.

"It's also where our prince is allegedly being held captive by the Whispers."

"The Whispers are across the sea!" I shout. "Any talk of Castian's abduction is Alessandro's doing."

Leo looks down at his lap and picks at a loose thread. "Actually, they're not."

Anxiety tightens in my stomach. "What?"

"I couldn't put this to paper, Lady Ren. The Whispers never boarded the ship to Empirio Luzou. We've heard tell they have a new leader and are recruiting heavily—not just Moria but anyone miserable with the king's taxes and drafts. They mean to fight, and they publicly claim to still have Prince Castian."

"Margo is going to get everyone killed," I say, slamming my fist on the table. I think of the Illusionári in my old Whisper unit. Her fierce blue stare, the rage that powers her to keep fighting. She was the warrior I was supposed to be. I wonder how she would react if she knew that Dez was alive and that he didn't come back to any of us.

"What else?" Castian asks, beginning to pace in front of the fire. "Was there anyone who didn't drink the wine?"

"Duque Arias," Leo says.

Castian freezes, and scoffs. "That giant man-child? I don't believe it. For what crimes?"

"He confessed he'd broken into your rooms the night of the festival. I've never seen anyone sweat that much in my entire life. Something about a wager he lost and a book? It didn't seem important." Leo's eyes bounce nervously from Castian to me. "It's important, though, isn't it?"

"Arias was always a sore loser." Castian swears under a heavy breath and retrieves the captain's log from the inside pocket of his vest. The leather is aged and the parchment yellow, a letter *A* stamped on the front.

"What's so special about a book?" Leo asks.

"I need your word that what I'm about to tell you can never be repeated to anyone else."

"You might have asked for secrecy after you revealed your magics to me, but of course, you have my *word* as a flirt and a baud," Leo says in a single breath. "My prince."

"It's not the book but the map it contains," Castian explains, tucking the item back for safekeeping. "We've been searching for a weapon that could turn the tides of Puerto Leones and put a stop to my father's reign."

"What is it?" he asks.

"It's called the Knife of Memory," I say, meeting Castian's eyes briefly. "For most of my life I believed it was a myth. The stories say its power can do impossible things."

"Right now, we need the impossible," he says.

Leo nods gravely. "That's why you needed Lady Nuria's help to procure a ship."

"Now my father knows I'm in possession of this map."

"I suppose it's a good thing the king believes you to be kidnapped?" Leo offers the thought as if it's a good thing. But deep in my bones I feel something is wrong.

"Did you bring *any* good tidings?" Castian demands.

"Two good tidings, in fact." Leo grins at the prince's glower. "There is a woman in the port city of Salinas who owes Lady Nuria a favor, and she's got no love for the crown. They call her the Queen of Little Luzou, and she can get us the travel documents and ship we need. I have here a personal letter of request from Lady Nuria, along with the promise of funds."

Between his artful fingers, Leo holds an envelope the color of the deepest red, like the lipstick Nuria favors. He flips it like a playing card and returns it to his vest.

"What do you mean by 'we'?" Castian asks.

Leo stands and gestures to his body as if he's presenting the star of an opera. "I'm coming with you to Salinas. Or Little Luzou, as the locals prefer to call it. I've heard—"

"No," the prince says, tugging on his bootlaces. "You'll slow us down."

"Castian and I don't know what we're going to face."

"I've been risking my life for years," Leo exclaims. "Besides, I speak three languages, can charm my way into the royal vault, and I mean no offense, but you and His Royal Highness don't exactly have the best intrapersonal skills since you don't actually like people. Lady Nuria agrees that you two are the best hope for Puerto Leones, but you need help. And a witness in the event you should kill each other."

I shake my head. "You don't even know where we're going."

"I don't have to. I'll go to the ends of the known world to help you find this knife if it'll put an end to King Fernando's rule."

"I can't protect you," Castian growls.

Leo takes a deep breath and is unwavering in his stare. "Let me do this, my prince. If I am not with you, then I will murder the new justice and be jailed, or my role as a spy will be found out and I'll be jailed. I don't care about protecting me. I care about helping you and Lady Ren with your quest."

"Cas," I say softly.

I can practically feel the inner workings of the prince's mind. Assessing the risk of a third person in our party. Of trusting someone new at a time like this. But now that I think on it, I *want* Leo with us.

"Very well," Castian relents, and extends his hand. They shake their alliance. "We'll tell you everything on the road. We should leave now, as we have nearly seventy-five miles to cover from here to Citadela Salinas."

While Castian maps our route, I change out of my dress and into black travel clothes, tuck a knife inside my boot, and drape a scarf around my neck. Castian arranges a gold necklace with a gleaming diamond beside the flower vase and says, "For Doña Sagrada's troubles."

Leo pulls back a curtain and watches the revelry outside. "People are dropping like drunk flies at court. I don't see the Second Sweep's horses, but I heard them say they'd be blocking the main road between tollhouses."

"Good thing we're taking the woods," Castian says, and pulls on his illusion of Wilmer Otsoa.

"Are we all getting a disguise?" Leo asks.

"It's too dangerous," I say. "If we get separated, our illusion wouldn't hold and my magics would be found out."

Silently, we file onto the balcony. The grounds of the inn are nearly empty, save for an old man asleep in front of the dying firepit. I climb over the railing first and slide down the shingles on the roof, grateful I'm wearing gloves to avoid splinters. I toss my pack into some shrubbery and launch myself down. The shock of the landing travels up my hip. While I wait for the others, I steal two oil lamps from the courtyard.

"This way," Castian whispers.

Shouts and off-key ballads come from the village square. Drunk stragglers stumble their way home. A carriage of fortune-tellers and performers begins a journey south. We keep our heads covered with sheer scarves, silvery moonlight illuminating our path.

As we pass the stables, a figure stumbles out and collides with Leo. It happens so fast that I can't stop the man from grabbing Leo's arm.

"Pardon me," the stranger says, holding his oil lamp high. "Leonardo?"

I freeze when I hear his voice. It's the Duque Sól Abene, having just relieved himself on the shadowy side of a stable. The front of his breeches is still open, and his shirt stinks of ale. Leo tries to pull out of his grasp, but the duque is strong, even in his inebriated state. I hear Castian mutter in the dark behind me. Barely out of town and we're already getting caught. Even if Castian used all his strength to cloak us, it would reveal him as an Illusionári.

Duque Sól Abene moves the light to my face and gasps. "Wait a moment—I know you."

Castian grabs the duque and slams him against the stable wall, trapping him with an arm against his throat. "Don't touch her."

"Do you know who I am? I am the lord of this provincia, and that girl is very valuable to me!"

The horses begin to wake. If we scare them further, we'll draw unwanted attention.

"I have to take his memory," I say, panicked.

The duque spits in Castian's face, then turns as far as he can to Leo. "Boy, don't be a fool. The king will gut you for treason himself—"

Castian clamps a gloved hand over Duque Sól Abene's nose and mouth. "Get me rope."

Leo runs into the stable.

We can't kidnap him. He'd struggle at every turn. There is only one thing I can do. I bite the tip of my glove and tug it free. The whorls of my magics illuminate the dark. Pain fractures my line of sight, and pressure builds at my temples. Soft white light races across my skin, burning, ready to search for a memory.

I squeeze Castian's shoulder. "Stand aside."

"You can't." Castian shakes his head. Do I imagine the worry in his eyes? "You know you can't."

"You know I have to."

The lord bites the prince's finger. Castian hisses and removes one hand long enough for the duque to shout, "I'm going to kill you myself!"

Leo runs back, waving the rope in his hands. "We're going to be caught if we don't keep him quiet."

"Listen to me, Anton," Castian says, using the duque's given name. "If you don't stop trying to scream, I'm going to let the Robári empty your mind until you're nothing but a walking carcass. Nod if you understand."

The duque nods.

"It'll be one memory," I assure him, but my words feel distant.

Castian holds the man down, and I bring my fingertips to his temples. I open myself up to the warmth that flashes through my bones. My power is like a line cast out to sea, searching and searching for a place to sink its hook. Instead of a memory, though, I feel the well of a void. A splintering ache breaks my mind apart. I can't help but let loose a scream, and then I bite my tongue.

"Stop it, Nati! Don't." Castian drops his illusion, and I fall on my knees. He is the Príncipe Dorado once again. He breathes hard and fast, his gaze glistening and torn between Anton and me. "I'll fix this."

"My prince—she has ensorcelled you. She has done something— Moria *bestae*!"

"That's right. I am a Moria bestae," Castian spits, so full of anguish I have to look away.

There's a grunt and the wet sound of a blade sinking into flesh twice, then a final exhale. Castian lowers him to the ground, arranging the body in a sitting position. Cas looks at the blood on his hands. When he brushes his hair away, crimson streaks his forehead.

"We have to go *now*," Leo says through gritted teeth.

I cast one final glance at Acesteña, where a night of mirth will turn into a bloody dawn.

6

CASTIAN DARTS THROUGH THE PATH IN THE WOODS WHERE YESTERDAY HE caught a rabbit for me. Since we left that seaside cave, we have traveled along the Sól y Perla ocean cliffs, through burned villages, muddy ravines, the Obsidio Mountains, and now this. I have kept telling myself that I do not trust the man I only ever knew as the Bloodied Prince, the Lion's Fury—but isn't that what I have been doing since we left the safety of the cave? Isn't that what I owe him now that he has taken a life for me?

Fear drives me forward, helps me focus through the maze of my own thoughts. Leo keeps pace beside me. Everything in the dark is terrifying. Leaves brush against each other, as if the trees are hissing at intruders. Little beasties chitter and blink, eyes glowing from tree hollows.

When I traveled with Dez and Lynx Unit, I learned how to tamp down my fear of the dark. Esteban never made it easy. On our very first scouting trip together, he filled my bedroll with grasshoppers, which woke me up screaming in the middle of the night. After that, I started sleeping farther away from the others, a knife within reach. Esteban never trusted me and never let a day go by without making sure I knew that. But when the Whispers were attacked and dozens killed, I wasn't the one who gave away their location—he was. I wonder if he's following Margo's lead the way he always did. I wonder if he's sorry. I wonder if I've been treating Castian the way Esteban treated me.

"Here," Castian announces, his voice like the crunch of gravel.

I cast a glow with my oil lamp over a small clearing enclosed by boulders. Leo pants as he falls to his knees, but he doesn't complain of the exhaustion. He takes the waterskin I offer and props up his pack as a pillow.

"We'll rest until daybreak and resupply in the next town," Castian says. "I'll take first watch."

"Cas—" I have the undeniable urge to reach for him. For a flash, I can see splotches of blood dried on his forehead, like he couldn't rub it all away. He turns from me quickly, but I've already seen the red rimming his eyes.

"Please, Ren," he says, positioning himself against a tree like a sentry. "Rest."

Anger and hurt twist in my gut. He should have just let me take the duque's memory. Instead, he killed this man for me, and I do not know how I can repay such a debt.

At first light we're on the move again. We don't stop until we enter a hamlet with three market stalls—one for eggs, one for cabbages, and one selling beads to ward off Moria magics. The vendors are so old that they look like fruit dried in the sun. We buy eggs and keep heading south.

The road is crowded, but not with soldiers. Those who were denied entry to Acesteña because of the Second Sweep have set up camp. There is no telling how swiftly Duque Sól Abene's men will be out searching for his killer. Perhaps they are turning Acesteña inside out trying to find us, and we have endangered people who were kind to us. Because we don't want more trouble, we choose dirt roads that cut through yellow canola fields. Leo does most of the talking, detailing the chaos that ensued after he helped me escape, and I tell him about Dez.

For miles there is nothing but us, the tall golden flowers, and clear azure sky. Leo whistles the tune to a familiar song, and Castian keeps glancing over his shoulder, his hair a golden tangle in the cool breeze. For the first time, I can exhale properly.

It is late afternoon by the time we reach a tavern in the next village. The sudden stench of sweat, leather, and sharp cheeses makes my eyes water. Tired farmers and travelers are hunched over pints and plates of fried sausages and potatoes. We find an empty table in a shadowed corner and collectively groan as we sit.

"This looks like the perfect place to either rest your feet," Leo says, green eyes taking in a drunk sloshing his ale, "or lose several teeth in a brawl."

"There will be no brawls," I say, massaging the knots in my shoulder.

A round, surly barmaid lights a candle stub at the center of the table and takes our order. We pay extra to have our eggs boiled and our waterskins refilled from their well. The clatter of plates and the lute player in the corner provide enough cover that we won't be overheard.

The barmaid sloshes our pints onto the table. Leo dries the surface with his sleeve before taking a sip. "I say you've been quite resourceful if you've survived this long on foot. Where are we? I don't believe I've traveled in this part of the Sól Abene provincia before."

I unfurl our small map on the table. "We've made it sixteen miles or so southwest of Acesteña, which puts us here, near the old castle ruins."

"We could make it to Salinas in seven days by foot if we had access to the main roads," Castian asserts, dragging his finger from where we are, straight down to the southernmost point of Puerto Leones.

"And if we stop only to sleep," I point out, retracing our path. When my index finger touches his, Castian draws back his hand and picks up his pint.

Leo jumps at the sound of the tavern door slamming open. A new wave of locals and weary travelers file in. I scan their faces out of habit. Several burly bald men with red scars crosshatched over sunburned faces. A group of women cackling at a joke I can't hear. My heart gives a squeeze when I notice someone in a forest-green hooded cloak, the kind the Whispers tend to wear. But as the traveler folds her cloak over the back of her chair, I realize I'm only seeing what I want to see.

"What happens when we board the ship in Salinas?" Leo asks.

I meet Castian's eyes and know we're in agreement, but then the barmaid makes a beeline for us with our meals. Castian throws an arm around Leo's shoulder and pulls him in. He laughs as if the two of them are old friends. Watching the prince's demeanor change so quickly is dizzying.

"Not here," I tell Leo.

I glance around the room once again, unable to shake the

sensation of someone watching me. It can't be another occurrence. My head doesn't feel as if it's splitting open. Then I see her face—for a moment. A flash of dark hair falls over her eyes. Sayida?

I stand quickly, drawing the attention of other tables. "I have to go to the privy."

"Marcela," Castian says, gently catching my scarf before letting it slip through his fingers.

"I'll be fine," I whisper, and move toward the door.

The girl I saw is gone, her pint and a bowl of stew untouched. A drunk swipes the glass and knocks it back, while another helps himself to the food. She can't have gone far. I hurry outside. The single dirt street of stalls is boarded up and quiet, save for fat rats clamoring around scraps. Clouds gather on the horizon, bright with the first hint of sunset. It smells like moments before a storm.

I try to remember the last time I spoke to Sayida in the safe house. Her power of persuasion helped me uncover part of my past and led me to the truth about Castian. What can I possibly say to make her forgive me?

A word spoken around the corner catches my attention.

"Whispers."

I creep closer to listen.

"You're a dead man if you think joining the rebels is what's best for your family," a hard, alto voice says. "You're not even Moria."

"And you're a dead man if you think breaking your back for a worthless king is any better. All I'm saying is, hear them out."

A third voice shushes them. "Quiet, you two, before Madrigal comes outside to make sure no one's pissing on the wall."

"I've made up my mind, Eggar. I'm going with the Whispers to Crescenti. I'm going to fight."

Yes—there's a chance I saw Sayida. There's a chance she also saw me and ran. I lean against the wall to process what I've heard.

The Whispers are recruiting, and they're gathering in Crescenti for a fight.

My entire body freezes when the tavern door swings open and Castian runs out. His panic makes his illusion waver like light on glass. The Bloodied Prince, then Will Otsoa. When he spots me, I press my finger to my lips and quietly lead him back inside, where angry drunks are beginning to shout. It's a sign we shouldn't linger. We quickly devour the thick chicken stew and get back on the road.

"If I might suggest," Leo says when we step outside. "We should not spend the night in town."

"I know a place." Castian turns to the horizon. "The ruins of Galicia."

"Isn't that—"

He nods slowly, but he's already walking. "My mother's castle."

7

THE LAST HOME OF QUEEN PENELOPE IS A CRUMBLING EDIFICE THAT LOOKS more haunted than safe refuge. With dark clouds gathering, we need a place where we won't get rained on. But I recall how Castian's entire being changed when Doña Sagrada spoke about his deceased mother.

"We don't have to stay here," I whisper at his side.

"It's perfect," Castian says, gesturing to the moss and weeds growing on the collapsed stone of the right wing. "What better legacy do I have than ruins?"

"Charming," Leo mutters.

We follow a dusty corridor to an open hall. Stone steps lead up a dais to the remains of a rusted throne. Around us are marble columns trimmed in gold and statues of ancient kings and queens.

Birds have made nests in the eaves and divots in the walls where paintings and tiles must have been ripped out. I try to imagine what the throne room might have looked like once, but it reminds me more of animal remains scavenged down to bones.

Castian stands in front of what used to be a floor-to-ceiling window, now overlooking overgrown countryside. Some of the stained glass remains, enough to see a partial rendering of the Father of Worlds in the First Heaven. For the Leonesse and their god, that section of the afterlife was reserved for kings, queens, and their royal lines. But for the Moria, the First Heaven was for those pure of heart, no matter their blood. How did Queen Penelope, a high-born woman from the Sól Abene provincia, give birth to not one, but two Moria sons?

When he turns around, bathed in the last rays before the sun sets, I find it impossible to look away. His gaze takes in the bits of rock and dirt on the floor, the ripped tapestries, the nests abandoned at the sound of our intrusion. He shakes his head softly, biting his bottom lip, as if he's trying to stop himself from screaming. Bypassing Leo and me, he stalks through a dark archway.

"Castian," I say, as if calling his name will lasso him back, anchor him here.

He stops. I see a sliver of his face in the shadows. His voice is grave. "I'll make sure we're alone."

"We should stay together. Surely no one likes to spend the night in abandoned castles."

"Except for us, naturally," Leo offers. "We'll find somewhere the roof won't crush us in our sleep and build a fire so we don't freeze to death after it rains."

With that, Castian is gone, and I'm left with this strangling sensation in my throat. "He's so—"

"Like you?" Leo clears his throat, a catlike grin brightening his features.

My indignation makes me trip up my words. "We are *nothing* alike."

Leo mumbles something that sounds a lot like "sure" as we light our way through a shadowed corridor.

We opt for remaining on the first floor, in the event we have to escape, and find a small sitting room with a fireplace and most of the windows boarded shut. Velvet drapes collect dust and holes from field mice. The marble floor is cracked at the center.

"I don't know if I've told you enough," I say as I gather up the broken legs of a wooden chair. "But I've missed you."

"And I you, Lady Ren."

"You don't have to call me that. We're not at the palace anymore."

"Ah, but I've grown fond of the name." He rolls up the ruined rug in front of the fireplace to make room for our bedrolls. "I was relieved to learn that you were well, though I was surprised to hear you were traveling with the prince. I'm still trying to decide what has shocked me more—that your former lover is not only alive but also the long-thought-dead *Prince Andrés*, Castian's Illusionári abilities, or that you've been together so long and he isn't dead."

"I'm glad you're amused, but we are together by necessity, not choice." I stack the broken wood inside the hearth and remind him how my people betrayed me. "If I had stayed with the Whispers, they would have killed me."

"They never deserved you," Leo says. "And yet, when we return from our quest to save the kingdom, they will bow at our—your—feet."

"I don't want anyone to bow to me," I admit. "And I'm done trying to find atonement. The Knife of Memory will right the wrongs of the past. The Moria and all people of this land will have a future."

"And you?"

I deflate with a sigh. "A small cabin deep in the Luzouan jungles, perhaps."

"And the Príncipe Dorado?" Leo raises his brow suggestively, and I give him a playful shove.

"Castian will become king, I suppose. We haven't talked much about what comes after. I don't know *how* to talk to him sometimes."

"He did kill someone for you," Leo reminds me. "I know some of his courtiers prefer jewels and excursions to the salt baths of Citadela Zahara, but as you said, you're not a lady."

"A man is dead, Leo."

"Believe me, I know that." He runs his finger through a thick line of dust on the mantel and rubs it into a ball. "I knew Duque Sól Abene well. He was like many of the other elite men in the kingdom, always taking so much from his people. Do you know why his fifteen-year-old daughter was sent to Dauphinique to study?"

I shake my head, my skin prickling in gooseflesh at the sudden severity in his voice.

"He'd sold her to a count to pay off his gambling debts. When Lady Nuria and Queen Josephine found this out, they intervened on the girl's behalf. Duque Sól Abene was punished by having his taxes raised and his daughter sent away to a foreign court. Does that mean he deserved to die that way? I cannot say. I have never killed anyone, but to save us? To save you? I want to think I would have the strength to do it."

"Did I mention I'm glad you're here?"

"You should be." Leo begins laying out our bedrolls around the fireplace. "Pardon me for asking, but—what happened to your magics at the stable? Did the justice harm you?"

The question makes me want to laugh. Méndez surely did, and in more ways than I'll ever be able to unravel. But I recount to Leo what I can about Cebrián, the king's twisted Robári whose powers were altered to steal the magics of other Moria. I have to shut my eyes for a moment, and even then, I see the pulsing silver scars that run all over his face and torso like a living alman stone. "Until we figure out what can be done, *if* anything can be done, Castian and I agreed I shouldn't take memories."

"After what happened with Duque Sól Abene, you're right." Leo cups a handful of dust and splinters and tucks it in the center of the tent of logs.

I use Castian's fire starter and strike the flint stone against the steel rectangle, then blow gently until the smallest flame bursts and spreads. When I was with the Whispers, little tasks like this helped me focus and keep my memories together. But fire used to be a trigger. One minute I could run into a burning house to rescue someone from within and my memories would stay put. Then I'd see a spark at the corner of my eye, or Esteban would ignite the wick of a candle, and I'd be paralyzed with memories from the Gray.

Now that I've faced the truth of the palace fire that changed my life, I'm not afraid to watch this one catch, even if I fear the way my magics seem to be changing.

I take a shuddering breath before an occurrence sinks in, as if I've conjured it with these flames. The vision pools before me:

> *Ladies wearing billowing gowns glide in dancing circles. Two little girls dressed in matching white lace race across the room while adults drink and laugh. In a corner, a young bard sings a familiar song about a beautiful queen lost to sea.*

Hands shake me. Leo's eyes come into focus.
"Ren, wake up!"

Someone is screaming. There's the sound of glass shattering and curses. *Cas.*

"Wait here," I say. I grab an oil lamp and run through dark halls, following the echo of his rage. Perhaps coming here was a mistake. Perhaps he isn't ready to face his monsters.

I find the prince of Puerto Leones in what must have been a nursery. A bassinet is overturned, the white lace brown with age and dirt. Cracked porcelain dolls litter the floor. Broken soldiers. Plush lions with spools of cotton guts spilling out.

"Cas," I whisper.

He whirls around. He's breathing fast, bright eyes roaming the damage as if he can't tell what was already destroyed and what he added to the chaos. In the spill of moonlight, I can see glistening tears stream down his face. He focuses on me, and a small figurine clatters to the floor. His arms remain outstretched, ready to strangle every ghost in this place.

"I thought I wanted to see our old room again," Castian says. "Then I couldn't stand to look at any of it."

My boots crunch glass. "Because you don't want to be here or because it doesn't align with your memories of it?"

"Both." He runs his palms down his face. I see the moment an idea sparks. Hesitation. He wants to ask me something but he's afraid. Somehow, I think I know what he wants, because I would want the same thing.

"Show me," I urge.

Castian extends a palm straight ahead, and the room changes with the threads of his illusion. The chipped paint and cracked walls are whole once again. The rusted door handle shimmers back into a polished lion. The bassinet is white and upright, and a second small bed is beside it. There is the faint image of two boys—Castian with his golden curls and Andrés with the bald head of a newborn.

I see a woman with long wheat hair, a crown of emeralds around her pretty head. Her skin is a golden tan, and she walks slowly, as if every step causes a deep ache, but she goes straight for the boys. The image flickers, and before she reaches them, everything disappears into darkness.

I want to believe that Castian and I are nothing alike, but I felt his rage and hopelessness in his illusion. We are both orphans in a war older than us, and for him to be the leader this kingdom needs, he must be whole. He's been pretending for as long as I have. Perhaps longer.

"I never forgave myself for what happened to my parents," I confess, picking up the figurine he dropped—a wooden soldier. The detail is exquisite, with a tiny sword raised in a fighting stance. "My friend—Sayida—used her Persuári magics to make me remember that even though I was wielded as a weapon, I was too young to control my powers. I don't know whether that feeling will ever quite go away. I know she's right, but if I'm honest with myself, deep down I know it's my fault that I never saw my mother again."

"I never went to her," Castian confesses. "She called for me while she was ill. Even my father ordered me to return. But I wouldn't. I hated her for being a drunk and treating me like I was invisible. Then she died." There is so much anguish in his voice. I have felt that way all my life, and I don't wish that on anyone. Not even Castian.

"How could she have done this to us?" he asks me.

I wish I knew. I wish I could understand. When the queen of Puerto Leones conspired with the leader of the rebel Moria to fake one son's death and blame it on the other, did she realize it could have all gone so wrong? I have never been good with words, so I wrap my arms around Castian. Slowly, he holds me back. His palm is cold against the base of my neck, and I feel his heart beat quickly against my chest.

"Only the dead can say, Cas."

"Do you ever want to be someone else?" he asks softly, his breath warming the skin of my ear.

I breathe deep and shiver. "Who do you want to be?"

"A good man, perhaps."

I think of how torn Castian looked before killing the duque. I think of the furious, terrible prince he portrayed with illusions. I think of the little boy who was my friend.

"Do you remember our childhood pact?" I ask.

"I'm surprised you remember it."

"I told you." I feel my chuckle vibrate between us. "Things have been coming back to me slowly."

His whole demeanor changes. "Is it a pact if you stabbed me first and *then* explained what we were doing?"

I step back and take his hand in mine, palm side up. At the center is a tiny white scar, like a grain of rice. I have the exact same scar at the center of my right hand. The memory came back to me while we were in that seaside cave after we ran from the Whispers. I used to think it was just another one of the scars that riddle my body.

"It was your fault," I say.

He looks affronted but doesn't pull his hand from my hold. "Mine?"

"*You* were the one who told me the story about two friends who made a blood pact. And I said we should do that. You went somewhere and returned with a . . . kitchen knife, I think it was?"

"It was my *ceremonial* prince dagger," he corrects, brushing the length of my hand, from my wrist to the tip of my middle finger. "You didn't even wait for me to be ready. You just stabbed."

"Some things don't change," I say, and find that I'm smiling. When I look up, so is he.

"We promised to never be apart. And then everything burned."

"We're here now."

When we press our palms together, something strange happens. My magics spark and the light of my whorls come to life. Afraid that I'll take a memory from him, I jerk back.

"I'm sorry. I didn't mean to do that."

He grasps for me, his hold gentle. "I trust you, Nati. You can't hurt me with your magics. Remember?"

They say that the Lady of Shadows moves the stars into the destinies of each and every person born under them. Dez said that he trusted me once, and his entire life was utterly changed. What if destiny brought Castian and Dez into my life? Pushed me onto this path with my oldest friend?

Warmth unwinds from the apex of my chest, as if a spindle is coming undone. I am afraid of this feeling. I am terrified that spending these weeks with Castian has made me soft to his past. But if Castian doesn't deserve forgiveness, neither do I.

Castian's hold on me becomes a caress along my hands. He claims that I shouldn't be afraid of my magics around him, that he is not scared of me. But doesn't he know how terrified I am of him?

"I should find my gloves," I say, and step back. I welcome the cold filling the distance between us. "Leo will think we've been devoured by ghosts."

Castian clears his throat. He walks past me, out of the room. "Haven't we?"

Back in the sitting room we've claimed as camp, Leo has spread our bedrolls near the fire. His suggestive stare slides between Castian and me. I ignore it.

"Look at what I found!" Leo points to a coppery object with flecks of teal patina. "I haven't seen an alfaro since I left Zaharina."

Castian sits beside him and picks up the small metal dome

perforated with dozens of stars. A lamp that marks constellations. "This was in my nursery—our nursery."

Leo digs into a pocket of his pack and withdraws a stub of a candle. He lights the wick and Castian places the dome over it. The perforated holes in the copper illuminate the ceiling with stars.

"I had one when I was little," I say, and join them, leaning back on my arms to get a better look. "My father made it out of tin. It was supposed to be the constellation of the three maidens, but my mother laughed and said it was a fine, if unrecognizable, attempt. I couldn't sleep without it because I was afraid of the dark."

"Which constellation is this one?" Leo asks.

Castian watches the stars flicker on the ceiling. "I'm not certain."

"Well, in my provincia of Zaharina," Leo says, "where we invented these—you're welcome—they're given as gifts for significant dates. The constellation represents the time and placement of the sky on a worthy occasion. Weddings. Births. Deaths. Though for the death, they're given to the family, not the deceased, naturally."

Castian shrugs as he takes off his boots. "I was born under the Father Giant constellation and my brother under the World's Star. This is neither."

"Perhaps it was your mother's, then," Leo says.

"Perhaps."

The rainstorm and roaring fire play a rhythmic beat that makes the silence easy, comfortable almost. I clean my boots and lay out my socks near the fire. Castian sharpens his dagger and stares at the flat of the blade.

"What happened to this castle?" Leo asks.

At first, I think Castian is going to ignore the question. He's quiet for too long. His blue-green eyes are dark pools as he stares at the alfaro between us. "My mother's family did not survive the plague, and so there was no one to defend the castle during the insurrections around the country. It was not only the Moria rebels but others from provincias across the kingdom who still harbored hatred toward the crown. According to the records at least, a small band of Sól Abene rebels joined them. What was left was taken by scavengers."

"That explains what I overheard," I say, resting my chin on my knee. "Locals of this region are joining the rebel cause. What I don't understand is why the Whispers would attack Queen Penelope if she and Illan were cohorts?"

"Only the dead can say." Castian reaches out to spin the alfaro dome, making the constellation dance. "I suspect that it could have been to throw off her involvement with the rebels or that she had Moria blood, even if she never displayed any power."

"She could have been one of the Olvidados," I suggest. Esteban's grandmother was one of the forgotten, people born to Moria families but without any magics of their own.

"Someone in her family must have been. I fear I do not know my mother's line as well as I should. I've been through her possessions and have found nothing. All I know is she was a young queen with a tragic life and an even more tragic end. She remains a mystery to me even in death."

Leo leans back with his arms behind his head, staring up at the star-speckled ceiling. "When I was a little boy they used to sing songs about the golden queen of Puerto Leones. She is not forgotten. One day they might sing songs of you, too."

"They already do." Castian flashes a wicked grin.

I throw my sock at him, which he catches. I expect him to grimace, but he only laughs and tosses it back at me.

"One year, my father banned the bards at court from singing my ballads. I used to think that he hated the sight of me because I reminded him of my mother. But now I think that he was always afraid I would do as he once did. He killed every member of his family with a claim to the throne. After the news of Andrés's death, I overheard my father telling my mother that perhaps it was for the best."

"I will never understand you royals," Leo says. "King Fernando is certainly going through a lot of trouble seeking your safe return from the rebels."

"As long as the people believe the Whispers are holding me captive, I'm an excuse to wage the war he's always wanted."

"He's more paranoid than ever. Dangerous." Leo sighs, the fear deeply etched in his green eyes. "This Knife of Memory better be more than a myth."

"When I lived with the Whispers," I say, twisting the ring on my finger, "some of the elders spoke of the great power that our goddess, the Lady of Shadows, could wield. She shared that power with the Moria, but after millennia of life, she created a weapon that would sever her immortality. She hid that weapon, only to be found by the worthy Robári of the Moria people. Most of us believed it was a pretty story to make us forget that we were fighting a never-ending war. But there were others who truly believed its existence."

"I heard about it from my nursemaid, Davida," Castian says, then worry furrows his brow. I remember what the older woman meant to him and how he's tried to protect her. "Do you know if she's still at the palace?"

"I haven't seen her since the festival, but I believe she left the capital safely with a small band of servants."

Castian lets go of a pent-up breath. "Good."

"What about the logbook?" Leo asks. "How did you discover that Duque Arias was in possession of such a map? Does he know where it leads?"

"Arias is a sore loser and a fool, but he's no traitor. He doesn't know what he had in his possession." Castian drums his fingers over his chest. "Forty years ago, my father went on an expedition. The crew consisted of my father, Duque Arias's grandfather, who was a naval officer at the time, and a command crew. Every name on the crew list is now dead, except for my father."

"Suspicious!" Leo gasps.

"If you call murder suspicious," I say.

"What does this logbook and voyage have to do with the king and the Knife of Memory?"

Castian spins the alfaro once more. "I believe the Knife of Memory has been used on this kingdom before by my father. That it could be the cause of everything wrong in Puerto Leones."

Leo sits up on his elbow and frowns skeptically. "Are you saying that a mythical *knife* is to blame for the animosity your family has fostered?" For the first time since I've known him, he's angry. "So my young husband's death was simply because of magics and not because your father created the order of justice to persecute Moria?"

"No. That's not what I mean. It's more complicated than that," Castian tries to explain. "I've spent years trying to piece together my father. To understand why he is a monster."

"Perhaps the wine that year was a bad vintage?" Leo offers.

But I say, "Monsters are made."

Castian looks at me and nods. "This expedition was a turning point for my father. He was a prince. He was engaged to be wed. He was poised to be named my grandfather's sole heir. But then he returns from the voyage and his betrothed had died of a fever while he was at sea, and he slaughters every Fajardo in sight and crowns himself king. He goes on as if everything before that coronation never existed."

Leo is rendered speechless for a moment. The candle in the alfaro sputters and leaves a trail of smoke as it extinguishes.

"I have been through all the rooms in the library halls and spent years searching records. The year after my father's expedition, the plague happened. That same year every map in the kingdom was replaced. The Arm of Justice was created. And he married my mother."

"It could be coincidence," I suggest. That's the first thing I said when Castian gave me the same explanation days ago. "Or King Fernando used the Knife of Memory to change the fate of the kingdom and our history."

"If that's true, then why didn't he use it to complete his murder of the Moria?"

"Moria legend does say that once used, the Knife of Memory returns to the Lady of Shadows's resting place," I answer.

Castian holds up Admiral Arias's logbook. "And my father no longer has the coordinates. The island detailed in these pages doesn't exist on any known map. The charts are unknown, even to me."

"I want to believe. I do," Leo says doubtfully. "I hope this Knife can sever King Fernando's link from the world. But what if this expedition was one of those soul-searching journeys noblemen take to find their true purpose in life? As you said, he was meant to be married. I've heard all the royals take them for their constitution. Not to mention learn the ways of romance at seaside brothels. Did you not go on one?"

"Mine were a little different," Castian says through gritted teeth.

"*Leo*," I warn.

Raising his hands in defense, Leo says, "I'm only repeating what my lady Nuria told me."

"I've been searching for years, reading every tome in the royal libraries and halls, and even traveling as far as Dauphinique and Luzou. But there was one ship that was supposed to be lost at sea that caught my attention. The *Leon del Mar*. I found the manifest, but there was no information about where it had traveled, only that Admiral Arias was there. The admiral died long ago, but when I was at the Arias estate I began my search. To Duque Arias, it's a keepsake from his grandfather's last voyage that he likes to show off when he's drunk. And now, my father knows I'm in possession of it…" Castian trails off, watching the fire's embers. I add another broken piece of wood.

He tugs on the scruff on his chin. "Time is of the essence. We have to risk taking the main roads to the port of Salinas and meet this Queen of Little Luzou."

I think of the way I used to travel with the Whispers. We took risks every time we left the safety of our borders. "I have an idea. But it'll take up most of the coin we have, and neither of you is going to like it."

"I trust you," Leo says, then curls up on his side.

I grin, sinking into the weight of the days to come. "Remember you said that tomorrow."

8

"IF WE MEET IN THE SIX HELLS, I SWEAR, RENATA CONVIDA," LEO WARNS, HIS nostrils flaring.

"Be quiet, you'll scare the geese," I hiss.

This cart of geese is being delivered half a day along the southern road to Vahía Caña, in the direction we need to go. Laying down between crates of the noisy fowl shitting and pecking is the least of our worries. We pass through several checkpoints, with only one close encounter. A zealous soldier wanted to unload and inventory the crates, when by providence the first goose bit him hard enough to draw blood. The farmer gave the bird to the soldier for his troubles.

From Vahía Caña we bribe a desperate farmer to sell us his horse and cart. He'd had a bad crop, and what he had he'd handed over to the tax collectors. Cas and I lie on the bed of the cart covered in itchy hay while Leo sings the entire time as he drives. We ride through the night until the wheel breaks, and we leave the wreckage in a gulch. The ancient horse trots away, back toward the road we came from.

We are covered in filth down to every pore and rarely in the mood to talk. But we don't stop, and little by little, we make our way to the southernmost point of the kingdom, where we will be one step closer to the Knife of Memory. We sleep in a stable, a pumpkin patch, and a vineyard. That's where we overhear that a large shipment of wine is headed to the Cliffs of Jura. We split up and sneak onto the wagons. From there comes the true nightmare. The last cart is full of fertilizer, which is dropping us about ten miles outside Salinas. Only a small mountain stands between us and the port.

We climb out of the cart, caked in manure, and make our way up the rocky slope. There is not a single cloud in the sky or trees to seek cover from the sun. Clad in fertilizer and undergarments— to make less of a mess we stowed our clothes in our packs—every part of me itches. I can hardly stand the stench of myself, but I keep pushing until we reach the mountain peak for a rest. Leo nearly weeps as he slaps at the clouds of stinging flies that follow our trail.

Castian unshoulders his pack, grabs a scarf to protect his eyes, and climbs atop a boulder. Past an outcrop of trees and rock formations is a long road that leads to Citadela Salinas and a pristine ocean that appears the palest turquoise along the shore and the deepest cobalt where the horizon meets the sky.

"It's so colorful," I say, surprised.

"That's what I love most about port citadelas," Leo says, breathing through his mouth. "We should make camp at the hot springs and wash up. We cannot, *will not*, meet the Queen of Little Luzou in this state."

Castian laughs quietly, but retrieves his pack and mine, and carefully maneuvers the rocky terrain downslope. Leo and I eagerly follow the promise of a bath. Tufts of emerald-green plants and a copse of spindly trees give way to a network of steaming pools hidden by shady trees. I shut my eyes at the reprieve from the sun. A breeze carries the echo of birds and stench of sulfur. Suddenly, a numbing sensation creeps up along my hairline. I whirl around but I see nothing but trees. Castian and Leo watch me carefully, reaching for their knives.

"Nati, what's wrong?"

I shake my head, and the feeling ebbs. "This place feels familiar."

Castian's brows knit, forming cracks in the dried muck on his face. "The Gray?"

"I'm not sure. My mind has been quiet." Too quiet perhaps, but until we've secured our passage to hunt for the Knife, I can't worry about myself. "Come on. You smell dreadful."

His body shakes with laughter, his teeth a white strip between mud and manure. Leo and Cas set down our packs and undress in moments. Leo wades into the closest spring with an exaggerated sigh but Cas throws himself right in, scrubbing muck from his face.

On the stone lip of the spring, I cut our only bar of soap into three rectangles and toss two at the boys. Then I peel off my undergarments and step into the steaming water. It's hot at first, but my muscles unwind and my itchy skin is relieved. I lather the soap on my body as if I'll never be quite clean, rubbing my skin raw. I wash my hair and finger comb the tangles free, inhaling the scents of sulfur and soap as if they're my final breaths.

When I'm as clean as I'll get in the woods, I wade in the shallow water into one of the bigger spring basins. Green lichen clings to the rock and soft steam rises on the surface.

"This is nice, isn't it?" Leo purrs, after a while. "Three friends taking a moonlit dip."

"The moon isn't out yet." Castian rolls his eyes skyward. The wet ends of his hair look like tarnished gold curling against the broad span of his shoulders.

"Give it a minute, my prince." Leo is clearly delighting in this situation. He reaches down to the muddy bottom of the spring and scoops up the white clay, dragging it across his cheeks and down the bridge of his nose. "You can't rush the moon."

"If I didn't know better," Cas says, wrinkling his forehead, "I'd say you enjoy making *your prince* angry."

"Pardon me, but I thought there was no prince from here on out, but a Will Otsoa." Leo beams at me. "Lady, is your husband always like this?"

A wave of water crashes over Leo's head, the clay streaking down his cheeks. "All right, I deserve that."

Ripples dance around me. I try to suppress my laughter but I can't, and soon the three of us are joined together in the delirium of exhaustion, and the reckless hope of what is waiting for us. Castian and Leo sit side by side, their elbows resting against rocks, faces tipped to the light dancing between the trees. As they talk about lords and ladies of the court, I sink below the warm blue waters. I search the Gray, dig through the faces that rest there for someone who walked through these trees. There must be a reason these hidden springs feels so familiar, but nothing jumps out.

"How are you feeling?" Castian asks when I surface.

"Never better." I force a smile. I know that we made a promise of honesty to each other back in Acesteña, but this isn't exactly a lie. I feel fine in this moment.

Leo bites on his lip the way he does when he's afraid to ask a question. "Would you tell us if something were wrong?"

I sit up, crossing my arms over my chest. "What do you mean?"

Leo and Castian share a conspiratorial glance. What is this non-verbal conversation I'm not privy to?

Leo raises his brows. "Do you remember talking to us in the middle of the night?"

"No, but I talk in my sleep," I assert. By the worry on their features I wonder if this was different from my usual muttering. "What did I say?"

"You were asking us when your husband was coming home," Castian says. "I tried to wake you, but I realized you were already awake. At least, your eyes were open. You called me your justice."

I rack my mind for memories of last night. I don't dream, not truly. Sometimes there is a pitch-black of the void. Other times, I relive the memories I've taken.

"I feel fine, Cas," I say softly. I'm too tired to argue. "I told you my power feels different. Perhaps I took one memory too many, and this is the consequence. Justice Méndez was the first Hollow I'd created in so long."

Castian doesn't push, but I can see the strain there. He presses the heart of his palm where our twin scars are.

"Leo," I say tentatively. There is one thing I haven't asked. "Méndez—"

"I did not want to bring it up until you were ready, Lady Ren." Leo sighs. "King Fernando gave him mercy."

"Mercy he didn't deserve," Castian says darkly.

Steam rises, cloaking us in warmth, and the three of us drift closer. I have an overwhelming sense of safety, more than I've had in a long time. That is the only reason, I think, that I allow myself to speak.

"When I was a girl, I would have denied that Méndez was an evil man. He was the closest thing I had to a father after I'd been kept from my real one for so long. But I see it now—men like King

Fernando, like Justice Méndez, they show kindness when they need power in return."

Leo takes a tiny bit of clay and taps it on my nose. My smile is weary, but my heart gives a squeeze. "I am sorry," Leo says. "I never knew my appa. He was a soldier. All I have are the stories my sweet amma told me. He was very charming and unbearably handsome, naturally. I am my father's son."

I gently splash him. But when we stop laughing, I add, "He must have been brave, I'm positive."

We both turn to Castian, who's creating illusions on the water, bright fish that leap from the surface and fade away with the cascade of his fingers.

"I suppose it's to no one's surprise that my father was cruel," Castian confesses. "I was never studious enough, fast enough, strong enough. Yes, I'd displayed potential in bloodshed, but he never relented. Still, there were days when he'd dote on my mother in the gardens or when he'd take me on a trip to the Islas del Rey. I wasn't old enough to realize that there were foreign emissaries in the gardens watching us be a perfect family. Or that our sailing expeditions were an excuse to execute his enemies at sea without a trial."

Castian stands abruptly, water falling off him in rivulets. His body looks carved from marble. Deep scars crosshatch along his shoulders, his ribs, beneath the golden trail of hair that starts from his belly button, down to parts where I avert my eyes. I am slammed with the memory of those girls from Acesteña who lusted after him while he chopped wood. The feel of him pressed against me when I threatened a kiss out of him. Then before that, the memories I stole from Lady Nuria of very intimate moments between her and Castian. The way he touched her, like he was learning how to recognize her with his eyes closed.

I swallow the utterly ridiculous knot in my throat. Except my eyes meet Leo's, who is beaming with amusement. I swim away from them.

"I'm going to set a few traps before we lose the light," Castian announces. For a moment, he watches me watch him, and there's the flicker of a rueful smile. It's like trying to find the same star in a field of blinking ones—there and then gone.

"Would it be so terrible?" Leo asks once we're alone. He washes the dried clay from his face.

I wring out water from my hair and tie it back. "What?"

"You are dense sometimes," he says, exasperated. "I mean, would it be so terrible to let yourself admit that you care for him?"

"Stop."

"Ren, you're my friend. And I might go so far as to say I am your best and only friend in the world at the moment. It is my duty, nay, my mission to tell you the truth. The way you two look at each other could incinerate entire forests." Doubt quirks his eyebrow. "If you don't destroy each other first, that is."

Preposterous. That's the most ridiculous thing he's ever said to me. My entire body crackles with energy at the thought. "Yes, we're finally getting along. But I could never—I won't."

I splash out of the spring, leaving him behind muttering something that sounds an awful lot like "Could have fooled me."

I am not naive enough to deny that there *is* something between us. Castian and I are connected in a way I never expected. But my feelings for him are so tangled with hate, with bitterness, with the worst memories I carry. He is strong and beautiful and has shown more kindness than I ever thought he was capable of. But he's also mercurial, with a well of untapped rage. Castian is a trick of the light. Not to mention, Dez's brother.

I find my way to our packs and hurry to dress. I've barely finished tying the drawstring of my trousers when I feel another presence beside me. I whirl around to tell Leo to never speak another word about Castian and me, but it isn't Leo at all.

Three strangers are in our camp. My body flashes hot with panic, and then I'm lashing out. I block a punch that flies at my face. I do not call for help because I can't endanger Leo and Castian. Instead I run, and the intruders give chase through the downward slope of bare trees.

The terrain is difficult in the setting sun, and I hear one of them fall and cry out. My heart thunders as I find a rock. I stop, counting on my attacker's momentum, and crush it against his face.

"I'll help Uri," one of them shouts. "You grab her!"

"I'm trying!" the one I just hit snaps.

I freeze at the familiar voice. He lands a punch between my shoulder blades, and I stumble forward. I throw myself into the fall and land in a crouch, sweeping my leg across his feet. He rolls into a standing position, fists up. Dressed in deep greens and browns, and sporting a red gash across the otherwise smooth brown skin of his cheek, is a boy I never thought I'd see again.

"Esteban?"

His wide brown eyes take me in. Panting, he staggers back a couple of paces. "Ren! What are you doing here?"

"I should ask you the same thing."

Esteban glances nervously over his shoulder. "This is a Whispers' camp. You know this."

I think of the sense of familiarity I felt coming up here. It *was* from a memory. One of mine.

"Where are the others?" I ask. Margo. Sayida. *Dez.* I should tell him that Dez is alive!

He grabs me hard by my shoulder, frantically whispering in my ear. "You have to run. If the others see you, we'd have to bring you in."

"We want the same thing. Implore Margo that we are on the same side."

"It isn't Margo that we have to worry about," he says darkly.

"If not Margo, who?"

Then I feel the buzz of magic along my skin. As if someone has walked on my grave. I look at his hand on my shoulder. Of course— he's using his Ventári magics to peer in my head. I shove him, and the whorls of magic on my palms ignite. He groans and cradles his abdomen. I remember putting pressure on his wound when the rebel stronghold was attacked. Even with the best Moria healers, his injury isn't fully healed. It is unlike Margo to send out patrols that are compromised. But do I have the right to question what the Whispers do anymore?

"What have you done to yourself, Ren?" Esteban watches me with a fear I remember too well. "I can't read you—"

Before he can finish, his two companions catch up to us.

"Robári!" The youngest boy cradles an injured arm. His gaze falls on my marks, still glowing. "We're to bring them in!"

"What have you done to yourself?" Esteban asks again, and this time his words are heavy with lament. It frightens me.

"I didn't do anything," I whisper. But I know I'm wrong. I let Cebrián tinker in my brain. I used my power one too many times.

I close my glowing hands into fists, ready to fight all three of them if I have to. Then heavy boots come clamoring down the mountain. Torchlight. Red uniforms. I count six of them, but only one steps forward and hooks an arm around my throat.

"What have we here?" he says, cupping his fist over my mouth. He leans in close, murmuring at my ear. "It's me."

I never thought I'd be so relieved to hear Castian's voice. I feel his damp hair against my face beneath the illusion.

"*Run*," I shout at Esteban.

He begins to shake his head, but the others have already left him. Cowards. No matter what, none of us left our unit behind. We always went back for one another.

"Go!" I shout. I hope he knows me well enough to hear the certainty in my voice. "I'll be fine. You know I will."

"I'm sorry, Ren. For all of it," he whimpers before he turns and bolts. Something has shattered him and left only fear. What has happened to the Whispers?

I release a terrified breath and fall against Castian. His illusion flickers, then vanishes as he brushes my hair back to make sure I'm unharmed. The five guards with torches become Leo holding two oil lamps.

We hurry back to our camp. I stepped on a jagged rock and lean on Castian for support. When the pain grows too strong, and I can't bite down on the splintering sensation shooting up my foot, Castian gathers me into his arms despite my protest.

"You're injured, and you'll make it worse," he says, his face too close to mine. I hold on around his neck and contemplate choking him for being so frustratingly rational.

"I know that," I relent. "I don't like feeling helpless."

Leo glances back, holding the lanterns in front of him. "You don't like help either, Lady Ren."

Though he doesn't make a sound, I feel the vibration of Castian's laugh.

"Thank you," I murmur.

I watch the outline of his face, a silhouette haloed by moonlight. "You don't have to thank me for saving you, Nati."

When we get back to our camp, I slink out of Castian's arms. The packs are overturned, the firepit half built. They must have dropped everything to find me. I can't describe what that makes me feel, so I busy my hands. I clean my wound, use a bit of cooling salve, and wrap a clean strip of cloth around my foot while Leo finishes building a fire, and Castian goes to check his traps.

He returns with a brown rabbit and begins butchering it on a slab of stone. "That boy. You knew him?"

I nod. "Esteban. He was from my old unit."

"That makes two members of your old unit you've encountered lately," Leo says. He fans the budding cinders until they catch. "The girl in the tavern and now this."

Three. Dez would make three, even if he just left a note.

"We should be prepared, if we see them in the citadela," Castian warns. He wipes the back of his hand on his cheek. "They could be recruiting. Or perhaps they're going to try to forge an alliance with the Queen of Little Luzou."

"No," I say, hurt catching in my throat. "The Whispers seem to be after Robári. They were going to take me."

Castian looks up from the bloody rabbit in his hands. "I won't let that happen. *We* won't let that happen."

"They're recruiting magicless Leonesse," I say, my mind turning to memories of when I was a child at the palace. "They're snatching up Robári the same way the justice did nearly a decade ago."

Castian snaps a branch in half and whittles the bark clean off with a few jerks of his blade. "I've been thinking about this since Leo arrived. Because of my stepmother, the king has the Dauphinique fleet at his disposal. He's drafting from every corner of Puerto Leones. He's urging the elite families of the kingdom to gather their forces. How many Whispers would you say were left, Nati?"

"Forty," I estimate. "Perhaps fifty."

Leo feeds small branches into the fire. "Why go through all the trouble of amassing such forces against an army of rebels that's woefully outnumbered?"

"Precisely," Cas muses. "Something you said hasn't been sitting right with me, Leo. My father has never done anything altruistically. He has to see a return."

Leo's face scrunches up with thought. "Do you mean the matter of Lady Las Rosas?"

"Aye. My father could have sent Leyre Las Rosas back to Luzou and seized her father's land. He *chose* to offer this bastard daughter property and soldiers he could otherwise command. Why?"

"Do you know her?" I ask.

Castian shrugs and places the rabbit on the spit. "I remember her from one of our diplomatic voyages to Empirio Luzou. I was twelve, just finished my first year of military training. My father was furious at me because I was sick the entire voyage and I embarrassed him. I hid most of the time, but I remember Lord Las Rosas asking my father whether he could recognize Leyre and have her reared in Puerto Leones."

"And?"

"My father said no." Castian watches the animal fat drip and hiss into the flames.

"Could he be trying to make an alliance with the empress of Luzou?" I ask. "If Leyre has a title, she could be an ambassador between the two kingdoms. Though I can't believe the empress of Luzou would ever consider allying with him. She's challenged the king's war against the Moria."

"Whatever game my father is playing, I'm going to ruin him before he's finished. The Knife of Memory will wipe him from existence, and he'll never taint the world again."

That night, when the fire crackles and the sounds of the mountain howl, I can't sleep. Castian keeps watch, using his illusion as cover. Curled on my side, I shut my eyes, but my mind is a dance of memories. Slowly, one slips forward, unfurling like the shadow of wings:

> *Castian is a boy in the palace gardens. He's singing for me while I lie in the grass. He says the song is about his mother. Méndez calls my name and Castian runs while I pretend that I got lost in the hedges.*

I push the memory away, lovely as it is, because it softens my heart. I can't afford that. I may not be a Whisper anymore, but I am still a rebel and I have a queen to meet.

9

DESPITE YESTERDAY'S TROUBLES, THE THREE OF US SNAKE OUR WAY DOWN THE mountain, climbing over swells of rock, dry brush, and pale white flowers with black centers. Ocean moisture thickens the air as we reach the bottom.

We stop and use the last of our water reserves to wash the mountain dust from our faces, and change into more presentable clothes. Leo winces and slaps the side of his neck before pulling on a green tunic that brings out the jade of his eyes. I catch sight of his deceased husband's gold wedding band resting over his heart before he tugs on the laces to reveal just enough of his chest. He grunts, then slaps the top of his hand. "I forgot about the mosquitoes."

Sitting atop a boulder, Castian keeps an eye on the main road. He glances back, a sly grin on his face. "Clearly they have not forgotten you."

"It's a terrible thing I'm so delicious." Leo feigns humility. "Clearly, you have nothing to worry about, my prince."

Castian smirks. "Thank you for bearing that burden for both of us."

It's strange to see them this way, trading playful barbs like they're longtime friends. I'm not entirely sure whether I'm jealous because Leo is my friend, not his, or because Castian and I can never truly have that kind of relationship. Honestly, why limit myself? I can be jealous of both things, I suppose.

Leo helps me with the hook closures of my blue Carnaval dress and braids half my hair. When I glance up, Castian quickly turns his face back to the road. He doesn't need to change out of his black tunic and breeches because he'll be under an illusion.

"Why is she called the Queen of Little Luzou?" I ask.

"The true name of this citadela and port is Salinas," Leo explains, jabbing a hairpin across my scalp. He used to do this every day while he was my attendant, and it might be the only thing I miss. "But to the locals, this is Little Luzou."

I scoff. "I can't imagine King Fernando would allow even one of the elite families to carry on with such a title."

"Ah, but the Queen of Little Luzou isn't from any of the elite families of Puerto Leones," Leo says.

"Oh, I assumed with her connection to Lady Nuria that she might have been."

"After years of plague, so much of the Leonesse population was decimated," Castian says, leaping from his perch to retrieve his pack. "But it was worse in the port citadelas and the larger villages. Salinas used to be second only to Riomar in trade. With half of Salinas on death barges, the only person left to run the city was a decrepit priest, and the citadela was desperate. My father granted authority to the last remaining official, an ambassador from Empirio

Luzou. She brought in workers from the empire, so many that travelers and locals began calling the citadela Little Luzou. The ambassador was its queen. But when fighting with the Moria resumed, and Luzou's leaders publicly criticized my father, he tried to expel all Luzouan-born people."

"That's what he did to the Moria," I say.

"The Queen refused to leave," Castian continues. "She kept the city running, and as a test, she called off her soldiers and anyone loyal to her. Pirates ravaged the port for months before my father allowed her to stay."

"But wouldn't she be ancient by now? I know the Luzouan claim to have miracle waters that let them live for ninety years, but this is still Puerto Leones."

"Ah, but like all monarchies, the title has been passed down," Leo says. "I believe it is her daughter who has been elected by the citadela to take up her mother's mantle."

"Can they do that?" I ask.

"My father does not need an insurrection from one of his highest-taxed and most profitable ports. As long as the alliance is convenient to him, of course."

Leo retrieves Nuria's red envelope from his pocket and offers it to me. I reach for the thick parchment, and a pinprick of pain shoots through the back of my eye. *A fisherman carries a metal cage full of crabs down this road.*

I inhale a sharp breath, but when I open my eyes, Leo and Castian haven't noticed my brief occurrence. The prince is working on his own magics.

When Castian creates an illusion, it is like watching a tapestry be woven right before my eyes. Illusionári magics appear instantly, but when you look closely, truly look, you spot the iridescent threads that make the whole. His hair darkens to stark umber ringlets, and his irises become two rough-cut emeralds. His mouth, however, remains the same shape buried around a black beard decorated in gold string as in the ancient days of Zaharina. With Leo beside him they could easily be brothers.

"Who are you supposed to be?" Leo asks.

"May I introduce Álvaro Talamanca, the emissary of Duque Albajada." Castian folds himself into a bow.

"Why can't you be Wilmer Otsoa?"

"Because she'll appreciate someone with a title. Trust me."

"The Queen of Little Luzou is said to be a fierce woman with a reputation that would even make the Matahermano sweat. My apologies if I wasn't clear when I first arrived—Lady Nuria was answering Ren's letter, not yours, Prince Castian. Ren should be the one to make the request."

"I have spent my life at court," Castian counters. His royal ass is showing. "I have been at countless diplomacy—"

"But we aren't at court," I say. "We're fugitives."

"I can do this, Ren," Castian says, leveling his strange new eyes with mine.

Nerves twist at the pit of my stomach, and a dull pulse spreads to my temples. What if I stand in front of this woman and freeze because of an occurrence? What if my skull decides to split open with memories as we're making a deal? If I tell Cas and Leo my worries, they'll ask about my state every hundred feet. For now, Castian has to be the one to do this.

I slap the letter against his chest. "Let's hope your illusion extends to your charm. You're not as handsome in these frocks."

I realize the mistake I've made before the words finish leaving my mouth.

His mouth quirks playfully, his body languid in a way it hasn't been since that night at the palace. "You think I'm handsome?"

Leo, who simply cannot contain himself, bursts into laughter. Grasping at the last bits of my pride, I hurry ahead of them and down the dusty road leading to Little Luzou.

The road into the city is crowded with wagons and foot traffic and leads to a set of steps that empty out on the highest point of the citadela. Down below are the narrow streets that this part of the kingdom is famous for, paths that create a layered maze right through the white cliffside. A single road for horses and carriages zigzags from one side of the city to the other, but we take the first of thousands of steps leading to the piers. Each building we pass displays brightly colored shutters and doors. Flags of Puerto Leones fly along the water and from the glint of a mansion where the Queen of Little Luzou lives.

But the truly breathtaking part of this southernmost point of Puerto Leones is the port itself and beyond. The sea glistens in the sun. There's a haze along the horizon. Salty wind makes the anchored ships bob, sails and ropes moving just so.

"I don't think I've ever seen this much color," I say.

"Everyone paints their door on the new year," Castian says. "Each color represents what the house wants to attract—health, money, love."

"Why stop at one?" Leo says, pulling his scarf over his face to shield his eyes.

I begin to laugh, but my breath is kicked from my lungs. Pain sears the inside of my skull as I stop halfway down the steps and I feel my whole being recede.

Where am I? My family is walking ahead of me. My husband takes my hand. "Lovely day for a wedding, isn't it?"

"It is," I find myself saying.

"It is what?" Castian asks ahead of me. Then he's doubling back, racing up the steps to stop me from falling. I'm forced out of the occurrence with a shudder.

"I'm fine," I lie. "The sun made me feel faint."

"Nati, but—"

"I said I'm fine, *Ambassador*." I lower my voice to a hiss. "Don't call me that."

I shove past him and descend. My heart races the whole way but I force myself to focus. I can beat this. I can do this.

The closer we get to the piers, the busier everything becomes. Women dressed in fine silks cut to the latest styles stroll in heels under lace parasols. Farmhands in loose, dirty tunics lead mules pulling wagons of sugarcane. There are people from all over the kingdom here, and the three of us don't stick out any more than we would elsewhere. At the bottom of the steps a commotion seems to have formed around a few vendor stalls. Castian and Leo catch up to me, and we move with the crowd to the center of the market. Local guards in brown leather hang back, and all eyes are focused on the three people at the center of the crowd. I've seen something like this before in villages with more archaic ways.

This is a trial.

The woman who seems to be doling out the justice is petite, with black hair twisted in an elegant braid. She has light brown skin and high cheekbones accentuated by the severe pout of her ruby mouth. She wears a ruffled silk blouse in deep sea blue and fitted trousers. There's a blade strapped at her hip, but it looks too intricately dec-orated to be anything but ceremonial. Her wide eyes are rimmed with kohl, accentuating the elegant tilt at each corner. She wears rouge like a Dauphinique woman and a string of braided gold around her neck like the people in the empress of Luzou's court. I have no doubt that this is the infamous Queen of Little Luzou.

"Do you deny it?" she asks a young man in front of her.

His hair is shorn across the scalp like a recent soldier, or someone who has lice. He drops on his knees, his hands on the cobblestones. When his face crumples with tears, I think he looks so very young. A thief most likely.

"The guards aren't intervening?" I whisper to Castian.

Castian lowers his mouth to my ear. "They seem to have different rules here after all."

"I asked, do you deny it?" Her strong voice rises over the onlookers' chatter.

"No, I do not," the boy cries.

He looks up at the third person in this trial: a butcher wearing an apron smeared with blood. There, a scar, like a sickle on her cheek. Her face is mean, and her hands are calloused. For a moment, I wonder if that is what people say when they look at me.

"Three weeks now," the butcher says in the coarse coastal accent of the southern provincias. "Started small with giblets and pig's feet. Hunger has been a friend to us all, so I let it slide. But then he got bolder. A chicken here, a rabbit there. Then he made off with a lovely roast that was scheduled for Señor Alonzo. I'll lose their business."

The Queen holds her hand up, and the butcher goes silent. I find I'm holding my breath right along with everyone else, waiting to see what the woman will proclaim.

"You know the punishment for thieves," she says. "How convenient that you already have a cleaver."

The sharp intake of breath drains the blood from the accused thief's face. Tears stream down his face. He prostrates himself on the cobblestones.

"Please, I beg you. Our village has been raided three times in the last month and twice more before that. There's nothing to give, nothing! I was the only one of my brothers who wasn't drafted because of my bad leg."

The Queen's razor-sharp gaze falls on me, and then Castian, and

I feel my stomach tighten. Can she see through him, or does she recognize us as strangers? Perhaps this is what she does to intimidate. King Fernando has a similar way about him. He says more with his silence than with any cutting word.

"I leave it up to you, Romia. Take his hand"—the boy sobs once again—"or allow him to work off everything he's stolen. After that do with him as you see fit. But as your last apprentice ran off with a sailor not three nights ago, I know you are shorthanded."

The butcher's face only gets tighter, the hard lines of someone who has worked hard every day of her life. She looks at the boy, then at the woman mediating their dispute. The butcher picks up the cleaver in her meaty hand, and I picture her chasing the boy with it. She turns to the boy, bent over like that, and I can count the bones jutting through his tunic. She relents, and her hard exterior softens.

"I accept those terms," the butcher says, and the crowd expels a relieved sigh. There's even a cheer and laughter from some of the younger kids who'd wanted to see some violence. "It won't be pretty work, you hear that?"

The boy gets up, a smile splitting his face into weeping joy. He nods frantically. They both thank the Queen of Little Luzou and set off into the city's stone maze.

"What are you standing around here for?" the woman snaps. "Don't you have wares to sell?"

Everyone scatters.

"Come on," I say, tugging the sleeves of my companions. "It's her."

We cross the market and approach the Queen of Little Luzou.

But before we get close, brown-clad guards surround us, with spears at our throats.

The Queen's mansion is a five-story building toward the end of the pier, built as if it was meant to watch over the citadela. With a spear at my back, I march at a steady pace with the others, stealing a single glance back. After what we witnessed in the square, the Queen must be just. Still, those were her people, and we are strangers who dared approach her in public. It wasn't the introduction I was hoping for, but at the very least, we have her attention.

We're brought into a bright parlor with tall windows that let in the salt breeze. The Queen sits in a high-backed chair of black wood. Ledgers and scrolls are spread across her desk, where a few gold pesos tip a brass scale. I note a slender oil lamp, a bowl of pink fruit, and a lace fan—everything she might need to keep working late into the night. The strangest thing is a large stone turtle in varying shades of white and brown. Colorful beads are strung around its neck. I wonder if they mean anything, like the painted doors and shutters throughout the city.

I can't tell whether it's her hawk stare or my possible dehydration, but I have a sinking sensation in my stomach. I bite the inside corner of my lip so the pain can keep me grounded.

"State your query, travelers," says the Queen, unfurling a pleasant smile that conveys little patience for us. Castian clears his throat and approaches the desk.

"My lady," he says, bowing courteously. I wonder if it costs him anything as prince. But Castian has been a ruthless royal, a musician on his honeymoon, and a rebel on the run. What's one more disguise? "My companions and I seek to acquire a vessel."

"To what port?" she asks quickly.

He hesitates for the barest moment. "Porto Cebou."

"The capital of the Luzouan empire?" She scoffs. Shrewd brown eyes reassess us carefully. "I am not a ship's captain, and I do not sell passage. You're a stone's throw from the harbor at the other end of the pier."

"Ah, you see, therein lies the problem. We do not have travel documents out of the kingdom," Castian explains. I have never heard that waver in his voice, even though it's slight.

The Queen points at us. "There it is. Lead with the thing you want, Mister...?"

"Otsoa," Castian says, and stiffens slightly when he realizes that he's given the wrong name for the wrong illusion.

I catch Leo's wide-eyed expression with my own. Castian clears his throat again, nervously smoothing out the front of his embroidered jacket. "This is my wife, and my brother. We have a letter of request from a friend at the capital. Perhaps you know—" He reaches into his vest and two guards step forward.

Castian holds up one hand and reveals the red envelope. The guards relax, and he presents Lady Nuria's seal. The Queen breaks the red wax, and her clever eyes scan the elegant handwriting. I look at Castian, but he won't meet my eyes. That strange sensation in my stomach returns.

"Lady Nuria," the Queen says. "I owe her a very great deal. She was in this provincia recently. Brought wagons of grain and crates of fabric for the orphanage. She procured medicine for relief after hurricane season."

"Lady Nuria has always put herself before others," Leo says. Is that why she wanted *me* to speak to the Queen instead? To soften her heart to my plight as a memory thief on the run?

The Queen dismisses her guards with the flick of a hand. She fixes her eyes on Castian, taking in his clothes, his tousled hair. I suppose it's a good thing that he chose an illusion almost as beautiful as his true face. Then she looks at me, and I find myself holding my breath.

"Now, what are you all after?" she asks.

"I've been searching for my brother," Castian says, all courtly pretense from his voice gone. "And I mean to reunite with him."

"I thought this was your brother," she says, pointing at Leo.

"You can have more than one," Castian counters.

It's not a lie, not exactly, but I suspect a woman like the Queen can sense that.

She adjusts items on her desk. Moves a couple of coins from one side of the scale to the other. It doesn't quite balance. "That's not the entirety of your story, is it?"

"Lady—" he tries again, frustrated and impatient. I can sense how badly he wants this because I want it, too. I need it.

"I am no lady. My name is Perliana Montevang, and you will call me Señora Perliana or Señora Montevang as everyone else around these parts does. I'm sorry that you came all this way, but I cannot help you."

"You *will* help us," Castian says, his voice like the snap of a whip. He realizes too late that he's let his temper fly. "Señora Montevang, I beg you—"

"This is not begging," she says, leaning forward, her sharp nails spread out like claws. "Begging is what that boy did in front of the butcher so his hand wouldn't be cut off and hung for the strays to chomp. You come here with your pretty manners and pretty face. You come to me with a letter that shows how connected you are. Tell me, if you're so well connected to the palace why not beseech their help? Why not beg of the king?"

Castian's fists are at his sides. I feel this possibility slipping from my grasp. I squeeze his wrist, wishing more than ever that I had the power of a Ventári as strong as Esteban to communicate with him.

"We cannot beg of the king," I tell her. "The boy spoke of raids. Know that there will be more where that came from. But we are on more than a voyage to find his brother. We mean to stop this war before it starts."

"Who are you?" the Queen asks. When the lie begins to leave Castian's lips, she touches the stone shell of the turtle sculpture on her desk. Do I imagine the pulse of light, or is it the sun's rays? "I know you're wearing a glamour."

Castian takes a step back, but I grasp him tighter. His features are twisted in indecision, confusion, failure.

"I protect this port and these people," she says. "I have helped refugees. I have helped bad people, too. But do you know what they had in common?"

I shake my head.

"Honesty." Her lips pull back, showing all her teeth. "Now, get out."

As we're escorted from the mansion, I realize why I felt strange in her office. The turtle sculpture on her desk had the faintest glow. It was made of alman stone.

10

I RACE DOWN THE MANSION STEPS, PAST THE NOISY DOCKS AND VENDORS ADVERtising their wares. I have to keep going because if I stop, I must face the fact that we have come all this way for nothing.

"Ren, wait," Castian shouts after me.

I reach the end of the boardwalk—to my left is the glassy Castinian Sea, straight ahead, the marina busy with sailors docking luxury yachts and schooners. To my right I see an out—a sign that reads THE LIONESS OF THE SEA hanging from a rusty chain. Wood splinters off the open tavern door, weathered gray from years by the sea.

Inside the quiet Lioness, three patrons drink pints at the bar. The barmaid, a Luzouan woman with ink-black hair, points to an empty booth. I slide in and try to reel back everything I feel. The Queen of Little Luzou knew that Castian was an Illusionári. She had alman stone. Could she be a friend to Moria?

Castian and Leo quietly slide into the seat across from me. Leo picks at a paint splatter on the table, and when the paint splatter crawls away, his face twists with equal parts revulsion and disbelief. Soon, a Luzouan girl of about ten years old approaches. Her hair is braided in two long plaits, and her round, hazel eyes are piqued with curiosity. "What can I serve you? We've got a fish fry special but are out of the chicken caldo." She grins at a bright woven bracelet around Leo's wrist. "This is pretty. Can I try it on?"

"I'll tell you what." Leo chuckles, tugging the bracelet free and dangling it before her. "You can have it. It would look far prettier on you."

"Oh, thank you!" She holds it in her palm as if it's the most precious thing that's been given to her, and even though the intention is different, I can't help but think that this is what I must have looked like every time Méndez showered me with gifts.

"What are you doing?" the barmaid hollers, hurrying after her daughter. "Maya, I told you to take the orders, not bother the customers."

"She's not bothering us," I assure her. "We'll have three pints and three fish fry, please."

"Told you, Mamá," Maya says.

Relieved, the barmaid ushers her daughter away. When they're gone behind the swinging doors of the kitchen, I lose my smile and face Castian.

"What in the Six Hells happened to you back there?"

"We'll find another way," he says.

My anger simmers. I see red. "*How*? We spent all our pesos getting here. You can't fix this as—*yourself.*"

He sinks his face in his palms. "I'll write to Nuria again."

Leo shakes his head. "That would gravely endanger her. She's under constant watch. Her husband intercepts any correspondence.

Even letters from Lady Roca. A judge goes through her laundry. Need I remind you, her assets are frozen."

"I should have trusted my instinct," I say, more frustrated in myself than anything else. I've struggled with my magics and memories for longer than I've traveled with Castian. Why did I doubt myself earlier?

I imagine snaking my hands around the back of his head and slamming it on the table. I glance around the tavern and for a moment wonder whether anyone would care if I broke his face. Two of the patrons have fallen asleep in their seats, and the other stumbles out into the bright day. The barmaid carries over three pints and wipes her hands on a dirty apron.

"Salud," she says, though she doesn't linger.

"Salud," we repeat, drinking to our health and prosperity.

Castian sets down his pint and scrutinizes the moisture rolling down the glass. "What was I to do? Tell her the truth?"

"She was the single person that could help us," I remind him. "What do we do now? Without a ship, your logbook is useless."

"She wanted too much," he says.

I feel my eyes go wild, my body tremble. "We both knew we'd have to make sacrifices. At some point you're going to have to decide how much you're willing to give. How long are you going to hide the most important part of yourself?"

Castian leans his arms back and scoffs. "You've never had a funny bone in your body before, Nati, so why are you starting now?"

Leo takes in a sharp breath, then raises his hands as if he's getting between rabid dogs.

"Stop, both of you," he snaps. "Your husband might be right, Lady Otsoa. We *will* have to figure out another way." Before Castian can look too smug, Leo whirls on him. "You may want my head when this is all over, *brother dearest*, but the reason your charm failed in front of the Queen is precisely that. You thought she'd take one look at you and swoon. But you forget, you might be impossibly handsome, but even if you looked like a horse's ass, you used to have the only title that mattered"—he lowers his voice to a whisper—"prince of Puerto Leones."

I don't know whose mouth is open wider, mine or Castian's.

"How *dare* you," Castian seethes. He slams his fist on the table. It makes the drunk at the bar jump. The barmaid and her daughter chatter from somewhere in the back in rapid-fire Luzouan.

"You don't know how to talk to women who aren't there for the purpose of adornment or to take to bed," I say, and drink deeply from my ale.

Leo looks from Castian to me. "Why do you think the pair of you fight so much?"

"I don't want—I'm not trying to—" the princeling starts and stops, looks at me, then back to Leo. "I resent that."

"Oh? Your father's counselors are men. Every duque your father calls upon—"

"Every member of the justice, too," I add.

Castian frowns. "You've made your point."

A seagull flies through the open tavern door, walks across the bar, and drinks from the dregs of the sleeping patron's ale. The bird knocks the glass and wakes him. The drunk checks his pockets, and coming up empty, he staggers out.

Castian raises his glass and whispers, "Nuria and I were able to have an equal courtship. She is the descendant of queens."

"Lady Nuria was betrothed to you before you were both born in order for your family to secure her lands. When you cast her aside, no matter how noble you believed the cause, she was used as a bargaining chip to maintain your father's control of this kingdom. You might have been to hundreds of political meetings with dignitaries, but no one speaks of you the way the Queen spoke of my lady."

The barmaid and her daughter return. Maya carries one plate and her mother two others. The fish fry is crispy and golden, served with small round potatoes coated in crystal salt.

"Another round?" she asks.

We've barely finished our drinks, but I can see the desperation in her eyes, how empty this tavern is.

"Yes," Castian says, nudging Leo.

"My treat," Leo says dryly. He leaves a nice tip, and the barmaid beams with watery emotion in her eyes. She brings out another round, plus a small bottle of aguadulce and three small glasses.

"On the house."

When we're alone, and there's only the sound of the pier and the kitchen, Castian knocks on the table. In the blink of an eye, I can see his true form flash. It's for a moment, but a soaring sensation takes hold of me.

"Perhaps I should have done what Nuria wanted and told her the truth," Castian says finally. "But I've spent my whole life hiding—even these past few days with you, I've been someone else. If I become king, I will have to tell my people everything. Not solely what I have done in the name of my father, but that I have Moria blood, that I am an Illusionári."

"What are you afraid of?" I don't mean to ask it aloud but it slips. I've wanted to know since I saw the flecks of fear in his blue-green eyes the first time we fought.

"What if who I truly am, beneath the magics and illusion, isn't enough to lead Puerto Leones into a new age?"

I want to reach across the table and squeeze his shoulder, force him to look at me. I want him to know that I believe he can do this. That as angry as I am at him, I know he is fighting for our future.

The kingdom's future. But as the silence stretches, I can't find the right words.

"The good thing is, you still have time to figure it out," Leo says, diving into his potatoes.

Castian shakes his head, but a small smile plays on his lips. I don't have much of an appetite, but I force myself to eat because I don't know when our next meal is going to be. That was something I learned with the Whispers. Plus, it's my best excuse to not make eye contact with my princeling.

My princeling. The words sound ridiculous even thinking them.

My thoughts are interrupted by two men entering the tavern. They're dressed in violet silks and velvet worthy of King Fernando's court. One brings a handkerchief to his long nose and sneers in our direction. Maya steps out of the kitchen and freezes when she sees them.

"Be a dear, child, and get your mother."

Maya runs back. I look down at my plate, preparing myself for what is going to happen. It is what the Second Sweep said when we were in Acesteña, and it was what the thief said in the market today. Raids. The tax collectors have come again.

I glance at Castian, who gives a single shake of his head.

"Olya ginara, Anna!" the taxman says in a saccharine greeting using the Luzouan tongue.

"Señor Vernal, did you forget something?" the barmaid begins, her voice climbing to a high pitch. "I paid my share not six days ago."

Vernal glances back to the boardwalk, where two men in black wait to be summoned. They don't wear any official seals or carry weapons. By the looks of their muscles, they *are* the weapons. "The kingdom is in dire need, Señora Anna."

"I simply can't be here for another moment," the second taxman says, grimacing as his suede slippers barely touch the ground. "Give us what you have, lady, and we'll be on our way."

Castian's hand falls on top of mine. "We can't."

I know that we shouldn't get involved, but my heart doesn't see it that way. Anna reaches into her apron and hands over a fistful of coins, most of which were the ones Leo gave her. Maya yanks her mother's hand in protest. "That's everything we have!"

The coins fall to the ground, and Maya dives to gather them. The two brutes lingering outside are summoned, and Maya's scream pierces the air.

Castian exhales, and I see the moment he decides that he can't stand by and watch this happen. We scramble out of the booth and block the taxmen's path.

I turn to the mother and daughter and say, *"Go, now."*

The pair of men who make their way inside are built like twin ginger oxen with faces that have seen their fair share of fights.

"You must be new to Little Luzou," one purrs in a baritone voice. "Even the Queen knows it's best to leave the king's men to work."

"Is that what you call work?" Leo asks. "Scaring families out of their last coin?"

"No, this is." The brute swings.

I pick up a chair and crack it against his body. We are a fury of fists and kicks. The tax collectors begin to run, afraid of fighting, but Leo slams the door shut, bolts it, and hits one unconscious.

"What is the meaning of this?" Vernal shouts.

I channel the rage that is always beneath my skin. It is a living thing that slumbers, something that I have always hated, but in this moment I know it is all I have against them. One of the brutes charges at me like a bull, and I use his momentum to swing him against the brick wall. He swallows a grunt as he falls with a heavy thump.

"You can't do this," Vernal keeps shouting, backing into a corner and covering his face.

I try to block a fist flying at my head, but I'm too slow and it knocks me to the ground.

"Nati!" Castian shouts.

"Behind you!" I point, watching as the world slows down and Castian is hit over the head with a bottle. His eyes roll back, and I scream as his illusion unravels. His blond hair shines through, his face changes, and when he hits the ground, he is Castian, the kidnapped prince of Puerto Leones.

11

Vernal and his bodyguard are both startled into silence. They look at each other, then at the prince attempting to sit up, bleeding where the bottle cut him. Leo helps Castian stand.

"Is that—" Vernal begins to say. But I don't let him finish.

I yank off my gloves and slam my palms against each man's temples. I rip the memories from their minds, pain searing across my hands and behind my eyelids as never before. My vision splinters with pinpricks of lightning, and when I've removed all traces of this fight from all four men, I wrench my hands free. Leo tries to grab me as I stumble. Castian's illusion flickers like candlelight. He shakes his head, blinking until he regains control and is the emissary once again.

"We have to go," I say, standing on my own. My legs tremble. Shadows linger at the corners of my vision.

"Are you hurt?" Castian rasps.

"I'm fine." I can't think of the pain, the way my vision breaks like there's a storm in the distance. Instead, I focus on a new plan—I dig through the taxmen's pockets and withdraw a key. "Help me."

We drag all four bodies to the alley beside the tavern and prop them against barrels covered in barnacles. I pour a bottle of agua-dulce on their clothes. When they come to, they might think they've lost a day to drink or were robbed. With the taxmen's knowledge freshly embedded in my mind, we hurry down the now familiar boardwalk. Through the stolen memories, I realize they have raided local businesses nearly three times in one month—every tavern and shop, every artisanal stand and church. Their victims' faces swim in front of mine, begging and pleading for help. The taxmen's carriage is stationed a short distance from the Lioness tavern. I unlock the door with the stolen key, open the hidden compartment along the bench, and grab a heavy leather bag that jingles with coin.

"Let's go," I say.

"Go where?" Leo asks, eyes scanning the empty area. It's as though everyone has returned to their homes in fear of the collectors.

"To give this coin back to where it belongs."

From here, it is a straight shot back to the Queen of Little Luzou's mansion on the other end of the boardwalk. We climb up the steps flanked by columns, her guards letting us through out of sheer confusion at our sweaty, bloody state. I'm aware of Leo's melodic voice requesting an audience with the Queen, but as soon as I reach out and rest my aching body against the pillar, an invisible wave of remembrance passes through me, like the familiarity of the mountain we crossed. I recoil from the pillar, confused.

For as long as I've known, my mind created the Gray as my curse for the thousands of memories I've stolen. But this feels different—it feels like there is memory embedded in the pillar. Is that possible without alman stone? Perhaps there's a piece hidden within, or in the tiniest carving. I cautiously touch the stone once more, and Leo fades away. Gray figures spring to life as the world around me becomes a living memory. I hear voices arriving for a grand feast. I stumble onto the floor and sense the impression of every servant, every nobleman, every person who ever walked through here.

Ghostly figures walk in front of me, but when I reach for them, they vanish. He doesn't vanish, though. Dez. Andrés. The lost prince of Puerto Leones.

He's laughing, stumbling his way out of this very mansion. He tries to tuck his hair behind his ear, but there is only a scar, and the long black locks fall back over his face. Hands reach out for him, slender, delicate hands with dozens of gemmed rings adorning every knuckle. A woman grabs him by the open threads of his tunic, and her pink mouth curls into a devastating smile. "You're not leaving the party yet, are you?"

Then a tall woman, broad shouldered with a sword strapped at her back, clamps her hand on his shoulder. "Of course he's not leaving. The Queen wants to see him."

When I wake, I am keenly aware of two things: Dez was here in the Queen of Little Luzou's mansion, and I am not alone. My body is heavy, my sight so blurry that it's like looking through warped glass. Someone is brushing hair out of my face. My vision fights for space with the last memory. One that shouldn't be possible.

"Dez." My voice cracks.

But when my eyes clear, he is gone. I see only a strange room, and a glimpse of Castian slipping out the door. I try to get up. Light spots dance in my line of sight. I push the soft sheets off my legs. Needles shoot up my calves with every step toward the open balcony overlooking the sea. The sun marks the late afternoon, but of what day? Someone changed my clothes—I'm wearing silk trousers and a white linen tunic. I try my voice again, but I sound as if I've gargled with sand.

Every inch of the space is decorated in rich greens and blues. The most interesting piece in the room is a map made of marble pieces bolted to the wall. There's Empirio Luzou, its main continent and a thousand smaller islands rendered in various forms of jade. The Icelands to the north in the palest blue. But the continent that makes up Puerto Leones is divided into its five original territories. I let my fingers hover over the landmass that's labeled THE KINGDOM OF MEMORIA. Nowhere in the whole of the country is this allowed to be depicted. Once again, I feel the pulse of magics emanating from within—more alman stone. But a faint pain at my temples warns me not to touch the alman stone or pull memories from it. This is why Lady Nuria wanted me to speak to the Queen.

I sit on the corner of a chaise to gather my thoughts. Dez was here. How long ago? This is the second time I've seen him through someone else's eyes since that terrible day in Andalucía. What is he doing?

Stop following me. I'm already gone.

That is what he said to Castian—to us. If not for those words, I'd think Dez was on our trail, and not the other way around. I need to know what Dez wanted and what business he had with Señora Perliana.

I go in search of Castian and Leo, but when I open the door, they're already there, and they're joined by the Queen herself.

"We were beginning to worry," she says, with a cursory glance my way.

She strides in and the capelet around her shoulders billows in the sea breeze. She sits on a high-backed brocaded chair and the three of us follow, squeezing into the long couch.

"How long have I been asleep?" I ask.

"The afternoon," Leo says, squeezing my shoulder. Relief crosses his features. There's a bruise on his jaw from our fight. Castian, however, won't look at me. The blood on his temple is matted in his hair and the barest fault in his illusion, a swath of gold, peeks through.

"You've made quite a mess on my boardwalk," the Queen says, raising manicured eyebrows.

"We cannot apologize," I say. "They were—"

"Doing what the king's men do. Their jobs. They were collecting taxes."

Could Nuria have been wrong about her? Could *I* have been wrong? I chance a look at Castian, but his illusion-green eyes are focused on the map I stared at earlier.

"Still," the Queen says, tapping the armrests, "by the Great Tortuga, it was a beautiful thing to see them run to me for help from so-called *common thieves*."

Leo lets go of a deep sigh, but Castian and I are paralyzed with tension.

"Now," the Queen continues, "that coin is being redistributed throughout the citadela. Discreetly, of course. Because of what you've done, I am ready to listen to your request once again."

My companions and I share a look of understanding. So much needs to be said. But we have to start with what we're after.

"My name is Renata Convida," I begin. "My friends and I are searching for a weapon that can help us stop King Fernando's oncoming war without bloodshed. We cannot say more, as we don't wish to endanger you. But you've seen the state of Puerto Leones—the king drains each provincia until there is nothing left to give. He will keep raising taxes for his war against the Moria rebels, and the fighting won't stop there. If the king wins, if he captures more Moria, he will create weapons that could help him conquer the known world."

"And the three of you are going to stop an army?" she asks skeptically.

I remember Leo's doubt when Cas explained the Knife of Memory. It is a difficult thing to get people to believe in something they cannot see. Hope is as slippery as memory.

"Yes," Leo says. "The only other option is watching the atrocities of Memoria repeat once more."

"Even if what you are saying is true," the Queen says, "the prince has been kidnapped. You will find that citizens across the kingdom may be willing to endure war for their prince, no matter who has to die."

"Prince Castian isn't being held prisoner," I say.

"How can you possibly know that?"

"Because." Cas leans back with the air of the prince I thought I knew, the man I know now. His illusion fades, revealing his true face. The pull of his magic brushes against my skin. When he looks at me, his smile breaks my heart. "I was rescued by this rebel before my life could be threatened."

The Queen of Little Luzou's mouth parts in surprise, and I see the moment she realizes everything. That I am the Robári the king and justice want. "You're the one making all this trouble. The leaflets calling for your head don't do your beauty justice, my dear girl."

"They truly don't," Castian agrees softly.

I breathe through the spike of my heartbeat. "I suppose I owe a great deal to whoever had to describe me."

Leo clears his throat and straightens as if he's in a confessional box. "That would be my fault, Lady Ren. As Justice Méndez was not able to give his description, the king had the artist get instruction from myself and the servants who'd spent the most time with you."

I try to imagine Leo, verbose as he is, sabotaging my wanted leaflets. I can't help but laugh, and so does Cas.

The Queen shakes her head and rests a hand on her cheek. "And here I thought I'd seen it all. My, what have you gotten yourselves into."

Leo shrugs. "Dissent, treason, a little bit of performing if the occasion calls for it."

"As you can see, I am not a captive of the Moria Whispers," says Castian. "I am on a mission to secure the future of my kingdom."

The Queen of Little Luzou levels her piercing stare at him. Neither of them blinks. "And I suppose you will be different from your father?"

"In some ways, I am not," Castian says. "I have done terrible things in my father's name, and I will atone for all of it. I thought that if I could only outlast him, if I could wear the crown, then I could right the wrongs of my forefathers. The Moria are no more our enemies than are the kingdoms of Dauphinique and the Icelands or Empirio Luzou. Puerto Leones cannot thrive in the dark, and that is what this war will lead to. If that is treason, then I am guilty. But I am still the prince of this country. I am Moria. I will no longer separate those things from myself. I will put the kingdom before myself, and that is how we are different."

The Queen of Little Luzou nods slowly. She walks across the room and pours herself a glass of aged aguadulce. She stares at the marble map and drinks the amber liquid slowly.

"Once, when I was a bit younger than you, I told my mother I wanted to learn how to sail," she says, turning back to us. "And so she sent me out to sea with a ship's captain I'd seen in the port. I learned how to swab a deck and man the sails. I learned how to slice lemons for the cook, and most important, I learned that when you're set upon by pirates, you have to let go of some cargo. Otherwise it'll weigh you down, and you'll never be able to sail away."

"Your mother had you running from pirates?" Leo asks, slightly terrified, if not wholly amazed.

"We *were* the pirates." The Queen winks. "My parents remained in this kingdom because they loved their life here. They were like you, hoping to outlast the atrocities of the crown. That is why, like when I was at sea, I do everything I can for the people looking to me. Perhaps, Prince Castian, you are not who I expected you to be."

She finishes her drink, pours four more glasses, and carries them over to us. "You will have your vessel."

Leo squeezes my hand, and I grip his tight in return, if only to stop myself from screaming, *We did it!*

The Queen offers a conspiratorial grin. "Come sunrise, the same thieves who robbed the tax collectors will also have absconded with one of my cataval ships."

Leo raises his glass, and the three of us offer a hearty salud. "To that band of wily seagulls!"

Castian grimaces at the taste of aguadulce and the suggestion. "We are *not* calling ourselves that."

"A cataval ship?" I ask. "Those are luxury vessels, aren't they? They're not armed."

"Then don't get caught by the navy," the Queen offers. "Or pirates. Besides, it's small enough that a crew of three can sail it."

Castian and the Queen go back and forth for a bit longer, going over our ship's dock number, what to put on our forged documents, giving a hint of her extensive operation.

"I'll have everything drawn up now. It's been an honor doing business with you, Prince Castian."

He takes her hand and brings it to his lips with a rare smile. "That honor is mine, Señora Montevang."

"Wait," I say, knowing that my words are going to sink the buoyant sensation we all seem to be feeling. I take a steadying breath. "You ordered a man brought to you. He was dark haired and missing an ear."

She frowns, but nods. "Hard to forget. He and his group of newcomers showed up at my monthly feasts where all in Little Luzou are invited."

The Whispers?

"When was this?"

"Last night."

"Did they leave?" Castian asks.

The Queen cocks an eyebrow. "Do you think I keep track of every stranger in my citadela?"

I want to say yes but think better of it.

"We missed the feast?" Leo says, genuinely disappointed. Castian elbows him.

I meet Castian's eyes. Last night we were not ten miles away. Did Esteban tell him about seeing me? I remember that wretched note again. How did Dez arrive here ahead of us unless he had access to horses and the main road? Where is the boy who taught me how to disarm an opponent? The boy who once looked me in the eye and said, *I have never doubted you. I know we will win this war.* I thought that he would always come back for me. I thought I knew him well enough to find him. Perhaps I don't know him at all. What is he planning?

"Thank you," I say. "One more thing. Is there alman stone in your pillars outside the house?"

She shakes her head. "Only the finest Dauphinique marble."

"Oh," I say, disappointed.

The Queen tilts her head to the side, peers at my hands. Reflexively, I ball them up against my chest. Something like empathy flashes across her dark eyes. "I'll have supper brought up to you. Until then, I suggest you three remain together. While I trust everyone in my personal household, I'd rather your visit here have little fanfare. Apologies in advance, Your Highness."

When she's gone, Leo pours himself another drink and sinks into the bed. Castian follows me to the balcony overlooking the pier. Shoulder to shoulder, we turn to each other and, at the same time, say, "I'm sorry."

"I know how much you wanted to reunite with your brother."

Castian stares straight ahead at the setting sun. "I know how much you love him and wished to see him again."

I did.

I do.

"Perhaps learning the truth of his birth caused an irreparable change to Dez," I say. "When this is all over, I'm going to help him find his way."

Cas offers me a smile and the anxious coil in my gut unwinds. "If he lets me, I'll be there, too."

"Do you feel that?" Leo asks.

We turn to find him rubbing his arms, as if he feels a chill we do not.

"What?" Cas asks, genuinely worried.

"You two are in agreement. All Six Hells must have frozen over."

I pick up a small pillow and throw it at his head.

As promised, dinner arrives just after sunset.

"Only the finest for the prince of Puerto Leones, I give you a traditional Luzouan feast," the Queen says, supervising the delivery of the meal herself. She does not stay but posts a guard—a muscular woman named Alden—at the door.

After days of stringy forest game and hard bread, we devour the decadent meal of pork belly, bananas wrapped in paper-thin dough and fried until brown and crispy, rice sweetened with coconut milk, and buttered peas piled in large bowls. The main course is an entire fried fish for each of us, the red scales crusted with pink sea salt, and we wash everything down with goblets of a tart white wine made from Luzouan cherries and grapes.

"Enjoy this last stretch of freedom while we can," Leo says. "I've been on a luxury vessel only once with Lady Nuria, and by the end of the festivities, I wanted to take the life raft back to shore. Though we *did* try to fit thirty people on a ship meant for ten."

Castian chokes on his wine. He sets his glass down between the plates. "I can't remember the last time I laughed like this."

"That's how I won over my husband," he says, winking. "Enri said it was my gift. I feel that if I can't always be happy, I can at least try to make others feel joy."

"You're not happy?" I ask.

Shadows flicker against his face, cutting the soft angles of his cheekbones into dramatic points. "I will always find a way, even when it feels hopeless. Enri and I eloped so young—seventeen, barely. We'd known each other as children, but we didn't want to wait to start our life together. Two months later he was caught using his magics and killed. Part of me wished to leave all the hurt behind, but everything we've seen the last few days has made me realize how much I was hiding in the palace, even though I was in service of Lady Nuria. I find myself wondering how much of a difference I can make out here. What would my Enri say if he could see me?"

I place my hand on his cheek, brush my thumb over the faint bruise under his eye. "He'd say that you're brave and the very best friend anyone could ask for."

Castian nods. "He'd say that if there are more people like you, this kingdom will have a good future."

"Promise me you'll say that to yourselves. Both of you."

Castian and I hide our faces behind our wine goblets. I wonder if he feels the same way I do, that so much of what went wrong with Puerto Leones is because of us—because of me. I can't shake the uneasy sensation I've known for years. I owe Puerto Leones a great debt, one I will have to pay with my own blood.

12

IN THE HOURS BEFORE DAWN, WHEN THE SKY AND SEA ARE TOO DARK TO SEE THE seam of the horizon, Leo, Castian, and I set off for the docks with Alden, one of the Queen's personal guards. Her eyes are lined with kohl, and a curling tattoo covers her arms and neck. Her long black braid swings between the short swords strapped at her shoulders. Despite the severity of her appearance, her temperament is too bright for the time of morning.

"Dock ninety-four is on the other end of the marina, where reclaimed and impounded vessels are," she says. "Your belongings were moved while you were sleeping. It's early, but at the very least the winds are in your favor. The Great Tortuga will bless you with strong tides. I can't wait until the blockades are lifted. I sorely miss being out at sea. Had half a mind to beg my mistress to let me go with you."

I don't know much about sailing weather or the giant turtle the Luzouans pray to, but I will take any luck we can get. The citadela is slowly coming awake as a salty breeze rolls in with the tide. I concentrate on the shuffle of our boots and the squawk of seagulls as we make a brisk pace down the boardwalk toward the ships gently bobbing in the marina. I imagine stepping on the deck and feeling the freedom of being at sea. All at once the clang of bells shatters my thoughts.

I whirl around to find Alden. "What is that?"

"The city's warning bells—only the royal patrols can access them." She unsheathes her swords and forms a barrier between us and what is to come. "Run!"

Second Sweep guards storm the buildings and alleys that line the boardwalk. They drag people out of their doors onto the sand. Screams punctuate the cry of seabirds, the unrelenting clang of bells. When I spot a familiar face among the townsfolk, I realize two things: The Second Sweep is not after us, and the Whispers are still here.

"Ren." Leo pulls my sleeve. "We have to go!"

But I'm rooted to the boardwalk as Esteban throws a fistful of sand into a soldier's eyes and thrusts a sword through his throat.

Alden is caught between a rebel and a king's man. She swings her blades like extensions of herself, slashing across thighs and shins to bring her opponents down but never striking a killing blow. Little Luzouan guards spill onto the boardwalk, but they don't attack. They protect the stores, make curious citizens return to their homes.

Alden sees us watching and shouts, "What are you waiting for? If the port captains catch you, there is no getting out."

Castian tugs on my pack. "We have to get the ship."

A new surge of energy shakes me. I look at Esteban, then Cas and Leo waiting for me. Part of me wants to run toward the

Whispers, but I never felt hope with them, not the way I have with my boys on this journey.

So I choose them.

The sky bleeds with orange and yellow. I inhale deeply and hurry behind Castian and Leo past the melee, keeping my sights on the docks, on the purple-and-gold flags rippling on the wind.

Hands grab the back of my tunic. I whirl around and slam into someone. We fall on the cobblestones, and I bring my fists up. A man grabs my wrists, and I am unable to move.

Dez.

"Hi," he says, and pulls me up.

Dez.

His grip on my wrists loosens. His hair is tied back at the nape, exposing the healed skin where Castian cut off his ear. There's a new scar hidden behind the scruff of his dark beard, and another across his eyebrow. I both recoil from his touch and then feel myself return to him like the ebb and flow of the tide.

"Say something," he whispers.

Dez.

But I can't. Everything crashes over me. The last night we spent together. *I love you. I need you to know that.* The day I thought he'd died. The time he's had to find me. The message he scrawled on a bit of parchment because he couldn't or wouldn't face us.

I push him away, but his touch is familiar and solid. I squeeze my eyes shut because a fraction of my mind doesn't believe he is standing before me, even as he brushes a strand of hair behind my ear.

"Ren," he says, and something within me breaks.

I reel back my fist and punch him in the face. "How could you?"

"Let me explain."

Around us, the Whispers have overwhelmed the Second Sweep, whose bodies lie scattered on the boardwalk. Esteban is removing the uniform from the soldier he killed. Other rebels are leading the Sweep's horses into a line.

Dez pulls me into a narrow alley between two taverns, and we stare at each other. I can hear my heartbeat roar in my ears as the moment stretches, and I rest a trembling hand on his chest because a part of me doesn't believe he is here. Dez steadies my hand with his, and for a moment, it is just us in the dark alley. Then realization dawns on me, and I let go.

"You're leading the Second Sweep into traps," I say.

"It's the only way we've been able to accrue resources for our growing rebel army." Dez crosses his arms over his chest, rubs his lips together the way he does when he's thinking or trying not to fight with Margo. "I have to say I'm a little disappointed that you're not more thrilled to see me, Ren."

"I've seen you already." I remember the first memory that told me Dez was alive. "I saw you leaving on a ship at Sól y Perla. I saw you here in the Queen's mansion. Last night. We've been searching for you, but you already know that."

Dez looks away from me, resentment making his body tight. "Margo told me that you'd left with *him*. I didn't believe it until I saw you in Acesteña. I regret leaving that message. But seeing you together, well, I couldn't stand it."

Him. He can't even say *brother.*

"Did Margo tell you why?"

"It doesn't *matter*, Ren. You should be with us. We're your family. We're the ones, after all these years, finally fighting back." He cups my face in his hands. Warm tears threaten to fall from my closed eyes, but I can't seem to push him away. Dez is holding me. *Dez.* "Please let me show you. Things will be different this time. Chasing the Knife of Memory is a waste of your talents and will only lead to disappointment."

"How can you say that?" I ask. "You said you would do everything you could for our people. Is this it?"

"It's better than the alternative," he says darkly. "The Knife—it won't work. Trust me."

"Trust you? Dez, you didn't trust me enough to find me and tell me you were alive. And how can you possibly know that the Knife won't work?"

His golden eyes bore into mine. I used to think I could look into those eyes for hours, imagining that's what it felt like to be preserved in amber. A foolish, lovesick girl's thoughts. He swallows his words, turns to the chaos on the boardwalk. He's pleading with me, holding me tighter. I have tried to picture this moment since finding out he was alive, but this is not the reunion I envisioned.

"Please—trust me," he repeats. What can't he say? What *won't* he say?

"You left me behind," I manage, despite the way my heart breaks. "Stop following me. I'm already gone, Dez."

A tear runs down his face. He swipes it away, then steps back, his lips twisting into an angry scowl. "Go with him, then. See the ruin my *brother* leads you to."

Dez stalks away, and I follow him out of the alley. Three Whispers wielding stolen swords block his path. I recognize one from the mountain spring. His eyes widen in mutual recognition.

"I'm sorry, Commander Andrés," the boy says, pointing his sword in my direction. "But we have orders to bring her in."

Dez swallows hard. His fists go slack at his sides and says, "She is not to be harmed, do you understand me?"

"Dez." I hate the tremble in my voice. He's going to let the Whispers take me. "What are you doing?"

The rebel boy advances, then slumps to the ground, an arrow piercing his right eye.

"Up here!" A figure leaps from the roof and lands in a crouch. There's a bow in her gloved hand and a quiver of arrows strapped to her back. At first I think she's one of the Queen's Luzouan guards, with her two tight braids and burnished bronze skin. But she doesn't wear a uniform, only the black leather of someone accustomed to hunting in the shadows. "I'll take you to your ship—there's no time."

I run, and fight the urge to glance back at Dez. I'm afraid of what will happen if I do.

"Who are you?" I ask my savior, breathing hard as we sprint toward the docks.

"Someone who needs to get out of this kingdom," she says. "And I hear you have come into possession of a ship. Saving your life should be payment enough. If you don't like what I have to say, then toss me overboard. I don't imagine it would be too difficult as there's three of you and one of me."

If she knows about Cas and Leo, then how long has she been following us? I tell myself to grab one of her arrows and jam it into her thigh to slow her down, but what kind of payment is that when she saved my life? I note the leather across her chest is actually a thick breastplate of something like gator skin. Her body is slender but muscular.

She flashes me a feline smile. "Deal?"

Sharp whistles blow higher than the clang of bells, which stop as the sun sits on the horizon. Blue fills the sky. Behind us, a dozen rebels give chase.

"Deal," I shout.

She yanks an arrow from her quiver and aims. Once, twice. She stops to shoot again. I stop only to make sure Dez isn't among the injured, and I don't know whether I'm relieved or angry that I don't see his face. When we turn onto the deserted pier with our ship, I run faster. Leo and Castian are unfurling the single square sail of a cataval yacht in the morning breeze. Cas notices me and leaps onto the dock to uncleat the ropes.

"Get on board!" I shout at my savior. She swiftly hauls herself onto the ship.

"Who is that?" Castian shouts.

"No time to explain," I yell.

There's uncertainty in his eyes as he watches the stranger, but he simply nods, trusting me. He drops the ropes, and slowly the ship begins to drift from the dock. He climbs aboard first and extends his hand. I seize it. With one foot on the railing and the other in the air, I hold on to him and feel everything at once—relief, dread, safety. He is a lifeline from which I may never be able to become untethered.

We collapse on the deck as the wind pushes the ship into open water. My savior cackles like someone who enjoys the thrill of fighting. I breathe hard to steady my racing heart. But my relief is short-lived. Castian grabs the girl and shoves her against the mast. Leo stares at her with confusion, then at me.

I try to break them apart, but Leo stops me. "Wait!"

"Do you know what you've done?" Castian shouts.

Dread gathers in my belly. Who is she? Before I can ask, my savior speaks.

"I'm Leyre Las Rosas." The girl grins up at him but doesn't struggle. "I'm here to kill the prince, and I'm your only hope of finding the Knife of Memory."

13

"YOUR KNOTS AREN'T TIGHT ENOUGH," LEYRE SAYS.

"And you're rather smug for someone outnumbered," Leo says.

With Little Luzou behind us and the wind in our sail, Leo and I leave Leyre tied to the forecastle and walk across the deck to where Castian helms the ship. He's relinquished his illusion, and a deep frown cuts across his forehead, long gold curls blowing in the breeze. Leo's green eyes settle on me, and though he offers a smile, his worry betrays him.

"Before you say anything," I start, raising my palm. "The Whispers were going to take me prisoner, and she saved my life. Now I understand why she wanted passage on our ship."

Castian glances past me to Leyre. She flashes her teeth but doesn't seem concerned. Why would she be? She has her bounty in sight.

"I suppose now I know what my father wanted with her," Castian says, stroking the short gilded scruff of his beard.

Leo draws a small object from a leather satchel. "I found this in her belongings. I've never seen a sextant quite like it before. Look at the constellations etched on the sides. Diamonds, too."

I take the heavy metal piece. In the miniscule sparkling dots that represents stars, I recognize the precious rock that I've known all my life. "These aren't diamonds. They're alman stone."

"We will get answers from her," Castian says darkly. "Right now, we have to come to an agreement on what we do with her once we know the truth. After what happened with the tax collectors, Ren shouldn't take her memories."

Leo muses, "But Leyre doesn't know that."

"If we make a threat, we have to be willing to go through with it," I say. "We can't very well torture her."

"You won't have to," Castian says, so softly that his words could have been simply carried on the wind. I understand that he is willing to do this for me, for us. But my mind thinks back to the day when Justice Méndez forced me to watch him torture Sayida. Blood. Screams. The pounding of my own heart. I know Cas has killed, even before he murdered Duque Sól Abene in Acesteña to save me from the pain of my changing powers, but I saw the way it tore through him. I can't have him do that.

Leo runs a hand through his soft black tangle of hair. He startles, and I turn to see Leyre striding toward us across the deck.

"I find torture rather uninspiring," she says, grinning at me. "I *told* you the knots weren't tight enough."

She leans her back against the rail, massaging her wrists. "We had a deal, Ren. You'd listen to what I have to say, and if you didn't like it, you could throw me overboard. Not that I think you have the stones to do it since all you've done is tie me up. Rather ineffectively, I'd add."

I am in no humor for her. "You already said you were sent to kill Castian, what more is there?"

"That was one of the things I was sent to do. That was not my proposition."

"What do you want, Leyre?" Castian asks, pulling on the mask of the ruthless Bloodied Prince. "And remember, I don't need inspiration to make you hurt."

A sliver of fear must have found its way to her reason because our would-be assassin takes an uneasy step back. "I was sent by the king, it's true. He wants that knife you're after and he wants you dead."

"Charming man, my father," Castian says. I hear the chord of pain there and wonder if all children want their parents' love, even if they are monsters. "This means my father knows I'm not being held captive by the Whispers."

I picture King Fernando's face. That deep stare with eyes darker than his heart. I retrace the scar he left on my chest. It was supposed to prove my fealty to him. I bled for that man as a ruse, but blood is blood. "He's going to use your death to anger the people."

"Why you?" Leo asks Leyre. "I can think of a dozen people who'd like to get away with murdering the prince."

Castian balks. "Who?"

Leo scoffs and counts the names on his fingers. "Well, there's Alessandro. He has yet to consummate his marriage with Lady Nuria because he does not want to compare—"

"You've proven your point," Castian snaps.

"There's Duque Arias because you took his grandfather's treasures. Lady Fravela, who commissioned a wedding dress after you smiled at her, accidentally, I'm sure. Lord Sandoval's son, who lost his eye in Riomar…"

"Leo, that's *enough*," Castian barks.

"The high-born of Puerto Leones might hate Castian," I emphasize, "but they don't want him dead. Any one of those leeches would gladly kiss his boots for an opportunity to be near him."

A reluctant smile tugs at Castian's mouth. "Besides, my father would never make someone of their station dirty their hands."

"That's why he thought a bastard girl who'd do anything for her father would be perfect for the job." Leyre glances back at the port growing smaller and smaller. "King Fernando's arrogance is thinking I *want* to be Leonesse. I cannot help what my father is, but I have no interest in taking up his title or having a seat at court."

"Then why didn't you leave when your empress did?" Leo asks, pointing a finger as if he's caught her in a lie.

"Because I *am* a bastard girl who'd do anything for her father." Leyre sighs. "On the night of the festival, when the prisoners escaped, I broke my father free with two of my friends from the Luzouan naval academy. We left behind a man who was already dead, his face eaten by rats. When the king called me to his apartments, I thought he'd found out and was going to torture me. I was ready to swallow the poison capsule I keep in here." Leyre brandishes a small black pill before returning it to a hidden pocket. She gives a meaningful look to Leo. "None of the wine goblets were poisoned, by the way. And then he tried to trick me by making me this offer, thinking I was a fool. I don't want to kill you. I want to help you *end* the king of Puerto Leones for my family."

"Not for the good of the known world?" I ask.

Leyre sneers. "What has his kingdom brought my mother except heartache and shame? There is no room in my heart for morality. That's your lot."

Castian watches her for a long moment. Clearly he's made up his mind to let Leyre stay since he's not throwing her overboard. But can we trust her?

"Why did you wait so long to approach us?" he asks.

She grins and props herself up on the side of the ship, giving a cursory glance to the waves as if daring us to push her over. "I have been following Leo since he left the palace."

I remember the hooded figure I'd believed was Sayida. "That was you, wasn't it? At the tavern just outside the castle ruins."

"Yes," she says. "For the purpose of being completely honest."

"As opposed to half-honest?"

She flashes a crooked smile. "Precisely. I was afraid the prince might've remembered me from when we were children. I've been told I look the same as when I was a girl, but you know how princes easily forget."

"Do you *want* him to remember you?" I ask. A bizarre irritation scrapes in my chest.

Leyre quirks her eyebrow. "You jealous, Robári?"

"No," I grit through my teeth.

She laughs and I want to shove her off that ledge. But after seeing the way the Whispers moved, so unified, so ruthless, I know that we need all the help we can get.

"That doesn't explain how you knew to follow me," Leo says, rubbing his arms. I wonder if he feels guilty for having led her to us.

"I broke into Castian's apartments to see if he'd left behind a trace I could follow. That is when you and Lady Nuria came in. Surely you thought no one would dare enter the prince's private quarters, and it *would* have been a safe place to have your conspiratorial meeting if I hadn't already been there."

I glance up at Castian. "Can *anyone* break into your rooms?"

"Ah, but Nuria used a key," Leyre says, and winks at Castian.

"Out with it, Leyre," he presses.

"In the imperial navy we're taught to trust our bodies. Our senses. Soldiers who know themselves have impeccable instincts.

Mine said to follow Leo. And today, it was by the Great Tortuga that as I was following you to the dock, Renata was detained by that dashing Moria commander."

"You learned all that in your obligated military service?" Castian sneers.

"At least we aren't drafted at eleven," Leyre counters harshly. "We serve our sixteenth year in a division of the military, and then the empress grants us a boon to start a life or continue in the service. But do you know how many wars we're fighting? None. Unlike you Leonesse, arming children barely strong enough to wield a sword. So yes, I learned all that at the academy, and I managed to track you down. Don't forget, where I'm from, you're not my prince."

Castian is silent, his glare homed in on Leyre in a way I've never seen before. I imagine no one has spoken to him this way in his life. His anger and embarrassment pass quickly, and then he nods. "I'm sorry."

"What's wrong with her?" Leyre asks, and I realize she means me.

I can't move. I feel as if all sound has gone from the world for a moment before it comes rushing back again.

"Ren!" Leo yells, catching me before I hit the deck.

On the horizon, I see a fleet of ships flying brilliant purple-and-gold flags. Cannons rip the sky apart, iron and steel cracking the hull of enemy ships.

"We're being attacked!" I try to scream. I can't even raise my hand. My bones have turned to molten metal. I scream once more as a cannonball flies across the waters right at my head. It must be a memory, but it feels more real than ever.

I try to scream again, but my voice wheezes in starts and stops. A terrible, painful heat spreads from my chest to my spine. Castian takes me from Leo and carries me.

"Captain's quarters," he says, walking to the rear of the ship.

We're through a door, and I'm set on a mattress. Hands press against my face.

"She's burning up," Leo whispers.

"I can help," Leyre demands.

"You go drop anchor."

I float in total blackness until pain returns to my temples and remains there. The Gray. The occurrences. Cebrián. All of it has pushed me to a precipice, and if I take the jump, perhaps the pain will stop.

"I don't know what to do," Castian says, his voice unsteady. I want to reach for him, but my body feels weighted down. "What do I do?"

"I don't know!"

I can't answer them. I am trapped in the Gray, a cage of my own making. As I fall into the memory, the room slips away until there is nothing but cannon fire and sinking ships.

> *When I was a little girl, I was afraid of the sea.*
>
> *But here I am on the deck of the* Siren's Wrath, *and I cannot imagine a better place to secure the future and peace of my people. Gunpowder and smoke fill the air, a gray haze parts to reveal the sinking galleons of the Icelandian invaders. Soldiers keep attempting to load cannons, only to be crushed by their steel, then dragged through splintered decks into the open mouth of the Aeste Ocean. A few terrified souls accept surrender in exchange for their survival. Looking out into this great sea, so blue, so cold, I fear I would do the same.*
>
> *"Princess Galatea," he says, ever the picture of propriety. Fernando stands the six paces of distance required*

by his Leonesse customs. There's blood on his face, a scar marring his beauty. Though it is his first battle scar, he fought with the fury of his lion blood. The dark oceans of his eyes watch me with an intensity that leaves me both anchored and a little afraid. I have never been loved this way. I have never loved this way.

"Are you pleased with your victory?" he asks.

"I am. The kingdoms of Memoria and Puerto Leones have much to celebrate. I have a gift for you."

"You have already given me everything I ever dreamed, and more," he whispers, though his obsidian eyes brighten as I reach for my belt. The ceremonial dagger is encrusted with glittering sapphires. All Moria royals wear a blade like this in honor of the Lady of Shadows. It is a small gift for a future king, but I am pleased with how he accepts it and holds it against his chest.

"Come, my love," he tells me. "We are going to change the world."

In the chaos of battle, he glances around. He smiles, the secret one he reserves only for me. I grab hold of his chain-mail collar, and he wraps his hands around my waist. The glow of my alman stone washes his face in ethereal light. He traces a thumb along the pearlescent marks that curl along my neck.

When we kiss, we become the fire and the sea.

14

"REN." CASTIAN'S VOICE LEADS ME OUT OF THE OCCURRENCE, BUT THE MAN IN front of me is King Fernando, as young as he was in that memory. A memory that I shouldn't have. A memory that shouldn't exist.

"I hate you," I tell him.

"I know," King Fernando whispers.

I close my eyes for a moment and fall into the black void. How many more of these occurrences can I withstand? I do not regret leaving Dez and the Whispers behind, but I wonder if one among them might have some idea as to what is happening to me. I refuse to believe that what I have witnessed is a memory. How can it be? That girl—that princess—was a Robári. The alman stone emblazoned on her armor was in the shape of a peregrine falcon—sacred to the Lady of Shadows—and there were marks on her skin. They were different from mine, but I am certain they were Robári scars.

And she was embracing a young Fernando, *kissing* him. Even if I *did* dream, how could I ever imagine that? I haven't pulled any memories since the tax collectors, and besides, that memory was *hers*. I've never drawn from Memoria royalty...have I? I try to remember what the elders taught us of the old monarchs before they fell to Puerto Leones, but the names are lost to time.

A shiver racks my body, and the ocean's every ripple brings a deep uneasiness to my stomach. I crawl out of bed, but my legs won't hold me up. I knock over the glass at my bedside, and it shatters. Leo rushes in, breathing hard, then scoops me up and tucks me back under the covers. The world is spinning so much that even when I shut my eyes, the dark whirls.

"Drink," he says roughly.

It is so unlike him that I summon all my strength to sit up. Here in his presence, I allow myself to be weak in a way I can't with Castian. Leo, after all, has seen me at some of my worst moments.

"You're the reason I survived in the palace," I confess.

He smirks, but his worry makes him quiet. He cups the back of my head, helping to steady me. Instead of water, he pours brown liquid from a green glass bottle onto a large spoon. The silver is cold on my chapped lips, and I grimace at the bitter, oily taste of the elixir. I have to tell him about my dream, but instead, I remember being a little girl, sick with a fever that ravaged the village. My mother made a concoction of bitter berries, mushrooms, and lemon peel. Just like then, I almost spit it out. Just like then, the liquid is forced into my mouth.

"What is that?" I lick my dry lips. "It tastes disgusting."

Leo stoppers the bottle and sets it on the bedside table. For the first time I notice the red and gold decadence of the captain's quarters. Past Leo, the window shows a gray sky and a smattering of rain. The elixir warms its way through me, calming the anxiety in my gut. Even my muscles unwind, and for the first time I feel how soft the bed is.

Leo takes a seat beside me. He's quiet, and I wonder if he is sorry he ever followed Castian and me. His catlike green eyes blink rapidly, and a sad smile quirks at his lips. He finds clean cloth and soaks it in cold water, placing it across my feverish forehead and throat.

I hold his hand against my cheek. "Thank you."

He lets go of my grasp and busies himself sweeping the broken glass off the floor. His tread is heavier than usual.

"You don't have to do that," I say, and move the cold compress to the back of my neck where needles of pain still dig into my skull. "Whatever that miracle elixir was, I feel better. I have to go talk to Castian. I have to tell him something."

He looks up, startled for a moment, almost terrified. "Now?"

I rub my hands across my face. "I know what you're going to say. That I'm lying to myself. That it wouldn't be so terrible to... want him. Sometimes I do, and it *does* feel like the worst thing. Castian is just so..." I trail off, unsure of what I want to say. I have to tell Castian about what I've seen, but the occurrence seems to be overwhelming everything and Castian is on the surface. Leo stands there with held breath. "Part of me still loves the boy I knew."

He looks away, and I don't know whether it's my bleary eyes, but I think he's blushing. He pushes the broken glass into a corner.

"Cas is wrapped in my worst memories. He's so beautiful and so terrible. I don't know how to reconcile those two people, and it scares me. He's done awful things. But so have I. Being with him these few weeks makes me feel different. Better. And yet I want to hate him because I hate myself, even still. I don't want to feel this way anymore. I wish..."

Leo stands in front of me and brushes a damp strand of hair from my face. His voice is strangled, soft beneath the distant roll of thunder. "What?"

"I wish I had let Cebrián rip out every one of my memories because then I could start over."

I don't want him to see me this way, so I get out of bed. Every moment my mind is clear is an opportunity I can't miss, and we have an island to get to. "Tell the others I'm better. I'll be right out."

Leo hurries out the door. I yank on my boots and pull my hair into a single long braid. Thunder and lightning rattle the ship. When I stagger onto the deck, the rain has turned into a storm.

When I was a little girl, I was afraid of the sea.

The familiar words echo through my mind as I stare at the approaching black clouds. There is little difference between being out here and being back on land. They are simply two different kinds of storms, both terrible and ready to sweep us under.

"It's coming in too fast," Castian shouts over the wind. He runs across the tilting ship with sure-footed balance and takes his place at the helm while hollering commands. "Leyre, help him reef the sail!"

"We can't!" Leyre braces herself against the side of the ship holding a rope.

"It's our only way out of this!" Castian struggles with the wheel, straining to turn the cataval ship. "If we run downwind, we're done for."

For a moment, there is only the downpour and the scream of a gale force I've never experienced before. Surrounded by clouds and waves, I remember my memory of the sinking ships. Castian's hair is matted to his face, rain streaming over his parted mouth. An understanding seems to pass between Cas and Leyre. Then he lets go of the wheel. "Do it! Dropping anchor!"

"Stowing the sail!" Leyre releases the rope. It hoists her in the air, and she screams, not out of fear but sheer delight. Castian runs to help her, and together they are like twin water spirits gliding across the wet deck, shouting commands that Leo and I follow without question. I am driven by the fear of them falling into the roiling sea, and only when we have stowed the sail do I take a deep, calming breath.

"Get below deck!" Cas takes a last look at the lightning storm coming our way. "Hurry!"

Leo opens the hatch, and we slip down the ladder into the cold belly of the ship. We stack bags of potatoes to prevent any crates from tumbling down, but there is little we can do to keep the cooking ware and other loose items from tipping over.

"Now we wait for the storm to pass," Leyre warns, peeling off her wet clothes until she's down to her chemise. Castian and Leo do the same. As my teeth begin to chatter, I follow suit to prevent the cold from seeping further into my bones. Leo yanks open the door to a pitch-dark room. Chairs scrape from side to side, and the ship bobs up and down the troughs of waves. Down here, we are but shadows on top of shadows. I call my magics forward, but the light burns as if I've stuck my hand in fire.

"I thought I saw—" Leo curses as he trips over chairs.

There's some rummaging, the sound of our breaths, the crack of lightning. Leo's bellow of triumph: "Here we have it."

After the hiss of a match, we have a single oil lamp, and a stack of wool blankets. In the weak glow, Castian and I take up seats on one of the chaises. Leo sits on a gaming table with a red velvet top. Leyre chooses the floor, her back resting against the wall.

"How did you know that was there?" I ask, wrapping the itchy but warm blanket around my shoulders.

"While you were indisposed, I made sure there were no *other* stowaways."

Leyre rolls her eyes, seemingly unbothered by the threat of capsizing. "Need I remind you I was invited aboard, and I have done everything to save all of you ingrates. If not for me you'd be trying, and failing, to swim back to shore. Now, who has any good stories to stop my mind from imagining a hundred ways to die at sea?"

My last memory flashes before my eyes—the cannon fire, the Moria princess with the Leonesse prince.

"Come now, Leo, you must have court gossip, at the very least," Leyre presses. "And while you were snooping around the yacht, did you happen to find any of that delicious aguadulce?"

Leo rifles through a drawer on the side of his table and withdraws a clear bottle of the sugarcane liquor. "You're in luck."

She catches the bottle in the air, tugs out the cork with her teeth, and takes a swig. "If I was lucky, I wouldn't be here with you lot. But we all make sacrifices for the ones we love."

Castian takes the bottle she offers but doesn't drink from it. He watches her carefully. When thunder booms, he's the only one who doesn't start. "Why are you here, Leyre?"

"I told you."

"Your father is alive," Castian says darkly. "You saved him. The living don't need avenging."

She takes the bottle back, scrunching her features into a petulant anger. "Ah, but they do."

The entire vessel shakes. When I close my eyes, I can feel us moving on the ocean surface, hear how much harder the rain is beating.

"Do you know the story of the Princess of the Glaciers?" Leyre asks, and I realize that for all her bravado above deck, she's scared. Sails and pulleys she can control, but sitting with a group of strangers below deck, she can't.

"Never heard of it," I say, and reach over to take the bottle of aguadulce. After the smallest sip, I hand it to Leo.

"Honestly, what do the children of Puerto Leones learn, then?"

Castian's laugh is a low rumble I feel in my belly. "We learn about pirates."

Leyre flashes her crooked smile but waves her arms in time to her story. "It's a tale of a Luzouan princess from ancient times. She was taken by the barbarians from the southern icelands."

"There are icelands in the south, too?" Leo asks, passing the aguadulce back to Leyre.

"Of course," Leyre says, offering the bottle to Castian. "Sail all the way up north and you'll find ice. Sail all the way south, and you'll find ice. Luzou to the southeast. Dauphinique to the northeast. No one has ever been far enough west of Puerto Leones to find anything there, though. Truly, when you are king, you *must* do something about the education in your kingdom."

Castian grunts and takes a sip. "Get on with your story, Leyre, before the storm swallows us whole."

"Anyway, the princess of our tale was taken from Luzou by the Glacier King and kept in his ice palace. But being from the tropics, she nearly died."

"How did she survive?" I ask.

"An ice witch placed her under a deep sleep. The Glacier King, to prove that he *did* love her, went in search of a rare cure, a flower that only grows in Luzou. He brought a glacier with him to the northern tip of our continent. To stop him from turning the whole world to ice, every villager helped search for the flower. But on an island so green, so full of flowers, it was going to take every citizen to succeed."

"Did they find it?" Leo asks. "Don't tell me. No. Wait. Tell me."

"Yes, but at great cost. The Glacier King, despite bringing a piece of home with him, thawed, and when he thawed the oceans rose, and he began to drown. But as the princess woke, thanks to the villagers finding the flower, she'd become part ice and saved him. If you ask me, she should have let him sink to the bottom of the ocean and taken his lands for her own, then found someone who deserved her."

"Or just gone home," I suggest.

"She was away too long. Became too changed. Sometimes you return to a place, and it no longer feels familiar." Castian's voice is low compared to the waves, and the emotion in his words feels like a confession. "Not because it's changed, but because you have, and there isn't anything you can do to get that feeling back. It'll never be home again."

I think about going back to the small house in the woods where I lived with my parents for the first seven years of my life.

"That's bleak, Your Highness," Leyre says. "But you're right. For some of us home is a fleeting thing. I'm not naive. The Princess of the Glaciers didn't change because she fell in love. She changed because she needed to survive what should have been *un*survivable. I wonder, what happened to all those people who helped search for her cure? What happens to the people who live? What comes after?" Leyre rests her head against the wall, the room's shadows hiding her eyes. "I'm here because King Fernando hurt my family. I know my father was no saint, but how many children like me has the king left to drown? So yes, Matahermano. I *can* avenge the living."

Warmth spreads through my limbs, and this time when the ship shakes so hard it feels like it'll break apart, I count the silence between cracks of thunder. I count the number of times I catch Castian looking at me.

"Have any of you ever heard of a princess named Galatea?" I ask.

"Not in Puerto Leones," Castian says.

"Are you sure?"

"Believe me, every single tutor I had made me memorize the royals dating back to the very first of my line who settled in Vahía de Leones."

"Galatea of what kingdom?" Leo asks, picking at the fuzzy pills in the velvet.

Memoria, I want to say. The kingdom that belonged to my people. The temples and sacred sites were destroyed during each war, but judging from Fernando's appearance, this memory couldn't have been more than forty years old. Illan would have been old enough to remember her, my own parents would have been old enough to add to their collection of stories.

"Ren?" Castian calls my name, but they are all watching me now. How do I tell them what I've seen without sounding like a lunatic?

It doesn't matter, as the storm won't let me speak. Moments later, the ship rocks, and Leo's lamp shatters. Quickly, Castian smothers the fire with his blanket as Leo says, "I'm all right!"

"Hold on!" Leyre shouts.

I can't see anything. As the ship heaves, I grab on to the chaise bolted to the wall, but the ridiculous fabric is too soft and I glide right off. I can't be sure what is up or down or sideways. Lightning cracks so loud that I can practically feel it in my teeth. Then I hit skin and muscle.

"I've got you," Cas whispers. Calloused hands wrap around my arm, and I crawl to him. For a moment, it's like the entire ship is flying, weightless. I scream when I slip out of his grasp. He clutches me tighter, pulls me against his chest. We land in a crash, and I thank the Lady that we are in the dark and no one can see the relief across my face as Castian's weight pins me to the cushions of the chaise. I brush his hair back, and he leans his face into my touch. Heat radiates from the apex of my torso, my pulse a sledgehammer against my ribs.

"Cas," I murmur. If the ship goes under, if these are the final moments that I get to spend with him, what do I say?

"I'm here." His warm breath at my ear. My arms wrapped around his neck, determined to keep him with me if we get pulled out. I feel the undulation of the waves in the pit of my stomach. Hear Leo's yelps, Leyre's laughter, the scream of the storm, my intake of breath as my nose touches Cas's, and his lips brush mine.

And then there is silence. The rain stops.

"It's over," Leyre proclaims. I hear her scrambling for the door.

With the spell of the storm broken, Castian and I leap away from each other. I take in a deep breath and lick salt from my lips. Light trickles in to reveal Leo spread across the gaming table, his white-knuckled grip holding on for dear life.

"I think I swallowed a set of dice." He groans.

"How?" Castian asks incredulously, dusting himself off. There's a red welt on his back where something must have fallen on top of him. He shielded me. "You know, I've learned it's best not to ask."

The prince helps Leo off the table. I follow Leyre above deck to assess the damage. She runs around checking ropes and metal bolts, then inspects the mast and helm while rattling off a list of things for Castian to survey. Never having been on a ship, I don't know what she's looking for other than to make sure we can keep sailing. We're so far out I can't even guess the cardinal directions.

"Brilliant, isn't it?" She admires the storm speeding away from us. Gone is the melancholy that gripped her below deck, but I can't help but think of the story she told.

"That's not the word I'd use."

"You're lucky." She slaps me square on the back. "I've been through worse. But the Great Tortuga's blessed me yet."

Castian and Leo join us on deck and help raise the sail. I try to meet Castian's eyes, but his brow is furrowed, and his every movement is focused on the ship. The sun emerges from behind mammoth white clouds and dries the rain off our skin and clothes.

When we're finished, Leyre fetches her satchel, and Castian, the logbook. Together they chart the course that will take us farther and farther away from home. I remember the princess who became part ice, who changed to survive. I can only hope that when we return, there is a home to come back to.

15

BEING AT SEA IS AS WONDROUS AS IT IS TERRIFYING. EVERY DARK CLOUD CAUSES my body to clench with nerves, anticipating another storm. At night, the sky and sea are so infinitely black that the moon looks like silver flames illuminating the surface and brings a different kind of fear, the fear of falling into a void and losing control of myself. But there are moments—when Leo is up in the crow's nest with a spyglass, or Leyre and Castian are chasing the coordinates using the sun and stars, when I do my part by keeping the deck and cargo hold clean, when Castian sings along to Leo's filthy chanteys during supper— that I can't imagine another place I'd rather be.

For days that is our routine. Castian and Leyre spend most mornings poring over Admiral Arias's logbook and the maps in the captain's quarters. But the way to Isla Sombras is shrouded in more than the myths of the Moria. Combining the coordinates with Leyre's maritime knowledge puts the island between the kingdom of Puerto Leones and her home of Luzou, right in the middle of the Castinian Sea.

"How did the Moria hide an entire island?" Leyre asks on the third day. She attempts to instruct me on how to navigate with the sextant. But when I touch it, I feel the strange spark of power coming from the miniscule alman stones embedded in the metal. Even thinking of culling the memories summons an ache behind my eyes.

"The same way we've hidden from a murderous king for decades," I tell her, and hand the sextant back. "Magics and a stubborn will to live."

Despite the certainty with which Castian and Leyre navigate, I can see the doubt that plagues them. The fourth day arrives, and there is no Isla Sombras. Nothing but ocean for miles and miles.

After that strange moment we shared during the storm, Castian and I haven't been alone together. If there is a task that needs doing, I partner with Leyre or Leo, and he does the same. With a crew of only four, there is always something to do.

On the morning of the fifth day, Leo shouts, "Land!"

We all gather along the starboard side of the deck. But Leyre slams her spyglass shut and rubs her lips into a taut line. "It's a sandbar."

Castian rakes his fists through his hair and leans on the taut rigging. "We should be there."

"Do you *see* any other land nearby, princeling?" Leyre challenges. "By all accounts we should have seen first signs of Isla Sombras yesterday. Have you heard of this before, Renata?"

"A vanishing island?" I shake my head. "Before Castian, all I knew of the Knife of Memory was that it was a story. So much of the Moria history was lost."

"Perhaps it's the logbook," Leyre suggests. "Half his notes are ramblings about the fortitude sea air gives men. The rest are too vague to make sense of." Leyre clears her throat and takes on the voice of an old aristocratic Leonesse man and quotes it from memory. *"We followed the fixed point of the Marinera star until the island appeared, shrouded in mist and moonlight. Though I fear for the girl, the king is pleased. We carry on."*

I bite the inside of my lip. "Was the girl ever named?"

"No," Castian says.

I go over what we're sure of once more. "King Fernando traveled to the Isla Sombras with a crew who died during or immediately after the voyage. We know that for some reason, he has not returned to claim the Knife of Memory despite having the sextant. We know that though it does not appear on any map in the known world, we are at the coordinates of the island."

"What are we missing?" Leo asks.

"We aren't missing anything," Castian answers. When his eyes fall on me, it's like he can't look away fast enough. "We're lost."

While Leyre and Castian figure out where we went wrong, I head below deck to prep for lunch. There's something soothing in the monotony of peeling potatoes, even if part of me imagines different faces with every jerk of my knife. King Fernando. Méndez. Alessandro. Margo. Dez. Cas, even.

Leo knocks on the threshold of the mess hall. The skin around his nose is burned and peeling. He says nothing but picks up a brown spud and joins me.

"I used to hate peeling potatoes as a boy because my mother told me they had eyes."

"Once when my unit was trapped in this tiny town in Provincia Tresoros, we had potatoes for every meal. For *weeks*. I could barely stomach them after that."

He points to the sacks of potatoes. "Well, I hope you learn to love them again."

I wipe my brow and stab my knife through the same potato he's been delicately cutting since he sat down. "Out with it, Leo."

"I can't help but notice that you and Castian have been rather quiet since the storm. You barely look at each other, though I certainly haven't missed the longing glances you cast when you think no one is watching. You even chose to sleep down in the hammocks with us though he offered you the captain's quarters! Hells, I'd pretend to lust after the prince to have a nice mattress—"

"Leo," I groan, gutting a potato. I want to deny everything he says. We're lost, possibly off course because of the weather, and there is a war waiting for us back home. But right now, Castian occupies my every thought. I want nothing more than to tell someone about it, and Leo already knows how conflicted I am. "There was a moment during the storm."

Leo smirks knowingly, but keeps cutting, and the sound is oddly calming. "Go on."

"We nearly kissed." Saying it aloud forces me to relive the very moment. My belly squeezes with the sensation of being heaved into the air by the waves.

"Is that the first time this has happened?" he asks.

"No." Heat scrapes across my neck at the memory of him hacking away at firewood outside Doña Sagrada's inn, the way he practically growled as he kissed me back. I touch the base of my throat as if I can still feel the strain of his grip. "But that was under duress. And he asked me not to do it again."

Leo raises a skeptical brow. "Are you certain those were his exact words?"

"He said not to use him that way."

"Ah, that's different."

"I know this is the worst time to figure this out."

Leo sets a naked potato on top of my small pile. "I'm not sure I agree with that. In order for you and Castian to succeed, you have to be able to look each other in the eye. If there's anything you should have learned from your journey, it is that you work best when you communicate. Otherwise, what is all this for?"

"The future of the kingdom."

"Pardon me, Lady Ren, but you are used to fighting a battle you thought you'd never win. You always felt apart from the Whispers, and so you didn't let yourself truly imagine a future beyond the next spy mission. Here, I have chosen you. Castian has chosen you. Even Lady Leyre. You and Castian—that is no easy thing. Your hearts are entangled by your pasts, his brother, the future."

"I told you before, those complications are precisely why I can't imagine a future. Not with him. Not with anyone, really. Castian is going to be king. What will that make me? Royal spy? The king's former best friend and pretend wife?"

"You have to imagine a future." For all his humor, Leo understands me, deep down into the sad, ugly parts I don't want anyone to see. "Even one without Castian because I can't imagine a kingdom in any of the known world in which you aren't in it."

I pick up a new spud and squeeze it. I wish emotions were as easy to be rid of as memories.

"I suppose I'm trying to rationalize the feeling that came over me in the storm," I explain. "I'm familiar with the anticipation of a catastrophe. It can make anyone act impulsively. Back when I was with the Whispers, the rebels coupled up before a dangerous mission. Nearly every kiss Dez and I ever had was because we thought we were going to die. Being with Cas makes me wonder if any of that was real."

Leo thinks for a moment, rhythmically cutting a continuous

peel. "No matter the circumstance, it was real to you at that moment, was it not?"

"Yes it was, but I don't want to have the kind of heart that is easily changeable."

"I may not have known you for long, Lady Renata, but of one thing I am certain—when you love, you do it with your whole being. From the tips of your toes to the untamed baby hairs at your temples. You love so fiercely, that you would let it destroy you. It seems to me that there is a difference between being easily changed and being forced to outgrow that which harms you."

I haven't felt such ease with someone since I used to spend quiet evenings in the old rebel fortress with Sayida, doing simple tasks just like this. But my old life is still a fresh wound. It's been days since Dez chose to stand aside and let those Whispers take me. Esteban, someone who was nothing but rude to me for years, had urged me to run. But Dez, the boy I turned into my reason for fighting, just stood there as if our decade of friendship meant nothing.

"What did that potato ever do to you?" Leo asks, gently placing a hand over mine before I slice my fingers off. I was still cutting the white flesh in a single strip. Leo surveys our small mountain and grabs a pot to begin the fish stew.

"This is a lot of potatoes," I admit.

"I hope you're hungry."

There it is, the sensation I couldn't quite name—hunger. I'm hungry for so many things I didn't let myself feel before. Happiness. Laughter. The easy quiet of understanding. Friends, real ones. Kisses traded in the dark. Am I allowed to want these things at all? I suppose none of it matters if we can't find Isla Sombras. Leo's right. Castian and I work best when we communicate. And if he won't be the first one to talk, then I will.

I climb out the hatch and scan the deck, but Castian is nowhere in sight. Leyre is at the helm. When she sees me, she points to the captain's quarters. I knock, but he doesn't answer. I consider barging in, but then I lose my nerve. I have broken into cathedrals to steal back Moria treasures, sneaked around the palace of Andalucía, but *talking* to Castian evokes this response from me? I rub my palms on my tunic, suddenly remembering that Leo said I have unruly baby hairs. I feel utterly ridiculous and decide to turn around.

But before I do, the door swings opens, and Castian fills the doorway, surprised to see me. His golden hair is mussed, and I imagine him combing his fingers through it while he tries to think. He holds my stare. It is the longest we have looked at each other in days.

"I was coming to look for you," he says, something like dread and hope in the way he speaks.

"I'm here." I wince at how bright my voice is.

He beckons me forward. "Come in. You need to see this."

There's a hammer on the bed. The sheets are pulled tight around the mattress, and I can't tell whether he makes his bed every morning or simply hasn't slept in it. The cabin smells of leather and salt. I remember being in Castian's rooms, searching through his things for a hint of the king's weapon, before I discovered the weapon was a person. I was overwhelmed with the smell of the ocean. Now, that scent is everywhere all the time.

I point at the hammer. "Usually I'm the one ready to break things."

Castian brushes back his hair and smiles with his whole body, appearing just as relieved as I am. He crosses the room to a carved armoire bolted to the wall and fingers the new nails on the doors. "These swing open and creak all night. At the very least it's one thing on this ship I can fix."

"I thought you don't sleep."

He shrugs, and a sad smile tugs at his lips. "I still have to try, I suppose."

That falling sensation returns. I breathe deeply. "That's what you wanted to show me?"

"No. The reason I was going to look for you, well, it's what I just discovered." He walks around the captain's desk covered in maps, metal ships, several compasses, and a spyglass. Cas points to a page in the admiral's logbook. "I found her."

I feel a pressure behind my eyelids the moment I take the book in my hands. I've held it a dozen times since we left Little Luzou, but I don't remember this drawing in runny blue ink of a bird with spread wings, a long beak, and a fan of tail feathers. Beside it, the words *This is the end of the queen's flight. Queen Galatea is gone. This is my—*

The ink, which has been darkening with each passing second, is smudged, as if the quill had been dragged. The writer stopped midsentence and never finished. I flip to the next page, and the one after. Ten pages left and nothing. After a moment of stunned silence, a smell hits my nose.

"Aguadulce?" I hand the logbook back.

Cas nods. "Last night Leo and I were having a drink—"

"You and Leo?" I repeat. Is that why Leo came to find me this morning?

He smirks. "Are you jealous I'll steal your friend?"

"No, Cas. It's about time you had people around that you trust."

"Well, he can't hold his aguadulce." Cas slaps the logbook

against his open palm. "He spilled a glass on the pages, and I set it in front of the fire to dry. I didn't notice the change until today. When we were boys, Duque Arias spent a summer writing love letters to girls at court using invisible ink he stole from his grandfather. He was insufferable. But he did tell us that when exposed to heat, the ink appears. Admiral Arias was going to write more. An obituary? Something about this person."

I take the book back. My body buzzes with this information. "Galatea."

"You said her name before." Cas stands so close I can smell the herbs of his soap and see the pattern of scars on his chest. "But you asked about *Princess* Galatea."

"I have a memory. I don't know where it came from. It appeared when I fell ill. I saw a battle—on deck was a princess and the crest of her armor was this glowing peregrine falcon. It was made of alman stone."

"A Moria princess in one of your memories?" he asks. "Why didn't you say anything before?"

"Cas, there's so much of my magics I can't control. The last Moria royal family was said to have died decades ago. Before now, I'd never heard of a princess or queen named Galatea. But in my memory she was—" I sigh, the weight of the words on my tongue. "She was *with* your father."

Castian blinks his shock, then slowly grimaces. "As in...?"

I see Galatea on that ship, nearly relive the vibrant love that she felt when she kissed Fernando. My entire body wants to recoil.

The ship lurches on a wave. Castian wraps his arm around me, and we brace for a rough patch of sea. Outside the sky is clear, and we're sailing so fast that it almost feels like flying. When we're no longer in danger of falling, Castian releases me slowly. His palms linger on my waist.

"Why didn't you tell me?"

Because if my mind is breaking, I don't want you to know, I think.

"It's hard to believe without seeing it. I wish I could show you what I saw," I confess. I touch the crescent scar over the mound of his cheekbone. Then pain flares along my fingertips, like lightning coursing through my tendons. The whorls etched across my palm burst with light, and Castian jerks away. He cradles his face, then examines the skin there in a mirror.

He breathes fast and turns to me. "What *was* that?"

Numbness still buzzes at the very tips of my fingers. "I didn't mean to."

"Ren, I saw it." He takes my hand in his, tracing the pattern of scars with his thumb. "The image of them on that deck. You shared your memory with me. I didn't know Robári could do that."

"Neither did I. That's never happened before," I say softly. I shut my eyes for a moment. He isn't afraid of my touch or my power. He's *curious.*

"Have you ever heard of such a thing?"

"Ventári can communicate with other Ventári," I explain. "It may be plausible that others can combine our magics, too."

Cas gently pulls away, walking around the desk and staring at the maps and compasses. All these tools to help us across an ocean, but we can barely navigate each other. This is the longest we've been together in days, and I feel myself anchored by the way he touched me.

"What does this mean, Cas?"

"It means there's so much more to my father than I ever thought possible. It means that perhaps there's a reason why there is virtu- ally no trace of my father's first marriage." Castian faces the win- dow. He steps closer, body tense as he watches the calm sea, then whirls around. "Why have we dropped anchor?"

Marching on deck, we find Leo and Leyre leaning against the starboard side of the ship.

"What do you think you're doing, Leyre?" Castian asks.

She rests her hands on her cocked hips and gestures with the sextant overboard. "Congratulations, Your Highness. In half a day we've managed to sail in a circle."

Pale green and blue water hugs a snakelike sandbar.

"Are you sure it's not a different sandbar?" I ask, but even I wince at the suggestion. It can't be a coincidence.

Leyre flips the sextant back and forth, examining the eyepiece before letting out an exasperated breath. "I don't know what King Fernando meant by this being the one thing that could help us find this cursed Knife of Memory, but all it's done is get us lost."

I imagine her heaving it into the water, so I gingerly take it from her grasp and set it down. "There has to be an explanation."

"Why don't you find it, and I'll go clear my head and wash the stink off my skin." Leyre leans into Castian and sniffs. "So should you."

Leyre removes her clothes, revealing all the tan lines from where she rolls up her sleeves and breeches. On the railing, her naked body is a dark silhouette in front of the afternoon sun, before she dives into the clear blue waters below.

"Wait!" Castian shouts.

Leo eyes the water longingly as he unties the front of his trousers. He steps out of his clothes, all corded muscles as he follows Leyre overboard.

"This is mutiny," Castian spits.

I sigh. "They're not wrong."

"We've been out here for days!" Castian says, then closes the distance between us. He lowers his voice, even though we are alone

171

on deck. "We've done everything right. What if—what if Leyre's task wasn't to kill me but to distract us?"

"I can't say I completely trust her, but there was something in the way she spoke of her father, of the king, and her own anger—I trust that. I believe that." Castian turns his face to the side, but I lead his stare back to me with my finger along his scruffy beard. "Leyre's right. We have to clear our heads. You would say the same to me." Weeks ago, I would have never suggested such a thing. I would have simply agreed that we needed to keep sailing and then perhaps gotten us more lost. Now, we are surrounded by uncertainty with more questions than we have answers. "Look at it. We're back at this sandbar *again*. Perhaps we need to explore why."

I pull my tunic over my head. Castian sucks in a short breath, then turns to give me privacy. Ever the gentleman. I step out of my breeches and underthings, and add them to the pile with the others. I take a gulp of clean air and dive, cutting headfirst into the cool blue surface. The water amplifies my heartbeat. The sea is so clear, and for a moment, it feels like plunging through air. Bright orange fish swim across my vision, but they scatter when there's a fourth and final splash. Castian has finally joined us. His powerful limbs cut through the sea he's named after. I let myself float, suspended in the water's embrace. Something large swims under my feet. I open my mouth to scream, but then see a school of silver fish plucking away at the fins of a spotted toothless whale. I turn in the water to catch the others' attention, but when I look back, the whale is gone. Impossible—it couldn't possibly have swum away that quickly.

My chest begins to burn. I kick up to the surface, and swim closer to my friends. Leo is gathering shells on the sandbar while Leyre floats by with her arms tucked behind her neck, basking in the sun. Castian pads ashore. Sheets of clear water swoop down the muscular curve of his back. His long hair curls at the tips, and he squints into the distance—a sea god made mortal surveying the land above. I feel a tugging sensation in the pit of my stomach, a loss of breath.

"You're staring," Leo sings beside me.

I start and realize he's back in the water with me. He's holding a perfect spiral shell in his fist. I don't know whether I'm angry that I was, in fact, staring or that I was caught, but I sink beneath the surface, hiding every part of my face except my eyes.

"You're more worried than usual," Leo says.

I follow him to where we can stand, the bottom so soft it suctions my feet. "Yes, for a hundred reasons. There's something strange about all this."

I tell him about what I did to Castian with my magics. "I've never *shared* a memory with anyone before."

"Could your powers be evolving? Getting stronger?"

Another question I can't answer. I slap the surface of the water, making a tiny wave. "Ventári are the only Moria capable of reading minds, but that moment with Cas was something entirely different. It was like I let him into *my* mind."

"Perhaps it's a good thing. This way, you're not alone in the things you keep."

What would it have been like to share my memories sooner? I shake away the thought. "I fear this is the type of memory that will change everything."

When I'm quiet for too long, staring far out into the endless sea, Leo sprinkles water at me. "You can't say it's life-changing and then not tell me."

"It was of a Moria princess named Galatea," I say finally. He nods along as I describe her armor, the Icelandic ships. "And she was kissing King Fernando. You should have seen the desire and utter devotion in his eyes. That's the memory that came over me that first day."

"No wonder you were ill," Leo says, understanding dawning on him. "We didn't know what to do. Castian was half out of his senses. What does it all mean?"

"I don't know yet." The memory of my first day at sea makes me cringe. "But I never thanked you for taking care of me. Even if that tonic was disgusting."

Leo scoffs, running his long, musician fingers through the clear sparkling water. "You mean Leyre's dreadful sea sickness concoction? After she made us each drink some, she ordered Cas to feed it to you in hopes it would ease your malady. I think that was the moment I decided I liked her."

"But *you* fed me the medicine," I say.

The confusion on his features is chased away by a shared realization. Leo was not with me when I was sick. I snap my gaze to Castian across the sandbar, sifting sand through his fist.

I remember everything at once—how strange it was that Leo was so quiet, how he didn't speak but two words to me. I was seeing so many things that day I failed to realize it was *Castian* who made me drink, who listened to me say those things—Oh, my Lady, I said so many things. *Castian* glamoured as Leo! He let me bare myself to him.

He's so beautiful and so terrible. . . . I want to hate him.

"Wait, Ren!" Leo shouts, but I'm already swimming for the ship.

I climb the rope ladder and land on the deck in a wet heap. I tug on my clothes, my own words echoing in my mind.

It wouldn't be so terrible to . . . want him. Sometimes I do.

Castian's trousers are right in front of me. I throw them overboard. Humiliation colors my line of sight. I don't even know where

I'm going until I'm below deck and in the only place I can think of: the gambling room, where we hid the day of the storm. Leo and Leyre must have been here earlier because a game of cards is scattered on the red tabletop.

"What's gotten into you?" Castian slams the door behind him. His wet pants cling to his thighs. Rivulets of seawater run down his neck and chest. Everything I feel for him is due to proximity—it is because we are forced to be together every day. Hate and love and desire rolled into a storm I can't outrun.

"You tricked me" is all I manage to say. "You tricked me, Cas."

He stands right in front of me, eyes searching mine for an answer I cannot speak. "I did."

"Why?"

"You know why."

I shake my head; beads of salt water drip at my feet. "Help me understand."

He traces the outline of my shoulder, my arms. "I couldn't stand seeing you hurting—it killed me. I left Leyre at the helm and went to administer the draft. When you opened your eyes you told me you hated me."

"Cas—" I try to say that it wasn't his face I saw. It was Fernando's, but he glances at the floor and offers a sad smile.

"I knew that Leo was the only person you would let in, the only person who you'd trust to help you. I have never wished I could be someone else in that moment, and then I remembered I could be. I would be anyone for you. Hells, I'd be my own brother if that's what you wanted."

I remember Dez on the boardwalk of Little Luzou—reckless, brave, but now something else. Lost. Changed. I was so worried about how I have become different that I didn't stop to realize that so has everything and everyone around me.

"Don't say that. I don't want you to be Dez," I say softly. "I want you to—"

When I bite down on my own words, Cas becomes so still. The heat of his stare rakes down my mouth, to the wet clothes clinging to me. My heart beats so hard it feels like thunder in my ears.

"What do you want from me?" His deep voice wavers.

That is what I've been trying to figure out. I see the boy who was my friend in the palace, his angelic smile, our secret pact, how much it hurt to leave him. Then there's the boy I hated, the illusion of a murderous prince. The one whose public executions I'd heard of across the land. The man who danced with me and asked whether I remembered him. The prince I almost beat to death, and the Cas who is in this room now. I am startled to find that Castian is all those things, and I want him. But I can't bring myself to say it because when this is all over, I will be gone, and he will be king.

"Everything hurts all the time, Cas." I sit on the edge of the gaming table. "My power is becoming something I have no control over. I'm afraid of wanting anything at all. My memories of you, the real you, were so buried, I didn't even recognize you when we met again. How could you have remembered me after so long?"

He pressed his fingers to the center of his chest. "Because you're right here, Nati. I've kept you here as my light. When I have done wretched, cruel, *unspeakable* things, I thought that would be the moment that I'd rip you out of my heart. That I would reach a point when I didn't deserve a shred of goodness. But it never worked. In the moments that I wanted to give up, I remembered you. My friend who saved me from the worst kind of loneliness."

"Castian—" Why is it so hard for me to just say the things I mean? Isn't that why I went in search of him earlier? I was willing to allow myself to want, and now I am retreating like a creature of the depths, too afraid of the sun.

"What do you want from me?" he repeats.

I place my hand over his. A heady rush fills me. His pulse is frenzied. The pit of my stomach feels like a cavern, and the rest of me is falling straight through. That's what surrendering to this strange desire is like—falling.

I wrap my hand around the back of his neck and tug him closer. I shiver as our damp bodies press against each other. He stands in the open space between my knees, and I yank him back with me against the velvety surface of the table. His body presses hard atop mine, but he doesn't meet my lips. Instead, Castian brushes his mouth over my ear. When he speaks, his words warm my skin. The vibration of his voice permeates my body.

"What do you want from me, Nati? You have to say it."

"I want you to kiss me," I exhale, and the admission of this want leaves me breathless. I dig my fingers along the waist of his trousers, where his skin is still cool from the sea. He shudders, and I can feel how much he wants me with the pressure of him against my belly. He cups the sides of my neck, tracing the line of my jaw, drinking me in as our lips touch softly. It is the kind of tortuously slow kiss that deepens, awakening a spark of hunger. Then he pulls back, and I want him again.

"Kiss me and make me forget," I whisper.

It's the wrong thing. Castian's hands come down on either side of me. He sighs and takes my chin in his fingertips.

"No, Nati. When I kiss you again, truly kiss you, it will be to make you remember."

With a grunt he pushes himself off and walks away. I trace the ache on my lips, feel the chill he leaves in his wake. But before he reaches the door, there is the resounding pop of cannon fire.

My mind clears with a rush of panic. We clamor up to the deck to find a massive galleon ship with what appears to be a hundred people on deck. They've cast hooks onto our hull and are reeling us in like trout.

"Where did it come from?" Castian asks.

"I don't know," Leo says. "It appeared from the ether."

Leyre has her arrows drawn, but I see the terror that passes across her features. Us versus a small army. She meets my eye and gives a shake of her head, lowers her weapon.

The Queen of Little Luzou's words ring in my ears as sharply as our attackers' bells.

Pirates.

16

WE'RE PARADED ACROSS DECK, TIED TO EACH OTHER WITH OUR HANDS BOUND behind our backs. The pirates are not what I was expecting. Though I've only ever heard bedtime stories, I was preparing for a ship full of middle-aged men covered in filth and stolen gold. Dez used to say that pirates were simply wraiths without a cause or a country, stealing and killing for their own glory. But I am not entirely sure what to make of our captors. Boys swing down from the sails, and groups of young girls cease their wooden swordplay to stare. Weathered elders pause as we're herded by.

At the front of our line, I feel the brunt of their scrutiny. A boy of perhaps ten, with ruddy cheeks and a nest of red curls, opens up a hatch. Hands begin to shove me down, and my natural reflex is to struggle, but another pirate runs to stop us. She nearly doubles over panting, the sun reflecting on the deep brown skin of her bald head. In her hand is the sextant.

"Wait! Cap'll want to see them right away."

I lurch forward, but I'm overcome with a wave of calm. The breeze tickles the baby hairs at my temples. Music is coming from somewhere on deck, and I hear the slap of the red-and-gold flag above. My heartbeat slows, and then I'm walking up wooden steps and through a shadowed threshold. The wide cabin is empty, and we're positioned in front of a mahogany desk littered with parchment, quills, and coins from different nations. Deep purple velvet drapes are parted to let in the light. A boy runs in with a metal tray and sets down a pot of café and a clay mug. His wide eyes glance at the empty chair with relief before darting back out.

"Wait here," the bald girl murmurs, and her voice has a distant chime. She moves her hands slowly, like she's controlling the strings of a marionette. Copper rings adorn each of her fingers.

When she's gone, I fight the weight against my eyelids that tells me to be calm. Leo hums his favorite opera. Leyre grabs a coin from the captain's desk and brings it right up to her eye, laughing.

"Snap out of it," Castian growls.

"Snap out of what?" I breathe deeply and take in his face. He's upset, attempting to unknot his bindings and failing. Cas is so beautiful, even when he's angry. I mean to tell him so, but then the haze around my vision begins to lift, and the realization dawns on me. Copper rings. That pirate is a Persuári! Her magics are tempering our will to fight.

"Moria," I whisper as an entourage of four enters.

Two remain at the door, and two flank the desk. Daggers and swords are strapped to thighs, across chests and shoulders. But their metals are the most striking. Thick gold gauges stretch a woman's earlobes. Silver studs pierce delicate nostrils, even the skin below their clavicles. One of the boys wears a copper choker that looks like a strip of chain mail around his throat. They're Moria warriors, displaying their weapons and metals with pride.

The captain enters.

She's a tall woman, perhaps in her late fifties, wearing a scarlet tunic with black leather pants and boots with steel tips. Her corkscrew curls are threaded with silver and hang loose on her shoulders. At the hollow of her throat is a thin silver chain with a single blue gem. The necklace is the only thing that makes her look delicate, like a remnant from another life. She glances at us but says nothing as she removes her embroidered coat and takes a seat. She takes her time pouring a cup of café. Her sleeveless tunic shows off toned arms and medium brown skin riddled with scars. The markings arc everywhere—along her neck, her wrists, and even in the cleft of her breasts right over her heart. I realize her necklace and the rings on her thumbs are not silver but platinum. The rarest metal in the kingdom, platinum, enhances Robári magics. And that's what her scars are—Robári marks. Hers are thinner than mine, like threads of pearl. Like Galatea's in my memory. How is that possible?

She leans back. Rich brown eyes framed by arched black eyebrows take us in as she drinks her café.

"Captain—" I say, but she cuts me off with a wave of her hand.

"You'll have your turn to speak." Her voice is pleasant, though it has an edge. "You have been boarded by the pirates San Piedras, and you are now aboard the *Madre del Mar*. First I'm going to tell you what's going to happen. Everything that was in your possession, or on your ship, is now forfeit to me and my crew. You have two options: I remove all memory of these moments and drop you off at the next available port. Or, if you don't want me riffling through your tender mind, I can remove your tongue, and you will still be dropped off at the next available port. Either way, you will never speak about the pirates San Piedras ever again."

"What about writing?" Leyre asks.

The calming effects of the Persuári have completely vanished. All I'm left with is a sense of dread. Castian turns a bewildered stare as if he cannot believe she's uttered the words. One of the younger Moria pirates chuckles. The captain grins, and a spark of hope ignites in my belly.

"Then you shall lose your hands as well. I can make it your feet if you happen to have trained your toes in the skill of penmanship."

"Please," I cut in, struggling with my ropes. "By the light of the Lady—"

"We carry on," the captain finishes. Her dark eyes scrutinize me. "You are one of the blessed."

A Robári captain. Moria crew. I think of how we traveled in a circle, arriving at the same sandbar. How the underwater animals impossibly vanished. Only they didn't vanish. They simply went where the illusion couldn't reach.

"And you're the reason we can't find Isla Sombras," I say, more awed than angry.

The captain drinks from her cup. "We protect the island."

"Noble pirates?" Leo asks, laughing nervously. "Isn't that a good thing?"

"If you're protecting the island, then that means we were never lost," Castian says. He's the tallest of us, and though his voice is calm, he looks menacing. "We're here."

"*Nearly* there," the captain corrects, holding up a sharp nail. "When we trailed your ship along the coast of Salinas, I wasn't sure what a luxury vessel was doing so far from the mainland. But the longer we watched you, the more certain I was you were foolish enough to treasure seek. Now this has been found in your possession."

She gestures to the sextant and the logbook on her desk. Her face goes stern, a scar on her clavicle lights up, just the one. How is she doing that?

"Who sent you?"

"No one sent us," I say. "We are on our own."

The captain pours more inky café. She doesn't believe me. "The four of you simply bought a ship with false documents? Though there isn't one for the Luzouan girl."

Leyre smiles. "I don't need one. I'm not pretending to be anyone but myself."

I kick her shin, and she shoves me. With their arms tied, Cas and Leo can't do anything. The bald Persuári returns, urging a pleasant calm through my tense muscles.

The captain rubs the fingers of her left hand together. "Forgive me, but I can no longer give you a choice. I must remove your memories of this encounter. Normally, we'd never force this on anyone, but these are extraordinary circumstances."

Castian leans forward, and this time his voice is anything but calm. "Robári magics do not work on me."

"It's true," I say. I remember us tumbling across the floor, my hands at his temples. "I've tried."

"*Robári.*" She says the word as if it's a marvel. "This is the best catch yet. Then you will have to stay, as crew or as prisoners."

"We can't stay at all," I say. "You asked who sent us, but I've already told you the truth. We have no army, no allies. It is the four of us against the entire might of King Fernando, and there is one weapon that can help us stop the bloodshed between Puerto Leones and the Moria. You are the only thing in our way, and you are obviously Moria—why wouldn't you help us?"

"The kingdom of Memoria fell," she says, anguish in her voice. "The Moria are scattered. Nearly extinct."

"The Whispers still fight," I counter. "But they will all die if we don't get that weapon. Right now the king is assembling an army. The rebels don't stand a chance."

She barks a bitter laugh. "I used to be idealistic like you. You are a Whisper? I bet you revere Illan and listen to his empty promises of restoring the great kingdom of Memoria. Where is that kingdom now? Illan should have heeded my warning and left when he had the chance. What is he doing now but fighting a losing battle?"

"He isn't fighting anything," I snap. "Illan is dead."

The corners of her eyes crinkle ever so slightly. Then the Moria captain sighs deeply, reaches for a drawer, and brings out a bottle of clear liquor. The sweet tang of aguadulce fills the air as she adds it to her café. She raises the drink, like an offering, then takes a long swig.

"We know the dangers of the Knife of Memory," Castian says passionately. I see the mask he puts on in front of this woman. "I know that my father has used it before. We won't make the same mistakes. Test us, let us show you that we will do right by the kingdom."

The captain watches Castian and, as if seeing him for the first time, looks deeply ashamed. No, disgusted. "Spawn of the Lion."

He answers by bowing his head in acknowledgment of the insult. As her pirates start to chatter, she slams her fist to call for silence.

"Last I remember, the Whispers, along with your mother, dealt you a terrible fate. And your father has no idea of the power you possess?"

Castian flashes a crooked smile. "I'm still alive. What do you think?"

"Destiny makes fools of men who try to force the world to change to their whims." The Moria captain settles deep into thought. "I was there when we tried, and then when we failed. Believe me, I am saving your life by keeping you here."

When she says the last part, she only looks at me. I think of Dez saying that the Knife wouldn't work, that my skill would be wasted. Don't they understand? I never expected to survive this war.

"Do not let Illan's martyrdom ruin your future," she tells me.

I lean forward, and then it happens. The light of my magics sets fire to my ropes. Back in the king's dungeons, I once melted the chains off my wrists. I feel the heat lick at my skin, and I break free, stomping out the flames. I hold my hands out to her, but I do not expect the horror on her face.

"Illan isn't why I'm doing this."

"What happened to you?" She blinks, unbelieving. "Did he fashion you a pair of locked gloves to wear?"

"The only one to keep me locked up was Justice Méndez. Illan trained me. He did what he could for me when others told him I was dangerous."

"My dear," the captain laments, "where do you think the justice learned the design for your gloves?"

She takes another drink, this time of just aguadulce.

"And who are you to claim these things of Illan?" I snap. "You didn't even know he was dead."

Her smile is wistful, almost tragic. "I know—I knew a lot about Illan. He was, after all, my husband."

17

"You were married to *Illan*?" I shout.

"If I may," Leo interjects. "As we are presented with the very real possibility of having to live on this ship, may we know the name of our captor? And have our ropes removed?"

The captain looks up at an Illusionári nearly my age. The girl's hair is cropped short all around the sides, with a tangle of wheat-colored curls at the top. There's something about her heart-shaped face I can't quite place. She unsheathes a curved knife and cuts through everyone's restraints.

"As for introductions, I am Argiñe San Piedras."

Leo presses one hand on his abdomen, the other on his back, and bows. "Leonardo Almarada of Provincia Zaharina."

"Leyre Arang de Las Rosas formerly of the Royal Luzouan Navy." She *winks* at the captain.

"Renata Convida." What else can I add? Of the Whispers? Of the king's Hand of Moria? Of the burned forests north of Andalucía?

Castian rubs at his wrist. One of his golden curls falls over his eyes in a rakish sort of way. "I suppose I am Castian, prince of Puerto Leones, Matahermano, Lion's Fury, Príncipe Dorado, and heir to the Fajardo dynasty."

"That really is a mouthful," Leyre says with a grimace.

"You were *married* to Illan?" I repeat. He'd spoken of his wife, but I'd always assumed she'd died in a skirmish between the crown and the Whispers.

Captain Argiñe stands, resting her knuckles on her desk. She bypasses my question and says, "Let me see your hands."

Instinctively, I ball them into fists. When I was a little girl, after I created my first Hollow and the scars began, I was afraid of them. Justice Méndez couldn't explain what was happening to me, and I had no one else to talk to. My hands were in gloves most of the time, so even Castian never saw them. But when I was in the care of the Whispers, I learned that they were an abhorrent sight.

When Captain Argiñe extends her hand to me, I don't feel the same kind of shame. Only sadness. She runs her fingers along my scars. Tears well up in her eyes. "You poor child."

For a moment I wonder, is this the way my mother would have held me? Like I was something that needed to be protected.

I take a steadying breath. "I don't need your pity, Captain. I need your help."

She gives a weary sigh and lets go. "I will teach you how to control your powers. I will even allow Leonardo and Leyre to go free. But there is a reason I left the world and built a new one. Come and let me show you."

"What about Castian?" I ask.

The captain's dark stare lingers on the prince, as if she can't decide what to make of him. "We don't recognize Leonesse royals. But I extend the same offer to train with my Illusionári. *If* that is something you want."

We are outnumbered. We are outmatched. We are in the middle of the sea. Fight is not something we can do at the moment, but we will have to find a way off this ship. For now, the four of us follow the pirate captain back on deck.

"This galleon is a relic," Leyre says, running her hands along the polished wood. "From the Luzouan fleet thirty-five years ago!"

"Forty," the captain says. "This was one of the first constructed that year."

"How did you come by it?" Cas asks.

Captain Argiñe winks. "I won it off a merchant."

"You're joking," Leyre scoffs.

The captain stops, holding open a door that leads to the lower levels. "Do I strike you as the sort of woman who jokes?"

Leyre turns to the three of us and says, "I rather think she does."

One deck below is a busy marketplace. I breathe in the familiar scent of manzanilla and dried herbs, the medicinal poultices that Sayida used to make, a fragrant perfume made of lilac oil.

"You make your own cloth?" Leo wonders as we pass a couple of older men and women weaving together. "Marvelous."

"We make our own everything, when we can procure the supplies at a port. We might be on the brink of extinction, but I want to make sure we pass down our traditions."

There's a carpenter station. An older woman with cropped gray hair and brown skin is hunched over a table carving grooves into a slat of wood. The pattern reminds me of the intricate lines and symbols in the old fortress I once called home. With the captain as our guide, people shake our hands. They *want* to shake my hand. A middle-aged man greets me by making the symbol of the Lady over my forehead and telling me that I am blessed.

Castian marvels at the way these pirates trade anything and everything—from buttons and thimbles to bottles of homemade aguadulce and jars of preserves. A group of kids is playing a furious game of cards. Captain Argiñe walks up behind one of the boys and yanks his ear hard.

"No illusions, Hernán. Lose honestly or lose a finger."

The others jeer at him, and the tops of the boy's cheeks grow red. Next we pass through the kitchens, where I recognize the supplies we were given by the Queen of Little Luzou, even the potatoes Leo and I spent hours peeling and the pot to make the fish stew. We share a look of irritation, but then a girl in rolled-up hose and a dirty tunic runs up to us.

"Captain Argi," she says, "Elva says the bounty is enough to last us for the next month—"

"Enough, Jess," the captain clips. "See to it that everything is properly stored and that the apothecuras gets first pick of any herbs and medicine. We don't want another fever outbreak."

"Yes, Captain Argi." The girl gives a salute, then sticks her tongue out at me.

Perhaps she's younger than I thought. My chest feels tight, and my mind is heavy with memories of when I was her age. Fingers snake through mine, and Castian squeezes my hand. I wonder if he's thinking the same thing.

The entire ship is teeming with life. Families cluster in the crew cabins, and children swing from hammocks. We pass a small library, where two girls my age tenderly hold hands and read from the same tome. A line of women nurse screaming babies. We see rooms full of powder kegs and other weapons. I can taste the iron in the air. There's a brig, but it's empty.

How do they serve justice aboard a ship? Then I think about the options we were given—lose a memory or lose our tongues. With the Whispers, punishment was never dealt easily. There was a trial by the elders. I remember standing before the council themselves— what would have happened if they'd only listened to me?

I try to catch Castian's eye, but he's been pulled into conversation by a woman weaving a tapestry, adding row after row of thread. The image she's making has only begun, but it's a bright blue sky and the beginnings of a crown.

"It's beautiful," he compliments her.

She kisses both his cheeks. "May the Lady bless you, my boy."

I feel Castian tense, but he pulls on one of those smiles that hide everything. I don't think he's ever smiled at me that way, and I don't know whether I should be thankful or not.

Captain Argiñe leads us back above deck, exiting in the front of the ship, overlooking the bow as it cleaves the ocean apart. This isn't just a pirate ship. It's preservation in a way the Whispers never had.

"How did you end up helming a ship full of Moria, Captain Argiñe?" I ask.

"Now that we're good friends, it's Captain Argi. There are some Olvidados and refugees from other countries here as well," she says. "But this ship, the *Madre del Mar*, was meant to save the Moria. I warned Illan that King Fernando had become something wretched, that we had to leave. But Illan chose to rebel. He believed that the kingdom of Memoria could be revived. I believed the way to do that was to save the people, not the place. And so I left, and Illan did not come after me."

"It can't be easy," Leyre says. "You have what, three generations now?"

"Soon it'll be four. Our biggest advantage is our group of Illusionári, who hide us in plain sight. We get by."

"Through stealing and scavenging," Castian argues.

"Through strength and resourcefulness," Captain Argi corrects.

Cas raises his brows. I see the beginning of a spark in his turquoise eyes. "You can't do that forever."

"How do you think Puerto Leones has flourished? How do you think your father and his father and his before that got by? They believe they earned the lands beyond their borders, but didn't they simply steal and scavenge? At the very least we give our victims options. Puerto Leones won't rule forever. When the kingdom burns, we will be here, waiting."

"That's not a strategy," I say, raising my voice. "King Fernando has spent years experimenting on Moria to harness our powers. He's succeeded once, and he will do it again."

She licks her canine and watches the gray mist that skims the ocean surface. She grips the railing of the ship and says with certainty, "No, he won't."

"You haven't seen what he's done to Robári like me. Like us." I shake my head, my voice rising in anger. "Why won't you help us?"

Captain Argi stands inches from my face. Everything about her is made to be intimidating—the kohl around her eyes, her clothes, and even the way she twists her platinum rings while she deliberates.

Her smile is like the edge of a precipice. "I will show you."

As the sun sets, the crew gathers on the deck. The *Madre del Mar* is anchored in the calm sea. Oil lamps are lit in a circle as Captain Argiñe enters the gathering with the weaver Castian spoke to below deck. Her long linen dress flutters in the breeze, and even in the setting sun, the woman's eyes fall on Castian.

"Are you ready, Euria?"

"Aye, Captain Argi." The older woman nods, brushing soft, tight curls behind her ears. She extends her arms straight out, palm side up. Two gold cuffs ring her wrists. An Illusionári.

"Then let us show our newcomers what they have come to seek." Argi touches Euria's fingertips with her own.

I feel the pressure of magics in the air. The susurration of voices over the rustle of sea. Argiñe's memory scars light up all at once. There are so many on her skin, it's as if she has been set aglow from within. Beams of light fracture and waver like sunrays.

And then two figures appear on the deck. A young man with ink-black hair dressed in the Leonesse groom shade of azure. At his side is a young woman with obsidian hair that falls to her waist, crowned by white flowers. It takes me a moment, but I gasp and reach for Castian beside me. He recognizes them, too.

It's Prince Fernando and Princess Galatea.

As the image takes form, it is impossible to deny they're really standing there on the deck with us. Our night becomes day. Our sea becomes a garden. We are inside Captain Argi's soundless memory, brought to life by Euria's power of illusion.

Prince Fernando and Princess Galatea hold hands in front of a Moria priestess. On Fernando's sash is a golden lion. Galatea's robes are the traditional deep scarlet with a pattern of stars at the hem. A young Argiñe is part of the intimate gathering. Her face is free of the hard lines she carries now, and only her forearms show memory scars. Beside her is Illan, barely in his twenties. I recognize a man who looks so very much like the current Duque Arias—his grandfather. The others I do not know.

Fernando says his vows. Galatea holds him fiercely, her radiant joy so pure. The young couple leans forward and shares a deep kiss. Petals rain from the guests. Fernando gathers Galatea by her waist and lifts her into his arms. And when he sets her down, trailing kisses along his face, three arrows pierce her back.

I cry out as the image fades, leaving gray wisps, ghosts of a memory. I reach for Galatea at the same time Fernando does. I can see how shattered he is. A break within him echoes with his silent scream.

"This was Princess Galatea, the last daughter of the Memoria kingdom." Argi answers the question I can't bring myself to ask. "Fernando had just been declared heir and Galatea was to wed a Moria lord. They eloped against their families' decree."

"Who murdered her?" Castian asks.

A series of hisses comes from the crew. Several of the older Moria press thumbs on their foreheads as a warning sign.

"Your grandfather," Argi spits, then with a deep shame adds, "aided by Moria loyalists who would not see the union pass. Illan tortured the information out of the archers and discovered Fernando was also a target."

This is the end of the queen's flight. Queen Galatea is gone. Those were the last words Admiral Arias wrote in his logbook. He was at their elopement, and he was on their voyage.

Castian's strong grip around my arm jolts me back to the present. Disbelief is plain as he watches the Moria captain. I know in my gut that she isn't finished. A fissure of light travels from a scar along Argi's throat and down to her fingertip.

> *Prince Fernando appears, incandescent as he snatches a blade made of alman stone from a Robári boy. Fernando's intention is clear.*
> *Fernando crawls away from Galatea's lifeless body.*
> *Fernando wraps his fist around the Knife of Memory.*
> *Fernando stabs the Robári boy through the heart.*

I gasp. "He tried to bring her back."

As the memory fades, there is a collective sorrow across the deck. "Our Lady of Shadows and Whispers created the Knife of Memory to sever her own immortality. As a weapon it is divine. That is why she hid it on this island. But when Fernando tried to bring Galatea back to life, he corrupted its power and erased Galatea's existence from the world's memory." Captain Argiñe crosses the deck to face me. "When I tell you that you will fail, I say it because I have seen it. A power like that *can't* be trusted."

"We have to try," I say. "Didn't you listen when I said the king will keep making weapons to destroy the Moria left in Puerto Leones? He'll control us, the rest of the world."

Argi pinches the bridge of her nose. "He won't make another weapon. He can't."

"How do you know that?" I shout.

"Because he'd need the Knife of Memory to do it." Argi's scars glow, and she claps her hand around my throat. Her magic bores into me, forcing me to relive memories of Fernando's rage.

The images flash and flash. I shove her off and gasp for breath. I'm aware of my friends being held back by the Moria pirates. Slowly, I get up. Every memory and truth is harder to bear than the next—King Fernando once married a Moria princess. He tried to bring her back to life. But upon seeing the memory again, I recognize the boy Fernando stabbed through the heart. It was Cebrián. Fernando created the Ripper.

"When Cebrián failed to revive Galatea, Fernando tried to wield the Knife himself. Don't you see, Renata?" the captain says. "I was there. I saw the worst coming, and I knew to take my people and *run*."

I turn around and feel their fear and scrutiny. Families and friends bound together by survival—what the Whispers were supposed to be. "I don't blame you for all of this. But while I look at your faces and I see the sadness at listening to these stories, I know that's what they are to most of you. Stories. But to me, to my crew, this is everything. You've been gone too long to know what it means to be Moria under King Fernando's rule. It's your turn to see through my eyes."

I offer my hand to Euria, the Illusionári. I do not have to reach far for memories of the king and justice's cruelties. But when I try to share the memories, Euria's cry of pain ripples through the night. Her illusion crackles the air of the deck, each moment coming too quickly. I yank my hand away and break the connection, and we fall together.

"I'm sorry," I whimper.

Euria takes up my face in her hands. She kisses the tops of my eyes. Somehow *she's* the one crying. "What have they done to you, child?"

Everything. Nothing. I don't know.

When I look up, Leo, Leyre, and Castian are at my side. The ship's inhabitants slowly disperse below deck until we are left alone, pariahs, starboard.

"Are you all right?" Leo asks.

"No," I say. "We've never been closer or farther away from the Knife of Memory, and I'm more confused than ever. What about you?"

My question is for Castian, but he gives a small shake of his head, and I know he isn't ready to face what he saw of his father.

"We can take our chances," he says, quietly watching the black sea lap against the anchored ship. "Scale these lines back to our ship—"

"You will do no such thing," Captain Argiñe says, sidling up beside us.

"How can you expect us to do nothing after everything we've seen?" Castian asks.

"I cannot simply give you the Knife," she says. "It requires a cost. And only one of you can pay it."

Before the captain's dark eyes settle on my face, I understand she means me.

"You were right, Renata. I do not know what you have been through, and I cannot stop you from fighting a war I abandoned. But I can help you better understand your power so when the time comes, you do not make the same mistakes we did."

Something like hope ignites in my heart.

"Lift the veil!"

The captain's call is answered by a series of horns, the ringing of bells. Sails billow against the wind, and the ship soars over an ocean so dark, it is like sailing across the night sky. After a moment, land shimmers where there was none before.

"Welcome to Isla Sombras," she says. "The last resting place of Our Lady of Shadows."

18

THERE IS A MORIA LEGEND THAT SAYS OUR LADY OF WHISPERS WATCHED OVER all of us from her floating temple in the sky. But on nights when there were storms or the sky was not clear, she shaped her shadows into messengers—crows, porpoises, lynxes. The most important was a white peregrine falcon.

When I asked Illan how that was possible, he told me that the goddess was capable of anything, that she had many roles to play in watching her creation. I didn't truly believe him then, even as a child. But standing on the black sand beach of Isla Sombras, the only thing keeping me going is belief in impossible things.

By the glow of a lighthouse, the canoes that brought us ashore return to the ship for more passengers. Ahead of us a path snakes into the island, where Captain Argiñe says is a small village. Our destination is beyond the settlement, the temple of alman stone that crowns a hill. It glows under the moonlight, an incandescent beacon guiding me home.

The pirates have returned our packs as part of our agreement, and we make quick work of loading two horse-drawn carts with supplies for the four of us, plus Captain Argi and two of her hand-picked pirates.

"How has no one ever put this location on a map of the known world?" Leo asks.

"Moria magics," Argiñe says, tilting her chin up with pride. "Do you see that lighthouse? That is one of four on the island. Each houses a Moria of our blessed orders. Together they make Isla Sombras virtually invisible."

Leyre gathers a fistful of black sand and rubs it between her palms. "In Luzou, we have red sand beaches, but I've never seen anything like this."

Argiñe gives one of the horses a healthy slap. "I'm delighted our volcanic rock fascinates you, but we must begin our trek to the temple of Our Lady. Your training starts at dawn."

Leo glances nervously at the horizon, where the black blue of night is brightening. "Dawn is fast approaching."

The captain strides past him, her oil lamp exaggerating her smirk. "Then we'd best make haste."

Leyre chases after the captain, rattling off questions about sailing to the Icelands, while Leo strikes up a conversation with Elixa—the wheat-haired Illusionári girl of seventeen who struck me as familiar on the ship. The seventh member of our party is Maryam, who glides with the grace of a dancer, her coil of brown hair swinging at her back like a pendulum. She watches me with a curious, if wary, stare. Forgoing a lamp, she lights up the back of our caravan with the pearly white scars of her hands.

Already I have been around more Robári on this trip than in my entire life. I have so many questions, but as we set off on our journey to the temple, I concentrate on keeping up. The way is steep, and I slip in the black sand that covers the path. Castian shoulders my pack for me. I keep pace at his side, the barest thing to let him know he isn't alone. None of us are.

For the longest time, the temple doesn't seem to get any closer, but when we finally reach the stone steps, it takes all my strength not to fall on my knees and kiss the ground. There is a murmur in the breeze, seeping right through me, down to my bones—magics. This is a sacred place of power and history. I have longed for a fraction of this sensation, to know that I am connected to something other than just myself.

I am not a wretched power that takes and takes and takes—perhaps I am something more.

I have a vague recollection of falling into a soft bed in a small stone room within the temple. My sleep is a continuous loop of the moment I dove into the crystal-clear waters of the Castinian Sea, the simple quiet of being submerged. Glittering fish and then a second splash. Castian smiling underwater. I have never seen him so buoyant, so happy. He swims to me, and even though we should be surfacing for air, we don't need to breathe. We only need each other. His mouth presses against mine, firm and sure, just as he kissed me in the belly of our ship—before I ruined it by telling him that I wanted his kiss in order to forget. I don't want to forget.

And then I plummet, falling straight through until I'm kicking and screaming in a void.

When I wake, I'm on the floor of the room, the linens tangled around my legs. I seem to have only slept for mere moments. As promised, training begins at sunrise. Captain Argi is at the threshold, staring at me with confusion and mild concern.

"Do you always fight with your pillow when you're dreaming?"

"I never dream," I confess, rubbing sleep from my eyes, "but that was very much a dream."

These rooms, originally made for clerics and priests who devoutly worshipped the goddess, house the pirates San Piedras when they return from a voyage—and now us. The furniture is simple but made with great care: a sturdy bed and a narrow table with a water basin. I splash my face with cold water and dress as the stern Moria pirate waits for me.

"Where are my friends?" I ask, tying laces.

"Maryam and Elixa have taken them to the sparring grounds."

"Sparring grounds? In a temple?"

"Long ago, before the Knife of Memory was more than a myth, the priests who lived here were guardians. Each of them would have had to fight." Captain Argi shrugs, and I realize she's holding two tin cups in her hands. She offers me one, and I inhale the rich dark smoke of black, bitter café.

"I thought the island was invisible." I scald the tip of my tongue but keep drinking.

"Virtually invisible," she amends. "Those stationed at the lighthouses are but the first line of defense."

I follow her through the wide halls burnished in pink-and-orange sunrise. The alman stone is so full of memories that it feels like it's whispering to me. I run my fingertips along the cool surface and feel the energy.

"I've never seen anything like this before."

"At the height of the kingdom of Memoria, all our temples were built of alman stone. What better way to honor the goddess than to give her a capsule of memories for her worship?"

We step into an enclosed garden. The air smells like salt and wisteria. White clouds gather overhead.

"The priests who lived on this island must have had strong legs," I say, panting as we trek to a rectangular sandpit enclosed by tall columns. Captain Argi barks a surprised laugh. She rolls up the sleeves of her red tunic to her elbows. Her curls spill over her shoulders like black and silver ribbons.

"So would you if you climbed this hill every day. Now, tell me. Who are you, Renata Convida?"

"I'm a Robári," I say.

She sucks her teeth, kicks off her boots, and walks barefoot in the black sandpit. I follow her lead, positioning myself in front of her.

"Who are you in *here*?" The captain taps her gut.

"I don't know what you want me to say."

"I want you to answer with your instinct."

Brown larks flutter on thin branches, and insects cluster around the wildflowers while Captain Argi circles me like a hawk. The same whorls of magic that have burned my hands look different on her, like delicate carvings instead of scars. They glow and dim against her tawny brown skin.

"How are you doing that?"

"I think of one memory at a time."

The idea of that leaves me dumbstruck for a moment. I turn my hand over. "You can identify your memories to your scars?"

"Scars?" She frowns at the word. "I suppose they are scars. I've never given them a name. Blessings. Markings. Simply memories."

My markings stop just above my wrists and they're thicker, raised and angry. "Why did this happen to me?"

"The easy answer is that this happened to you because they did not train you. But the real question is, why weren't you? The kingdom of Memoria had been weakened by civil war before the bloody

Fajardo lions, and then it was beaten and erased and starved. Plague. Murder. War. The king and justice wanted living weapons, and they started with children like you. It is immeasurably complicated trying to understand our history, Renata, but the only thing you need to know, the only thing that matters, is that this is not your fault. This was done to you. Now tell me, *who* are you?"

"I'm a killer. I'm a weapon." I choke on the emotion welling up in my throat. "I'm no one."

"That is what they tried to *make* you. That is not who you are."

"What else do you want me to say?"

"Who are you?" Captain Argi kicks the sand and paces around me fast, demanding. "Answer me!"

"I don't know!" A hammering sensation pounds at my temples. Cracks of lightning strip the landscape of color.

Captain Argi's laughter makes larks take flight. "If you want the Knife of Memory, you're going to have to face the parts of yourself that keep you up at night."

Who am I aside from a girl made a weapon, vengeance in the night? There are things I have never spoken out loud. Not even to Illan, who was my mentor. Not even to Dez, who was my everything. But in this ancient place, hidden in the middle of the sea, I tell Argiñe San Piedras everything because I *do* know who I am. I am just afraid it won't be enough.

"I lived in a log cabin in the woods with my parents," I begin, taking careful steps in the sand. "I strayed from home, and soldiers found me. They took me to Justice Méndez. I became the perfect doll, the perfect weapon."

My scars light up as I speak. "The first time I stole a memory the magics burned me. The first time I made a Hollow I cried for days, but then Justice Méndez gave me treats, and I quieted. Then I had to do it again."

I stop and stare at the grains of sand beneath my feet. I have paced a trail within the rectangle.

"Remind your body to breathe," Argi says, and signals for me to keep going.

"There was a shy boy in the palace. He was always dirty and alone like me—he's the one who helped me escape when the Whispers attacked. The world outside was on fire. Dez found me in the courtyard and took me to his father. He never left my side, not even when my magics were wild. But we changed, he and I, and we left each other. We became different people."

"Describe yourself before." Argi's alto voice is soothing, like a guiding light through the dark. "When your magics were wild."

"Everyone I touched, I hurt. I pulled memories without thinking. When I was thirteen, the elders kept me in isolation for three months, until I could be trained properly. I tried to cut out the power from my hands with nails I dug out of the walls. All I got was an infection."

My heart beats so fast I feel dizzy, but I keep going. My past is a dam burst open, an artery cut to bleed out. "It was then, in isolation, that I discovered the Gray. Thousands of stolen faces and voices haunted me. They'd emerge while I was awake. I thought I was seeing ghosts, but it was only the stolen lives. I never really dreamed after that."

"Why was this morning different?" Argi asks.

I close my eyes and see the crystalline sea and Castian's smile. That's how I know it was a dream—because we were both happy.

"It was years before I made another Hollow," I say, wanting to keep me and Castian private. "And it was Justice Méndez. Ever since then, my magics feel wild again. I've been able to see memories by simply touching a surface. Memories I couldn't have taken."

Argi studies my hands again. The wrinkles between her brow

pinch together in thought. "You mentioned something called the Gray. Is that where your memories go?"

"The elders used to tell me it was the curse of the Robári, but I never had another Robári to ask."

"Curse *them*," Argi spits out. "There have been stories of Moria going mad in the past, overuse of magics and the like. But here's my theory: Because you gathered so many memories as a child, before your power had matured, the only way to stop your mind from breaking apart was to create this locked room of memories. The Gray could have very well saved you."

I wince at the pinpricks of pain behind my eyelids, a reminder that the Gray is still there. "It doesn't always feel that way."

"We all have limits, and perhaps, creating a Hollow of Justice Méndez was yours. We were given the power of a goddess, but we are still breakable things. Your mind is a muscle. It demands conditioning and care." Her memory marks flit along her forearms like shooting stars as her brown eyes come alight with realization. "Who you are is there, beneath the vault, and all we have to do is bring her out."

The ground seems to waver beneath me. "How?"

"We're going to destroy the Gray."

19

"I DIDN'T THINK IT WAS SOMETHING THAT COULD BE DESTROYED," I SAY.

Argi drops to her knees and begins to dig in the black sand. She glances up through her long lashes. "You created that wall. You can tear it down."

"But *how*?"

"The Knife of Memory requires complete access to who you are. The very root of you. We will chip away at the wall, piece by piece, until it is weak enough to break." The elder Robári plucks a pale, translucent crystal and cradles it in her palm. Unused alman stone. "This training ground was where Robári children dug through the sand to find their own crystals. You're going to return each and every memory that does not belong to you."

It is as if she has slammed her fists into my stomach. Return each and every memory? I blink away the frustration that burns in my eyes.

"I—I can do that?"

Argi's face softens with pity and regret, but only for a moment. She asks, "How many Robári were in your Whispers camp?"

"I was usually the only one. There was another boy four years ago, but his magics were weak, and he died on a mission. The elders always kept us separate."

She lets go of a deep, slow breath. "The damned fools. No matter—in this moment, what's most important is making room in your mind."

"And this will help me wield the Knife of Memory?" I ask tentatively.

Captain Argi's gaze sharpens on mine. "Claiming the Knife of Memory requires a test of self. Only Robári can wield it, but you must be in control of your mind or it won't work."

"What happens if it doesn't work?"

Argi's lips part, and she shakes her head slightly. "You won't return."

She waits for me to speak. What can I say? I knew that there would be a cost to wield the Knife's power and set the kingdom on the path of peace after ridding the world of Fernando.

"How do we start?" I ask.

"Do you know that feeling that builds when you're ready to enter someone's mind? It's a vibration, deep in the marrow. It's your power coming to life. Use it. Find a memory you wish to relinquish, and transpose it in this stone."

She places it in the heart of my palm. My eyes blur. I never, not once in a million years, would have thought this possible. What other knowledge of the Moria was lost when our people scattered, when the kingdom was reduced to ruin and rubble and everything was taken? Who might I have been if I hadn't lived with these stolen lives in my head for a decade? I listen to the sounds of the clearing, inhale the sharp scent of grass and the sea. Faces and sounds crowd all at once, and a jabbing pressure at the center of my forehead brings me to my knees.

"There are too many."

"Fixate on one."

I crouch beside her and close my eyes, listening to the jagged melody of her voice. One of tax collector Vernal's memories comes into view, and I settle in.

> I knock on the door, but no one is home. I walk around back, into the courtyard. I hear a shuffling sound followed by a whimper.
>
> "I know you're in there!" I shout.
>
> I stand aside, and Telmo kicks open the door. A man shouts and clutches his child. There is no time for this. If we do not fill the wagons by tonight, then it is my head on the line. I wait at the door as Telmo ransacks the house. Six pesos and one pesito.

A strange sensation tickles the inside of my skull. My eyes flutter open, and the stone in my hand pulses with a new memory.

"I could have done this all along." My voice breaks. Anger claws its way up my spine. "I lost so much time."

"You're here now. Your mind has to heal, Renata." Argi guides my fingers until I am cleaving my way into the cold earth and finding new crystals. "Again."

I sit and hold the alman stone between my palms. Excavating memories one by one burns my skin, retracing a past I wanted to forget. I see them all:

A boy runs through the maze of the palace dungeons, the passages get more and more narrow.

An old woman on the streets of Citadela Crescenti throws rice in the air after a wedding procession.

The horrific screams of a man unable to move, and Justice Méndez, the last thing he sees before his sight goes dark.

A servant girl gathering Prince Castian's sheets and bringing them to her face, inhaling deeply.

Dissidents waving the ancient flag of the queendom of Tresoros cut down in a dense forest.

A festival under the stars set on fire by the Second Sweep.

A rebel fighting on the streets of Riomar.

Someone running over a field of dead rebels.

The howling cry of a girl watching her entire city burn.

A priestess standing at the ruins of her temple.

On and on. Memory after memory. Each and every moment rushes out of my mind and into the alman stones I dig from the sandpit. My nails are coated in fine black and gray dust, cracked and ruined. My index finger bleeds where the cuticle is torn and blood bubbles along the seam of a cut. I wipe it on my tunic.

"That's enough for today," Argi says, resting a hand on my shoulder. "It will get easier."

"I don't feel different," I confess.

What was I expecting? The Lady of Shadows herself to emerge from the temple to give me a pat on my shoulder? Light to halo me as I transcend into a new form? Instead, I am sweaty and shaking, sand peppered along my arms and, well, everywhere. I fall onto my back and take fast, shallow breaths.

"Even the Lady couldn't undo your trauma in half a day, girl," the pirate scolds me.

"What do we do with these stones?" I hold one up and watch the soft, pulsing light within.

"Anything you want. Toss them to the sea. Drop them in the ponds around the temple. Leave them scattered here. Either way, they will serve as offerings to the Lady."

I stack several stones into a tower. "Who taught you this?"

Argi grunts as she takes a seat beside me. She tips her waterskin into her mouth and then offers it to me. The mineral water from the rushing waterfall behind the temple is the best thing my parched lips have ever tasted.

"I learned on my own," says the captain. "My father was a foot soldier in the Memoria army. He died fighting the Icelandian invaders and never got to meet me. He was a Robári, too. My mother died soon after I was born from a withering sickness. By then, the borders were shifting. Robári, already rare, were usually employed by King Umberto of Memoria.

"When I was thirteen, I was on my way to the palace when I stopped in a town bordering Puerto Leones and Memoria. The apothecura needed an apprentice, and I stayed and learned her trade. It wasn't until I met Illan that I would have access to some of the oldest books in the Memoria archives, and meet other Robári like myself."

The trembling in my bones begins to pass as she talks. There's something soothing about her voice, the way she recounts her story, letting her scars—markings—come alive. I wonder, how does she choose which ones she keeps on her skin?

"How did you meet Illan?" I ask.

Captain Argi puffs out a laugh. "Like all great love stories, he rescued me from my jail cell."

"Jail?" I sit up on my elbows. "What were you accused of?"

"A woman brought her ailing child to my apothecura. The babe was born with a weak heart that no form of magics or medicine could cure. The mother grieved. She accused me of using my 'curse' to hurt her child. Using our power wasn't forbidden then, especially not along a border town. But there I was, along with other accused Moria, when Illan rescued us."

I think of the orders doled out by the justice condemning Moria magics. Slowly, over the years, they have vilified us. "How old were you then?"

"Sixteen. I thought that no one would come for me. They didn't torture Moria yet, not in a backwater village like San Lita. We had bigger problems like feeding the population during the worst drought of the century.

"Even then there was a network of Moria. We'd been living under Puerto Leones rule for some time, dispersed into different parts of the kingdom. Illan was one of King Umberto's ambassadors to Puerto Leones. But really, Illan had been building the Whispers Rebellion with a chosen few, dreaming of the day Memoria would be returned to its glory."

Her laugh is bitter, but there's also a deep sense of loss and heartache. "We were so young then, and he was perfect. I loved his mind, his passion. He offered me a position with the Memoria embassy, and I took it. I never wanted our people to have to endure what I did. He brought me to the palace, and I was put to work."

Something cold passes through me. "Were you part of the Hand of Moria?"

The Hand of Moria is King Fernando's collection of Moria magics—one for each power. At least it was. He experimented on them, and he would have had me, too.

"No," she says darkly. "That would come later. I was assigned to protect Princess Galatea. She was only a few years older, and we were both Robári. I was the one who shepherded love letters between her and Fernando. Sometimes I wonder what would have happened if I had simply said no, if I had obeyed and made sure she was the picture of propriety—but anyone who went within mere feet of them knew they were like comets burning through the sky toward each other. The world was collateral damage. I suppose no one could have truly known what was to come. I buried her here."

"I saw her," I confess.

Argi tilts her head, a question in her eyes.

"When we first set sail I was overcome with a memory that I never took. At least, there's no way, is there? The other times these occurrences happened, I blamed it on the thousands of anonymous faces in my mind. But I still felt different, like something within me was breaking."

"You're stronger than you know, Renata," Argi says. "There's nothing wrong with you. Your power is simply attempting to grow, but because of this creation of yours—this Gray—it can't. It's rare, but there are Robári who are so rooted to their power, so strong, that they can see the impressions of memory in an ordinary object. Tell me when each occurrence happened."

I recount the market, Little Luzou, and the Queen's mansion. For each one she has an explanation.

"An impression when you brushed against a market stall. The stone steps. The column."

I shake my head. "What about Galatea? It's not very well likely that she was on our ship once."

Argi's smile is wide. She inhales the air and looks at me as if I've just told her of a miracle. "You saw Galatea's battle on the sea. Its winds, its droplets. All of us leave behind something on this world, Renata. Some of us can simply see it more than others."

"That doesn't make sense," I say, examining my own scars. My Robári marks. "I'm not rooted to my power that way. I've tried to get rid of it more than once. That isn't strength; it's weakness."

"Perhaps there is a part of you that has accepted who you are, and the rest of you has yet to realize it." Captain Argi reaches down and gathers a handful of sand. "Memories are slippery things. As hard to hold on to as grains of sand. But not for Robári. Illan should have known better. He failed you."

I want to argue with her, but she's right. I was so grateful that he gave me a home that I didn't realize I was simply being used in other ways.

"Do you ever regret leaving Illan?"

"Never." She looks up at the clouds, twisting and molding themselves into new shapes, always in the midst of change. "That is, until you told me he was killed. Now we'll never have the opportunity to see which one of us was right in the end."

I laugh, knowing that my old mentor would feel the same way. She laughs with me, and suddenly, I start to feel the absence of the memories I gave up, and my laughter turns into sobs. I cry like something has split within me, and the wave of emotions I buried for so long bursts forward. I have tried to make myself small and likable and normal. I have tried to be someone who is not me. I have tried to be a weapon again and again because how could anyone want me or love me if I was anything but?

When my tears stop, she does the strangest thing. Captain Argiñe San Piedras hugs me.

"This isn't over." She brushes my hair back and anchors me in place. "I'm only going to ask you this once. Are you sure you want this path?"

"I do."

She tips my chin up, and I dry my tears. "Then there is someone I want you to meet."

20

When we walk back the way we came, past tall overgrown hedges and rows of apple trees, I hear a soft whisper in the wind. A voice that has only begun to grow louder since I have arrived in Isla Sombras.

The temple of the Lady of Shadows and Whispers echoes every step, every breath, and even the wild beating of my own heart. Light streams in from the ceiling, turning the alman stone and marble into a shimmering plane where her statue is the focus. I have seen the Lady depicted on the inside of armor before battle, and in two-foot sculptures in hidden sanctuaries, but I have never seen this—a monument of her that seems to stretch up to the sky. A halo of stars encircles her head, and long waves of hair reach down to her feet. In one outstretched hand she holds an orb, and in the other, a knife that can only be the one of myth.

"Isla Sombras is where the Lady chose to sever her immortality," Captain Argi says. "The first Moria order who lived here erected this temple in her name."

"This is where you've been all along," I whisper.

My words carry, and Argi gives me a temperate smile. "She is everywhere, and she is always with you."

I want to deny it because I have felt alone for so long, but then a chorus of laughter spills from nearby. I follow the sound outside, to the sprawling front lawn, where my friends are making their way back from their day of training with Elixa and Maryam. As they get closer, I take in the blooming bruises on their bare arms. Leo uses a wooden staff to walk. Cas is smiling as he talks with Elixa. She's loud and boisterous, communicating with her entire body. After just a few moments, Castian looks up at me leaning against a column. How does he always seem to know where I am?

I wave and bite my bottom lip to quell the urge to run to him and share every single extraordinary thing I did today.

"Where did you learn to fight that way?" Castian asks Elixa.

Elixa rests a wooden sword against her shoulder. "A retired Luzouan warrior on the *Madre del Mar*."

"Is it retiring if Josefino still taught aboard our ship for another twenty years?" Argi asks, taking the temple steps down and embracing her girls in greeting.

"*Josefino Edin*?" Leyre asks, stopping suddenly. Her green eyes go wide, and she stumbles on her words. "He's a legend in my empire. All right, take me back to the ship now please."

Argi chuckles softly. "Alas, he rests with the Great Tortuga. But his daughter has returned to Empirio Luzou."

"You raise warriors, though you do not fight," Castian asks her. "Why?"

The captain steps a few paces toward him, leaving little room between them. The prince of Puerto Leones is a head taller, but Argi's presence somehow dwarfs him. "To protect ourselves from your family."

"When Castian is king, you won't need to fear the Fajardos," Leo says, ever the diplomat.

Castian flashes a smile, but his blue-green eyes darken with doubt. "When my father is gone, it will be a new day for us all."

"Let's start by washing your filthy hides in time for supper, eh?" Argi slaps his back in good cheer and guides us around the grounds and back to the living quarters.

Leo is the first to dive into the bathing pools. The steaming water is piped in from nearby hot springs using a mechanism I've never seen before. I try to imagine the life of the clerics who chose to dedicate their lives to protecting the Knife of Memory. Isolated, but at peace, they'd wake up every morning surrounded by the healing quiet of green hills and the sea.

After I wash, dress, and arrive in the kitchens to help, Maryam bandages my broken nails and cuts with a manzanilla balm and strips of linen. Leyre and Castian are tasked with preparing the turkey, while Elixa and Leo exchange musical numbers as they chop onions and garlic.

"Imagine living on that ship and only having heard one of Delgado's operas. And *The Nymph's Reply to the Huntsman* isn't even his best work. You sweet, deprived child." Leo sighs, eyes glistening with onion tears.

"Why do you look so pretty when you cry?" Maryam asks, genuinely confused.

"He was a stage actor," I say.

"If I'd only learned all your exhaustive fighting techniques when I was cast as Capitán Brava in *For the Love of the Maiden Cuerva*," Leo preens.

Elixa gasps. "Tell us everything!"

Castian and Leyre return in that moment with a decapitated and plucked turkey. He chuckles and says, "Oh dear, he's got a new audience."

"You poor souls." Leyre offers condolences, but winks at Leo.

And then he sings the ballad of a sea captain who fell in love with the maiden of death. I can't help but glance at Castian. I can't remember the last time he smiled this way, not peering from the corners of his eyes for danger, and not wearing the illusion of the arrogant, murderous prince. He's an ordinary man among his friends.

Then I think, *No. He'll never be ordinary, and neither will I.*

It was a pretty thought for a while, though.

"You'll have to take off your ring," Maryam says, her sure voice pulling me back to the present. She gently taps my index finger, where blood has begun to scab over the cut.

"Some of those alman stones are like spearheads," I say.

The young Robári waits for me to take the emerald wedding ring off before she coats my finger with a sweet salve. I almost forgot I was still wearing Castian's ring. He turns to me, and the look on his face is unreadable. I wish he would say something, but instead, he waits for me.

Heat slithers up my spine and settles across my chest as I offer it back to him. "This belongs to you."

"You're *not* truly married?" Maryam asks, and suddenly I realize how young she is, even if she's sixteen.

Elixa gives her fellow pirate a warning glance. "*Maryam.*"

"It's quite all right," Castian says with a crooked smile. "I'm sure we're both relieved we're no longer undercover."

I remember watching him tie and untie knots on the deck of our ship. That's what my insides feel like as he plucks the ring from my palm. I force myself to laugh.

"Don't worry, Lion Cub," Leyre says, wiping her forehead with the back of her wrist. "We'll find you a right and proper queen consort. There's a woman in my former unit, heiress to a banana fortune—"

"If you want a marriage of convenience," Leo says, twisting the cork from a jug of what looks like cider, "I'm fairly certain your step-mother's cousin is eligible, as they're all out of princesses. Though that will make for a rather awkward Sun Festival once you depose your father."

Castian is surprisingly good humored about the subject of his future queen. Meanwhile I'm sure the reason there's a ringing in my ear is because I'm screaming inside.

"And here I thought you harbored such ambitions for yourself, Leo," Castian says, leaning against the wall, letting the words fall off him like deflected arrows.

Everyone laughs, but Leo rolls his eyes. "Hardly. I prefer my men with a dash more charm, and you're *far* too moody."

Everyone continues to flirt with the idea of Castian's future, going as far as planning his next three political marriages. I join in the game because if I stop and think for too long, I will remember that yesterday I let myself contemplate a future with Castian. There is no future—when I claim the Knife of Memory, I will face two paths: I will either pay the cost of its magics or I'll never return.

When night falls, Elixa ignites torches in the courtyard. Our food is arranged on a long wooden table. Garbanzos and tomatoes dusted in pink salt and coated in chopped herbs. Black and purple olives drenched in oil. Bread slathered in honey and spicy pepper flakes. The turkey is golden brown and stuffed with sweet onions, and after a day of training, we devour the meal and wash everything down with a cold pear cider.

Elixa is curious about our travels, but Argi interrupts by discussing where the pirates have been and how their next voyage will be to explore the unknown worlds, chasing other Moria myths.

"Why not settle here?" Castian asks, his gaze roaming the courtyard lit by torchlight and fireflies.

"There is no farmable land and but a single river and lake for fresh water. Isla Sombras was a place for pilgrimage and worship. It was where we trained future generations of Moria priests and holy orders. Now it is a refuge. But it is ours."

"How do you account for population growth?" Leyre asks. "What happens to families on your ship?"

"We can only sustain so many," Argi explains. "Those who want to expand their broods have the option of settling in ports with open borders like Luzou. The rest, so long as they are on the ship, drink irvena tea until they're ready to decide. Speaking of which—" Argi gestures to Maryam, who runs inside the kitchen and returns with a brewed pot.

Everyone sips their tea, and I can't help but notice the blush that creeps up Castian's neck and ears.

"Don't forget we trade off in seasons between the ship and the island," Elixa says in her sweet, high-pitched voice.

"But," Maryam says tenuously, "that will change when you are king, yes? We will be allowed to return?"

Castian sits up taller. The humor in his eyes morphs into an earnest stare. "On my word, whatever that is worth to your captain, I will keep my promise to your people. Our people," he amends.

Argi doesn't discourage the girl, but she drinks from her pint instead of acknowledging Castian's vow.

"Were you born on the ship?" Leyre asks Elixa.

The girl shakes her head, round cheeks turning pink. She touches a pendant I didn't notice before, tucked in her tunic. A tiny gold seashell. Reaching for Maryam's hand, they thread their fingers together and share the look of young love. "After my citadela was ransacked, my sister and I tried to hike up the coast, but we were separated. I stole a fishing raft and was out at sea for a day before Mar spotted me from the crow's nest, where she likes to read the stars. I don't even know *how* she saw me, but here we are."

"I'm slowly starting to believe in impossible things," I say.

Beside me, Castian rests his forearms on the table. I brush my little finger against his. He's still for a moment. Then he covers my hand with his. We are pressed skin to skin, our thighs touching. Every time I focus on it, I feel my pulse race because neither of us moves away from the other.

"Captain," he says softly. "When you captured our yacht, you said something to me. How did you know that I was an Illusionári?"

Argi's eyes light up with memory, the glow skating from up her arm along a river of markings. She's quiet for a long time, and we cling to that silence until she finally breaks it. "After what happened here with Cebrián, I fled Isla Sombras. Made my way back to Puerto Leones, where Illan kept me in a safe house. Your father wasn't far behind. Rumors had spread of his elopement and his sudden voyage. While he was away, his family spread lies about his wife to keep her identity secret. When Fernando returned, he slaughtered his entire family and had the Moria royals murdered. Illan assured me his rage would quell, and I waited there.

"Over the course of weeks, I realized things were changing. There seemed to be no memory of the Moria royal family or Galatea as Fernando's first wife. Not even among the Moria. It was like she'd been erased from the world. I believe no one but those of us on that expedition remembered her."

Our silence magnifies the sounds of the night.

"Months passed," Argi continues. "There was even a moment where I almost believed I'd made up the entire voyage. We waited for Fernando to strike against our people again. Instead, his patricide was forgotten when he announced his wedding to Penelope of the Sól Abene family."

Castian leans forward at the mention of his mother's name. Argi sips her cider and rubs her lips together. "I began my network of Moria spies while Illan still pretended to be loyal to the king. When Queen Penelope had you, Castian," Argi says, "she discovered that you were an Illusionári. There must have been Moria blood in her family, though she did not have magics herself. She confided in Illan, and together they schemed. I grew tired of the Whispers and their inaction. I bought a ship and convinced Penelope to leave with us. She was afraid, and by then she was pregnant with your brother. Illan convinced her to stay. They devised a new plan to keep your magics secret."

Castian blinks away the emotion in his eyes and retracts his hand from mine. "Did the Knife change him?"

"That's difficult to say for certain." Argi takes a deep breath. "When King Jústo wouldn't sanction his marriage, Fernando eloped. When Galatea was murdered, Fernando tried to wield a sacred power that did not belong to him. When he failed to revive his love, Fernando slaughtered those responsible for her death. The Knife of Memory magnifies power, but it cannot change a person's heart."

"Are you worried it will change me?" I ask Castian.

His body goes rigid, and all I want to do is wrap my arms around him and tell him that I'm going to be fine. But looking at Cas, I see an anger I know is mirrored within my own heart. What if the Knife of Memory manipulates that into something terrible? I remember what Argi showed us on the ship—Fernando's desperate need to control life and death was the beginning of a long road of cruelties. What will make me different if I use the Knife to destroy him? What will it do to Castian when he kills his father?

"What if—" I begin. I can feel the absence of every memory I've culled and placed in alman stones today. "What if instead of erasing Fernando from existence, we show the kingdom who he really is?"

"Hmm," Argi rasps.

"Is it possible to create such an illusion?" Elixa asks her captain, considering the possibility. "The way you and Euria taught us has its limits."

Leyre's catlike eyes go from face to face. "But isn't the Knife of Memory divine?"

"You'd need a powerful platinum catalyst," Argi says, tugging her chin in thought. "Which the Knife does have in the hilt. And more alman stone to create the refracting light, as well as an Illusionári to stand with you."

"I will be with her," Castian says, then glances at me. "I will be with you."

"It could work." Argi grins and taps the surface of the table for luck. "Renata and I are working to make sure she is prepared to claim the Knife."

"What does that mean?" Leo asks. "You've said that before."

"The Knife of Memory requires a connection between itself and the Robári who claims it. Wielding it requires great power."

"I'll be ready," I say.

"Well, good," Elixa says, picking at the meat on the turkey bones, "because we were going easy on you today."

Leo chokes on his cider, and Cas gives him a gentle pat on the back.

"There's one thing you should know about sharing magics," Argi says, her eyes cut between Castian and me. "The projection requires trust. The question is, do you trust each other?"

I feel the pressure of his knee against mine. His eyes, so full of conflict, rake across my face. And together, we say, "Yes."

21

LATER THAT NIGHT, WHEN I CAN'T SLEEP, I WALK BAREFOOT DOWN THE HALLS OF the temple and trace my fingers along the smooth stone. Though there are no lamps, the warm glow of memory within the stone lights my path. I make my way back to the kitchen and find that I'm not the only person who is awake.

Castian startles when he sees me, very much a mouse caught nibbling on cheese, which is exactly what he's doing. He's in a pair of sleeping trousers. His tunic is inside out, as if he threw it on in a hurry.

"Hungry still?" I ask, sitting across from him on the rickety table.

"Ravenous." He finishes eating the cheese, drizzled with honey, and licks his fingers. I grab a clay mug and pour myself water from the pitcher. I remember the two of us as little kids sneaking off into the palace kitchens. My breath hitches as the memory lights up on my index finger, where my memory marks are thinning into delicate silver whorls.

"Nati?" Cas reaches for me.

"I'm all right." I put up a hand and smile.

His hair is tousled around his shoulders. There's something so vulnerable about him, and the more I look at him, the longer I hold my breath.

After a stretch of comfortable silence, I ask, "What's keeping you up, Castian?"

"Other than knowing the Whispers and my kingdom's army are marching toward each other and we may not arrive in time to stop it?"

"We will," I say, surprising even myself.

He exhales, but his posture is still tense. "I've always known there were things about my father that I would never understand. That there were secrets there. But I did not imagine this. It's like he's two different people."

"I used to think that about you."

He looks up, like I've struck him.

"I only mean that you lived under an illusion. And the man you are is different from the prince the kingdom knows."

Cas runs a hand through his gold waves. "My father would have killed me if he knew the truth. My mother, for all her faults, tried to protect me and Dez. I'm beginning to understand that, perhaps."

I break off a piece of bread going stale and drizzle honey on it, then lick the excess off my thumbs. "It startled me how much Dez looks like your father when he was younger."

Castian scoffs. "I think my brother would murder us both if we said that to him."

I laugh and remember how Cas asked me in Acesteña to tell

him about Dez. I couldn't do it then. But after the confrontation with Dez in the Little Luzou marina, something inside me broke and relinquished the guilt in my heart tied to him.

"When I was about twelve," I say, plucking a grape from the bowl between us, "a group of boys invented a game called wreck the Robári. It involved finding anything they could throw—large rocks, bottles, even a very big, very rotten pumpkin once. They'd aim these things at me when I walked from the dormitories to the training grounds."

Castian's face turns to horror, then anger. He begins to curse their family lines.

"It gets better," I say, somehow unbothered by the occurrence anymore. "When Dez found out what was happening, he made a list of every single boy. Then he filled their waterskins with his own urine."

Cas chokes on a grape and slaps the table. "Truly?"

"Illan gave him six licks in public, one for every boy. Dez didn't even cry—he laughed the entire time, which is terrifying in its own right."

"And here I thought court was ruthless," Cas says, shaking his head. "I know he's my brother, but that's disgusting."

"He grew out of it," I continue. "Mostly. He had this thing he'd do to every king's guard he'd beat. He'd relieve them of their sword, raise it, and just before landing a killing blow, he'd spare their lives and say, *Remember that it was a Moria bestae who spared your life.*"

Cas bites his bottom lip and sighs. "He kept the sword, didn't he?"

"Naturally."

"I used to feel sorry for the soldiers who returned to me with their reports after facing him."

"When did you find out that he was your brother?" I ask.

Cas touches the scar on the left side of his rib. A hot flash spreads across my body as I remember touching the twin of that scar on Dez. "During Riomar. I wanted to be alone after the battle. I had to relive every life I took. I hated the destruction of the day, while my men wished to celebrate. And the next thing I knew—"

I have this memory. Dez shared it with me. "Dez was climbing over your balcony and challenging you to a duel to the death."

Cas shuts his eyes, as if he would like to banish the incident. "You and Dez have that in common at least. And neither of you has defeated me."

I feel my mouth hang open with shock. When Cas taps my chin closed, frustration and desire coils in my belly.

"I saw the medallion he was wearing, and it was identical to mine. A gift from our father when we were born. Dez had his the day I thought he drowned. Then Illan arrived. I recognized him from the palace and I knew. I *knew* in my gut that my brother hadn't died. I spent months trying to piece together what happened."

"I'm sorry, Cas."

"So am I, Nati." He rips another grape from the cluster. Rolls it between his fingers.

I get an idea and rest my hands on the table in front of him, palm side up. "Can I try something?"

He nods and reaches for me without question.

I pull memories, only this time, they're my own. The heat of my magics move in soft lines across my skin, calling forth a series of memories of Andrés, the lost prince of Puerto Leones. Dez, commander of the Whispers Rebellion. I share my memories of the boy I loved. The man he was before his world shattered. The man I hope he still can be. Joy and anger. Purpose. Defeat. Hope. It's all there.

When I pull away, our fingers remain intertwined.

"Are you still in love with him?" Cas whispers.

"I don't know."

"I shouldn't have asked."

I trace my thumbs along the inside of his wrists, where his pulse is frantic. "Can you still love someone who breaks your heart?"

"Yes," he says softly.

"Then I do. I love Dez. Part of me always will." I swallow hard. "But so much has happened so quickly. We aren't the same people. Right now the idea of love is a luxury."

The whorls of my power extend up my left wrist in patterns that remind me of a cresting wave. My power *is* changing. Only this time it isn't Justice Méndez or Illan forcing me to manipulate my magics—I'm controlling it.

He leaps to his feet, watching the light course through my skin with panic. "Are you hurt?"

"I'm all right, Cas." I stand and brush the crescent scar on his face. "But I should go to bed."

"You go," he says. "I can't sleep."

I recall the one night we slept in the same bed in Acesteña. I woke up nestled in his arms. "When was the last time you rested?"

His thumb grazes the raised skin of my Robári marks. "That night. With you."

"Then let's go to sleep, Cas."

For a moment, his eyes trace down the skin of my neck, the open laces of the man's tunic Maryam left me to sleep in. He nods softly, and we walk hand in hand to my room. Heat ignites between our palms, right where our matching blood-pact scars cut. We lie down, facing each other. I draw the linens up over our legs. His lashes flutter, and he exhales.

"Good night, Cas," I whisper.

He drifts, uneasily, as if he's fighting the exhaustion in his body before he allows himself to truly rest.

At the start of our journey, I fantasized how easy it would be to rid myself of him—the Bloodied Prince who occupied so much of my hatred. Now, when I know our time together is coming to an end, I am overcome with a sadness I haven't quite felt before. *Can you still love someone who breaks your heart? Yes.*

As I follow into sleep, a delicate light wakes me for a moment. It's coming from me, a new silver coil of memory etching itself on the bare skin over my heart.

22

I NEVER BELIEVED I'D STEP FOOT ON LAND THAT WASN'T PUERTO LEONES TERRI-
tory, but here I am on a sprawling hill surrounded by people I want
to call friends. I shut my eyes against the warmth of the sun, and
when I do, my own mother's face appears. I call her memory to
me—a woman whose black hair and coloring I share. She's in the
kitchen grinding herbs into a paste, and I watch, awestruck by her
magic. This is a memory I keep. This is a memory that carves its
mark in the notch between my clavicles.

"There," Argi says, pleased with my progress. Alman stones
full of stolen pasts litter the lawn. "Hold on to it. Now, Castian—"

Though I can't see him just yet, I can imagine him standing a
little bit taller at my side, his serious countenance short of becoming
a glower as he listens to Argi's instructions.

"Illusionári are connected to alman stone in a different way from Robári. Our magics are the only ones that can cull the memories captured within, but you can latch on to those images and magnify them through the crystals—so long as you and Renata are in tandem."

Someone snickers, Leyre, I think. The laughter is silenced by Argi's sharp clap of her hands.

"First, Renata, you will share your memory, and then Castian, you usher that image through the crystal. Go on."

I blink open my eyes. Our training meadow is bleached of color by the midday sun. Cas edges closer to me, and with every step he takes, my face grows warmer. His blue-green eyes are filled with purpose, but he bites his bottom lip, the only hint that perhaps he isn't entirely sure of himself.

"Ready?" I ask.

He nods and extends his palms to me. I brush my fingertips along his calluses. I remember thinking once how coarse his hands were for a prince. I close my eyes and try to pull a perfectly pleasant memory of the ocean or exploring the woods behind the rebel fortress of San Cristóbal. But I'm close enough to smell the sweat on his skin, and instead I offer up the memory of him standing naked on the sandbar.

Castian's lips quirk, and his voice is low at my ear. "Is that what you see when you think of me, Nati?"

I raise my chin and squint my frustration. "I'm *trying* to focus."

"Don't let me distract you."

I retract the memory and wade back into my mind. I could do this yesterday. But now that everyone is watching and Castian is holding me this way, all my thoughts turn to him. And then I find the perfect memory—the night we danced at the Sun Festival. His eyes fly open. I don't want to share the horrors of my past with our audience, and those that are good I'd very much rather keep to myself. But this moment is a place in between.

Castian projects the memory through the prisms of the alman stone onto the stretch of green lawn before us. King Fernando is leading me onto the dance floor when Castian cuts in. I didn't want to notice his beauty then, his golden mane crowned by a circlet, the way he waited for me to meet his eyes. I remember the rage I felt that day because I still thought that he'd killed Dez. As I watch us glide across the lawn, I let that anger go.

The image fractures, and Elixa claps her hands. "You look lovely all dressed up, Ren."

"Thank you," Leo and I answer at the same time.

Cas and I try again, this time with the stolen memories. Violent fires and weddings. Faces I begin to recognize as rebels captured by the justice. For a long time I focus on those. If I let myself only think of Castian, then I'm afraid I will forget the reason we aligned in the first place, even if it hurts. When Argi decides we've had enough, I fall on the grass and dig my fingers into the dirt. My skin is hot from the sun and the burn of magics. The welcome cool grounds me.

"Captain, can you choose where those light markings go?" Leo asks. "For instance, if you were upset at someone, but you wanted to save the memory for later, could you put it in a—uhm—*delicate* place no one would ever see?"

Argi barks a laugh. "Why, of course. All the memories of my second husband are on my left cheek."

Castian frowns, confused, as he looks at the Moria pirate captain. "But there's nothing on your cheek."

"Oh, he *is* precious, isn't he?" Argi chuckles and shoots a wink at me.

Realizing the pirate's double meaning, Castian mutters a curse and shakes his head as we laugh at his expense.

"I can't wait to see King Fernando's face when you perform your little trick for the entire nation," Leyre says, stretching her legs in preparation of her training.

"First they have to perfect their *little trick*," Argi says. "I'd be a fool to let you return to the mainland before then."

"We'll do it," Castian says like a dark promise.

"Is this how all Moria were trained?" I ask Argi.

"Once." Argi picks at a spread of food we brought with us. "I remember how fascinated Fernando was with our techniques. He wanted to control his own Moria army. Before this so-called Hand of Moria you told me about, there was the council provided by ambassadors of Memoria."

I sit up and brush the dirt from my hands. Castian offers me an apple and I catch it in the air. "The one Illan was on?"

Argi hisses a curse between her teeth. "At first, Illan wanted to play the diplomat, show the Leonesse that Moria were capable of controlling their powers. But that was never enough for a king who wanted control of that power. Imagine a phalanx of Ventári at your disposal who can see your opponent's every move. A front line of Illusionári trapping the enemy in illusions so real their very hearts could stop in the battlefield. A fleet of Persuári assuaging the enemy to drop their weapons, or have them fall on their own swords if they did not want peace. Robári snipers and spies who could erase the memories of all who witness your crimes."

Argi shakes her head, but I catch the dozens of memory lights that flicker up her arm. "I suppose the only solace now is that most of our master strategists and teachers are either dead or on the *Madre del Mar* living their final days in peace."

"We can teach them," Elixa says with a bright fervor. "We can fight with them, can't we?"

"The only thing you will do," Argi tells her, "is whip these pampered Leonesse into shape."

Leyre scoffs. "I'm only half Leonesse, and if you served your year in the Luzouan navy, you'd never utter the word pampered in your life."

"Girls, take over," Argi says.

Castian stands beside Leyre, picks up a polished wooden staff, and sinks into a fighting stance to spar with Maryam and Elixa. They are equally matched in speed and maneuvers. However, Castian and Leyre have the advantage of experience with true battle. They've taken everything the young Moria pirates have taught them in their short sessions and used the knowledge to anticipate each strike. Maryam manages to get a hit across Castian's ribs, but he shakes it off and grins as if he enjoys the pain. It is such a contrast to the shy, soft smile we shared when we woke up curled against each other at daybreak.

"I can see why you have taken on this fight together," Argi tells me as we watch them train. "He must take after his mother because I see none of Fernando in this boy. Perhaps his passion? But where Fernando's came from a need to control things, Castian's seems to be the need to free himself and others."

There's a moment when Cas takes his eyes off his opponent and finds me watching him. Maryam uses that opportunity to swing and strikes him across the face. I wince, and a dark voice that sounds incredibly like Dez whispers at my ear. *What if that had been a real sword? He'd be dead. Your prince would be gone.*

Argi gives me a long look of knowing. "Have care with your heart, Renata."

"What do you mean?"

"I mean that you can't save the kingdom and save your love. Times such as these don't allow for matters of the heart."

I frown but say nothing.

On the other side of her, Leo purses his lips. "But times are always like this. You still married. *Twice*."

"I also left when Illan and I chose different paths. As for my second marriage, well, it's not my fault he couldn't handle his alacrán venom."

A look of terror passes between Leo and me.

"As if you're the only one who can tell a joke, Leo." Argi cackles. But her eyes crinkle as a memory lights up around her wedding band. "I loved Illan's brilliant, arrogant face with everything I had. I am glad he raised the son he always wanted, even if I disagree with the means with which he procured the boy."

I think of how different things would have been if both princes had been raised as brothers. Would Dez have learned his courage amid fire? Would Castian have learned kindness out of loneliness?

That is when Leo, ever the romantic, speaks his truth. "Pardon me, Captain, but your heart is open. Why else would a fearless pirate queen have dedicated her life to her people's survival?"

"I like you, Leonardo," Argi says in that scratchy voice of hers. "But you're wrong. Fear was the gift the world gave me. I pray I can give my people better than what I knew. That is how I keep them alive, and I want Renata to prepare herself for what is coming. Now in order for this gambit to work, the Bloodied Prince and Renata must create an illusion so seamless that the rest of the world falls away."

We nod and silently watch Castian and Leyre leap and strike their way against smaller, younger, but equally worthy opponents.

"What do you say, two pesos that my girls destroy your compatriots in the next match?"

Castian and the others return to where we sit, panting and drenched in sweat. "Two pesos?" he asks. "I should feel insulted."

Leyre snatches the waterskin before he can grab it. "The only thing that's insulting is how you drag your feet when you turn."

His eyes roll skyward. "My technique is flawless."

I shrug. "*I* beat you."

"The Whispers taught you to fight dirty." Castian's eyes flash with a mixture of anticipation and challenge.

"I still beat you."

Castian drops his staff at my feet. "Then I must defend my honor."

I flash a smile, accepting his challenge. Leo can barely contain himself as he hands me a wooden sword and a string to tie my hair back. Elixa sits giddily beside her captain and claps her hands. That sense of familiarity returns for a moment, and then Castian fills my line of sight.

We bow.

I think back to the training grounds at the Whispers' stronghold. Yes, we had to fight dirty at times, but we were also outnumbered, and using our magics was always a risk. The goal was to survive.

Castian and I spar across the meadow. He leans back, narrowly missing my blow, and flashes a smile that cleaves me down the center. Perhaps Argi was right. He has a predatory approach, never taking his eyes off me. My only advantage is using my speed to his size. I roll and pop up behind him. As if he expected that, he kneels and blocks my sword with his own, leaving me exposed. He has the killing blow, but he doesn't take it, and I trip up his feet. He yanks me to the ground as he falls, but I've got the upper hand, and I press my sword against his throat.

He raises his palms in surrender. Straddled on top of him, I feel the moment desire sparks in his eyes as he breathes hard beneath me. He lets go of a low grunt as I press the weight of my sword a little harder.

"Yield," I demand.

He shuts his eyes. He could easily flip us around and overpower me. But he doesn't. "I yield."

Leyre and Argi hand Leo a couple of coins. Now it's my turn to be insulted.

"Renata," Argi says, her café-dark eyes evaluating the scene before her with concern. "A word?"

Argi leads me down the hill where a gravel road begins. The wind sings a pleasant hum, but when I realize the ocean air is thick with humidity and the thinnest cypress tree branches don't move, I know it isn't the wind at all, but a voice. It calls to me from wherever this gravel road leads to.

"You can hear it," Argi says, her voice heavy.

"Is that the Knife of Memory?"

"It is." Argi takes a deep breath. "I need you to be honest with yourself. Do you truly want this path?"

"I choose it," I say. "I'm ready. Cas and I are so close to creating the illusion."

"Leo wasn't wrong today when he said that times such as these require open hearts. But for those who want to bear the power of the Lady's Knife, it is more complicated than that."

I understand her meaning. "Because of the cost of magic? I've already made it clear that I am willing to pay it."

"May Our Lady of Whispers, Mother of Shadows and the Eternal Moon, forgive me. I do not wish this fate on anyone. I see the way Castian looks at you. It is the same way Fernando used to look at Galatea."

"Castian is not his father," I say, voice tight.

"You look at him the same way," she says, her brow softening under overwhelming sadness. "When you came aboard my ship I saw your fury and your vengeance, but I did not see your love until today. It reminds me of what occurred here once, and I suddenly feel so very old."

My panic races through my bones. "What exactly happened when Fernando used the Knife? You showed me flashes, but I feel there's something you've held back. You said you wanted to avoid the mistakes of the past."

Argi shuts her eyes and turns away. She takes a step forward, her boot crunching on the pebbles that mark the road. It is like she's listening to the melody of the divine power calling to us both.

"When a Robári claims the Knife of Memory, you become an extension of its power. You can command magics that are divine, but there are limitations."

"I won't try to raise the dead," I promise.

"But would Castian? Would Leo or Leyre?"

The realization shouldn't slam into me the way it does. I know how magics work. I know that there is a cost for power. I know that all Moria have limitations.

"After you wield its power, Renata Convida will be gone. And those who love you, that boy who looks at you as if the world begins and ends where you stand, cannot try to bring you back."

"Renata Convida will be gone." I swallow, my throat so dry my voice is hoarse. "Where will I go?"

Argi brushes my hair away from my face. The gesture draws tears from my eyes because it isn't her face I see now, it's my own mother's. Smiling and beautiful and waiting. "You will become Hollow."

Somehow, I have always known that this would be my fate. Isn't that what Méndez told me once?

Well, if I was trained to be a weapon, then I will be the only one to wield it. This war doesn't need hundreds of martyrs.

Only one.

23

AFTER ANOTHER SESSION OF CULLING MEMORIES INTO ALMAN STONES AND SUP-per, I find Castian sitting in the green lawn behind the temple, where rows of juniper hedges obstruct the temple's glow. I take in the wool blanket, the bottle of cider, and the match in his fingers.

"What are you doing?" I ask.

He flashes that crooked grin and says, "Attempting to light a match."

I scoff and roll my eyes to the moonless night sky. "I mean *why*?"

"I discovered something," he says, lighting a white candle stub.

I crouch beside him and thumb off the cider cork. I try to drink through anxious knots in my stomach. I should interrupt, tell him that I finally know the true cost of saving our people. But Castian has come alive with a giddy sort of joy. I don't remember him ever being this way, even as a child. He rummages through his pack and brings out a familiar copper dome big enough to fit in his palms. The alfaro.

"I took it from the castle ruins," Cas confesses, setting the perforated dome in place and giving it a tiny spin. "It's pointless having an alfaro out here. But last night, when I first saw the stars, I realized the reason I didn't know the constellation before—it's not a constellation they teach us in Puerto Leones." I follow his gaze up to the heavens. Millions of stars wink at us, but one is brightest. The fixed point of the Marinera that we used to sail here.

"Maryam called it the Lion's Paw," he says, and exhales a laugh. "It corresponds with my mother's birth month."

"I suppose you were always born to be a lion, then."

"I wonder what other secrets my mother kept."

"Only the dead can say."

"I miss her." He takes the bottle from me and drinks. "I don't want to miss her, but I do. There is so much I want to ask, and I wasted it because I was angry and terrible. I've been thinking about what Leo said back in Little Luzou. I realize that I hurt the women I love."

"What do you mean?"

"I pushed Nuria away because I thought I was protecting her. I denied my mother forgiveness because I wanted to make her feel the anguish I felt for so long. I—I don't want to hurt you."

"We all have regrets, Cas." I brush his hair away from his face, and he leans into my palm. Women he loves. He loves me, but he hasn't said the words.

"Do you think that after all this is over," he begins, "that we can convince Argi to return? Not forever, if she doesn't wish it, but to share some of this knowledge with the Moria on the mainland?"

We.

"When the time comes," I say, "we're all going to make the best decisions we can for our nations."

He leans on his knee and spins the copper alfaro between us. "Say what you mean, Nati."

I bite my bottom lip and taste the guilt of all the things I'm not brave enough to say out loud.

"I didn't mean what I said," I confess with shallow breaths. "When I asked you to kiss me and make me forget. I don't ever want to forget you. I want every moment, no matter how cruel or perfect, because I wager we have plenty of both. When I'm with you, part of me wishes we could be other people."

"Why?" He touches my chin softly and guides my gaze back to his. "Why, Nati?"

Isn't it obvious? "Because you and I don't have a future together."

He looks away. "You don't know that."

"I do. *We* aren't going to make plans right now, Cas. Let's say we perfect the memory projection and then I retrieve the Knife. After that, what will I be to you? You are going to be the *king* of Puerto Leones."

"I know that," he says darkly.

I sigh, frustrated. "When I'm with you, I want to forget that I'm a girl without family or land or title. And before you say that you don't care about these things, know that the rest of the world cares. Your council will care. Your allies will care."

"Then I won't be king," he says, and every word is spoken slowly but with conviction.

"Cas—"

He takes my hands in his and gives a rumbling laugh. "Did you not expect your 'most ardent enemy' to say that?"

I remember the words I wrote to Lady Nuria beseeching her

help. It feels like ages ago now. Like we have outgrown our skin and bones and are becoming new versions of ourselves.

"Are you drunk to suggest such a thing?" I ask.

"The cider is watery at best," he says, "and no, I'm not drunk. We've been on this island for only two days, and I have never been happier. Except when we were in Acesteña."

I hate you.

I hate you more.

"We've done nothing but fight." My voice trembles with the weak excuse.

"I love fighting with you. I love that you question me. Correct me. I— We can stay here, Nati. Or reclaim our ship from the pirates and go anywhere, if you'd prefer. I will sail you wherever you want to go."

"You're not that great a sailor."

"I wasn't a good swordsman at first either, but I beat my body into form, didn't I?"

What about the Moria and the people who will be casualties of King Fernando's war? What about Dez and Leo and Leyre? What about Argi and the pirates San Piedras? What about us, Castian and me? Don't we owe it to the children who made homes in hidden libraries and under the wide kitchen tables of the palace? I feel the memory burn over my heart, light shimmering between the open laces of my tunic.

"What is that?" he whispers.

"It's you, Cas." I climb on his lap and sit astride him. We're face to face and inches apart. I summon the memories along my torso, the ones that I've chosen to keep. I pull my tunic off and feel the heat of his stare on my bare skin. "You said you'd kiss me again, truly kiss me. So do it."

I used to think that I was the hurricane and Cas was the eye of the storm. That I was the earthquake and he was the quiet before the ground split apart. But when he kisses me, we are every one of those things all at once. He takes my bottom lip into his and gently puts pressure there, parting his way with his tongue. The breeze blows cool against my skin, hot from his grip around my arms. His touch slides down my sides, encircling my waist. I feel every part of me come awake, reaching for him, wanting him closer still.

When he pulls back to breathe, I groan in protest. He laughs as he kisses me. "I'm not going anywhere. You can have me as long as you want."

"I want you always, Cas." I kiss him softly, memorizing the swell of his pert mouth, the salt on the skin of his throat. I want him forever. But even if he gives up his throne and family, I won't be there, and he needs to know that. My eagerness quells, but when he takes off his tunic, my words evaporate like clouds after the rain.

"Then you will have me always." He takes my hand and kisses the inside of my palm. I have always pulled away when Dez held me this way, afraid that my magics would hurt him. But I realize that I trust Castian in a different way—down to my bones, I trust him. I trace the line of bare skin along his trousers. Cas tilts his head back and hisses a curse at the night sky. I marvel at the lashes resting against his cheeks, the way his mouth parts with each intake of breath. *I* make him react this way.

When he presses his forehead against my chest, he guides me onto the blanket. Grass tickles my bare shoulders and for a moment, I remember another night like this. I smell the bright green of leaves, hear the ghost of a rushing river from the night before Cas took Dez from me. My heart flutters at both the memory and Castian as he peppers kisses down my stomach. I try to push the thought of Dez away, but that memory is never far. It feels different now, though, and I can see that it's what that night represents. The desperation of wanting to be close to someone. The need to keep them close. I kiss him harder, afraid it might be for the last time.

Tell Castian. The kingdom is waiting for us. Tell him that this can't last.

But nothing lasts except the earth and heavens and sea, and even then they change. The stars move. Clouds morph into something else. The earth erodes and makes way. Who will remember me when I am gone? I imagine the world Castian will build after. After this place. After me.

And then magics pulse between us.

The light from the alman stone in my pocket is warm, bleeding rays through the fabric. I draw it out, and it's hot to the touch. When we look up, we are in my last memory—beside the river. I whirl around, and the temple is gone, and one memory tumbles into the next. Cas pulls me against him as the forest falls away, and we are engulfed by flames. For a moment, I am back in the small village of Esmeraldas. The burning house turns into the flaming streets of Riomar and it feels so real, Castian lurches to his feet to fight the soldiers that fade like smoke as they run *through* us.

And then we're inside the palace gardens, hidden inside a hedge. There's a woman on the ground, her golden hair is tangled in the grass, and her crown has been discarded. She's barely breathing. Her eyes are red and swollen as a palace guard scoops her into his arms. This memory is of Castian's mother, the one and only time I caught a glimpse of her when I was a little girl in the palace.

He lets go of my hand, and the spell breaks. The illusion is gone. It is just us standing in the dark.

"We did it," I say. Together, our magics were strong enough to project not one but four illusions.

"That we did," Castian says, turning in place as the illusion recedes, and the faint glow of the temple, the silhouette of hedges comes back into focus. At our feet, the cider has spilled on the blanket, and the candle wax has pooled into the wool. I thread my fingers through his, and he brings my knuckles to his lips, still warm from our kisses.

"We can't stay here, Cas."

"I know." He pulls me close, embracing me with a promise to never let me go—a promise neither of us can keep. He kisses me again. "I know."

We dress, and march back into the living quarters to wake our crew.

24

THE FINAL RESTING PLACE OF GALATEA, PRINCESS OF MEMORIA, IS A GRANITE mausoleum with a white peregrine falcon carved of alman stone over the threshold. In a cave beneath lies the Knife of Memory. I clutch the purple wildflowers I gathered along the gravel path, but now I wonder if this gesture is childish and sentimental, unworthy of the warrior girl so full of life and promise.

Castian, Leyre, and Leo accompany me, as we all want to pay our respects to a princess whose fate and memory were severed from this world. As we follow Argi, Elixa, and Maryam inside, my eyes adjust to the white marble and alman stone, and I rub the prickle of gooseflesh on my arms.

Galatea's suit of armor is bolted to the far wall, and her tomb lies in the center. Its lid is a carving of a girl shrouded by a veil, an image so lifelike that the silk seems to have been frozen in marble as it fluttered in the wind. Her eyes are closed, and her hands are wrapped around a sword, a symbol of her warrior status. I place my flowers in the crook of her arms.

"You are not forgotten." Even though I whisper, my voice echoes.

Argi presses a faint circle carved in a wall. There's a deep groan as stone moves against stone. I push open the entrance to the cave and glance back at my friends. Argi's words earlier ring through my mind. *Have care with your heart.* But it's too late for that. Castian takes a single step forward, but he can't follow.

Summoning all my strength, I turn away and take the stone stairs down two at a time. With every step, I convince myself that I do have time. I can hear Leo sing once more. I can listen to Leyre's adventures before we land in Puerto Leones. I can tell Castian the truth, all of it. A small part of me wonders, *What about the others?* But how many times have I seen bodies cut down in the middle of a fight or rotting in a cell? Saying good-bye is a luxury I do not get.

My sandals barely brush the stone stairs, though somehow are as loud as my panting breath, the drum of my heart. I feel as if I am propelling down a mountain, into the mouth of the deepest cavern in the Six Hells, the level of the desolate.

The final step gives way to a narrow stretch of powdery white sand. The cave glitters with jagged crystals shooting out from the ceiling and the ground. A lake begins three paces from where I stand. There, at the very center of the sapphire-blue water, is a glinting light. The Knife of Memory.

I glance around the cave for some sort of raft or boat to carry me across and find nothing. It's about a half mile away. I'm not a strong swimmer, but I could make it, so long as there's nothing under the water. I remove my sandals and my clothes—nothing will weigh me down. White sand sucks at the soles of my feet as I step into the cold water.

I take a deep breath and dive in. The cold threatens to knock the wind out of me, but I kick my legs hard and swim. Bubbles and a clear blue are the only things in my line of sight. I concentrate on my steady heart, my limbs cutting a straight path. I surface for air, kicking to stay afloat. Above me the ceiling's jagged crystals glitter. That is when I hear the first voice.

Who are you?

Is the cave whispering these things to me, or is it a memory?

I keep swimming.

Who is Renata Convida? Sayida once asked that of me. She helped me uncover the memories of a little girl buried beneath the stolen ones. I couldn't answer that once, but I know now.

Stay for more. Lozar's words tumble through me. I offer a silent prayer for the Moria prisoner who reminded me that there was more at stake than vengeance for Dez, for a boy who did not come back for me. The water grows darker. Colder. I stop, a weight dragging me under.

Where is my Nati? I see a luminous light up ahead. My mother. She is in front of me now, chasing me around the house as she would when we played my favorite game of chasing forest spirits.

Show me who you are. The cave's voice finds me even underwater.

I push all my strength into my legs and swim, cutting across the sapphire cold until I can see it—a column of alman stone. The shaft vanishes into the deepest bowels of the cave. It is impossible to tell how far it goes. I swim toward it, my lungs burning. The stone is smooth, with eroded nooks and crannies where an ancient pattern of whorls might have been. I follow its length to the surface and gasp for breath. The glittering crystals that line the ceiling wink at me as I grab the lip of the column and heave myself onto the flat surface.

The Knife of Memory is driven through the top of the column, down to the hilt. It takes me a moment to recognize the chattering echo in the cave as my own teeth. My limbs are frozen and weak, but I crawl and grab the platinum hilt.

It doesn't budge.

The cave shudders and the column begins to sink. Water sloshes over the lip, wrapping around my ankles like cold hands.

Show me who you are, the voice asks again. This time the cavern trembles and bits of crystal fall like hail from the ceiling. One cuts my cheek. I think of Argi walking in circles around me, always demanding answers. Who am I? Nobody. Everybody. Slivers of crystal slice at my naked skin, the trickle of blood like fire on my cold flesh. And then, all at once, I know what to do.

I let the rest of my stolen memories go. They flit by in swirls of gray smoke. The remaining walls of the Gray splinter, my magics unfurling across my skin. I hold on to the hilt despite the ache in my muscles, the way my legs seize with cramps. I open myself to the Knife, and it feels as if someone has stepped into my mind with me.

I know who I was. Who I am. Who I will be.

I was a child. I was a weapon. I am a Robári.

I am going to return the memories of my kingdom.

The Knife slides out of the stone, and the cave explodes with light.

25

"I THOUGHT PERHAPS IT MIGHT BE BIGGER," LEO SAYS AS WE MAKE THE JOURNEY back to the ship. Leyre gives him a tiny shove, but I can't help but laugh, even if the cut on my cheek stings.

I finger the Knife sheathed at my hip. Every time I touch it, my skin goes numb with its power. When I returned with it to the temple, shivering and wet, our few belongings were already packed, and the others were ready to hike down the hill. Castian walks at my side, his quiet like a blanket around my shoulders. Then I feel his stare on me, and as much as I try to focus on the ships waiting in the distance, I think of his idea to run away together.

"Speak your mind, Cas," I say.

His brows shoot up, and something like pride possesses his smile. "You're different."

I feel different. The Gray is gone. Since I stepped out of the cave's lake, my Robári marks have stretched up to my shoulders. Out of habit, I search for the vault in my mind, but I only find pieces of my own life, things I'd forgotten. My father's voice. The children I used to play with in my village. The first time I lost a tooth. The smells of my mother's kitchen. There are darker memories—the Hollows I've created are still mine, even if their memories aren't. I see the dead of their eyes, their empty faces. And yet, there's room for more of me now. I take a deep breath and touch the hilt of the Knife again, feel the deep hum of its power in my veins.

I reach for him. "Do you like it?"

Cas catches my hand in his, and our fingers intertwine. "I hate it with every fiber in my being."

"Good."

Argi glances disapprovingly at Castian and me. It shouldn't matter what she thinks, but she's the closest thing I have to a mentor. I owe her more than I will ever be able to repay, but this thing between Castian and me feels right. Selfish as it is, I can't let him go.

We say good-bye to Argi and Maryam. Elixa will take us to the ship, and from there we will make for Puerto Leones.

"I have a gift for you," Argi tells me. She hands me a wooden chest as Moria pirates load the canoes that will carry us back to the ship.

"What is it?" I set the heavy box in our canoe.

Argi's crow's-feet are more pronounced when she smiles. "My, Renata, don't you understand the concept of gifts?"

"I don't care for surprises." I laugh and take her hand. "Unless you're going to give us some of our food back."

She pulls me into an embrace, and I press my forehead into her shoulder for a moment. Touching others used to come with a thread of fear. All I had ever been taught was that my magics were unwieldy and dangerous, that they made me dangerous to touch. I can't change what was done to me, but now I know the truth, and I return her embrace.

"Come with us," I say.

Castian nods, but something in the way he turns his head tells me he may have already extended this offer.

"As I told your prince," she explains, "when he reverses the orders against the Moria and disbands the Arm of Justice, my people will choose for themselves."

"And what will you choose?"

"I'm already home, little Robári."

I think I understand what she's feeling. If I went back to find my village, it wouldn't be home again, like the story Leyre told us of the princess and the glacier. She was gone for too long and wasn't of her world anymore.

"The Knife is bound to you now," she whispers in my ear. "It is your power to wield, but remember, you're an extension of the blade and it you. Reveal Fernando's sins to the land, and then let go."

"Will it hurt?" I whisper.

It'll hurt. I remember saying those words to Dez once.

"Will that stop you?" Argi asks. She brushes my hair back from my face and gets a good look at me. "I thought not. You are blessed, Renata Convida."

When we're back on our ship, we work in tandem—Leyre and Castian hoist the sail while Leo and I tighten the rigging. My heart is full, and I am ready to go home one last time.

In the captain's quarters, we gather around a map of Puerto Leones. Leyre sits on the desk and watches Cas move a ship across the board. She picks up the vessel meant to be us and plops it on one side of Citadela Crescenti.

Castian shakes his head. "The Oroplata gate puts us closer to the city, but the Ororosa gate is more secluded." He drags the ship to the crescent-shaped inlet that gives the city its name.

Leo taps the heart of the citadela on the map. "Now we need a place where you can cast the illusion without pesky fighting getting in the way."

I gnaw on my bottom lip and touch the hilt of the Knife of Memory for comfort. I add, "And it has to have alman stone."

"What about the Tresoros cathedral?" Leo asks.

"Leo, you're brilliant." Castian adds a wooden soldier to the map to represent us on land. "The cathedral faces the river—it used to be an old temple to the gods of Tresoros."

"And that would have the stone?" Leyre asks.

"When I was in the palace," I say, "Lady Nuria mentioned that her family lands were a source of alman stone and platinum, among other riches. Hence why Castian's family wanted to secure a marriage alliance with them."

Leyre scoffs. "So the Fajardos are gold diggers?"

"Among many things." Castian glowers. "The queendom of Tresoros was once the richest nation on the continent. Their temples were legendary. My father did love beautiful things, and even though the Tresoros cathedral was heretical, it was *saved* when he transformed it into a house of worship for the Father of Worlds. The carving on the ceiling has alman stone." He glances up at me. "Will that do?"

"It has to."

"And what happens after you use the Knife?" Leo asks. "I mean, what do *we* do?"

Castian leans on the desk and stares at the scene before him, probably imagining the fight ahead. "My father won't surrender, but we will provoke outrage. We will gather allies and take the war to his doorstep."

"The memory of Galatea and the king's actions will create confusion," I say, unsheathing the Knife and laying it flat against my palm. "There will be anger that we can harness. That's where Leo comes in."

"Me?"

"You will take a letter to Lady Nuria. Last you said she was traveling to Citadela Crescenti with Justice Alessandro."

Leo nods. "She wasn't given much of a choice to stay under his watch."

"Nuria is safe in her provincia. The people of the region are loyal to her family," Castian agrees.

I picture the fierce girl I met in the palace who wouldn't let anyone look down at her. "She will renounce the king and pledge her support to Castian."

Leyre frowns, unconvinced. "That is a lot of wager on one person. Are you sure you can trust her?"

"With my life," Castian says.

"So do I," I add. "With Lady Nuria and her forces, you will be able to spread dissent. I will also write to the Whispers to make a final plea."

"A letter?" Leyre scoffs. "You're the Robári who is going to wield ancient goddess-forged power. Don't tell me you're afraid of your own rebels."

An uncomfortable sensation settles in my chest. "Cas, you have to give my letter to Dez."

"Nati." Castian says my name, a question in the pinch between his brow.

Leo glances down at the map, and I see the moment when he realizes my intent. "You don't plan on surviving this, do you?"

Leyre snaps her fingers together. "You're the only one who can wield the power of that damned knife, but there's a cost, isn't there?"

"Cebrián is alive." Castian raises his voice. "My father survived. Why wouldn't you?"

"And look at what they became!" I shake my head. "Cebrián *shouldn't* be alive. Somehow he recovered from being a Hollow, but he was made into a Ripper. Not me. This is the cost, and I have to pay it."

Leo stares out the pitch-black window. Castian and Leyre begin to shout, but I can't answer their protests and questions.

Finally Castian slams his fists on the table. "How could you keep this from me?"

"You know why," I answer, then level my eyes to his. "This is my choice. I am done with vengeance."

The maelstrom of our arguing gives way to Leo's silent tears. He wipes the corners of his eyes with a silk handkerchief. I would laugh about how he managed to acquire a luxury item during times like this, but I suppose it is his own form of magics.

"Renata has made her decision," Leo proclaims, turning to Castian. "We have prepared as much as we can. All we can do is what Renata needs of us."

Leyre follows him out of the room, but not before shooting me a look that says, *I hope you know what you're doing.*

I hope so, too.

As I move to the door, Cas's voice rings out. "We are not finished, Nati."

I shut the door. "I wasn't going to leave. You can't sleep without me, remember?"

"How can you mock me in this moment?" He kicks off his boots and yanks off his stockings. I know he feels helpless, but I can't change this.

A part of me reacts to his anger, and it catches within me like embers in kindling. "We knew there would be consequences."

"It should be my price to bear."

"Why?" I approach him like the Lion's Fury he is.

His anger gives way to a chasm of things left unsaid. "Because I deserve it."

"And who would lead Puerto Leones?"

"Someone better," he says, each word an anvil. "Someone else. I should have known you'd do this."

My stomach tightens when I stand in front of him. I rest my palms over his heart. "I'm becoming predictable."

Cas takes a lock of my hair and winds it around his finger. "You are many things, Nati, but predictable is not one of them."

"I have to ask you," I whisper. "When the time comes—"

"No." He grabs my shoulders and moves me aside so he can walk as far away as the cabin will allow, cursing every god he's ever heard of.

"It has to be you. I trust you. I love you, Cas."

His chest rises and falls so rapidly that he places a hand over his heart, as if he could physically stop it from beating. "Then don't."

"Don't love you?"

"Hate me," he pleads. "I could endure your hatred. I would devour its fruit if it meant keeping you with me."

"We both know what being a Hollow means."

"*Please.*"

"I hate you, then." I rummage through the drawers of the desk and find a pair of leather gloves. I shove them against his chest. "And I challenge you."

He shakes his head, undoing the knot keeping his hair away from his eyes. He looks absolutely feral. He grips my arms and squeezes. "You'll lose."

"I won't." I bring my fist to his abdomen, but don't follow through. He doesn't even try to block me and shuts his eyes at his own mistake. "Because you let me win every time. You have to be the one to give me mercy when the time comes."

"The world has never deserved you. Neither do I." He lowers his forehead to mine. I kiss the tops of his cheeks and the crescent moon scar below his lashes. Taste the salt of his tears. I let my fingertips glide down the sides of his neck, and he shivers at my touch. My heart is a wild thing against my rib cage. I have never reacted to someone the way I do to Castian. We are intertwined, the same way I am connected to the Knife of Memory. I long for the years we spent without each other. I long for the future that is gone before it got a chance to begin. I long for my terrible, beautiful broken prince. My best friend and my heart.

"Kiss me," I whisper.

And he does.

Castian kisses me, and it is like I'm plunging back into that sapphire sea. For a long moment, I am breathless, clinging to him. He pulls away, and the blacks of his pupils widen in the lamplight. It's as if he is committing me to memory, and the thought of that rattles me.

I kiss him again and again because there isn't an *after* for us. I will never know the king he will be. I will never see the world he will create.

I will never.

I will never.

I nip at the tender skin of his throat because if there isn't an after, there is a here and now. He blinks rapidly until his eyes focus on me, then grips my arms tightly and backs me against the wall.

"You're going to be gone, and what will I be left with but to be your executioner?"

"You'll have a better memory of us, Cas." I pull the hem of my tunic over my head and throw it to the side. His gaze drops to the Robári marks on my body that now cover both my arms, then traces my clavicle and stops between my breasts. My memories hum along my skin, coming to life in pinpricks of light. "You're buried deep in my skin. Nothing, not this world or the Lady of Whispers, can take that from me."

"I love you, Nati," he says. "I love you, and I'm terrified."

"So am I." I stand on my toes. "And I love you, too."

Our lips collide, and I can hardly keep myself upright. My mind spins, dizzy and drunk on the smell of him. Salt and cedar. I meet his tongue with mine, a kiss so deep it is like we are searching for truth within the other. I pull back first and gasp air, but only for a moment. My heartbeat comes erratically as he strips off his tunic. I remember the first day I woke up in his arms in Acesteña, and how much I didn't want to admit that I wanted him then. He kisses my naked chest, lingering on each and every new memory and mark I've collected. He traces the blunt scar above my breasts. The one that his father made.

"I'm sorry," he says.

"It's all right." We wear our past on our skin, and it is unavoidable. I drag my finger along his ribs, down to the scar on his side. The one that Dez left behind. I kiss Cas's shoulder and bite down gently. He exhales a soft hiss when I undo the buttons of his trousers, and he tugs at the laces on mine. Everything feels so fast and unbearably slow all at once.

He steps out of his trousers, and I watch. I've already seen him naked, but I marvel at my reaction every time. I remember the way the sun gilded the tight muscles of his body that day at the sandbar. But this is more intimate. My clumsy inexperience shows when my pantleg gets stuck. Castian rumbles a short laugh but peels the rest of my clothes off, trailing his fingertips back up my leg as we fall backward onto the bed with him on top of me.

"Don't laugh," I murmur.

Resting on his forearms, he sinks into the hollow of my throat, parts my knees with his leg. I feel my breath hitch, and he presses a kiss to my lips. "I was laughing because the last time we tried to do this we created illusions that were decidedly unromantic."

"No illusions now, Cas." I trace the curve of his spine, to the hard muscle of his back and watch his eyes flutter. "There is just you and me."

Cas kisses me fast, crushing me with the weight of his body. He positions himself between my legs, kissing my inner thighs, the soft, scarred skin below my belly button.

When I feel like my entire body will shake apart, I call him back to me. His calloused palms grip my waist. I wrap my leg around his thigh and guide him onto his back. He cups my hips and our bodies line up together. I sink against him, sighing as the pressure of him builds in my lower belly, and then we're moving against each other in a way that is shy at first and then desperate.

Castian gathers me like I'm weightless and rolls me back onto the mattress. His hair falls around my face, and I lean up to catch the kiss he offers. He threads his fingers through mine, our twin scars burning against each other, and he holds me so tightly it is like he is afraid I will disappear right here right now.

I memorize every part of him with my touch. This beautiful, deadly, bruised prince that I will never know again. I will never.

Later that night, when we are tangled and sink into the exhaustion of being awake for more than a day, I go to sleep with a new realization. My heart has always belonged to Castian, even when the world would have it otherwise. We have simply been finding our way back to each other, now another memory lost to a great expanse of sea.

26

After three days at sea with the wind in our sails, Leo's call announces land ahead. But as we drift through the fog I realize that it isn't fog at all—it's smoke.

"We're too late," Leyre says, running to the ship's side.

Cannon fire rips through the evening sky before we reach the marina. Distant shouts follow. From our vantage point, I make out clusters of Leonesse soldiers on the streets. Pyres burn, and the streets of Citadela Crescenti, renowned for their never-ending revels, smolder.

It's quiet in the harbor as Castian guides our ship through the Ororosa gate. Thick clouds hang low in the humidity and mingle with smoke, providing natural cover. Our ship cuts through the scent of brine and gunpowder until we find an empty dock among the pleasure vessels and schooners.

"Are you ready?" I ask, but it's my own heart that stutters when I search for my friends on deck. Smoke hangs low, and every step is like cutting through clouds.

"Not yet," Leo says.

I turn to find him holding a wooden chest in his arms—Argi's gift. "We don't have time for that."

"I beg you not to be angry with me, but I was searching for weapons and opened it." Leo scrunches his nose and pops open the latch. A white glow spills from the inside. "And I thought you might like to wear it."

Leyre and Cas come up behind us.

"What is that?" Cas asks.

"It's Galatea's armor." I touch the white peregrine falcon of the platinum breastplate, fit for a Robári. The delicate chain mail sleeves rattle against the deck as I take it out. I close my eyes and see her—Princess Galatea of the Memoria kingdom with her raven-black mane and defiant stare, waiting to change the world. Did she know Fernando's true heart or was she blind to it?

"Leo," I begin.

He bows his head. "I would love to help you into your armor one more time."

Before we disembark, Castian's illusion turns him back into Will Otsoa. He didn't want to return to Puerto Leones as a stranger, but to reach the Tresoros cathedral without interference, we need to risk using his magics.

I touch the Knife of Memory sheathed at my right hip. Leyre adjusts the strap of her quiver, and Leo touches the breast pocket of his leather vest, where he carries two letters. Castian's magics settle over our skin. To preserve his strength, he glamours away our weapons and, in my case, armor.

The moment we step onto the dock and tie up our ship, the harbormaster waddles over with a patrol guard a few paces behind.

"Entry papers," the woman croaks. Her eyes linger on Leyre, with her mixed Luzouan and Leonesse features. Castian hands over the ship's manifest and our forged documents. I try my best not to move—the illusion might turn my armor into a merchant lady's dress, but it won't cover up the sound of clinking metal.

The harbormaster licks her thumb and flips through the parchment folios. "Where you coming from?"

"Got tired of losing at Señora Perliana's gambling parlors," Leo says, starting when the eerie quiet of the citadela is disrupted by a loud *boom*. "Though perchance, we chose the wrong season to visit Citadela Crescenti with our coin?"

The woman smiles with teeth yellowed from smoking. She gives the seals on our documents another look, then steps aside. "The Second Sweep will rid the streets of the Moria infestation, worry you not. Though there is an extra tax today on account of our troubles."

Castian hands over a bag filled with tin illusioned to appear as gold pesos. The harbormaster narrows her eyes at me, and my insides clench.

"Has the fighting gone on for very long?" I ask, forcing my voice into a soft, high pitch. "I'd hate to spoil my fun."

The woman's lips become as flat and pink as a worm. She weighs the purse on her palm and steps aside.

"They've been at it for days now," she continues, "but if you want a good place, the Belen quarter on the north crescent has been cleared of rebel filth. Mention Navira for a discount!"

Citadela Crescenti is known for its decadent festivals and Tresorian artisanal markets selling tapestries, chiffon silks, and shimmering jewels. But as we take the cobblestone street that stretches from one tip of the harbor to the other, all I see is smoke and ash. The locals are gone or hiding in their homes, leaving the battleground to the king and Whispers.

With Castian's illusions, we are a trick of the light right in the open, invisible ghosts crunching broken glass and rattling by as we run down gray cobblestone streets past smoldering piles of broken furniture and anything else that will burn. The shutters of the narrow brick buildings are drawn closed. Some balconies wave the Puerto Leones purple-and-gold flag, but I spot a window with an open shutter that waves a cobalt-blue banner, the one from long ago when this territory was still the queendom of Tresoros. When we turn the corner, I fight the urge to scream as we freeze in the middle of the street. Second Sweep soldiers ride directly toward us.

"How long before the king sends the rest of his army?" a soldier with a cracking voice and brown whiskers asks. "One battalion is hardly enough to keep the rebels at bay."

I look to Castian, who acknowledges this news with a nod. This is just the beginning of King Fernando's fight—perhaps we aren't too late.

"Could be a fortnight by the looks of it," a second soldier answers, grasping the reins in a gloved fist. "We've turned out this quarter already. Even Luna's getting testy."

"Ye named yer horse?" the third of the riders sneers. He spits on the ground and wipes a smear of wet blood on his cheek. "The rebel bestaes aren't here. If they are, they're using their unnatural magics. How're we supposed to fight against that?"

The three of them make the symbol of the Father of Worlds over their torsos.

"Why can't the king pay the ransom for the Bloodied Prince, eh?" Luna's rider grumbles. Luna huffs in our direction, trying to course correct even though she can't see us. Leyre reaches for a bow, Castian for his sword. But then a flaming bottle shatters against one soldier's helmet. The spilled oil spreads flames across his tunic, and his screams scare the horse. I lunge away before it can trample me. The other Second Sweep soldiers gallop down the street, chasing rebels running atop the brown-tiled roofs.

"*Run*," I say.

We don't stop, zigzagging through alleys littered in filth and pyres of garbage. I want to scream as I leap over the bodies of fallen Whispers. Seagulls scavenge at the concave faces of young Leonesse soldiers. I force my legs to keep moving and remember Doña Sagrada, the innkeeper who pleaded for those drafted from her village. These are King Fernando's men, children who sacrificed their lives for the lies of a mad king.

Shattered glass from the explosive bottles litters the cobblestones. Anything that can catch fire does—awnings, market stalls, delivery carts attached to horses and goats.

The way to the desolate square around the Tresoros cathedral is clear. A statue of the Father of Worlds looks down from the roof of the ancient church. He wears the sun as a crown and his hands hold orbs representing the unknown worlds. Every time I've been in a cathedral and listened to one of the royal priests speak, they emphasize that King Fernando's reach over the continent is like that of their god. But beneath all that I see the knots carved into the stone, the patterns of what this place once was—a temple of long-forgotten deities.

When we're sure the four of us are alone in the cathedral, Leo bars the heavy doors shut using an altar boy's staff. He mutters, "Definitely going to the first hell for that one."

I swallow the emotion that threatens to escape when I meet Castian's stare. He relinquishes the glamour over his face so that he is Castian again. I grab him by the collar of his tunic and kiss him.

I love you.

I hate you.

We don't have to say anything, in the end. I push him away and take my place at the altar. It feels like blasphemy to stand here in a place of the king's priests. Outside, a series of booms make the air vibrate. Screams follow and then utter silence.

I unsheathe the Knife of Memory.

I remember the whispering cave in Isla Sombras—the power radiating in those crystals, in the hilt, in me. Thousands of threads appear all around me. Each one glows and pulses differently, and they crosshatch the air like the constellations in Castian's alfaro. These are the threads of memory that can be severed by the Knife. The white crystal blade thrums with power. It wants to be used. But I am not here to cut someone from existence. I'm here to return the memory of one person, to show the kingdom who she was.

Light emanates from the blade. Castian watches me, and I shake my head, knowing what is going through his mind. A desperate, selfish part of him might want to stop me, but the king he is supposed to become won't let him. I need him to complete his end of the illusion when it's time.

I shut my eyes to draw on the memories of Fernando and Galatea trapped within the alman stone blade. The ringing in my ears grows, like howling wind trapped inside these walls. I thrust the Knife of Memory into the air, feel the heat of my own magics illuminating the whorls of my skin. Castian reaches for me, ready to make the connection.

Nothing happens. The blade goes dead.

"What's wrong?" Leo shouts.

"I don't know."

The doors of the cathedral break open. But it isn't the Second Sweep who stands at the threshold. It's Dez and Margo, part of my old Whispers unit, along with a half dozen other rebels.

"Enough of this, Ren," Dez says, extending his hand. "It's time to come home."

27

BOUND AND BLINDFOLDED, WE ARE MARCHED OUT OF THE CATHEDRAL. SOME-
one is fighting, and I recognize the sound of fists on bone, the
pained grunts of falling. Others are running, their boots crunching
on glass. There's the cry of a child from up high. I try to listen for
my friends, but we are all silent as the Whispers guide us through
the dark.

"Look at the *queen* of Puerto Leones." I recognize Margo's voice
beside me. "After everything, parading around with her Bloodied
Prince."

I hiss a curse at her. "You have no idea of what we've been
through. You and Dez are going to get our people killed."

She makes a sound of disgust and spits. "Do you know what I
see, Ren?"

"Are you aware that you blindfolded me yourself?"

I feel a shove at the center of my back. "I see a traitor who left with the enemy."

I throw my head back and laugh. "You used me as bait. You left me in Soledad to be taken prisoner."

"We would have come for you," she says.

It's the lie that tips me over the edge. I heard her conspire with the remaining Whisper leadership to abandon me and hunt for the threat of Robári. I let the sound of her voice guide me and kick her. Margo fights back, knocking me to the ground, slapping me, then trying to pin my bound hands against my chest. I hear a muffled protest nearby.

Castian.

Argi was correct. In the back of my mind, I couldn't let go of him. Is that why the Knife didn't work?

"Enough of this," Dez shouts. I can imagine him standing between us as he always had before. His honey-brown eyes cast to the ground as if he was disappointed in all of us, but especially the dirt.

I feel Margo yanked off me, then I'm hauled to a stand. Hands turn me and nudge me to keep walking. Though I can sense Dez's presence close, no one puts their hands on me again.

"We're on the same side, Ren," Dez says.

I hold up my hands, the ropes scratching my wrists. "It doesn't feel like it."

I collide into him, and he grips me by my hands and undoes the knots. I remove the rancid cloth from my eyes and blink the night into focus. As I suspected, we're away from the harbor, farther inland, where sprawling estates speak of wealth.

Dez and I scrutinize each other. His eyes take in my armor, lingering on the alman stone at the center of my breastplate. I note the new bruise blooming on his cheekbone. His black hair is loose around his shoulders, and his clothes are covered in soot. There's a bandage around his forearm. He turns away and I track his gaze to three Whispers who create a blockade that separates me from Castian and Leo. Leyre, however, is nowhere in sight. A pang of nerves works its way through me. Where is she?

"Where are you taking us?" I ask.

Margo shoulders between us, removing a key from her inner pocket. "To the new Whispers."

I arch a brow at Dez. "The *new* Whispers?"

"There is hope, Ren." Dez pleads with me. "Let me show you."

My heart races as we cut through the grounds of an abandoned estate. Most of the homes we passed were dark or boarded up. Either the wealthy merchants are hiding in their cellars, or they had the means to escape the city before the first of the king's army arrived. Margo unlocks a door on the side of the house. The hinges squeak as she steps aside to let us in. How did the rebels find a place like this? Perhaps Lady Nuria is aiding them—she was Illan's ally once, and this is the provincia of her ancestors. But if Nuria was helping them, we wouldn't be bound.

I inhale the damp of cold stone as we descend into the cellar and adjust to the dim light of torches at the end of an archway. I tip my head back to get a full view of the domed brick ceiling. Casks of wine are stacked along one wall, and bottles line the other. Crates and wood chips litter the floor.

Dozens and dozens of Whispers hurry in and out of other rooms and dark halls. The youngest Moria are cleaning the bloody armor and weapons taken from the Leonesse soldiers. Others carry crates of empty bottles, probably to make explosives. I scan their faces for Sayida's luminous black eyes and Esteban's familiar glower, but there are so many people.

All at once, everyone stops to look at me. A little girl runs toward me, pointing at my armor, but an older boy yanks her back. Their voices fill the room with speculation.

"Our fearless leader has returned with a great bounty," says a familiar voice.

My body reacts before my mind does. I feel the ghost of magics against my skin, reaching for my Robári powers. I convince myself that I'm wrong. He *can't* be here.

The Ripper. The Robári who had been held prisoner by King Fernando and Justice Méndez for decades. The one who tried to revive Galatea and failed.

"You were right," Dez replies, though I notice the white knuckles on the hilt of his sword. "They were in the cathedral where you said they'd be."

How could they have known? I fight the urge to hold the Knife, lest they think I'm going to attack.

"Come closer, Commander Andrés. We are all allies now," Cebrián says.

Dozens of tapered candles drip wax in the nooks and crannies along brick walls. Behind a maze of crates and sacks of grain and flour is a table covered in maps, seals, and bread crumbs. Cebrián rises from a high-backed chair, his long nails scraping against the leather armrests. His strange Ripper marks are more pronounced than I remember. Silver veins extend around his eyes and along his throat, more like running blood than Argi's delicate carvings. There's a violence to it.

His silver eyes widen at the sight of my armor. "Aren't you quite the warrior?"

"Aren't you quite the rebel?" I ask.

But after what the justice did to him—the years of torture and experimentation on his magics—nothing can change his sickly gray skin, his ashen hair, or his eerie silver eyes.

I feel the unused power of the Knife of Memory through our connection, like a flint spark in my veins. In that moment, Cebrián's eyes fall to where it rests at my side, and now Dez's words make sense. I look up at him, but he won't meet my eyes. "You said the Knife wouldn't work because *he* told you it wouldn't."

Dez's features tense. The way he looks at me I know he's trying to tell me something, but it has been so long since we were united in our goal. I used to be able to know his every move, anticipate where he would attack. Now, nothing.

"Be angry with me, Renata," Cebrián says, his voice cloying with practiced patience. But there's an unsettling spark beneath his eyes and his placid smile. "We do not want to fight with you. On the contrary, ever since you ran away with Prince Castian, I have advised our leaders that now is the moment to unite."

With a small wave of the Ripper's gnarled fingers, one of the Whispers moves to undo Leo and Castian's blindfolds and restraints. I notice the furrow of Dez's brow—how many more orders has Cebrián given without Dez's approval? If there's a rift in this alliance, I can play on it.

"I thank you," Leo offers the boy who's freed him, but the niceties are a habit. He's afraid, but not of the Whispers. We both notice Castian's fury, the way his eyes ignite with rage at the sight of Cebrián. "Please, Cas, we are *guests*."

Cas slowly surveys the cellar. The maps. The weapons. The scores of people who have gathered to watch us, though instead of a meeting of allies, it feels like another trial. Then Cebrián's words settle in.

"He's your *adviser*?" I ask Dez.

"Cebrián knows what we're up against," he says.

On the outside, Dez is still every bit the bloodied, bruised warrior I've always known. The beautiful, reckless boy who runs into a fight because he has no other choice but to win. The shift happens slowly. That stubborn lock of hair that always gets in his eyes, finds a way free. He goes to brush it back, but it's like he suddenly remembers that his ear was cut off by his brother, that he did lose, that he gave up. That is the moment I see the change in him, the doubt that seeps in, that wasn't there when we were together. I catch Margo's concern as Dez defers to Cebrián and by the glee in the Ripper's silver eyes, I know Dez's insecurity is exactly what he's after.

"Who is she to ask questions?" a voice hisses in the crowd. "She left us."

"Please, my friends. I was not my best when Renata and I first met," Cebrián says. "I'd been held captive by King Fernando for four decades. Though sometimes it felt like centuries. But after she so heroically freed me, I ran as fast as I could before I realized that there was nowhere for me to go."

Is that what Cebrián thinks happened? *He* was the one whose brute strength tore open the windows. He's lying to bring the Whispers closer, but why?

"The king took everything from me." Cebrián raises one of his hands and lets his memories glide along his skin, the same way Argi showed me how. "And with your help, Renata, we will bring Puerto Leones to its knees."

I take a step forward, turning so that the only people at my back are Cas and Leo. "My help?"

"Why, yes," Cebrián says, voice like a snake in grass. "We were hoping to find you along your travels and retrieve the Knife of Memory together, but you kept slipping through Commander Andrés's capable hands."

Another slight at Dez's leadership. Why is he standing by and letting Cebrián speak to him this way?

"If you want to work together," I ask, "why stop me from using the Knife?"

"Did I?" Cebrián grins, and the effect is skeletal. "Or were you simply unable to command its power?"

"I—"

"You aren't strong enough to do what needs to be done. But I am." He steps forward, unclasping the robe to reveal his scarred, naked torso. He's allowing the crowd to see the marks that cover nearly every inch of him, marks he carved by ripping the magic out of Moria. "*I* have wielded the Knife of Memory once, and I will do it again."

Slowly, the Whispers move toward Cebrián, seemingly drawn to him. Dez used to have this same magnetism. Everyone wanted to cling to the power behind his words. Now that boy stands beside Cebrián, not like the commander of the Whispers, but a henchman.

"Félix, come, come, as we've practiced." Cebrián extends his arm. I'm reminded of birch trees near my old home, bark so white it looked like a field of bones. The boy's chest rises and falls like a trapped rabbit. His brown hair is pulled back in a knot, and white scars feather along the tawny brown skin of his face. I note the gold cuffs on his ears. Without hesitation, he latches on to Cebrián's fingers, and images flicker around us. It's the same memory Argi showed us, but from Cebrián's perspective.

Fernando crawls away from Galatea's lifeless body, the sapphire-blue water of the cave lapping at their feet. He sees the Knife of Memory glowing in the sand. A young Argi is bleeding from her forehead and coming in and out of consciousness.

Cebrián sees the Knife, too, but Fernando wraps his fist around the hilt first. They tussle in the sand until Fernando forces Cebrián into a chokehold. Fernando whispers something incomprehensible. Ribbons of light spill from the crystal blade, and then Fernando pierces Cebrián's chest, again and again. There is so much blood and light piercing out of each wound.

"Impossible," someone whispers.

"A miracle," another sighs.

Cebrián releases his grasp from Félix, who tips his face in reverence of the Ripper. "As you can see, I am the product of Our Lady's light. When King Fernando turned the blade on me, the goddess saved me. She and I are the only Moria to have survived its power. She gave me a second chance at life, but that was taken from me. I have made my way back to my kindred, my Moria. I simply needed you here, Renata." He waits for all eyes to turn on me. "Now, relinquish your bond with the Knife and turn over its power to me. Help me bring King Fernando to his knees."

Cas watches the crowd as if he's contemplating who is the biggest threat. I see what he does—we're outnumbered and backed into a corner of the cellar with no way out.

"We are in this fight together," I say. "Killing the king will not help our cause. Let me return the memories he's stolen and expose his sins to the people."

Cebrián's laugh is a low rumble. "Return the memories? You're trying to save a sinking ship when you need to let it go. The strong will swim to shore. The weak will drown. Which one are you, Renata?"

The Whispers nod in agreement. Dez's fists tense at his sides. Margo touches her gold starfish necklace, which I know she does when she's nervous. Is that fear I see in the blue of her eyes?

I hold the Knife's hilt and feel for the connection. It's still there, tugging at the power inside me. "This is not the way."

"You have not been here, Renata. Look at all we have accomplished by taking the fight to the king!" Cebrián raises his hands in the air, and the crowd cheers, a dangerous spark buzzing among them. "Now that we have the goddess's weapon, we can destroy any memory of Puerto Leones and its stain on the known world. We could start the world anew. Why would you stand in the way of that?"

His eyes dart to Castian, pinning the blame on him.

Castian, the Bloodied Prince who stands tall and faces them. He takes a calming breath, and closes his eyes, drawing illusions over his face. Will Otsoa. A Zaharian ambassador. Duque Arias. And then he's Castian again. "I am not your enemy. I am one of you. Renata can do this. Help us. Help *her*."

Cries of bewilderment and disbelief echo in the domed cave. I want to remember the surprise on Margo's face for as long as I live. But it's when Cebrián's mask of peace falls that concerns me. The half-moon shadows under his eyes darken, and the veins of light glow as if reacting to his anger. Did he think Castian would hide forever?

"Give me the Knife," he snarls.

I hold the hilt tighter and lean toward him. *"No."*

"Very well." Cebrián sheathes his anger long enough to turn to Dez. "I suppose we'll have to resort to stronger methods, don't you think, Commander Andrés?"

At Dez's order, two Persuári subdue Castian and Leo and drag them through a dark passageway. I try to run forward, but Dez stands in my way. He takes my hands gently in his.

"Ren, please. This is the only way to finally have peace."

"No, it isn't." I recoil at his touch. "You could *trust* me."

His brow furrows, and I see the hopelessness that tugs at the corners of his eyes. "This is what we have to become."

"If you think I'm going to give Cebrián that kind of power, then you don't know me at all."

Dez looks down the passage where Castian was taken. "I suppose I don't. Take her."

28

It isn't a stranger who ushers me away, but Sayida. At the sight of her, I am overcome with the urge to cry. She is exactly the same—her stark fringe of lashes, the curtain of black hair brushed taut, away from her face. Her diamond nose ring winks like a star in the dark halls of the cold cellar. But as she guides me away from the crowd, from Cas, I find I'm not afraid. Part of me knows that she's using her Persuári magics.

"This is all wrong, Ren," Sayida says. "You were supposed to come back to us."

I try to hone my senses, but all I can focus on is the sadness in her voice. It makes memories of the last time I saw her swell.

"I have missed you so much," I confess. "But I don't regret leaving. I didn't belong with the Whispers. Do you see it now?"

Sayida unlocks a door, and I enter a storage room. There is an oil lamp on a barrel, and cedar wood shavings cover the ground. I sink against the wall, my body weighed down by an invisible force.

"I'm sorry," she says, and sits at the threshold.

Then her magics fade quickly, leaving me with an overwhelming tangle of emotions. Doubt in myself. Fear that Cebrián is right. Worry for Cas and Leo. And Dez—he has no idea the "ally" he has made.

"The Sayida I know wouldn't want innocent people to die for the sake of King Fernando."

"A lot has changed since we forced you to choose Castian. But so have you." She exhales deeply. "You seem—alight. For as long as I've known you, there's been a terrible burden on your shoulders. It isn't gone, but it's eased, as if someone is helping you shoulder it. Would you tell me if it was him?"

I don't know why, but her acknowledgment of that makes my voice waver. "Yes, it's Castian. But it's more than that. I wish I could show you." Then I remember, I can. She takes my hand, and I share the memories of Isla Sombras, Argi, and the pirates San Piedras. I show her the terrifying beauty of being out at sea. Elixa and Maryam training us to fight. Leo and Leyre—who has disappeared. When I break the connection, I rub the palm of my hand to quell the sensation of power.

"You've had quite an adventure with the prince," she says.

"We have never forgotten our purpose," I assure her, my voice sharp. "I know Dez chose you because you've always been the one to make me see reason. But if I hand over this kind of power, he could make things worse."

"But *you* can wield it?"

"I've never wanted power. All I want is to set things right and return what was stolen. I don't trust Cebrián. He's a liar, and he's manipulating Dez."

"I may not agree with his methods," Sayida says, getting to her feet. "But he is the strongest of us. He is a miracle."

I shake my head with frustration. The Whispers have lived in the shadows for so long they're starved for a divine sign to remind us that we are blessed. How can I show them otherwise?

"He is a lost soul who has been tormented for decades. He is full of vengeance and hate. Why can't you see that?"

"Because I *have* to see the good in him. I saw the good in you."

"I am *nothing* like him, and you're wasting your time."

"I can see that." Sayida shuts the door and turns the key.

I pace so long that I leave a clear imprint in the dirt floor around the barrel. I have to believe that Castian and Leo can handle themselves. In the meantime, I go over what happened in the Tresoros cathedral. I felt the power of the Knife, opened myself up, forged the connection—and nothing happened. What does Cebrián know that I don't? Argi's words ring in my head:

It is your power to wield, but remember, you're an extension of the blade and it you. Reveal Fernando's sins to the land, and then let go.

I breathe out a low sigh. Did I let go? The last thing I was looking at before the Whispers arrived was Castian. I clung to the sight of him because I was afraid. I was afraid, but I was *ready*. I unsheathe it and lay the crystal blade flat against my palm.

"What did I do wrong?" I ask.

Part of me, the part that recently learned to believe in impossible things, expects the Knife to answer back. Slowly, I feel a deep ache. The blade quietly hums in my hands, like the tail end of a bell chime.

Not a chime, I realize.

Screams echo from somewhere in the cellar. Cas? Leo? Cebrián was tortured by Justice Méndez himself, and I know what that can do to a person. Still, there is nothing that Leo or Castian could confess that would give the Whispers information. No, Cebrián's torturing them to break me. With the hundred rebels present, they could have easily overpowered me and taken the Knife of Memory. But that wouldn't solve Cebrián's problem of me being connected to its power—unless they kill me. Would Dez allow that?

I sheathe the Knife and bang on the door until the sides of my fists ache. My hands tremble, trickling blood from where I tried to twist the nails and screws on the locks. After what feels like hours of hearing my boys scream, Sayida opens the door. Her eyes are hard and distant. She's been under Méndez's knife before, and the screams must have echoed through every part of the cellar. "Come."

I run, and she does not try to stop me. I take panicked shallow breaths and let the light of my Robári marks guide me. This is how the justice used to play with his prisoners. He'd set them free, let them think they were going to find their way out. Some escaped, but most returned to his torture table. His cells became worse than unmarked graves.

I turn the corner and find Cebrián standing right where I left him in the cellar. There's a figure at his feet, and it takes me a heart-beat to realize it's Cas. The Ripper's pale hand yanks on Castian's hair. Leo is on his knees with his mouth gagged and arms tied back. Cebrián has them lined up for slaughter.

"Stop him," I beg to Dez, to Margo, to Esteban. Other Moria bear witness but don't move. I plead with Sayida close behind me, but she joins the others.

"Renata," Cebrián says softly. "I hope your time alone has given you space to reflect. That is how *I* spent my days in Soledad prison, listening to the crush of the waves." Cebrián pulls on Castian's hair to expose his throat. His blue-green eyes are unfocused, and his arms are slack at his sides. He's barely able to remain on his knees.

"Stop it," I shout.

"Andrés. Did the prince not take your ear? Nearly gut you like river trout? Perhaps that is a place to begin." In a breathless moment, the Ripper plunges a dagger into Castian's side. He breathes hard, but grinds his teeth to stop from screaming.

"Cas!" I shout. Someone holds me back and takes a stand between us.

"We never agreed on this," Dez says, looking down at Cas.

Cebrián raises a thin finger. "Our friends need to understand what we are willing to do for our people, don't you think?"

Dez swallows and nods once. He falls back and pulls me with him. I throw my elbow at his face, but he clutches it with a vise grip and pins my arms at my sides. I throw my head back, but I only hit the solid mass of his chest.

"You know the only way to stop this is by turning over the Knife," Cebrián says, his voice even and calm as he removes the dagger from Castian's side. There's something about the Ripper's manners that remind me of Méndez, how he'd blame the victims on the table for their own pain. Leo screams through his gag, nearly doubled over on the floor. Cas can barely stand, so Cebrián tugs on his hair harder.

"Your silence is my answer," says the Ripper, and takes Castian by his ear, slicing half of it off in a clean sweep. My vision blurs, and a scream rips from my chest. I have been here before, and the living memory of it tears through me as Castian bellows. He falls on his face, then rolls to his side, wood chips sticking to his bloody wound.

"Stop it! Stop it, please. Dez!"

"We've seen enough," Dez barks as he lets me go.

What if this isn't real? What if it is? I have to believe that no matter what has happened, he is not the kind of man who would simply stand by and watch his own brother be killed. That the tremor in his voice is because a part of him, deep down, cares that Cas might die before things are settled between them.

"Have we?" A cold rage passes over Cebrián's face as he pulls Castian against his chest and threatens the dagger against his throat. Red runs from Castian's ear, and his eyes roll back into his head. The gash at his side spreads across the fabric as he bleeds out. I know what Cas would tell me to do. He would sacrifice his life for the good of everything. He would fall on Cebrián's knife if he had to. But this isn't sacrifice. It's torture.

Leo screams and screams, attempting to crawl to me.

"Ready the next one," Cebrián says, sparing a glance at his next victim.

I blink away tears, and I can see them both, my ridiculous, beautiful boys laughing across yellow fields and mountains, fighting side by side.

I unsheathe the Knife of Memory. My throat is raw, but I say, "Let them go."

Cebrián's smile unfurls as the grip on his dagger goes slack. "Release your connection from the Knife, Renata."

I remember the cave, the whispers of the magics. I imagine the thread that connects my power to the primordial, ancient goddess who created this weapon. *Who are you?* she asked. I am a thing too easily broken—that is why I failed then and now. The very air around us sighs, and the Knife of Memory goes cold in my hands. I can't feel the hum of its chime or the spark of magic in my veins.

"There," Cebrián exhales. He lets go of Castian, who slumps to the ground. Tears roll down Cas's temples, and he cradles the wound at his side. "I am overjoyed we could come to an agreement."

I get to my feet and close the distance between us, the Knife flat against my open palm. Cebrián's face is expectant, triumphant. Even without my connection, the Knife of Memory is still a weapon.

I thrust it upward.

Cebrián, somehow expecting my move, sidesteps and grabs my wrist, then twists the blade from my grip. In one swift motion, Cebrián clutches the hilt with both hands and slams it into Castian's chest.

"No!" Dez shouts.

Everything inside me splinters. The air is ripped from my lungs, and the cellar descends into chaos. Margo is screaming, too. Sayida gasps and falls beside Castian, clutching his chest. There's a ripple of emotion among those present, and as the illusion falls away, I understand why.

Where Leo once knelt is Castian, whole and alive, sobbing on his knees. I let him fall against me, shaking at the solid feel of him. Beside us, the dead boy with the crystal blade protruding from his chest wears Castian's face for a moment before his crooked nose and brown eyes reveal Félix.

"*Where* is Leo?" I demand.

"Locked away for safekeeping." Cebrián plucks the knife out of Félix's heart and wipes the blood against his trousers. "Let that be a lesson to all who will stand in my way. I'm disappointed in your resolve, Andrés. It is clear you do not trust me, and that the Whispers are in dire need of new leadership. But worry not. Tonight, we ride to the capital. We will destroy the kingdom of Puerto Leones once and for all."

29

THE WHISPERS LOCK US IN A STORAGE ROOM WITH A SINGLE WATERSKIN. WE can hear victory cheers fading in the cellar as they follow Cebrián back out into the citadela. Dez paces, Castian lunges against the door, and Leo sits nearby. I lose track of time. Every time I close my eyes I see Castian die over and over.

I suppose that was what Cebrián wanted—not to kill the prince, but to leave me with the memory of it. Dez said Félix was from Citadela Riomar, an orphan and new recruit who wanted revenge for his family. I wonder whether he offered up his life for Cebrián or was surprised at the very end. I should have known it was a trick, but Dez's worry gave me pause. None of the Whispers believed that Cebrián was capable of this. I warned them, and once again, they didn't listen to me.

"Nati," Cas whispers, crouching in front of me.

I feel the absence of the Knife of Memory, like a gash in my chest, too. I take off my breastplate and rub at the ghost of a wound. Castian takes my hand and presses my fingers to the center of his palm. I feel for the rice-grain scar there. "I am right here."

But when our eyes meet, I see the fear we share. I see him die again, and I break. I touch his face, and he kisses the inside of my palm. The moment is so intimate that I forget we are not alone.

Leo clears his throat and busies himself rummaging for something to eat. Dez is watching me with something worse than betrayal in his eyes. He opens his mouth to speak, then chokes on his words, and resumes his pacing.

When Cebrián ordered Dez to be locked up with the rest of us, I thought that he'd beat through the door or that perhaps Margo would have interceded. But Cebrián has instilled the fear of the Six Hells and guaranteed the loyalty of the Whispers. I was foolish to discount him, to think he'd simply run out of the prison to what? Start a life? Resume the one he was taken from? Forty years of captivity by the crown and justice. I should have known he'd want revenge. Wouldn't I?

I pull my hand away from Castian, avoiding the look *he* gives me. Though he recovers and gives me space.

"Are there any hidden passages?" I ask.

"I don't know," Dez says, avoiding looking in my direction. "Esteban was tasked with scouting while I was on the streets fighting *his* men."

"They're your men, too, brother," Cas taunts with a cruel grin. "You keep forgetting."

Dez charges Castian, who's on his feet in a single breath. I hear the crunch of bone and Castian's groan as he spits blood on the floor.

"Don't make me regret sparing your life for her sake," Dez growls.

Castian swings hard and knocks him on his back, heaving. "Her sake? You stood by and let that lunatic torment her because you're consumed with jealousy. If you'd joined me when I begged for your help, I wouldn't have had to endanger her in the first place."

"Stop," I say, but my voice doesn't carry beyond their fighting. Castian is wrong—they would have needed me in the end. This was always supposed to be my path.

When their shouting turns into flying fists, I grab an empty crate and toss it in their general direction. It won't hurt them, but they snap out of it.

"Oh, look," Leo says, loudly trying to defuse the argument. "Wine. A good vintage. If I'm going to perish down here, I might as well be drunk."

Dez sweeps raven locks out of his bruised eyes. He offers Leo a begrudging smile. "I'll join you. I'm sure Cebrián has alerted the Second Sweep of our location to cause a diversion for his escape."

Castian touches the tender skin on his jaw and winces. His anger seems to clear, and he slumps beside me, offering a sheepish stare. "I'm sorry, Nati."

Dez's eyes widen with questions I can't answer. "Why in the Six Hells do you keep calling her that?"

"It's what my father used to call me," I say.

"I see," Dez mutters.

"Whilst you were pretending to be dead," Leo reminds Dez, "our dear Robári discovered a great many things about the Príncipe Dorado. For instance, they've been friends since they were about wee high."

"You were the Moria boy from the palace that helped Ren escape." Dez looks Castian up and down and scoffs. "Of course you were."

Castian reaches over to Leo and snatches the bottle. He drinks, wipes his mouth with the back of his hand, and returns it. The four of us sit like the cardinal directions on a map, and Leo places the wine in the center. I explain to Dez as much as I can. I tell him of the island and the pirates San Piedras, of Argi and her marriage to Illan, of my armor belonging to Galatea. Through it all, he either stares at the hard-packed dirt floor or shakes his head in disbelief.

"You have no right to be angry with her," Cas says. "When I told you the truth about who you were, you ran."

Dez snatches the bottle from Castian's hand. He takes a deep breath before drinking. "And I regretted it as soon as I left. You don't know what it was like for me. It felt like my entire world had ended. To have you show up in that cell and tell me that we were— brothers—that a monster was my father. And then to join you on a search for the Knife of Memory? I ran. I'm not proud of it. I found passage, and after a day of being out at sea, I knew I had to come back. I took the life raft and rowed back to shore."

"You're wrong," Castian says. "I do know what it's like to have your entire world shatter. It happened when I thought I was responsible for your death. And it happened again when I discovered you were still alive."

I want to go to both of them. The strongest boys I know, who can barely look at each other. I rub my hands for warmth, but when that doesn't work, Leo passes me the bottle of wine. I try to imagine Dez rowing in the dark, making it back to Puerto Leones. How did he find the Whispers? Why did he push me away?

"Cebrián said that we slipped through your fingers," I point out. "But your note told us to stay away. Why did you lie?"

Dez cranes his head back, as if he's asking Our Lady of Shadows for forgiveness. "Because you weren't tracking me. I was tracking you."

My heart gives a leap. "What do you mean?"

"I mean the Whispers needed the Knife of Memory. I knew you'd left with *him* to find me. Esteban helped, using his magics to peer into the minds of strangers to listen to your conversations. I'd persuaded the servants to tell me everything they knew about you. I knew you wouldn't give up your search for me, and so I left that message and waited for your next move."

"To Little Luzou," Leo says.

"But you got there first," Castian says, watching his brother carefully.

"With Cebrián's tactics, we had access to horses."

An uneasy sensation moves under my skin. Cebrián's tactics. "If you wanted the Knife, Dez, why did you try to stop me from leaving on the ship? Was that just to bring me back to the Whispers? To put me on another trial?"

"Of course not, *Ren*. Cebrián." Dez says the name like a curse. "He told me that Robári who successfully use the weapon become Hollows, but he'd survived it and claimed he could do it again without having to sacrifice you. I was supposed to join you in retrieving the Knife and then take it from you. But seeing you together—" He stops abruptly, taking the bottle back. "I messed up."

I process his words slowly. He would have joined us. He would have been on that island, shared in our meals, and then taken the Knife from me. He would have made a fool of me. My anger bleeds to the surface. "You would rather Cebrián wield the power and destroy the entire kingdom?"

"You did it for *them*." Dez shouts my hypocrisy. "Perhaps Castian would have let you die, but I was trying to save you."

"I don't have to let Nati do anything," Cas says as he snatches the bottle. If he grips the glass any tighter, it'll shatter. "It was her choice."

"Stop," I whisper, and rest my hand on his shoulder. Almost instantly, Cas's anger breaks.

Dez shuts his eyes and squeezes the bridge of his nose. "You could have chosen anyone—there are millions of people in this entire wretched kingdom—but you chose *him*. You watched him kill me. How long did you wait, Ren? A day? A week? Do you know what it felt like seeing you in that forest, or seeing you in that crowd trying to reach me, and realizing the pain I was going to cause you?"

I snap my gaze to him. I always wondered whether he'd seen me running toward him. I swallow the emotion in my throat. "I—"

"Did you even mourn me?"

I shove my finger in his chest. "I remember that moment every day, Dez. Of course I mourned you. I'm still mourning you because when you had the chance, you *left* me."

"I came back." Dez wipes at a single tear rolling down his cheek. "But you weren't there. You were with him. The Whispers still needed me. Margo and I picked up what was left of us, and then Cebrián came to us."

"It's done, Dez."

Castian leans his head back against the brick wall and shuts his eyes. Leo practically feeds him wine like a baby bird. The princes of the realm, the dissidents, the rebels. The boys who have my heart. And they're all fools—and I'm a fool right along with them because I love them in different ways. All three of them.

We wait, listening to the chitter of mice, the groans of the old estate. I shut my eyes and imagine what it would be like to simply rest. Leo nudges closer to me and I rest my head on his shoulder as he draws shapes in the dirt with the sturdier wood chips.

"What do we do now?" he asks.

"Cebrián is going to use the Whispers as cannon fodder so he can get his revenge," I say, sick with disgust.

"And we're locked in here," Cas whispers. He and Dez run their hands through their hair, then huff a sigh at the exact same time.

Leo leans in and whispers, "I see it now."

"You don't see anything," Dez barks, and yanks the bottle from Castian, who crosses his arms over his chest and stews.

"Fernando will be prepared," I say.

"Don't worry," Dez says. "Cebrián will have another Illusionári disguised as Castian to get through the gates."

Castian sits up suddenly. "Wait—my father already *knows* that I'm not being held captive."

Dez's face falls. Questions trace lines across his brow. "What do you mean?"

"My father sent Leyre after us," Cas says firmly. "She told us that he knew I was plotting against him and searching for the Knife of Memory."

"Who in the Six Hells is Leyre?" Dez asks.

Leo scratches the side of his head. "A treasure hunter and former sailor in the Luzouan navy that the king hired to track down his son and steal the Knife of Memory."

Dez's lip quirks. When he looks at me with sly eyes, I remember every time he made me laugh. The way he'd make the most miserable nights on the road bearable simply with his presence. "I'm surprised at the company you're keeping, Ren."

"It doesn't matter now. Leyre ran when you attacked us in the temple," Leo says. "She's probably halfway back home now."

I gnaw at the inside of my lip because I want to believe that he's wrong, that Leyre was simply caught in the cross fire and was separated from us. But I know that she needs to get away as far as possible or face her betrayal of King Fernando. I don't blame her for choosing to live.

"Did the king want you dead or alive?" Dez asks.

Cas shrugs. "Dead, but it wouldn't have mattered. He would have used me either way as an excuse to decimate the Whispers."

"That's why we were racing to get here," I tell Dez. "We thought the city would be overrun with the Second Sweep. We overheard the soldiers saying they were still waiting for reinforcements."

Dez's features go rigid as he stands, his mind working through everything we know. "The king's known for weeks that we weren't holding you, and yet he's only sent enough soldiers to keep us distracted."

"He's waiting for something," I say.

Leo lets the dregs of the bottle fall onto his tongue and grimaces. "What I don't get is, if King Fernando sent Leyre after us, who put him on the path? Lady Nuria would sooner drink poison than reveal your secrets."

"We didn't tell anyone else," I say.

"I did." Dez breathes fast. "I told Cebrián. When he first came to us, he claimed he wanted to join the Whispers to exact revenge for what was done to him. I felt sorry for him. I thought we wanted the same thing. I didn't even tell Margo or the others of your quest to find me, to find the Knife."

"When my father created the Arm of Justice," Cas says, "he and Méndez had been trying to replicate and harness the power of the Moria. Weaponize it. Cebrián is as close as they ever got because he'd already been *made*."

A cold dread seeps down into my bones. "He's not going to kill Fernando. He's handing the king a way to make more Rippers."

Dez picks up the bottle and throws it against the wall, then releases a string of curses and shouts. Leo looks at me out the corner of his eye and whispers, "I *definitely* see it."

"We have to get out of here," I say, putting my breastplate back on with shaky fingers. "Now."

There's shuffling above us and the ceiling wheezes. Heavy boots stomp downstairs. The four of us stand, with nothing in the way of weapons except bottles of wine and a few planks of wood. Dez can lull the Second Sweep; maybe Cas can cast illusions as a diversion, and I can steal memories. It all depends on how outnumbered we are.

Leo holds out the jagged points of the bottle neck. I look at Castian, then Dez. One day, I'm going to have to stop saying good-bye to them. Today, we have to live a little longer. Muffled voices come from the other side as the door cranks open.

"It's us! It's us!" Leyre shouts, holding up her hands. Her cheeks are flushed, and her green eyes dance with mischief. Behind her is Lady Nuria, decked in a leather-and-metal breastplate and shimmering chain mail.

Leo charges Leyre, hauling her into his arms. "We thought you'd left us."

I pile atop them, feeling the reverberation of their wild, relieved laughter.

"There wasn't any time," she explains. "I saw a way out, and I took it. I went to find help."

Lady Nuria squeezes my shoulder and pulls me into an embrace as Castian steps into the dark hall. "I'm glad you survived each other."

Dez is the last one to step out of the storage room. He's cautious, eyebrows furrowed as he takes in Leyre and Nuria.

"I hope you brought a small army?" he says.

Nuria turns at the sound of Dez's voice. I spot the moment she sees Castian's features in his brother, from his muscular build to the vulnerability in his amber stare.

The Duquesa of Tresoros raises her chin in challenge. "I brought that and so much more."

We follow her down the hall, where three Whispers are waiting: Esteban, Margo, and Sayida.

Esteban clutches Dez's forearm, and they clap each other on the back. "We were wrong to leave you behind."

I know it takes all of her, but Margo closes the space between us and says, "What he did to Félix—you were right. I'm sorry."

"How is Cebrián traveling to the capital?" I ask.

"By boat. The streets are unusually quiet," Margo says, noticing the troubled stare Dez and I exchange. "We doubled back while they were boarding. That's when the Second Sweep resumed their patrols."

"What is it?" Sayida asks.

"There's more," Dez says, and divulges our suspicions about Cebrián's treachery.

"And now the Ripper has a head start," I say.

"How are we going to catch up to them?" Leo asks.

Lady Nuria trades a knowing smile with Leyre, and says, "By river, of course. But first, there's the small matter of my husband's blockade."

30

LADY NURIA'S GUARDS ARE WAITING FOR US OUTSIDE THE MANOR, ROUGHLY three dozen clad in her family's livery of silver and cobalt blue. They carry a flag with her personal crest—three mountain peaks and a sun at its center. Residents peek through their windows, watching us go by like wraiths in the rising dawn.

Nuria, the descendant of queens, leads the way. When I first met her, I was stunned by her beauty and her candor. Discovering that she was one of the rebels' biggest allies only reinforced my respect for her. But now, she feels like a saving grace when I was ready to lose all hope. As we march toward the harbor, I know there is no going back for any of us. We are declaring war on King Fernando and sacrificing our lives, titles, futures, our everything.

"Tell me, Lady Nuria," I say. "What does your husband think you do all day in that grand mansion of yours?"

"As one of my attendants has been in my suite serving as a decoy for the past three nights, I don't believe he's noticed my absence or that I've been building my own rebellion."

"He doesn't deserve you. He's a wretch."

"Believe me, I know. Disgraced and divorced before my twentieth year." Nuria's melodic throaty voice manages to sound delighted despite her sarcasm. "Mother would have been so proud."

"She would be," I assure her.

As the sun comes up, she's impossible not to look at. Her armor highlights the hourglass figure that entranced so many at court. The sword at her hip is simple, with delicate carvings along the hilt. Her tight curls are swept back in a knot, framing luminous, nearly black eyes full of furious hope. Her brown skin is clear of any powders and kohl from court, but her mouth is still the red of a promise made in blood.

Nerves begin to set in as I catch the scent of the harbor. "Are you wearing *color* on your lips?"

"Of course, Renata," she says. "We're staging a rebellion, not attending midday mass."

My laugh is lost in the thunder of horses suddenly filling the streets. Second Sweep soldiers cut off our route. I recognize Pascal, who tried to stop Carnaval in Acesteña. He orders his men to stand down as he dismounts.

"Lord Commander!" Pascal says as Castian steps forward. Then his eyes take in Lady Nuria, her men, and the small group of rebels. He's so perplexed that he clings to niceties. "Lady Nuria? Justice Alessandro was not expecting you. Either of you."

"Stand down, Captain Pascal," Cas says. "I am well, as you can see. Lady Nuria rescued me, and we are escorting these rebels to the capital."

Pascal shuffles closer, hand at his hilt. "We were given orders to take you to the king himself."

"Were you?" Castian grins, and the demeanor of the confident prince I know returns, the edges of him glinting under the coastal sun. "I'm sure my father has been very worried."

The soldier stares at Castian, as if he is trying to piece together the truth. The men don't trust their eyes because they have been warned about Moria. And yet, here is the kidnapped prince, alive and well—not the prisoner of war they've been told that he is.

"Let us through," Castian commands, lowering his voice to a familiar cutting edge. "I will be sure my father gives you and your men a commendation for aiding in my return."

But I remember this Pascal. I've known soldiers like him my entire life fighting alongside the Whispers. He turns and runs back to his men, and they begin a series of warning whistles and bells, alerting the entire citadela. Castian curses and unsheathes his sword just as Pascal and the Second Sweep regroup, ready to strike. While the Tresorian soldiers move in tandem to form a barricade, Nuria gathers us around her.

"There are four streets between us and the harbor," she says, pointing due south past her warriors, where a line of Leonesse soldiers wait in a blockade.

"We can spread out and flank them," Dez suggests.

Nuria casts an appraising smile at him but shakes her head. "The pathways on either side are part of the lower district. They'd never recover from the damages."

"Then empty out your coffers, princess," he shoots back.

Nuria looks shocked. I don't think anyone has ever spoken to her this way before, but it's Esteban who speaks up.

"She's right," Esteban says. "Not to mention the alleys become narrower. We'd be pinned down. We should take Calle Oropuro instead—it was designed to cut a direct line from harbor to harbor."

Nuria beams delightedly. "You know your history."

"We'll *be* history if we don't move now," I urge.

All around, shutters are slamming open, and people are watching from the five-story row houses.

"We lead them along Calle Oropuro," Castian says. "Flush them out and then double back. Leo and Leyre will take two of your soldiers and get the vessels ready to sail."

Dez rubs his beard, then points to Margo. "You and Castian must create an illusion."

The prince and the Whisper glower at each other, but nod. Dez finishes dividing our strengths, and we have our orders to proceed.

Lady Nuria glances back and says, "We have to—"

"Stop them!" The grating voice of Justice Alessandro interrupts her. He shoves his way through the Second Sweep, and we follow Nuria to the front of the line. When he recognizes his wife among us, horror twists his thin pink lips into a snarl. "Get *back* here. How dare you embarrass me this way."

"Good morning, dear husband," Lady Nuria calls sweetly. "I thought I'd come in person to let you know I want a divorce!"

There's a moment of utter silence, followed by laugher from both the Tresorian guards and the Second Sweep. Alessandro might quite possibly be foaming at the mouth as he shouts, "Lady Nuria is in league with the rebels. Arrest her. Arrest them all!"

And then the thin morning peace shatters.

"Sayida, with me!" Dez shouts. Their magics ripple in the direction of our attackers. Some soldiers slow and fight against the sensation that tells them to stand down. But others, like Pascal, keep charging. Some people are sustained by war for so long they cannot see a way out, and neither Sayida nor Dez find a sliver of peace within him that they can manipulate. But still, we get past the first of four blockades with Nuria's soldiers making quick work of the stragglers.

Alessandro climbs atop a carriage. He bellows commands and orders to kill. "Take my wife and the Robári alive."

What cruelties must he be dreaming up for us? Would he make Méndez proud? I channel my anger into my fists. Out the corner of my eye, I see Cas and Margo fighting side by side. I can't help but hear Argi's voice telling me my love for him is a distraction, then correcting my posture, my stance, and I barrel harder against those who would cut me down. Four Second Sweep soldiers have Esteban and me trapped, and the two of us stand back to back.

"Do you remember the scrape in the Sedona Canyons?" Esteban pants.

"I still have the scar," I recall, touching the mark on my left arm.

"Good."

He stops an oncoming blow, gripping the soldier's wrist. I see the way his eyes become dilated as they do when he peers into someone's mind. But now he's able to predict every move the guard will make. Within moments, the man is disarmed and unconscious. Seeing Esteban as the bigger threat, the others descend on him, leaving me to attack them from behind.

One soldier catches on and hurls me to the ground. Her weight digs into my ribs, her blade at my throat. Esteban runs up behind and slashes the backs of her knees. She falls with a deep scream.

"Thank you," I say, breathing hard.

"You were right, Ren. About everything."

"Fight now. Apologize later." I squeeze his hand. "That's two!"

We press our advantage, but the third barrier is a cavalry of two dozen horsemen. Nuria's soldiers regroup around her. I think we need to retreat and follow around the river, but the way around is blocked.

"Cas," I say, and tug his sleeve.

The people of Citadela Crescenti are emerging from their homes. They wield clubs, brooms, kitchen knives, machetes. I believe one woman is even brandishing serving tongs in one hand and a frying pan in the other, oil dripping on the cobblestones.

"Nuria," Castian says, and the duquesa looks up. The ancient silver-and-cobalt-blue flag of Tresoros spills out of window after window. The people join us and cry out her name, while the cavalry shuffles from side to side as they try to retain control of their mounts. Straggler foot soldiers rush our group, and the people fight with every tooth and nail and machete in their possession.

"We need to scare the horses," I say.

"Hey, Lion Cub," Margo shouts to Castian.

"Don't"—Castian kicks one guard in the chest, whirls around, and stops a second from cleaving his golden head in two—*"call me that."*

Margo's laugh is wicked as she takes his hand. They combine forces, and the pulse of their magic is instant. A wave crests high above, glistening in the morning light. People scream "Glory to the old gods! Glory to the heavens!" as it crashes down the Calle Oropuro.

"It's a trick, you stupid beast!" Pascal shouts at his horse just before he's thrown off.

"Last one!" I shout.

The final barricade is a single line of soldiers that stands between us and the harbor, but then the Second Sweep regroups. Pascal and his cohort are ready to charge. Somehow Alessandro has made it back to the front line.

"Last one," Dez mutters, wiping sweat from his brow. He looks down at me and winks, as if to say, *That's all?*

"You have nowhere to go," the justice shouts. "Lower your weapons and submit yourself as traitors to the kingdom of Puerto Leones."

"Never," Nuria snarls as she marches on. "Your days of cruelty and murder are over."

I see the moment Dez looks at her, really looks at her, and falls into place at her side. Castian and I join her on the other.

"How dare you talk to me like that?" Alessandro spits. "Who are *you* but the prince's castoff?"

"I am the daughter of queens!" Nuria's voice splits the air. "The Arm of Justice must come to an end. And it starts, dear husband, with you."

There's a guttural sound. An arrow pierces the throat of the man directly beside Alessandro, who lets loose a horrid scream, as if it's his neck that is spilling blood. As we look around for the source of the attack, a familiar horn splits the air.

In the harbor is a small ship flying the flag of the pirates San Piedras. Dozens of Moria hang from the rigging and perch on the port rail. The king's men are confused, turning their backs on us, and we press our advantage.

"Apologies we're late, Renata," Maryam booms, pulling back a hood. "But stealing a ship is no easy task."

At her side, Elixa draws an arrow and aims it at Alessandro. "The next one goes in *your* throat."

The justice shouts orders, but it's no use. We have them pinned down. The pirates San Piedras flow from the dock and soon move like a unified force with Lady Nuria's soldiers. More citizens pour into the street throwing anything and everything at the justice and the king's men, all of them shouting the name of Nuria of Tresoros.

After the Second Sweep is subdued, we leave them at the mercy of the people of Crescenti and board four river boats. We race against the current, knowing we can't stop until we reach Andalucía.

31

PART OF ME ISN'T READY TO RETURN TO THE CAPITAL CITY OF PUERTO LEONES, but I have no choice. Leyre takes command of our barge, calling out the rows. Castian is deep in conversation with Sayida and Maryam, introducing my former unit to the pirates who reeled us in at sea and changed everything.

"Where's Captain Argi?" I ask Elixa. We stand at the back of the boat, watching Citadela Crescenti grow smaller and smaller.

She flashes a smile. The wind blows the nest of curls atop her head over her eyes. "After everything you showed us, we couldn't stay behind. But you've met Captain, she's set in her ways. She did give me a message for you."

"Oh?"

"She wanted us to thank you for helping her remember."

I look back at where Castian sits. We haven't been able to talk alone since the last night on our ship, but he catches my gaze, and we simply share a moment of relief that we have another day together.

A sharp cry draws everyone's notice. "Elixa?"

My friend turns at the sound of her name. At the front of the boat is Margo. Her eyes are wide, a look of stunned disbelief on her face. That's when I see it—the same long, pert nose, the same sapphire-blue eyes and dry laughter. All at once I recall feeling like I'd met Elixa before. She'd said she was from Riomar. I remember Margo's greatest hurt was that she survived when her younger sister hadn't. But her sister did survive, she was just lost for a time.

"Margolina?"

They push through the small crowd and hug so tightly that they seem to fuse together. Margo takes the girl's face in hers. "I thought you were dead—I thought—"

Elixa touches the scar visible though her peach fuzz at the side of her scalp. "Almost was."

Tears spring to my eyes, and I look away. In the barge behind us are Lady Nuria, as well as Leo and Esteban. More soldiers and pirates are packed in the last two boats. The air is rich with dirt and the new green of the season. Thick emerald trees line the shores and frame small wooden houses on stilts. Entire families watch our boats proceed up the river. I wonder if they have an inkling of what we plan to do.

"This will work," I whisper to the river.

"It has to," Dez says, standing at my side.

I lean back to stare at him. "Do you remember that fishing village where you hid in a barrel of squid to escape from the soldiers?"

He smirks, golden eyes sparkling with memory. "Vaguely."

"If you could survive that stench, you can survive anything."

He picks at a chip in the wooden rail. "How am I supposed to survive losing you?"

I breathe deeply. If I speak, the emotion in my throat will spill into tears, and I've shed enough of those for a lifetime.

"I will take this moment, however," Dez continues, "and say that I was right."

Of course, he's laughing—typical Dez. "About what exactly?"

"Our whole lives you've been afraid of who you are." He takes my hand and cups it in his. The intimacy feels strange. I think of the night we spent by a different river, right before we splintered apart. "But I have always known that you were the very best of us."

I bury my face in his chest. I don't want him to see me cry. I don't want another reason to be weak when I have to face Cebrián and King Fernando. Dez brushes a hand over my hair and kisses my head.

I look up. "You will make a great leader, Dez. I always thought so."

His lashes appear darker when they're wet. "When Castian showed me the truth, I thought I'd go mad. Instead, I left. I never got to ask my father if—"

"Illan loved you. It was a terrible thing that he did, but he loved you." I give him a nudge. "Look at Margo. She's found her sister again. Do you know what Castian did for most of our trip?"

Dez grimaces slightly and leans on his elbows on the rail. "Do I really want to know?"

I slap his chest. "Be serious."

"You were born serious," he says with a sigh.

I roll my eyes. "He wanted to know what you were like."

I glance at Castian, who watches me with that intensity of his, and I feel drawn to him. But for now, he needs something more than I can offer.

"Did you tell him about what an extremely humble yet entirely courageous commander I was? About the scores of times I eluded his impudent soldiers—"

"Talk to him," I whisper. "Please. The only way this ends is with the three of us. Together."

Dez nods once, licking his lip. He doesn't say yes, but he doesn't say no either.

"I'll try," he tells me.

When it's time to alternate rowing, Dez takes the seat beside Castian. I watch them row side by side staring straight ahead. There is a moment when Dez says something and Cas laughs. A sensation pinches my chest, and I don't have to look to find the memory etching into my skin.

It takes a day and a half of rowing, but we know we're there when the river opens onto the lake just south of the capital and the glittering towers of the palace loom in the distance. My heart is a fist beating against my chest until we disembark, leaving the river boats moored in tall grass.

We march toward Andalucía. Severed heads, fresh and still dripping with blood and sinew, line both sides of the dusty road that leads to the city gates. This is our warning to turn back. Sayida, Margo, and Esteban must feel it, too, because we exchange glances. We have been on this path before, the day we tried to save Dez from his execution. This time we have something we did not have before. This time, we are not alone. Margo, Castian, and Elixa take the lead, cloaking us with their Illusionári magics.

The long dirt road cuts a clear view of the tightly packed buildings, some with foundations so old that they look like weary travelers slumped against each other for support. Ahead, a line of soldiers bars the gates—King Fernando is expecting us. But that is not the most striking thing about the jewel of the country.

Andalucía's palace is a work of magnificent architecture with four towers connected by sky bridges. Each tower glitters under the sun, a flagrant shrine to the Fajardo family name. I have lived in its rooms, haunted its halls, witnessed its hideous underbelly. But I have never seen it glow. A silver aura surrounds the structure, pulsing like the light within alman stone.

"What is that?" Dez is awed beside me.

"It's Cebrián," I say. "He's using the Knife of Memory."

"How can you tell?" Leyre asks.

Leo shrugs and waves a dismissive hand. "I'd say the palace turning into a giant candle may have something to do with it."

But it's more than that. I touch my fingers to the white peregrine falcon on my breastplate, and a ripple of magics passes through me. I have given up my claim on the Knife of Memory, but that connection has left a sliver of itself within me, thin as spider silk.

Rows of jumpy Leonesse guards flank the entrance gates. They can hear our boots, the rattle of armor, but they can't *see* us. Slowly, Castian and the other Illusionári lower the glamour, and then he strikes the first blow, piercing like an arrow through their defenses. The Tresoros soldiers create a wedge for the rest of us to push through the capital's streets. The stink of gutter water mingles with burning pyres of garbage that warn denizens their city is under attack.

Leo and Sayida are tasked with evacuating the servants in the palace while Cas, Dez, and I go in search of the king and his Ripper. But now that the time has come I hesitate. I have survived hundreds of fights and skirmishes, but in this moment I feel the love for my companions more than ever before. Perhaps that is the root of what Argi warned me about. And yet, I prefer this version of myself.

"Go, Renata, now!" Margo shouts, cutting down a soldier with a brutal strike of her sword. She picks up his and pants as she wields both. Something passes between us. It isn't friendship or forgiveness—it is acceptance. "I'll see you in the Third Hell."

The Third Hell, the one made of eternal white flame, is already here. Cebrián's silver form is stepping onto the balcony.

Suddenly, the reverberation of power ripples through me. A cord tugs in my chest. "We have to hurry. Something is wrong."

Castian points. "Are those—?"

Bodies climb onto the sky bridges, onto the ledges of windows, the lip of balconies.

"Those are Whispers," Dez says.

"The north tower," Cas orders, and we race after him.

The north tower. Fernando's throne room. He would be in the place he carved as a shrine to his victories, a place where he has people bow and bleed in his name.

When we reach the sky bridge, King Fernando's guards spill onto the opposite end. My body aches from days of motion. Weeks of heartache. Years of clinging to a life I haven't always wanted. Still I fight, slashing and punching my way to the fate I have chosen. Cutting through the waves of King Fernando's soldiers is like trying to swim upstream, but we reach the other side, where light shines from the open doors ahead, and I steel myself to step inside.

King Fernando sits on his throne made of alman stone, leaning on one armrest. He's dressed in his preferred black silks, and knowing what I know, I wonder if a part of him has never stopped mourning. He leans forward, his eyes tracing the armor I wear. Does he recognize it? Can he? The spell lasts for a moment, and then he lets loose the low rumbling laugh of a victor.

Spread around the dais are Whispers who chose to follow Cebrián. I recognize Javi, the beginnings of silver veins tracing at the corners of his eyes. Olivia, a Persuári who could scale up any tree or building as if born for the task. Enriqua, a Ventári who always managed to stretch food for days when our stores were down to scraps. More and more of them stand as if they're petrified in place.

"What did you do to them?" I ask.

King Fernando's black eyes come alive at my questions. "I have improved my Hand of Moria. I was missing a Robári, Renata, but here you are returning to a place you claim to loathe. And you've returned my son to me."

Cas and Dez exchange a fierce glance, and then the elder prince of Puerto Leones approaches his father. "She brought back both of your sons. Father, allow me to introduce Andrés, prince of Sól Abene, commander of the Whispers Rebellion, and second in line for the throne of Puerto Leones."

Dez cocks a smile, drinking in his father's quiet rage. "I prefer Dez de Martín. We rebels like to be brief as we are constantly on the run."

"Brief isn't how I'd describe you," I say.

Now it's our turn to laugh at the king.

Fernando is rendered speechless. He stands, stepping as close as he can, but careful to remain far enough that neither of his sons' swords can strike. As the king takes in Dez's features, there's a brief moment where he might recognize himself in the shape of his eyes, the set of his lips. But then it's gone—there is no light in him, no relief that the son he'd believed dead as an infant is standing before him.

"How?" he asks.

"It appears my mother thought it best I was raised far away from you," Dez says. I glimpse at Castian, but his features do not betray emotion.

Fernando's eyes crinkle at the corners. "I'd suspected your mother of being sympathetic to the Moria plight, sending food and aid to rebellions. I blamed it on her weak heart. I had no idea that she'd given me not one but two monstrous sons. Sometimes I regret killing her. But you have freed my conscience."

"What did you say?" Castian breathes hard and fast, taking predatory steps toward the throne.

"I poisoned her," Fernando confesses, the way someone might say, "I ate supper" or "I went to market."

Fernando stands, places his hands on Javi's shoulders. The boy doesn't even flinch. He's a boy made of stone, a weapon. "I needed to secure the Fajardo name with new heirs. The people loved her, and I feared that if I had her committed or her family suspected my involvement, there would be an uproar. Instead, I poisoned her drink myself, every day, little by little. To the court she was simply a drunk, a queen gone mad with sorrow. Pity, such beauty gone to waste."

I remember the last memory of Castian's mother—on the grass of her garden, red, swollen eyes like she'd run out of tears. Poisoned.

"Puerto Leones continues to owe you a great debt, Renata," Fernando says coolly, but I see how he trembles. "I have spent *decades* attempting to harness and tame the power of Moria, but I was never able to re-create the events that led to Cebrián. I suppose I should thank you for your service to the kingdom."

"I am going to *kill* you," Castian threatens, and I believe him.

"No, my son." The king eyes Dez. "My *sons*. You are going to become my weapons. You along with every Moria on this continent."

I think of the Whispers standing, waiting for Fernando's command, and Margo, Esteban, and Sayida, and all the Moria pirates down in the citadela fighting for our future. I take Castian's and Dez's hands in mine.

I feel the connection of Dez's Persuári magics, like the brush of a feather along my skin. I am certain he is sharing with me his certainty, his love. And I know that I have to go.

"Do it!" Fernando commands.

The living statues come alive. Their eyes are pools of starlight as they attack the king's sons. I slip between them and climb onto the balcony, shielding my eyes against the light radiating from Cebrián. Hundreds and hundreds of threads ripple from his heart. Each one extends far and wide, connecting every Moria to him. When I look down, I see the faint thread at my own chest.

"Isn't it beautiful, Renata?" he asks. "I know you can feel the power of the Knife of Memory. It never truly leaves you. There is always part of you that hungers for that connection. It is—"

"Like hearing the voice of the goddess," I finish. Because he's right. I *have* felt the voice of the power I gave up. Different voices call to me now—Castian shouting his brother's name, my friends in the city below. I used to think that if I destroyed the Gray, I'd have room for my own thoughts. Now I know that the strongest voices are sometimes the people we love.

You're vengeance in the night.

This is not your fault. This was done to you.

The world has never deserved you.

Where is my Nati?

I am left with only two options. To sever Cebrián's connection with the dagger I must either convince him to relinquish it willingly or kill him. I am tired of bloodshed.

"Cebrián, hear me," I say. He turns slowly and tilts his head to the side, fists clutching the glowing Knife of Memory against his chest. His liquid-silver irises hone in on mine. "Remember that day in Soledad? Remember how desperately you wanted to leave that place? You escaped, so why did you return to him?"

Cebrián casts his eyes to the perfect cloudless blue sky that has no idea the world below is burning. "He is all I have ever had. I have no family. I have no one. I have a single memory, one I relive, and that is my own rebirth as what I am."

I recognize that emotion—being dragged so far down that nothing will ever be good again.

"I know what it's like to be used for your power," I tell him. "When Fernando's done with you, there will be nothing left. What was done to you is unspeakable. But it *was* done to you. It wasn't your fault. Please, let me help you with this burden, Cebrián."

He shakes his head, releasing one hand to wind a thread around his finger. A painful tug jerks me forward. "No. I will help you with yours. After today, there will be hundreds like me."

"No," I say. "There won't."

You were born to be a weapon. If I do this, Justice Méndez will have been right, and I accept that if it means saving the people I love.

Cebrián thrusts the crystal blade at me, but I duck, and he slices through air. I catch his arm and twist, and he bellows. I don't stop, don't hesitate. With the Knife of Memory in my hand, I ram it into his throat. Blood sprays across my face as I lower him onto the floor. His final breath is gurgled, and then the light in his silver eyes goes out.

"May you rest in her everlasting shadow," I pray.

Then I feel the hum, the spark, the heat, of the ancient power in my grasp. I am an extension of the blade and it me. I hurry back into the throne room, where I find the new Hand of Moria on the ground. King Fernando is on his knees, shouting for guards who do not come, his crown tossed to the side. Castian and Dez, covered in fresh cuts and bruises, point their swords at his throat.

When he sees me, Castian releases a sigh of relief.

"Hold him still," I say.

The brothers grip their father, who screams as I press my

fingertips to his temples. My magics race through me, connecting with his mind. The terrible things he did at Isla Sombras are in the Knife, but I realize, with his confession of killing Penelope, there must be more locked in his past. I pluck his secrets like rotten stone fruit, and it tastes bitter.

When I let go, Fernando slumps to the ground. Castian hands Dez his sword and approaches the throne with me.

"Are you ready?" he asks.

I have to be. I am.

I take his hand in mine and raise the Knife of Memory with the other. The light of the alman stone grows brighter and brighter until Castian and I are standing in a white space without ceiling or floor.

Argi's last words echo through my mind again. *Reveal Fernando's sins to the land, and then let go.*

The release is the hardest. How do you let go of a life before it's barely begun? My heart swells. One day I will have to stop saying good-bye to Cas and Dez. I won't say it at all.

32

It starts with her first death.

    Galatea is a princess, a bride, a girl in love. Three arrows pierce her back, and her light is gone. But when has the world cared about another dead Moria, another dead girl?

    Fernando holds his young wife in his arms.

It follows with her second death.

    Galatea is a body growing colder and colder in the belly of a ship. The crew is lost at sea for so long, the only thing that keeps them afloat is fear of a furious, mad prince. When they reach the Isla Sombras, Fernando and his faithful crew carry Galatea into the cave while Admiral Arias remains aboard. Cebrián swims across the blue lake to retrieve the Knife. For a moment, he is drowning. The cave rains shards of crystals. Fernando shields Galatea with his body.

The Robári returns with the Knife of Memory, and he calls its ancient power to him. But the blade will not be used to violate the laws of life, and the girl remains dead. The power blasts through the cave, rattling the water into waves, and the crystals fall and knock Argiñe and two other Moria soldiers unconscious.

Fernando crawls away from Galatea's lifeless body. He sees the Knife of Memory glowing in the sand. Argiñe bleeds from her forehead and comes in and out of consciousness, begging the king to stop.

Cebrián sees the Knife, too, but Fernando wraps his fist around the hilt first. They tussle in the sand until Fernando forces Cebrián into a chokehold. Fernando whispers, "Your power is mine. You will bend to my will."

Ribbons of light spill from the crystal blade, and then Fernando pierces Cebrián's chest, again and again. There is so much blood, and light cracks out of each wound. Fernando slashes the throat of the Illusionári. Stabs the Persuári through the heart.

He crawls back to Galatea, and while he holds her, he doesn't hear the girl's footsteps. When he looks up, Argiñe bludgeons him with the hilt of her sword.

He wakes. He is on a ship. He is on the sea, and everything is gone. The island is gone. She is gone. There is a part of him that has been carved out.

He slaughters his traitorous parents and crowns himself king. She should have been his queen. The taste of blood becomes a hunger.

He remembers Galatea every moment of every day and realizes that the rest of the world doesn't share his grief. He searches for her face in his mind, but when he sees her, it is like standing at the mouth of a precipice. He cannot, will not, fall. He finds those who witnessed his voyage and failure and slaughters them. When he draws blood, when he fights, when the world is on fire, he has control. He will never be powerless again.

After many months, he unlocks the cell. The face that stares at him is skeletal gray, but something is there that wasn't before. Life. Power. Magics.

King Fernando has work to do.

It will never truly end.

The life and memory of Galatea is severed, but the soul of the world leaves impressions. She is the susurration of the wind. The lyric of a song that strikes a chord. The myth of a saint who fell to earth. The dregs of a love that was doomed before it started.

When we begin to fall under the pressure of our illusion, Dez appears between us and shoulders our weight.

"I've got you," he whispers, black waves falling over his eyes.

Pain and surprise passes through Castian's eyes at the sight of his brother looping his arms around our torsos. The heat between us radiates, emanating in waves of magics. Though the world is changing, I have never been more at peace. Selfishly, I want to hold this forever.

The palace trembles, and chandeliers fall to the ground and splinter. Images gather like storm clouds. *Fernando drowning a boy. Fernando poisoning Queen Penelope. Fernando slaying Admiral Arias.*

Each additional memory I gathered from him is refracted, magnified through the light of the Knife of Memory.

Everywhere in Puerto Leones people will turn to the illusions cast in the sky, in their kitchens, in their common rooms. They will call them ghosts. Miracles. They will call themselves witnesses.

When it is over, and the throne room returns to focus, I hear our heartbeats racing at different speeds—mine slow and steady, Castian's like hummingbird wings, Dez's heavy with a new burden, even Fernando's, erratic with the knowledge of what is coming next.

Fernando, barely strong enough to stand from his knees, croaks out, "Son—"

Cas takes sure steps toward his father and picks up his sword.

"Mercy," the king begs.

"You took my mother from me," Cas says, his golden hair wild, his blue-green eyes bright with unshed tears.

Dez holds their father by his arms, and Castian drives the sword deep into Fernando's heart.

Blood runs from the dead king's slumped form. I watch the scarlet river snake toward my feet.

"Ren?"

There's the clatter of metal.

The cold of the floor.

The red behind my eyes.

Castian pulls me onto his lap, and he says my name over and over. The Knife of Memory vanishes from my grasp, and I feel its pull, taking me with it.

There is so much I want to say to him, to the world, to myself. So much more on the tip of my tongue. But first, there is a place I must go.

"Nati," he cries.

And I ask, "Is that who I am?"

33

"You are," she tells me.

We are back in the cave beneath Isla Sombras. The crystals above me wink at the sapphire water below my feet. I walk across, my toes pressing against the ripples without breaking the surface.

"I am?"

The woman stands upon the column, holding the Knife of Memory. I have never met her, but I know her all the same. She is the voice of hope that refuses to be snuffed out. She is the dream I keep chasing.

What had Argi known her as? The name comes to me. "Our Lady of Whispers, Mother of Shadows and the Eternal Moon."

Her face is somber, but her skin shimmers as though she is made of stardust. Her dress is like a rippling sea swathed around her waist and shoulders, and her hair, a curtain of twilight. "You have returned my blade."

"Why are you here? You became mortal. You—"

She turns the Knife of Memory point side down. "I created the Knife of Memory to sever my immortality. I fell to the world for some time, but it did not take. Now I am a memory. After my mortal life was over, I returned here, forever tied to the weapon that was supposed to give me peace. The Knife is the one thing I can't sever—some veins are buried so deep nothing can excavate them."

I think of the fable I heard in Acesteña about the woman who sacrificed herself for rain. I wonder if, somehow, its origins can be traced back to the Lady of Whispers.

"Why not destroy the weapon?"

"I've tried," she says, her voice like the crush of waves. "Believe me. That's why I hid it here and tasked the guardians of this temple with it. But so much has been corrupted."

"Then fix it," I snap. The jagged crystals above me flicker like distant stars mocking my existence. "Make it right."

The goddess looks at me, and when she smiles, all I want is her forgiveness. "I can't. I have done my part, and I failed when Fernando perverted my magics with his violent actions. He attempted to wield a power that was not his to claim and so erased Galatea's life. Twisted the power of the Moria in a way I'd never imagined."

"But it's over now," I say.

"It will never be over. Men like Fernando exist and will continue to exist."

"Then we do nothing?"

She smiles again, that tragic smile that says everything I need to know. "You do nothing. Your work is done, Renata. All you have to do is choose."

"Choose what?" I don't understand. "Did Cebrián have a choice?"

"Cebrián's path is different from yours."

Is it, truly? "Tell me what to do."

"Don't you hear them?"

I listen closely. Murmurs rise from down below. My feet, for the first time, feel wet and cold across the soles.

You promised, Leo says. *You can't leave her like this.*

Please. Give me a few more days. Castian.

It's been two weeks, Leyre whispers.

Leave us, Dez says.

I can't do it.

Then I will. If you won't, then I will.

Castian laughs darkly. *We both know, brother, that you don't have it in you.*

Then the silence returns, and I find myself alone. "What do I have to choose?"

My words echo. The Knife of Memory hovers in the air over the column.

A part of me wants nothing more than to sleep. My work is done, she said. *Let go,* Argi once told me.

I hear his voice again. *Please. Please come back to me.*

So I let go, and sink into the cold blue water, to the fathomless depths of the cave.

34

Who am I?

I try to swim and realize I am on a bed, tangled and thrashing underneath blankets. After a moment, the name comes to me. I am Renata Convida, and I have no idea what this place is. I am in a bedroom, for certain. But whose?

Every inch is a deep blue, somber like the colors of the bottom of the lake in my dream. I slip out of the soft sheets and pull on a heavy robe far too large for me. These are men's clothes, and by the looks of it, a very wealthy man at that. I wash my face, and because the clothes are far too big, I go in search of something else to wear and to discover more about this place.

Finding only men's clothes, I remain in my sleeping tunic and robe. The bedchamber is decorated with oil paintings of ships and wallpaper that looks like the sea itself. When I sense I am being watched, I turn and startle at the enormous portrait of a queen with golden hair and skin. She peers down at me, and my first thought is that she looks so very sad. My second thought is that I have been here before.

I step out the door and into a living area. There's a couch with a blanket that looks like someone might have slept there uneasily. I pick it up and inhale the ocean scent. I look down at my hands and notice pale, pearl markings. They carry up my arms, and as I lift my sleeping tunic up, I discover they also run across my chest and belly. I tighten the dressing robe around my waist, and leave the room, bumping into a servant girl who waits just outside.

"Hello," I say. "Can you tell me where I am?"

Her doe eyes blink rapidly. "Yer awake!"

She runs, and I chase after her. "Wait!"

A feeling pulses against my eyes. Remembrance. Recollection. The sensation of walking across someone else's life. My breathing becomes labored, and my bones feel like hollow reeds ready to bend.

"Please," I shout. "My legs are about to give out under me!"

My thighs cramp when I reach the landing at the bottom of the stairs. A new mystery is solved—I am in a palace. Servants and ladies in dresses gape at me as I descend. I am suddenly very aware that I am practically naked beneath my dressing robe, and perhaps that is not permitted at a palace. After I catch my breath, I follow the brown-haired girl through a garden made of hedges. Cypress hedges, the name pops into my mind. When the breeze winds around me, I catch the floral whiff of wisteria and the harried cries of the servant girl.

"She's here! She's . . . she's—"

"Calm yourself," a pleasant voice rumbles.

When I step into a small clearing, I find the girl who ran away from me. Perhaps I'm some sort of prisoner, as she has clearly come to alert someone of my presence. Two young men of roughly the same tall height and broad build stand in the garden near the statue of a weeping angel. When they see me, shock stills their features. I note their fine silk and brocade and take several steps back. I am *certainly* not dressed to be wandering around a palace.

The dark-haired one breaks into a deep smile. His tangle of black waves is tied back, and the scar tissue where his ear used to be startles me. He's got the shadow of a beard, tanned skin, and eyes the clearest shade of honey. The golden-haired boy seems to see a phantom. His eyes are blue-green, filling with tears. He reaches for my hand, and I flinch.

"Ren," the dark-haired boy says.

"Do you know me?" I ask.

Something must dawn on him, because he sighs and extends his palm in a greeting. "I'm Andrés, but you call me Dez."

"Pleased to meet you, Dez. Where am I?" I ask, and turn to the quiet golden boy. "And who are you? I just woke up, and I'm starving. I—I don't think I'm supposed to be here. I don't even remember how I got here or what day it is."

Dez smiles and says, "It is the tenth day in the month of Primanocte. And you are our guest, and very much supposed to be here."

"Oh." I sigh, relieved. "Very good."

Dez slaps the other young man on his back. He hisses, "Don't be rude, brother."

"I'm Cas," he says, clearing his throat. "I live here."

Dez makes a sound of frustration, then gives instructions to the servant girl while Cas retreats and vanishes into the gardens. From Dez, I learn I have been sick for two weeks, but he doesn't tell me what my illness was or how I came to be with them. He reassures me that food will be brought to the chambers I was sleeping in and a bath will be drawn. He tells me that everything will be clearer soon, but did not suggest how soon, and the entire time I walk back to my room I feel as though he should be speaking to someone else.

While I wait for my food and bath, I explore the rooms in my apartment. Everything is beautiful, carved from fine wood and inlaid with precious metals and rare gems. But something small on the bedside table catches my attention. An alfaro. The copper has turquoise flecks on it and a dozen holes punched in the surface. Inside is a stump of a candle. I light it, shut the drapes, and watch the constellation illuminate the ceiling.

I think of the two handsome young men downstairs. They knew me. I knew them. But I struggle to conjure memories of them, or anything, before I woke.

I'm Cas, he said. *I live here.*

I drift off, staring at the flicker of stars on the ceiling. When I close my eyes, I feel something tug loose. It is a thread that unspools and unspools.

> *A little boy with dirty clothes and bright blue-green eyes.*
> *"Who are you?" I ask.*
> *"I'm Cas," he says. "I live here."*
> *"I'm Renata Clara Convida. I live here, too."*

And then I remember everything. Everything.

35

I am Renata Convida, and I know exactly where I am. I'm in Andalucía, the capital of Puerto Leones. I rush to the curtains and throw open the large windows. I feel the moonlight against my marked skin and listen to the cacophony of the city. There's music and shouting from the brothels and taverns, bartering from the night market, and then the acute sound of arguing at the gates and the crash of bottles. I watch soldiers break up the fights, and the evening resumes.

I'm tempted to go outside, but fear takes root in my gut and keeps me planted indoors. What if nothing has changed? What if everything has changed? Maybe this is my chance to get what I always wanted—a chance to start over.

After my memories return, I speak to no one for two days and stay in what I've realized is Castian's room. I've broken into these chambers before, but they feel different now. I wait for him or Dez to find me, but they keep their distance. The only person that comes in or out is a shy servant girl who runs my bath and brings trays of food three times a day. The blanket on the couch tells me Cas must have slept there while I was gone. I carry it into bed with me, inhale the scent of leather and salt, and sleep.

I sleep so long I get sick of it.

On the third day, visitors arrive. Leo and Nuria.

Nervous to see them, I pretend that I'm still getting dressed. I can hear their worried whispers in the adjoining room.

"We shouldn't disturb her," Nuria mutters.

"There's going to be a wedding and a coronation," Leo says. "She *has* to be there!"

"These things take time."

A coronation? A wedding? I thought that I wanted to be someone else, or even no one. But I *am* someone—I am Renata Convida—and at the sound of Leo's voice, I realize that I never want to be anyone other than who I have always been.

I step into the living area. Leo is dashing as ever in a violet suede suit and artfully coiffed hair. Nuria wears black trousers tapered to her figure with a high-collared capelet and corset that make her look regal.

"I go to sleep for a few days, and people are already getting married?" I ask.

Leo gasps and embraces me so hard we almost fall over. I hold his face in my hands and kiss his forehead.

"Look at that," he says with airy charm. "One look at me and everything came swimming back to her. My power is extraordinary."

I sob and laugh at the same time. As I eat the food they've brought, Nuria and Leo catch me up on the goings-on in the kingdom. A meeting of delegates from the provincias will be held after Castian's formal coronation. The Arias family has been given additional lands after the discovery that Fernando killed the admiral. Lady Soria is pregnant with her third child. General Hector and Castian's former nursemaid have eloped. It seems that the entire country is arriving in droves to meet the lost prince and the new king.

"That's wonderful," I say, and find I can speak the words without choking. Leo scrutinizes me out the corner of his eye but says nothing.

"Castian and Andrés have been campaigning together," Nuria says. "The Arm of Justice has been disbanded. There is some resistance, but that was expected."

"I've seen fighting in the streets."

Leo nods gravely. "There are those who call for Castian's head for patricide."

"Really, it's the anti-Moria sentiment. They don't want a Moria king." Nuria drinks, and though righteously frustrated, she doesn't seem as worried as I'd expect.

"We are coming up with ways to bring the people together," Leo says. "Even the empress of Luzou is returning for the coronation. Castian has asked Leyre to be the new ambassador between Luzou and Puerto Leones."

"What about Fernando's wife, Queen Josephine?"

Nuria takes a sip of her wine but arches her brow. "She was granted asylum, but she has chosen to return to Dauphinique. She is pregnant, however, and the child could make a claim to the throne when older."

I press my hands against my temples. "I suppose that's a matter for another day. Have you heard from the pirates?"

"Captain Argi has sent word. They're coming ashore for the festivities." Leo takes my hand and squeezes, as if he's afraid that I'm going to vanish in the next moment. When Nuria sets her goblet down, I notice the sapphire ring on her finger. Castian's mother is wearing it in the portrait just in the other room. I feel a knot in my throat, an ache that swells and spreads.

"You're getting married," I say, smiling as best as I can.

Nuria blanches. "It's not what you think—"

"No, no, of course. It makes sense. The country is in turmoil and—"

"It's Dez," Leo blurts out, nearly bouncing off the chaise. He covers his mouth but keeps talking. "Lady Nuria is marrying General Andrés."

Nuria laughs and pats his knee. "As you know, Renata, the Fajardos and the Tresoros families had a marriage alliance from the time of our grandfathers."

"But Castian can make that go away," I say. "You don't ever again have to marry someone you don't want."

"That's the thing," Nuria explains. "The country needs stability. The people love me. They will fight for me should we be threatened. I have to lead them. What better way than to maintain this treaty?"

I remember the way Dez looked at her in the cellar, during the skirmish in Crescenti. "Dez agreed to it?"

"It was *his* idea." Nuria flashes a devilish grin behind her wine. "I thought it might be odd considering Castian was my first love, and they're brothers, after all."

Leo shrugs. "Renata did it."

I throw a pillow at his head and feel my entire body blush. "By the Lady, I missed you."

Nuria beams with delight. "I find we are very much the same in some regard. And it would be divine to finally be married to someone I can actually take to bed. Now, Renata, spare no detail. I do *not* want to go to my wedding night unprepared."

That's the thing about coming back to life, I now feel ready for anything.

That night I go searching for him. I peer in our library, my old room, the courtyards, the gardens, but I find the king of Puerto Leones in the first place I should have looked. The kitchens. My breath comes too fast, and my racing pulse makes me dizzy.

Cas is sitting alone at a wooden table with his feet hooked on the bottom rungs of the stool. His tunic is rumpled, sleeves pushed up to his elbows. He slices a piece of olive oil cake with a thick layer of frosting. When he turns and sees me enter, he's startled. I cross the room and stand in the space between his knees. He cups my face and drinks me in with his stare. I lean into his calloused palms.

"I'm sorry I didn't find you sooner," I say, and kiss his cheeks, his jaw, his closed eyelids, his moon-shaped scar. "I was afraid. But it's impossible to be in your room surrounded by your things and not think about you every single moment."

"Nati." He sighs, pulling me against his chest.

I cradle the back of his neck and touch our noses together. I climb on his lap, and he runs his hands along my spine, pressing me against him. When we kiss, I see the stars. The constellations of the alfaro he left at my bedside. The ones engraved on the sextant.

The ones we kissed under on a hidden island in the middle of the sea. I pull him tighter, memorizing the beat of his heart against me.

"I heard you," I whisper. I can't explain the place I've been to. Not yet. But I want him to know that it was his voice that led me out of that dark water.

"Let's go upstairs," he says.

I chuckle against his lips. "It *is* your room. Where have you been sleeping?"

"The gardens," he says, and kisses the line of my jaw. "The library." His voice strains as he runs his palms down the thin fabric of my sleeping tunic. "Anywhere I could wallow and brood."

"I suppose nothing has changed while I was gone," I say.

"Everything has changed, Nati. You changed everything."

The fervor in his voice tears something within me. I kiss him desperately, touch him everywhere. Suddenly, he shoots to his feet and slams himself against the doors, locking each entrance. I sit up on the sprawling wooden table and try not to think of what the cook would say if she saw us here. When he returns to me, he kisses me for so long my lips feel beautifully numb. Warmth melts along my skin as I pull up my tunic and guide his hands up the inside of my thighs.

"There's cake on your face," I tell him.

He looks confused, then indignant when I slather a finger of icing on his cheek.

"God, I love you," he says, even as he shakes his head, pulling off his shirt.

His broad chest, which I have seen so many times, has a new marking—a tattoo of soft black lines right over his heart. It's a peregrine falcon, the open wings feathering out over his pectorals.

I trace my fingers along it, then tug on the strings of his trousers. They fall around his knees in a soft crush of fabric. "Why did you do this?"

"It reminded me of you." He lowers himself again over my face. "Then I realized you're already a part of me, under my skin."

The vulnerability in his words leaves me shaking. I answer him with a kiss, the rush of wanting to be closer to him even though every part of our bodies is touching.

And I know this is the perfect way to say good-bye.

36

It is going to be a beautiful coronation, but I can't stay. I've already said my farewells to the people I love more times than I would like.

The palace is filled with lords and ladies, representatives from Dauphinique and even the Icelands. The pirates San Piedras cause an uncomfortable ripple among the gentry as they enter in their best silks and leather armor, bringing the energy of a powder keg in their eyes. The empress of Luzou arrives with her extensive entourage, and I swear Leyre has never looked happier. Castian pardoned Lord Las Rosas, and it seems that both parts of her life now fit.

I'm told there will be a place for me next to Cas tomorrow on the balcony overlooking the citadela market square in the east tower. I slip away to take a look while everyone is busy cleaning the rugs, polishing the crown and scepter, and making sure those protesting the first Moria king of Puerto Leones do not incite violence.

When I look over the square, I remember the riot, the day Cas supposedly beheaded Dez. I go back further in my mind and see the streets on fire, the forest fire that claimed my family's life. I try to imagine standing here beside Castian as—what, exactly? The king's lover? The king's Robári? I try to imagine Castian sitting on the new throne made of gold and marble, staring at the spot where he killed his own father, reminded every day of his patricide, of the Whispers that he and Dez slaughtered, no matter how just. I try to imagine myself returning to the balcony where I killed Cebrián.

I think back to the glittering cave and the choice the Lady of Shadows presented me with. Did Cebrián return to the cave? Did he find his peace? She said that his path was different from mine, but deep down I'm not certain that's true. I simply had people who wanted to save me. A tight spiral of light burns its way on the inside of my wrist.

"Don't do it," a voice says behind me.

I turn around to find Dez. He's dressed in silver and cobalt blue, the colors of his fiancée's house. His large muscles look constricted in the doublet and fitted trousers, and he keeps running his hand through his oiled hair, which Leo continuously yells at him about.

I smile wide. "Don't do what?"

"I know what you're thinking, and you're wrong. You should stay here with us. I just got my brother back. I can't lose you."

"I'm right here, Dez," I say, which is not exactly a lie. I am here. I simply didn't specify for how long.

I try to speak with Castian before the coronation proceedings, but there are simply too many people primping him. There is even someone to make sure the king's sash is placed in the precise way. Cas, of course, looks like he'd rather be naked on a sandbar with the sun darkening the freckles on his ass. But he takes everything in good stride.

We have one moment to ourselves. He finds me in the garden, the one where we once danced together. His eyes drink me in, and every doubt vanishes when I step into his arms and devour his kiss.

"Steal away with me to the library?" he whispers.

I accept the hand he offers. My gown, a turquoise blue that fades into green, was selected by Leo. It's brighter than anything I've ever worn, and feels like being embraced by the sea that was our home for a little while.

"Cas—"

"There you are!" Before I can even start, Leo, Dez, and several people whose jobs I'm not entirely sure of grab Castian and rattle off a series of things going wrong. Protesters are camped in the courtyard, and a drunk ambassador is being held at a tavern without coin. Castian gives me an apologetic look, still reaching for me as they drag him away. I try to hide my disappointment, but Dez knows me better than most.

"I'll talk to him," Dez assures me, and plants a kiss on my cheek.

I slowly make my way through the hedges, passing couples coupling and revelers reveling. Back in the ballroom I search the crowd for a familiar face. I spot the pirates gathered in a corner watching the passing crowds. Out of all the Whispers, I've only found Margo, who is never far from her little sister.

"Come, Renata!" Argi says. "It's a party, but you look as if you're going to your funeral."

"Did you hear the news?" Elixa asks, her cheeks red with joy. "Maryam and I are going to stay with my sister."

"What about you, Robári?" Argi asks. "I've got a spot in my crew if you're up for it."

I glance around at the glittering people of the kingdom. Castian has Dez and Nuria and good, loyal people around him. Me? I am like the Princess of the Glaciers, and Castian's own words from our days at sea ring true. *Sometimes you return to a place, and it no longer feels familiar. Not because it's changed, but because you have, and there isn't anything you can do to get that feeling back.*

I try to imagine being part of this kingdom, and I know, in my heart, that I can't.

Not now and perhaps not ever.

Your work is done, Renata.

Argi gives me her knowing grin. "What do you say?"

Moments before the coronation, Argi is waiting for me outside my room. She's got a bottle of amber liquor and a crystal goblet that she most definitely stole.

"Ready?" she asks.

And I feel I can honestly say, "I am."

I strap my small satchel across my chest with the few things I can carry—one change of clothes, an alman stone, a quill, a seashell I stole from Castian's room. I can sell or barter the dress. These are my worldly possessions.

The trumpets sound, and a wave of applause fills the air. I tell myself not to look back, to just keep walking out of the gardens, out the servants' door of the palace. I can smell the wet cement that is still drying, solidifying the kingdom's decision to fill the dungeons and shut them forever. I hear the ecstatic noise of the crowd welcoming their new king. People flood the streets, and I know that if we had left any later, we would never have been able to get out of the capital.

Argi, thankfully, talks most of the way as our carriage ambles down the road. Two of the younger pirates who were thrilled to attend such a celebration name all their favorite moments and unload their pockets of things they pilfered. I lose track of time, and we're at port by nightfall. The Riomar night market bustles with travelers. Stalls offer grilled scallop pinxos, and fortune-tellers divine the futures of gullible sailors spilling from the taverns and brothels. Torches light the boardwalk where people take a moonlit stroll.

We reach the end of the harbor and disembark. The *Madre del Mar* is a welcome sight with her billowing sails and colorful flag.

"Welcome home," Argi says, and grins as she leads the way up the ramp. "We set sail at first light."

I glance at the towering masts of the *Madre del Mar*. A gaggle of younger pirates San Piedras sit along the rail with a single oil lamp between them, greeting their captain. Argi watches from the deck and pours herself a drink of her stolen liquor.

I take a moment to breathe in Puerto Leones one last time. Sizzling meats and fish from the food stalls. Strong aguadulce and cider. Dyes from the industrial sector. I can find these things, and perhaps even more wonders, at any port.

But a deep longing coils in my stomach because there is one thing the rest of the known and unknown worlds don't have.

Distant shouting draws my attention to the boardwalk. The crushing gallop of hooves seems to tremble the entire dock. Vendors lean out of their stalls, sailors stop what they're doing, and more pirates gather along the ship's railing. Even before he's close enough to recognize, I know it's him. Castian, the king of Puerto Leones, blazing toward me on a steel-gray Andalucían horse. Cries of awe and disbelief echo through the market.

The steed rears to a stop, and Cas dismounts. There's dirt on his new tunic, and his sash is very much out of place. He is windswept and panting, and when I see him, my body takes over, and I quickly close the distance between us. He gathers me against him, fingers digging into my waist as I reach for a kiss he denies me.

"You would leave me?" Hurt tears through his features.

I grab the front of his doublet. "You have a country to lead."

"No, I don't." Cas's smile is defiant, like a man daring lightning to strike. "Not anymore. But my brother does."

"Cas—" I want this. I want this more than anything. "You can't do this. Not for me."

"You and I both know what it's like to not be able to return to the world, to feel like you don't belong to it." His hold on me softens, and he caresses the bare skin of my arms. "I don't care if we're in the middle of the sea or on one of the thousand isles of Luzou. Hate me, love me, have me. Wherever you are, that's my kingdom, Nati, and you are my queen."

I push up on my toes and kiss him, aware of the cheers and whistles that go up at our display.

Castian leans back and shouts, "What do you say, Captain? Do you have room for another on your crew?"

Argi takes a swig from her stolen goblet, then slowly her smile spreads. "It would be my honor."

The tension I've held since I returned to this life releases. I trace the edges of Cas's face, a face I had committed to memory with the intention of never seeing it again. Now that he's here I don't want to let him go. He is etched in every good and terrible memory, and I no longer need to separate them as I know who we are—we are a broken past and an unspoken promise.

"Well?" Captain Argi shouts as she pounds the side of her fist on the ledge. "Do you want a formal letter? Bring the Lion Cub on! The horse, too, while you're at it."

Cas and I come aboard the *Madre del Mar*—a king without a crown, and a Whisper who will never again be silenced.

EPILOGUE

THE WEDDING OF KING ANDRÉS AND THE DUQUESA OF TRESOROS WAS SET TO last for eight days and nights in Citadela Crescenti. On the eve of the ceremony, when they were to exchange bridal gifts, King Andrés unveiled his present to his betrothed: a marble statue commemorating the one-year anniversary of the rebellion she led in the citadela streets. She bought him a new hat.

As the new king of Puerto Leones stared at the open box, he wondered if he knew his fiancée at all. Their arrangement had been sudden—a proposal he'd made on his own with the understanding that his people needed stability. No one at court understood the people quite like Lady Nuria. It was true, he hadn't quite expected to become king, but after talking to Castian, he knew that to save the two people dearest to him, he would lead. And marry. And, apparently, wear a hideous hat.

"Are you disappointed with your groom's gift, Your Majesty?" asked the future queen of Puerto Leones, biting her bottom lip.

A perfect supper for four was laid out on their balcony. King Andrés looked at his beautiful betrothed and adjusted the hat on his head. It was purple and gold, and the outlandish feather kept falling between his eyes. It was a near replica of the hat King Consort Jávalez of the queendom of Tresoros wore in 89 A.C.

Dez was positive he'd told her how ridiculous he thought the hat, but perhaps she misunderstood "I wouldn't wipe my own ass with something so hideous" with "Please give it to me as a wedding present."

Every day with Nuria for the past year had been surprising. He'd admired her beauty and strength from the moment he saw her, and he'd believed that they would at least grow to be very good friends and allies. But he hadn't expected to fall in love with her so deeply. To want to spend every day getting to know her. How fervently she cared about their people. How she blushed every time he looked at her, and he looked at her often. How she fell asleep reading on her chaise. He thought he understood her, until the moment he opened the hatbox and she looked positively delighted.

"It's—" He considered lying to her, but how could he lie to her, his future queen? He pulled it off his head and ran a hand through his black hair, the ends curling in the citadela's humidity. "I hate it, I'm sorry."

She cupped his face and pressed a kiss to his lips, and then she laughed. She laughed and laughed, even as the balcony doors opened and two strangers walked out. They were well dressed but bore no affiliation to a provincia or household. Dez shot to his feet and reached for his belt. Where was his dagger? What if his enemies had sent assassins? And then the illusion fell, and on the balcony stood Renata Convida and Castian Fajardo. The king looked at his future queen, whose smile was as wicked as her kiss.

"You tricked me."

"I did," Nuria said. "Now, my love, are you disappointed with your groom's gift?"

Castian walked across the balcony and extended his hand to his king and said, "Hello, little brother."

Dez never imagined that he would be overcome with relief at the sight of the Príncipe Dorado, but the four of them spent the night drinking and eating and trying to catch up on the year's absence. There was sorrow and joy, but most of all, there was aguadulce. They were alive and they were together.

Nuria made Castian and Renata promise to return at least once a year because she knew Dez would never work up the courage to ask.

They made port at the same time the following year to meet Dez and Nuria's firstborn daughter.

"She takes after her mother," Ren said, holding Nuria Illiana in her arms.

"The goddess provides." Castian winked at his family.

"Very funny," murmured the king, but his easy smile faltered as he cleared his throat and said, "But she has our mother's eyes. At least, I believe she does."

The little princess then reached out and squeezed her uncle's finger with all the might of her tiny fist. "She does."

"When are the pair of you coming home for good? Aren't you seasick yet?" Queen Nuria asked, candid as she was radiant. "I know this little one would love to grow up around family. Perhaps a cousin or two to play with?"

Castian and Ren looked at each other, trading secret smiles. They both answered, "Soon."

They gave the same answer the following year at the memorial of Riomar, which coincided with the birth of the second princess of Puerto Leones, and the year after during the baptism of the king and queen's third child.

They said "soon" once more when the twins were born a year after that.

Dez knew he might never truly get Ren or his brother back. He'd never be able to understand what she went through, but he would make sure the next generations of Robári would have the security that was taken from her.

Puerto Leones was entering its greatest age. Moria returned to their homelands, and Provincia Memoria was rebuilding temples and universities. But King Andrés knew peace was a fragile thing. It needed the utmost care and attention, but no matter how much he and his queen tried, the old veins of hatred excavated by his birth father thrived once again. A group calling themselves the Lion's Heirs took to the streets, breaking out in violence against Moria. They longed for King Fernando's old ways. They denounced the heretical king. They were only just starting.

Once Dez would have responded in kind. He would have met those who opposed him with the same violence, the same rage that, years later, was easy enough to spark in his heart. But he would never be his father—his birth father—not ever. Dez had learned when he needed to ask for help, and on the eighth year of his brother's yearly return from self-imposed exile he said, "Prepare yourself, brother. We celebrate now, but there will come a day when I will need you to fight by my side."

"I will be there," Castian promised.

The known world was a bigger place than Castian and Renata imagined, and that first year aboard the *Madre del Mar*, they reached distant shores. Earned the calluses that came with being just another hand on deck. Learned the alchemy of turning strangers into family during long days and nights on foreign seas. From the elders, Castian learned the trade of his people—how to carve runes, how to understand the constellations. Ren schooled her fingers in the art of weaving with the legendary Euria and wrote down every story, every myth, every legend, so that the Moria would never be lost again.

Finding a home for two people who'd never truly had one was a peculiar endeavor, because neither the prince nor the rebel knew what home felt like other than when they were together. They might have been satisfied untethered to land, returning to visit family and loved ones but once a year. It was enough, for a time.

On the eighth anniversary of the day they left Puerto Leones, they pulled on a new illusion and wandered into the provincial town of Acesteña. Doña Sagrada's inn had never before hosted such esteemed guests. In attendance were the Lady Leyre Las Rosas and her wife, Ambassador Leonardo Almarada, and several generals and admirals. Even the king and queen were present. Everyone, local and guest, witnessed their marriage.

Long after sunrise, the newlyweds fell into the same bed they'd shared years ago under the names Wilmer and Marcela Otsoa. They were different people, but in some ways the same. He still couldn't sleep without her at his side, and she reached for the ghost of memories long gone. Their scars ached, and they dreamed of the people they couldn't save, and worse, the people who hurt them. But they'd also learned to laugh often and freely. They made friends of strangers and danced until their feet ached. They were so close, but so far.

That same year Argiñe San Piedras finally retired as captain of the *Madre del Mar*. Her crew followed her, making the long landlocked pilgrimage to the border town she'd once called home. All but Castian and Renata. The ship was now theirs, and there was a new crew to break in.

And on the ninth year, Castian and Renata did not make port in the kingdom. They weathered a hurricane in the Castinian Sea. And when the thunder stopped and the rain fled to the horizon, they held their twins in their arms.

Leonardo and Penelope were born in the eye of a hurricane. That, along with their family's history, would be the thing that always defined them. They lived on the Isla Sombras for a year before a letter arrived with King Andrés's seal.

As Castian had promised, they were going home.

The *Madre del Mar* still sailed under a new generation of pirates San Piedras, but that's another story. Ten years after Castian Fajardo and Renata Convida left Puerto Leones, they were welcomed with great fanfare in the new capital of the kingdom—Citadela Crescenti. They brought several crates of gifts from Empirio Luzou and the southern icelands, and each carried a child in their arms.

Castian and Renata inhaled the sprawling citadela from the balcony of their palace apartment overlooking the sea.

"I hardly recognize it," he confessed.

"Some might say the same about us."

The truth was, Ren could have spent another decade on their ship or in a foreign empire or even in a glacier cavern as long as she had Castian and their children at her side. And yet, Puerto Leones finally called to her again.

Renata Convida, the girl who'd once lived a thousand lives and more, took her prince's hand in hers.

And she would never let go.

ACKNOWLEDGMENTS

As always, I owe everything to my family. To my brother Danny Córdova and our parents. Caco and Tío Robert #Robcos4eva. To Mami Aleja. All my cousins, aunts, and uncles—I love you all.

To everyone who worked on this book, especially Kat Cho for her guidance. You got your seafaring brigands, girl! To the fantastic Little, Brown Books for Young Readers team, especially my editor Alex Hightower, Marisa Russell, Savannah Kennelly, Victoria Stapleton, Sherri Schmidt, Jen Graham, and my publisher, Megan Tingley. To the phenomenal Hodder & Stoughton crew: Kate Keehan, Niamh Anderson, Maddy Marshall, Molly Powell. Thank you to Juliet Mushens at Caskie Mushens. To Glasstown Entertainment, especially Diana Sousa, Maha Hussain, and Olivia Liu for your enthusiasm and hard work promoting *Incendiary*.

To Billelis for bringing Ren and Cas to life with your breathtaking art.

I am eternally grateful to my writing babes. This particular road was incredibly difficult, and I couldn't have emerged from this endeavor whole without you: Dhonielle Clayton, Victoria Schwab, Natalie C. Parker, Tessa Gratton, Gretchen McNeil, Katie Locke, Patrice Caldwell, Adam Silvera, Ryan La Sala, and Victoria Lee. Thank you, Mark Oshiro, for being the first person to say, "How dare you?" after *Incendiary*'s cliffhanger. To my loves: Natalie Horbachevsky and Sarah E. Younger, with a special shout-out to Beth and Chuck Younger and their lovely home, Water Winds, where a majority of this book was edited. Thank you for sharing a bit of your paradise with us.

A special thanks to the teams at Fairy Loot, OwlCrate, the Latinx Squad, and United by Pop for supporting this series. Every book lives as long as it finds its readers, and you have helped me reach so many.

Finally, to every single librarian, bookseller, reviewer, blogger, bookstagrammer, booktuber, and book lover who has given the Hollow Crown duology a chance—thank you.

The world is yours to change.

Love,
Zoraida

© Sarah Elizabeth Younger

ZORAIDA CÓRDOVA

is the author of many fantasy novels, including the award-winning Brooklyn Brujas series, the Hollow Crown duology, *Star Wars: Galaxy's Edge: A Crash of Fate*, and *The Way to Rio Luna*. Her short fiction has appeared in the *New York Times* bestselling anthology *Star Wars: From a Certain Point of View*, *A Universe of Wishes*, and *Come On In*. She is the coeditor of *Vampires Never Get Old* and the cohost of the writing podcast *Deadline City*. Zoraida was born in Guayaquil, Ecuador, and raised in Queens, New York. She writes romance novels as Zoey Castile. When she's not working on her next novel, she's finding a new adventure. She invites you to visit her at zoraidacordova.com.